THE PAST NEVER ENDS

Jackson Burnett

*Jackson
Burnett*

12-14-12

**Deadly
Niche
Press**

Denton, Texas

Deadly Niche Press
An imprint of AWOC.COM Publishing
P.O. Box 2819
Denton, TX 76202

ISBN: 978-1-62016-003-9

10 9 8 7 6 5 4 3

Prologue

The image shimmered, then burned.

Attorney Chester Morgan swam another lap in the indoor pool. The cold and wet enlivened, awoke. Did he have a brief due that day or a court appearance scheduled? He tried to remember but ...

The image would not fade.

The early morning light glowed through the opaque windows of the Downtown Vivia YMCA in diffuse gold, and the bitter scent of chlorine hung in the humid air.

Morgan remembered.

He could not forget.

William Harrison had been a good swimmer—like everything else he had done. Competent, straight, no fanfare. His every act done with modest ease.

Morgan treaded water.

William Harrison at sixty-four swam in this place as if thirty-four. He had graduated from Princeton when Princeton meant gentleman, scholar, and athlete. Morgan dove underwater to eerie silence.

The image would not fade.

Lawyer Morgan admired Oilman Harrison, what he knew of him. In the hour or two before downtown offices opened, William Harrison had swum with the rest of the businessmen and women at the Downtown YMCA as if he were one of them. Harrison was, and he wasn't. Why didn't he build an indoor pool at his mansion? He wouldn't have noticed his lawn smaller or his dollars fewer if he had. Morgan popped his head out of the water and heard footsteps echo.

The footsteps had echoed that day, too.

Morgan didn't represent William Harrison. He didn't represent anyone like him, and didn't really want to either. Morgan was subservient to no one except the law and his own conscience. He told himself that again as he gently stroked the water.

Harrison was wealthy: old oil money. He inherited most, made some, and lost a lot, but Key Petroleum, Inc.—Harrison's family company—didn't go under during Oklahoma's oil bust of the nineteen-eighties and it didn't sell out in the nineteen-nineties. On the southwestern prairie, an occasional sign would flash a gold neon key unlocking a blue lock, marking an old filling station Key Petroleum established years ago.

Chester Morgan pushed off from the turquoise-tiled side of the swimming pool and the water spread against his body as he swam another lap.

He would not forget.

William Harrison spoke honest words with grace and knew the name of the attendant in the locker room and every member of that young man's family. The oilman's picture at charity fundraisers never appeared on the society page of *The Vivia Daily Sentinel*. Harrison didn't waste his time with them. Yet, an anonymous donor saved the opera from bankruptcy one year and had funded a library for the neglected and dilapidated east side. Harrison was different perhaps.

Morgan hadn't really enjoyed his morning swim since ...

Would the image haunt this room forever?

Morgan floated on his back and looked at the acoustical tiles on the high ceiling. He wondered.

Harrison's Key Petroleum, Inc. operated clean and fair. Unlike some small independent oil companies, Key didn't conduct business as if its corporate logo was a bulls-eye for Vivia's trial attorneys. The company filed suit only when it had to and when it knew its cause was just.

Morgan had heard stories: A Key lease hound—better at persuading farmers to sign oil and gas conveyances than at black jack—got into trouble with some Las Vegas loan sharks. William Harrison paid them off from his own funds and never collected anything back except loyalty. Key Petroleum refused to sue a contractor who defaulted on a drilling job and cost Harrison thousands. It would have forced the contractor, an old friend, into bankruptcy. Some things are more important, the oilman knew. Harrison and his company had made it through all the crashes and booms of that roller coaster industry, though, an accomplishment not allowed to the spendthrifts, gamblers, or incompetents.

Morgan closed his eyes and saw it again.

Harrison—thinning silver hair and apple green eyes, tall, gracefully aged, lean, and a tan face wrinkled with life and living. He had an ex-wife somewhere and an estranged daughter somewhere else. He lived by himself and sometimes even his shadow seemed solitary.

Morgan swam another lap and got out of the pool.

The image shimmered, then burned.

The image of William Harrison's lifeless body floating alone in that same YMCA swimming pool would not fade.

Chapter One

Madge Jorgeson provided the best free trip in Vivia. She had operated the elevator in the DeSoto Building since 1968. For more than the last thirty years or so, no one who rode with her ever felt dizzy from riding too fast or jarred from a sudden start or stop or threatened by devouring automatic closing doors. The DeSoto now stood alone in its splendid art deco. Seven stories of shiny silver, black marble, and mirrors. No others like it, and no changes really since 1928, the year it was built. Well, perhaps one—a powerful boom box squeezed between Madge's tall chair and elevator wall. She listened to talk shows and music all day.

"'Gonna be a hard winter if it's this cold in October, isn't it?" Madge said as Chester Morgan stepped into the elevator on his way to his fourth floor office.

"Yes, ma'am," he agreed, his face still tingling from the prairie-driven wind which had blasted him on his walk from the Downtown Y. "Yes, ma'am."

"The greatest threat to this country is the decay of its moral fabric. We must be vigilant," said a clear voice with an accent from nowhere. *"We must be foes of obscenity and degradation in all forms—"*

"When did you start to listen to evangelists, Madge?"

"Or our culture will seethe into life-sucking degeneracy like San Francisco or New York and that is why—"

"That's no evangelist; that's the—" Madge started.

"... purging Ninth Avenue of all vice and pornography—in whatever form it may take—"

"That's the new chief of police."

"... is this administration's top priority."

"Not so new now, I guess. Scary, isn't it?"

Kurt Hale had been brought in from some Southern California desert town to fulfill the mayor's campaign pledge two years ago: A law and order police chief. Reported crime was down but so too were alive arrests—too many hooligans were committing suicide by shooting themselves in the chests just as the police arrived to apprehend them.

"Whatever you say, Mister Morgan."

The elevator soothed to a stop.

Every year, the American Bar Association chooses three law offices as best designed in the nation. Any of these could be plopped down in any American city, and no one would know from which metropolis or region it came. A lot of law offices are like that. Others advertise: A framed copy of a jury's two million dollar verdict in the lobby; or an old deed to ten acres of bottomland in Ohio with the senior partner's family name on it; or newspaper clippings on hall walls flashing the brilliance of the attorneys who office there; or decorator furniture glitzy with gaudy wealth.

Chester Morgan's office was like none of these.

A huge oil painting of colorful, humorous cowboys and cowgirls and UFO's hung on one wall of the reception area—a payment in kind from a client who might become an avante garde Western artist. On another wall, two portraits—Morgan's grandmother, a Progressive Wisconsin Republican who as a young woman came alone to southeastern Oklahoma to help the Choctaws. The other—his grandfather—a white-haired eccentric Mississippi evangelist who after a revival one night married the Yankee woman and took the tent down forever.

The furniture was estate sale special and bargain basement comfortable and looked like it belonged in the De Soto building except for a big, gray metal desk—vintage World War II and bulletproof—near the middle of the room. One of the ugliest, but most utilitarian, pieces of furniture built. Morgan would never get rid of it; the best trial attorney he had known practiced behind it for forty years. Now a young woman sat there with a pencil in her mouth, her right hand on a computer's keyboard, a phone to her ear, and her other hand in a file drawer. Shawn—the receptionist, bookkeeper, business manager, courier, brawn, and face of the law office.

Morgan smiled at her as he picked up his messages and went into his office. It all worked at this moment. He was here and ready. Morgan had been appalled when the attorney for President Reagan's assassin, after his most famous client's acquittal, said, "Another day, another dollar." Morgan felt like that some days, too, but he wouldn't admit it and never before cameras or journalists. Being an attorney was a matter of trust—not only to your client but to yourself and to that ephemeral goddess: justice. Too many days end feeling like "Another day,

another dollar" and perhaps the law practice was no longer trust
but pandering, prostituting yourself and her. It all worked just
now. In the mornings, it felt like trust.

Chester Morgan began to return his calls. Mrs. Delano was
worried about the probate hearing that afternoon for her late
husband's estate. Chester assured her it would go fine, no
problems, he would take care of her. Mr. Miller had been sucked
into another pyramid scheme and he wanted Chester to look at
the papers. Mail a copy in, I'll look at them, Morgan told him.
Chester picked up another message, began to dial, and stopped.
He looked at the picture of Cassie on his desk. His wife, now ex-
wife, six years past. Where had the last post card come from?
Wyoming? Vermont? South Carolina? He wanted to believe he
didn't remember.

Rat-tat-tat! A knock like fingernails tapping at the door. He
knew the knock and yelled, "Come on in." The door flashed open.

"Mister Morgan, I know you don't like appointments first
thing in the morning ..." began the slender, tall woman who
dressed like a model from Vogue albeit one whose wardrobe is
budgeted from an administrative assistant's wages. Marylin, the
world's best legal secretary, continued speaking, "but this man
called at 8:01 this morning and said he had to see you. You know,
urgent and important. He said as soon as possible. I believed him
so—he's waiting out front. As you say, you never know."

"No, you never do," replied Morgan. "Incidentally, it's a good
morning, isn't it?"

"They all are. When I quit thinking that, I might as well drive
to the morgue and turn myself in—save the ambulance expense."

Morgan had heard that before, but had wanted to hear it
again.

"We really have enough to keep us busy," he said. He paused.
"What does the man need?"

"He wouldn't tell me. Acted kind of scared. And, as you
say ..."

"I know. It's either real bad, nonsense, or neurotic. It won't
hurt to talk to him a minute and see I guess."

Morgan looked at the form new clients or potential clients
had to fill out. Alan Kinman. 24 years old. Kinman Lawn Mowing
Service—sole proprietor. Gave an address in Follette District—a
decaying east side working class neighborhood.

A gaunt young man with sunburned pink skin and muddy-water colored hair followed Marylin into the room. He wore Buddy Holly black-framed glasses with fingerprints on the lenses and a face scarred by acne. Marylin introduced Alan Kinman. He carried a high school yearbook and a newspaper.

"Have you been to see an attorney before, Alan?" Morgan asked.

The man strained to speak and then shook his head.

"For a lot of people, it's like visiting the dentist," Morgan said.

Alan Kinman tilted his head and tried to smile.

"Except that it doesn't hurt as much—most of the time."

He did smile—an awkward, crooked smile.

"Let me tell you how I practice. First, everything you tell me is kept confidential unless you tell me otherwise. Likewise with what you tell Marylin or Shawn. Even that you are here is confidential. In return, I expect candor. The law depends on the facts and the facts of every case are different. My questions may seem irrelevant or may embarrass you. They aren't, and aren't intended to. I simply need to know so I can advise you properly. Do you have any questions?"

The skinny man shook his head tight.

"You have given me information about you," Morgan continued, picking up the client intake sheet. "You should have some information about me. I grew up in Southeastern Oklahoma and graduated from the University of Oklahoma law school fifteen years ago. I've been practicing here since. I represent individuals and small businesses. I may not be the best, but I try my best and—"

"Henry Voss says you are." Alan Kinman said, his voice pinched like the high scale of an oboe.

"'Henry refer you?"

"Yeah."

Henry Voss operated a two-lift garage and rarely said more than two words at a time. Chester Morgan had represented him for over three years and the most Henry Voss had ever said after a job well done was "OK." Morgan decided to take a bottle of Jack Daniels to him the next time his car was in the shop. Maybe not for Alan Kinman but for the compliment.

"Well, what can I do for you?"

Marylin had been watching Alan Kinman. She began to take notes.

"I-I don't know if you can help me. I-I don't know if I need a lawyer—or what." The man's voice squeaked. He twisted his head, shook it, and took a visible breath. "There's something about a whole situation that-that doesn't seem right."

"Sometimes they aren't."

"I—I don't know exactly where to start." With blank eyes, the pock-faced youth looked at Marylin and turned red. A big tattoo of the Sacred Heart on the back of his left hand seemed to pulse.

"Do you need anything?" she asked. Her voice soothed, eased. She did it well.

"No. I'm fine. Well, you see. You see there was this girl. We went to Bryan High School together. Her name was Tanya Everly."

Morgan nodded.

"She-she was a real pretty girl. She was my friend." Alan Kinman looked down and was silent. "She liked me. I've got a picture of her." The newspaper slid from his lap as he popped out of his chair and fumbled the yearbook open onto Morgan's desk. "There she is."

Morgan looked. The pages stayed flat as if opened there many times before. Tanya Everly. Light hopeful eyes. An elfin face, pudgy cute with baby fat. A take-you-in-and-cuddle-you smile and a glob of bleached blonde hair mussed cheap. Kinman was right. She was a pretty girl.

"She's dead," Alan Kinman said. "She's dead."

"I'm sorry."

The young man shuffled through the pages of the newspaper and awkwardly folded it back together. "That doesn't tell it all," he said as he handed it to Morgan.

A four-line *Vivia Daily Sentinel* obituary from three and a half weeks before. Name, age, address, next of kin, funeral home.

"There's nothing else in the paper about it," Alan Kinman said. "Nothing nowhere."

"You would think a person's life would deserve more than four lines but, for most people, that's all they print," Morgan said.

"Yeah, but they didn't say anything about *how* she died. That's-that's why I come to see you. You see, it didn't happen the way they all said it happened."

"What do you mean?"

"She always wanted to be a singer, but she never made it out of Kiowa Heights. Y'know what that means." He paused to silence. "Y'know, sex for sale. Getting naked for money, that kind of thing. I hated she lived like that but she did. I don't know if she had any choice."

"Sometimes people don't, and sometimes they don't think they do."

"Well, somebody killed her." His voice burst louder and pitched higher. "They say it was an accident but somebody killed her."

"How do you know somebody killed her?"

"I just do. I-I just know it. The kind of people around her and everything."

"You know, Mister Kinman, when somebody tells me they have a friend who is having a legal problem, most of the time there's no friend at all. It's that person who is having the problem. Or somebody calls me up and says their brother-in-law's attorney is telling them something and they want to know if that attorney is telling them right, there is no brother-in-law. It's just somebody wanting a free second opinion. You come in here and tell me you know it's a murder, but you can't tell me why. You know what that makes me think?"

Alan looked down and madly clicked his fingernails against each other. "I guess it's kind of like those cartoons on television I saw when I was a kid. The bear goes to the beehive to get the honey and the only thing he gets is all the bees coming after him and if all the bees come after me, that's okay. I...I may never have done nothing right by her when she was alive but I'm going to do this right, if I never do anything else. It wasn't no accident, and they can't honestly say it is."

"Who says it was?"

"The police. That's who."

"How do you know that?"

"Her mom says so. Everyone down in Kiowa Heights knows the cops are just treating it as an accident. 'Just another hooker. Treat it as an accident.' Don't have to deal with it that way."

"If there were any way to turn it into a homicide, the cops would. Have you asked anyone at the police department about it?"

"Do you think they'd listen to someone like me?" the gaunt young man asked, stated.

Morgan thought and looked at him. "You want me to find out for you?"

Alan Kinman nodded.

"Why do you think it's a murder?"

"I guess I don't know if it is. Maybe I just want to know it's an accident but if-if not, I want to make sure the right things're done, legal things. Not-not have her treated like some poor dead girl who didn't mean nothing to nobody."

"Where did she die?" Morgan asked.

"Dunno."

"How did it happen?"

"Dunno. That's what I'm telling you. I don't know. People aren't saying and something ain't right."

Nobody said anything. Chester Morgan looked through the yearbook, set it down, and thought. Finally, he said, "I'll look into it. I charge one hundred and thirty dollars an hour. I'll see what I can find out."

The skinny, young man nodded. "I'll pay you the best I can."

"I know you will."

"I'll keep these," Morgan said nodding at the newspaper and book. "They may help. If you call, and Shawn or Marylin tell you I'm out, or with a client, or on the phone, I am. Leave a message. If it's an emergency, ask to speak to Marylin—she'll take care of you as well as I can, if not better. You'll see what goes out of this office on your behalf and what comes in. I return my calls."

Alan Kinman stood and his hand jerked across the desk to shake Morgan's. "Thanks," he said and was gone.

"Boss," Marylin said, "Why this time?"

"Yeah, I know," he said. She had asked and he had heard the question before. Sometimes he had better answers. Sometimes he thought someone had been cheated or unfairly hurt. Sometimes he just thought somebody needed to be represented. Sometimes he didn't know. This time he did and, for anyone else, it may not have been enough, but for Chester Morgan, it was. "Look."

He opened the yearbook where high school students scribble names and benedictions and Godspeed. The page was practically bare. A few friends had signed the book—most nothing more than a line and a name. A "Good luck next year" written here. A "So long, Cheeseface" and a "Don't be a dick" written there. But down in the corner was a long paragraph surrounded by bursting stars and big hearts and signed "Love, Tanya."

Marylin looked at him.

"I know," he said. "I know."

Chapter Two

A fat oily-faced man, twenty-five years old or less, puttered behind the counter with a recruit's enthusiasm. His starched blue uniform squeezed his beer and steak girth. He carried no gun. A green-faced computer glared at the man while two or three people, including Chester Morgan, waited in line at Police Records in The Corral, one of Vivia's solutions to crime.

According to the U.S. Census Bureau, Vivia, Oklahoma in 1998 was an urban area. With a quarter-million people, skyscrapers, freeways, and concrete, it was, but not comfortably. Born of the Land Rush, the oil boom, and before that, the railroads, the city happened, not wanting to be more than a big small town. At this time, a big small town no more.

Old Vivia sits on the east side of Cottonwood River. A trading post in the Creek Nation of the early 1800's, a railway stop later, Old Vivia lives its past of exiled Indians, the Old South, freedman blacks, sharecropper whites, and corruption bred from opportunistic railroads and grasping interlopers. New Vivia, on the Cottonwood's west bank, ignores its fortuitous history: its one-day birth by grants of free Land Run earth. Smooth streets, tall shiny buildings, and prosperous white suburbanites who believe any problem can be solved by the right cowboy in a white hat.

Maybe that was why Vivia's police chiefs in the 1980's and 1990's all had gimmicks—shoot-from-the-hip solutions that promised but didn't work. Solutions that appealed to and soothed the fears of New Vivia, but ignored the reality of Old Vivia and its past of exploitation, injustice, and prejudice, and the vice deemed virtue of New Vivia: greed.

The Corral, Vivia's new police and detention complex, had been the gimmick of the last chief of police. More space to lock 'em up, more space for an urban fighting force and thus less crime. The city then erected this post-modern structure remarkably reminiscent of Tombstone, Arizona's most famous landmark. From then on, it was known as The Corral, the building to conquer crime, the building with empty space where computers should sit, and one man to work the desk in Police

Records because there was enough money to erect the monstrosity, but not enough to equip and staff it.

Morgan wouldn't have used a computer if one had been available. He didn't really know how and didn't want to learn, so he waited and thought and doubted.

He should have told Alan Kinman to come here himself. Kinman didn't need to pay him to get a copy of the incident report, a public record.

Other clients, though, had retained him for stranger, less necessary things. Mitzi Doran, for example, an eccentric and wealthy seventy year old whose real name was Virginia, hired him once to meet with her twenty-six year old fiancé's parents to convince them she had no interest in their son's money. It should have been obvious. The young man was built like an Austrian weightlifter and had never worked in his life. Or Andrew Davis, an SMU-trained attorney and vice-president of a chemical manufacturing company. Two months after Morgan became a lawyer, Davis called a senior partner at the twenty-five member law firm where Morgan then worked. Davis, whose company was a good client, insisted an attorney go with him to a meeting that afternoon with state environmental regulators. Somehow Morgan was the only lawyer available. He knew nothing of the company, had no background in the chemical industry, and no knowledge of the complex and esoteric regulations to be discussed. "Do you still want him?" the senior partner asked. Davis insisted, and Morgan remembered spending the afternoon in the meeting with eyes glazed and of no use to the brilliant vice-president of the chemical company, but Andy Davis was glad his attorney was present.

Clients intuitively know when they need a lawyer, even if they shouldn't have to hire one to get their problems resolved. Ralph Heftern's brother owed Ralph fifteen hundred dollars. Ralph wanted Morgan to send a letter threatening a lawsuit if the money wasn't paid. "He'll pay," Ralph said, "if you send him the letter."

Morgan persuaded Ralph to talk to his brother first. "Okay."

Ralph called Morgan back the next day. "Did you talk with him?" Morgan asked.

"Nope," Ralph replied. "Called him and he hung up on me." And Ralph usually told the truth. Morgan sent the letter and the brother sent a check for fifteen hundred dollars in the return mail.

Maybe Alan Kinman knew he couldn't get what he needed. Maybe this trip to Police Records wasn't really necessary but maybe it was. It won't cost him too much and maybe it will help him—what? Get over a lost love? Like anything could. Like anything could bring Morgan's own Cassie back.

"Yes sir?" the blue-uniformed records clerk asked. His voice had a good-natured rural twang to it.

"I'd like to see the report for this date and this victim," Morgan said, sliding a request slip to the man. "The only address I have is someplace in Kiowa Heights."

"Tanya Everly," the clerk said as his pudgy fingers typed information into the computer and then stopped. "Here it is. Tanya Everly. 90403918.DBAM.CD. Let me pull it up for you."

"Actually I would like to see the file," Morgan said.

"Well, with these computers, you can get just about everything you want just by pressing the right buttons."

"Really, I would prefer to see the file."

"Oh, it'll just take a second. Here let me show you." The clerk hit a few keys and turned the monitor so both he and Morgan could watch.

The screen went blank.

"Sometimes it takes a few moments," the man explained.

Nothing happened.

"Let me try it again. Sometimes these things don't work like they ought to. You know, demons in the wires or something," the clerk said. "90403918. DBAM.CD." The clerk hit the enter button and the screen went blank.

"What does all that mean?"

"90403918 is our file number. DBAM.CD means death by accidental means, case closed. Investigation finished. It'll be here in a minute."

It wasn't.

"Do you suppose the investigation wasn't really completed?" Morgan asked, looking at the solid green screen.

"Heck no. It's got to be deader than a door nail before it gets those CD's after it." The uniformed clerk punched the buttons again and pointed at the screen. "See. If there was an investigation going on, there would be two asterisks after DBAM or whatever we thought it was and then there would be some asterisks down here saying something like 'Refer to Lt. Johnson' or something. But on this one, it says CD and if it says CD, it is once and for all, absolutely flat out dead."

"Why don't you go get me the paper file?"

"Guess I'll have to. It'll be a few minutes."

"I've got time."

Maroney returned in a few minutes as he had left—with nothing. "I found out why that didn't come up on the computer. It's sealed. Chief's orders."

"Oh, I guess the investigation is still going on."

"No. Now buddy, I told ya, it wouldn't get those CD's after it if somebody was investigating."

"Well, then, I ought to be able to see it."

"Hell, even I couldn't see that report if I wanted to. I mean it is locked up tighter than a Methodist's billfold. Hope you aren't a Methodist."

"Don't worry about it. Do you know why the file is sealed?"

The file clerk shrugged and looked over his shoulder. "Never known it to happen before," he whispered.

"Nothing on the computer to indicate it was sealed?"

"No. There wasn't."

"Let me see your supervisor." Morgan handed his business card to the overweight oily-faced man.

"You don't want to do that, do you?" the young man whined.

"What's your name, officer?"

"Maroney."

"Listen, you didn't make the decision not to give me that file, did you, Officer Maroney?"

The file clerk shook his head.

"Then go get me whoever did or your supervisor, okay?"

The overweight clerical worker waddled away. Morgan didn't want to get the kid in trouble; the guy was just doing what he was told. Morgan imagined a zealous bureaucrat with nothing else to do sitting in a windowless room reviewing files, deciding which ones were fit for the public's view and which ones weren't.

A short man with greased back hair, a face wrinkled from tobacco and the sun, and with a hard glint in his eyes, sauntered to the counter.

"I'd like to see this file," Morgan said pushing the request slip in front of the man.

"Ain't here," the short man sneered. He stared intimidation.

"What do you mean it isn't here?"

"What I said."

"Where is it?"

The man shrugged. A blink of the eye and that movement would have been missed.

"Tanya Everly," Morgan said. "Death by accidental means. The file is closed. No investigation pending. It's public record." Morgan heard his own voice getting louder and knew his soul cursed government bureaucrats even as he continued, "Maroney said..." Morgan looked at the fat young man and paused. A drop of sweat rolled down the young officer's puffy cheek. "Maroney said I could talk to you about it."

"If Maroney told you it was gone, why talk to me? I got better things to do."

"Thought you might be able to tell me where it was and when it'd be back."

The hard little man shrugged again. They must teach them that when they move to desk jobs, Morgan thought. "Out of luck," the man said.

"We'll see," Morgan said. "What's your name?"

"Why do you want to know?"

"Curious."

"Hightower. Orin Hightower."

Morgan left Maroney to be chewed out by the veteran Hightower for doing his job. Morgan felt sorry for the kid who was trying to do what he was suppose to—honestly. The way elementary school kids believe all police officers are, but who learn all too often otherwise when they become adults.

Morgan located a pay phone and slipped in a couple of quarters. They had the report, Morgan thought. Someone did. Maroney had told him that much and maybe more.

"Morgan's Law Office," the young female voice said.

"Shawn, I need you to start on something immediately. Go to our library and find the most recent cases on—"

"Chester!"

"Mandamus."

"Chester, you need to—well, okay, wait a minute here. Mandame—what?"

"Mandamus. We're going to have to get a writ of mandamus against, I guess, the chief of police. A court order requiring him or his department to do its job, to provide a simple incident report. Find the cited cases, too."

"Chester, I'll do it, I'll do it, but you need to talk to Marylin right now."

Shawn transferred the call to Morgan's private secretary.

"Boss," Marylin whispered. "Mrs. Delano is here waiting for you. Her husband's probate hearing is at two."

Morgan looked at his watch. Five till. "Oh, man. Apologize for me—profusely. Tell her I'm running on attorney time. A half hour behind most people and—"

"A half century behind the rest," Marylin finished.

"Please get Mrs. Delano to Judge Powers' courtroom as fast as you can. If we're first up, I'll try to get it continued to the end of the docket."

Morgan hung up the phone. Late for Judge Eldridge Powers' two o'clock probate docket and Judge Powers didn't brook delay. Didn't brook much of anything. He could, and might, dismiss the whole case. How would Morgan explain that to Mrs. Delano who had never imagined life without her husband? He couldn't and he knew it.

Morgan's heart beat fast. He lifted his feet and walked as fast as destiny.

Chapter Three

"All rise! The District Court of Vivia County, Oklahoma is now in session. The Honorable Eldridge Powers presiding."

Morgan stepped to an empty chair near a counsel table as a snowy-haired man in a worn black robe entered the room and said, "You may be seated." Judge Eldridge Powers, as flexible as the marble that lined the walls and almost as old.

Morgan picked up a copy of the docket and saw *The Estate of Ralph Delano, deceased*, mid-way down the first page. Had he the breath, the attorney would have sighed. If Mrs. Delano arrived soon, he might escape Eldridge Powers' task-taking and might not have to spend the entire afternoon listening to the formalities of probate.

Judge Powers called the first case. A young attorney seated her first witness, a middle-aged man with arms like Popeye's and thick fingers adorned with gaudy rings. The attorney began questioning. "State your name. Where do you live? How were you related to ..." Morgan tuned out. In probate court, the questions were always the same and the answers only varied by names and dates—most of the time. The grandeur of being a courtroom attorney, he thought, hurrying and waiting, always more of the latter it seemed.

Morgan looked around the courtroom. Attorneys, plenty of them, and their clients who don't need the process at all—most of the time. Probate insures one's last wishes are carried out according to one's last will and testament. A well-drafted and managed trust can transfer property at death and avoid the probate process altogether, but not all attorneys recommend trusts, and sometimes they shouldn't. In probate, the court's supervision protects one's estate from vultures and thieves—some of the time, but most of the time, the deceased person's wishes are carried out without objection, creditors and taxes are paid, and the lawyers take home a nice fee for simply officiating in legal ritual that serves little purpose.

The attorney concluded her direct examination and Eldridge Powers determined the document presented was, in fact, the decedent's last will and testament. The man with a pawn shop's inventory of jewelry on his hands took an oath and became the personal representative, the current gender-neutral title for executor or executrix, of someone's estate.

Judge Powers called the next case. No one responded. In a louder voice, he said the name of the decedent and the attorney again.

Silence.

"Case dismissed."

Morgan looked at his watch. Four minutes past two. The fate of the Delano case almost, Morgan thought, and what accomplished? Someone would have to pay another two hundred dollars in court costs and the process begun again and that would cause at least a month's delay when the case simply could have been continued to allow for slow watches, bad traffic, emergencies, or, yes, mismanagement of time.

Morgan shook his head. Probate court. Forty-nine hundred little rules, Morgan thought, half of them written in the arcane language of the Oklahoma Probate Code adopted at statehood and little changed since; a fourth of them hidden in thousands of pages of appellate court decisions; and, in Vivia County where Eldridge Powers presided over the probate court, a fourth of them unwritten and known to lawyers only by unpleasant experience and spoken word. Forty-nine hundred little rules, Morgan thought, and most of the time they make no difference. Except to the Honorable Eldridge Powers.

Judge Powers, a brittle-bodied man with a soft library-and-office pallor, carried the faint twang of his Iowa boyhood in his voice. He had been appointed to the bench in the aftermath of a judicial scandal more than twenty-five years before. Judges, from the lowliest justice of the peace to the most senior members of the Oklahoma Supreme Court, had taken money in exchange for desired outcomes. Eldridge Powers remembered his legacy and went by the book even more than the book required. Lawyers dreaded his court; for in his odd school-marmish way, Eldridge Powers often embarrassed more than judged.

"In the matter of the estate of William Harrison, deceased," the judge announced.

Morgan tuned back in as did others in the courtroom. William Harrison, deceased. Morgan remembered the morning of his death. The image of the body in the water returned. It would not vanish.

"Thomas Haney of the law firm of Massey, James and Peterson represents the proponent. Is the proponent ready?" Judge Powers asked.

"Yes, your honor," said a lawyer Morgan did not recognize.

"Anyone present in opposition?" the judge asked.

Silence.

"The jurisdiction of this court depends upon the heirs and beneficiaries being given notice of their right to object to the probate of the decedent's will," the judge continued. "Written notice was published in *The Vivia Daily Sentinel*. Thomas Haney's sworn written statement on file—his affidavit—proves the heirs and beneficiaries have been mailed a copy of the written notice of their right to object. None are present, and none have elected to object. Randolph Harrison, the proponent, seeks the admission of a lost will into probate. Mister Haney, call your first witness."

Thomas Haney walked quickly to the bar in front of judge's desk, looked at the court reporter, and said, "I am Thomas Haney. I'm an attorney licensed to practice in Oklahoma. On September Four of this year, William Harrison, a resident of Vivia County, Oklahoma, die—"

"Aren't we forgetting something, counselor?" Judge Powers asked.

Haney stopped and thought. "I don't think so, but if the Court believes we have, I will certainly try to accommodate."

Judge Powers looked at him. His eyes half-twinkled, half-glared through an old fashioned pair of gold wire-rimmed glasses. "The oath?"

Haney's a novice to Judge Powers' courtroom, Morgan thought. Some judges require attorneys to take oaths before testifying. Some don't. Eldridge Powers always did.

"Since I am an attorney," Haney sputtered. "I thought I didn't need to be sworn—"

"Mister Haney, do you know of any law which excuses a witness from taking an oath simply because he may be a lawyer?" The jurist grinned.

Haney pressed his shoulders back and looked into the judge's face. "An attorney is bound in all his representations to the court to tell the truth."

"Everyone in this courtroom is bound to tell the truth, Mister Haney," Judge Powers replied. "Are lawyers known for being exceptionally honest?"

Muffled laughter murmured among the spectators. Thomas Haney locked his hands behind his back. Silent. His face white.

"Mister Haney, raise your right hand."

Haney hesitated for a moment then raised his hand and Judge Powers administered the oath. As Thomas Haney recited basic information—date of William Harrison's death, his residence, and heirs, Marylin escorted Mrs. Delano, a small-framed woman with hair spun and as shiny as a new nickel, through the courtroom's rear doors. Morgan nodded and the two women took a seat behind the rail with the other lay people.

The attorney continued, "On July seventh of this year, I drafted a will for William Harrison. He signed it in the presence of two witnesses in his home on July twenty-eighth of this year. I acted as the notary and saw him voluntarily sign it. I have an unsigned copy of the will from my file that I ask to be marked as proponent's Exhibit One."

The judge's court reporter marked the copy of the will and handed it back to Haney.

"Exhibit One is a true and correct copy of the last will and testament I saw William Harrison sign and I saw properly witnessed. The will names his son, Randolph Harrison of Vivia, Oklahoma, Personal Representative. It mentions his daughter, Jocelyn Harrison of Seattle, Washington, and leaves her nothing. Twenty-five percent of his net estate goes to United Oklahomans for American Values, a charitable foundation, and the remainder of Mister Harrison's property goes to his son, Randolph. The original will was identical to this copy. William Harrison called me two days before his death and told me the will was still in his possession at that time. After his death, the signed will could not be located despite all reasonable and good faith efforts to do so."

"Do you seek to have the lost will of William Harrison as evidenced by Exhibit One admitted into probate?" Judge Powers asked. He tilted his head and watched to see what Haney would do.

"Not at this time, your honor," the attorney replied.

"That's good because in Oklahoma it takes two witnesses to prove the existence of a lost will."

"You are absolutely correct, Judge. I call Randolph Harrison as my next witness."

A well-built man who may have been thirty or thirty-five or forty-five years old stood. His charcoal-dark hair fell in waves too naturally, his tan glowed too evenly, and his fashionable suit hung too casually. Randolph Harrison took the witness stand.

After preliminary questioning, attorney Haney handed the copy of the lost will to Randolph Harrison and inquired, "Are you familiar with this document marked as Exhibit One?"

"Counsel!" Judge Powers interrupted as he tapped a pencil on his desk. "Move on to your next area of inquiry. This witness isn't competent to testify about the existence of a lost will, assuming the terms of the will are as you state."

"They are, your Honor."

"Then move on. A beneficiary will not testify in this court about a lost will."

Haney took a deep breath. "With all due respect, Judge Powers, every day, I am sure, people who are named personal representative and who are also beneficiaries testify in this very courtroom about wills being admitted into probate."

"You are correct, Mister Haney, they do, but their testimony relates only to whether the document is the *last* will. They are not testifying about whether the will ever existed at all. And, in my court, no potential beneficiary—as Randolph Harrison is—will ever testify that a will existed, was signed, and then lost until the Oklahoma Supreme Court tells me otherwise."

"May I make an offer of proof, your honor?"

Haney's been in a courtroom before, Morgan thought. An offer of proof is an attorney's statement of what the evidence would have been had the judge not ruled it inadmissible. An appeals court could then decide whether the judge's decision was right. Without an offer of proof, a judge's ruling stands and even in uncontested probates, you have to protect the record, especially if Eldridge Powers is on the bench.

Haney's offer of proof summarized Randolph Harrison's proffered testimony: Exhibit One was an unsigned copy of William Harrison's last will. It was signed, witnessed, and had existed the week before his father's death.

"The offered testimony by the primary beneficiary of the alleged lost will of William Harrison is not allowed into evidence. Exceptions allowed. Continue."

"Did you make a diligent search to locate a last will and testament executed by your father?" Haney asked.

"Yes, I did, but I found none," Randolph replied.

"How do you explain that?"

"In his latter years, his organization of his personal affairs, not his business affairs, fell apart. He couldn't remember where he put things. And, what organization he had made no sense. I can hardly find anything. It's like he'd lost interest."

"No further questions," Haney stated.

"Do you wish to move the admittance of the lost will into probate?" Judge Powers baited.

Thomas Haney clasped his hands behind his back and looked down into his file.

"No," he finally said. "I call my legal assistant, Cindy Bateson."

A tiny woman stood. She wore a navy one-size-too-large suit and her face looked as it would if her dress had dropped to her knees. Cindy Bateson approached the witness stand and raised her hand in a slow and uneven movement.

"—the truth, the whole truth, and nothing but the truth, so help you, God?" Judge Powers concluded.

"I-I do."

"For the record, you are Cindy Bateson and you work as my legal assistant at the law firm of Massey, James & Peterson, is that correct?"

"Yes."

"You are familiar with Exhibit One, is that correct?"

"Y-Yes." Cindy Bateson glanced around the room.

"It is the unsigned copy of William Harrison's last will and testament, is it not?"

The youthful woman nodded.

"You need to answer out loud," Judge Powers instructed.

"It is," she said.

Haney's leading her, even on the easy stuff, Morgan thought. He doesn't want her to say anything except what he wants her to say. Morgan knew; he'd tried enough jury trials.

"You know of your own knowledge, do you not, that William Harrison signed the original will?"

The legal assistant shifted in the witness stand and paused. "Yes," she said softly.

"He brought it by the office several days after he signed it to ask me a question about it, is that correct?"

"I believe so, yes."

If I were the judge, Morgan thought, I'm not so sure I'd believe. Maybe she's scared or has never testified in court.

"And, you took a call from Mister Harrison for me the day before his death where he made reference to that same will, did you not?"

Bateson leaned to the side and tugged at her skirt. "If I remember correctly, yes."

"No further questions," Haney said. Then, triumphantly, "The proponent, Randolph Harrison, moves that the lost last will and testament of William Harrison as evidenced by Exhibit One be admitted into probate."

"Denied," snapped Judge Powers.

"We have proven the existence of the lost will of William Harrison by two witnesses," Haney said. His voice, now tense, pitched tighter. "Therefore, it should be admitted."

"While you may have put on evidence of the terms of a lost will and of the will's existence at the time of death—although the court is not entirely convinced you've proven the will actually existed at the time of William Harrison's death—you have not put on evidence of its proper execution or signing."

"Your honor, I was the notary. I testified I saw two witnesses sign the document and I saw it signed, too."

"Then we have the testimony of one witness, don't we?" Judge Powers asked. "Who are the other witnesses? Who else saw William Harrison sign this will?"

"I didn't bring my notary log with me. I don't remember."

"So they aren't present either, are they?"

Haney shook his head. "Your honor, I know now that every story I have heard about you is true. With all due respect, will the court allow this humbled attorney a continuance to let me subpoena those witnesses here for the presentation of such evidence?"

Judge Powers grinned. "Motion granted. The case is continued one week to reconvene at this same place and time." He called the next case and the probate docket regressed to its measured sameness.

The image of William Harrison's lifeless body returned to Morgan. He shook his head as if that would force it from his mind. It didn't. William Harrison was dead. Now only evidence of his life remained. In this courtroom, his material legacy would be disbursed by intricate ritual of law and Eldridge Powers' whim as if the man never existed. How far outside, and inside, this courtroom, did his other legacy—the one not bounded by material possessions—extend? Randolph Harrison walked to the rail to speak to Thomas Haney.

The image seared and would not fade.

"In the matter of the estate of Ralph Delano, deceased. Attorney Chester Morgan represents the proponent. Is the proponent ready?" Judge Powers asked.

Morgan stood. "Yes, your honor."

"Any opposition to the probate of this will?" the judge asked.

No one spoke.

"Notice of this hearing," the court continued, "was properly published in a newspaper of general circulation in this county. However, Mister Morgan, there is no sworn affidavit of mailing on file showing that all heirs and beneficiaries have been mailed written notice of their right to object to the admission of the will. The court wonders whether this hearing may proceed. Please address this issue before presenting evidence."

Morgan thumbed quickly through his papers. The judge must be right, he realized. He did not see a copy of the sworn statement proving he had mailed the notice.

"Chester," the elderly judge said. "How do you suppose this happened?"

"I don't know. This is not the way I usually practice law, your honor," he said. "I should have checked my file more closely." Better to admit an honest error and try to fix it than to pretend it hadn't happened, or that it was someone else's fault in this court or in any court, but especially in front of Eldridge Powers.

"Any suggestions, counselor?" The judge set the bait. He smiled and fractured light reflected off his glasses.

I'll take it, Morgan thought. This time he is wrong. "May it please the Court. Eleanor Delano, the proponent, is the sole heir and beneficiary of Ralph Delano, her late husband. Therefore, she is the only person who must be mailed written notice of her right to object. Mrs. Delano is present. No affidavit is required. The Oklahoma Probate Code specifically states a person who attends a hearing waives receiving written notice of that hearing."

Morgan had him, but did the judge know it?

Eldridge Powers said, "Mister Morgan, the Probate Code also provides that the Court shall issue written notice, and proof—proof, Mister Morgan, an affidavit, a sworn written statement—shall be made of the mailing of that notice of the right to object to all known heirs and beneficiaries. Isn't that right?"

"Yes, but since Mrs. Delano is here, that is conclusive evidence she received notice of the hearing and has no objection to the court conducting this hearing. There is no error, no harm done, and the law doesn't prevent this matter from proceeding. In any event, my client is prepared to testify under oath she received written notice by mail as required," Morgan stated. "The court reporter, as always, will transcribe her testimony. The sworn proof of mailing notice will then be in the record, if it so pleases the court."

"It doesn't." Judge Powers opened a green statute book and read. "An attorney for the proponent may mail the written notice required and proof of that mailing *shall be* made by affidavit." He closed the book. "It doesn't say proof shall be by testimony; it says by affidavit, a document you—the attorney—prepare and file, not something the court reporter types up."

"Your honor, Mrs. Delano is here. She is the only person by law who has a legal interest in this probate. She obviously had actual notice."

"She may be and she may have," the judge replied, "but the court has no authority to hear this case until the affidavit is filed. I give you one week to do that, Mister Morgan. This hearing is continued until it is reconvened at this same time and place one week from today."

"Judge Powers, I have practiced in front of you for many years now and you know that affidavit will be filed in as much time as it takes to print it, sign it, and deliver it to your clerk. To save Mrs. Delano the inconvenience of returning next week, would the court kindly consider hearing her testimony now and reserve ruling until this case is reconvened next week?"

"Mister Morgan, Mrs. Delano could testify all afternoon as far as I'm concerned, but since this court doesn't have jurisdiction to hear the case, it would be the same as if she said nothing at all. Would it not be? Next case."

Outside the courtroom, Chester Morgan met Marylin and Mrs. Delano. The brown and black diamond-patterned dress

Mrs. Delano wore came from K-Mart. Maybe Sears. Her eyes gazed flat and sad.

Morgan hated the next part. He had done it and said it before and would certainly again. "Mrs. Delano, I made a mistake." He paused. "I failed to file a sworn statement the law requires. I'm sorry, but we're going to have to come back next week."

"If that's what we have to do," she said.

"I'm afraid it is. There will be no charge for today's time, and we'll adjust your bill for your inconvenience for having to come to court twice."

"I appreciate that, Mister Morgan," she said. Their footsteps echoed against the marble-covered walls as they walked to the elevator. Then she said, "Mister Morgan, I heard what the judge said, but I don't understand it." She stopped. "This gets put off a week because no piece of paper says I was notified of this hearing when all the judge had to do was look up and see me?"

"Yes, ma'am. That's what the court decided." Morgan, tempted by his client's words, wanted to say something else. Instead, Morgan said what he knew he should. "Judge Powers did not have to make the decision he did, but he did. Though the words of the law are black and white, their application rarely is. In some cases, the lack of the affidavit could have made a difference. In this case by law and common sense, it did not, but the judge decided otherwise. We are bound by his decision whether we like it or not, whether we agree with it or not. He is the judge."

The doors to the elevator opened.

"That may be, Mister Morgan," Mrs. Delano said, "but I wonder whether he has ever lost someone he has really loved. Having to come down here and deal with all this is like living the loss all over again. Mostly, I just want it all to be done with, to get on with my life. Other times, I don't want it to be. I want to hear my Ralph's car door slam and see him come into the house. Sometimes I hear him out in the garage fiddling around with his tools, but then I know I don't. You can grow attached to someone over forty-seven years."

The three entered the elevator.

Morgan thought of the yearbook picture of the pretty girl with the mussed blonde hair and the life that was William Harrison's.

"Sometimes it doesn't take that long," he said.

The doors closed.

Chapter Four

Through a high window, late afternoon sunlight shone into the library of Chester Morgan's office and onto a stack of recently opened books on a dark wooden table. Nearby, another pile of books sat—research started, but incomplete, for an opinion promised to a client by week's end and, on the other side of the table, a yellow legal pad lay, scribbled with an argument for a brief due in two days. Thick sturdy volumes, posted from wall to wall and ceiling to floor, held thousands of stories of disputes, their resolution, and the rules applied. In this calmest room, Chester Morgan picked up an opened book from the new stack and looked for the word "mandamus" in the text.

The written opinions of judges constitute the law, so most attorneys think, believe. The statutes, much argued and debated by the peoples' legislatures, serve merely as markers and guides. Morgan hadn't always thought so, but law school and practice had taught that not all conflicts can be anticipated nor can enough rules be made. The common law—judges' decisions determining what the law is and shall be—had its origins in medieval England and still governs disputes today. The common law: written decisions made by appeals courts based on real quarrels between real people where nuances of fact can be weighed to distinguish just from unjust, right from wrong. Thus, most lawyers know the law as story and resolution, then a different story with a resolution changed by shade because the characters and setting and tradition compel a different ending. The written opinions of nine or five or three individuals are the law. The law of the land, written by judges appointed and not typically elected by the people.

Morgan found the word *mandamus* and started reading story and resolution, what the Oklahoma Supreme Court had written about the remedy he would seek for Alan Kinman and for others, perhaps, stonewalled by police bureaucracy.

"Hey, Chest, so what's this about making the chief of police do his job anyway?" said Shawn. The tall, strong, do-everything receptionist-business manager leaned against the library doorframe.

"The Alan Kinman file you opened this morning—"

"'He the goofy looking guy in today as soon as you were?"

Morgan looked at the young woman—unblemished, unscarred skin, the appearance and texture of magnolia in bloom; ruler-edged straight and white teeth paid for by parents with a yawn's effort and the excitement of paying a utility bill; a body muscled to perfection, some by labor, but most by devotion to itself. She would finish college and go to law school or earn graduate business training without obstacles.

"He was in this morning," Morgan said. "The police won't turn over an incident report about the death of a friend of his."

Shawn shrugged. "Not to you either?"

Morgan shook his head and told her of the overweight recruit with the computer and of Orin Hightower, his mason-strong fortress-building boss. As Chester finished, Marylin brought in for his signature the affidavit to be filed in the Delano probate. "Make three copies of that, please," he said as Marylin left the room.

"So, what do you do? Mandamus the police department? What is that—Latin for some bizarre sex act? With the whole police department?"

"You seek your mandamus, and I'll seek mine," Morgan said. "Do you remember the case of *Marbury versus Madison* from any of your college classes?"

"The U.S. Supreme Court is the ultimate arbiter of the law and of the Constitution," Shawn replied.

"The case stands for that principle, but this is actually what happened: President Adams appointed Marbury to be Justice of the Peace for District of Columbia, but Marbury received no formal commission, no badge. James Madison, a later-appointed Secretary of State, refused to give it to him. Marbury petitioned the Supreme Court to order Madison to deliver the commission. He technically sought a writ of mandamus, a written mandate, ordering Madison to do his job. The Supreme Court decided it had no constitutional authority to issue that writ."

"Great civics lesson, Chest," Shawn said.

"Just trying to give you a head start when, and if, you ever make it to law school," Morgan replied, looking again at his book.

Marylin returned with the Delano document and copies.

"Shawn," Morgan said, "file the original affidavit of mailing in the Court Clerk's office. Take a copy to Judge Powers' chambers. Bring the other copies back here and mail one to Mrs. Delano."

Shawn took the papers from Marylin, looked at the library table, and said, "I don't know if I'd mess around with that mandamus thing when there are more pressing, and more profitable, things to do."

Morgan touched the other pile of books and remembered the yellow legal pad at the other end of the table. "Yeah, I know. Always thinking of business, aren't you?"

"That and ..." Shawn turned to leave. "Eighteen and a half minutes of silence."

"You're too young to remember that," Morgan said.

Shawn stuck her head back into the room. "They teach it in history class, Chest."

The receptionist disappeared, her energy left the office, and Morgan felt dated—too young to feel old and too old to be young. Shawn, twenty-one or twenty-two, had learned of Richard Nixon and his ineptly erased tape in history class.

"She may be right," Morgan mumbled.

"What's that Boss?" Marylin asked.

"If we ask the court to order the report be made public, what would keep the police from simply saying it had been lost?" Morgan said.

"The truth?" Marylin replied.

"Maybe," Morgan said, sliding the book he had been reading across the table. "But the report's there and sealed, or it's not. Either way, we've been lied to once."

Marylin sat at the table and folded her hands. She smiled. A dimple twitched. "Mister Morgan, I know what we should have done first. Call Jeff McNally. He'll get the lowdown and dirty."

"I had thought about it, but I'd hate to do anything that might get him in trouble," Morgan said.

As a young cop, Jeff McNally had been discharged from the Vivia Police Department for conduct unbecoming an officer. Morgan had represented him before the Civil Service Commission. McNally had gotten his job back, had since been promoted to a mid-level position, and, in truth, would do whatever Morgan asked.

"You worry too much about your clients, Chester," Marylin said. "He lives every day by himself."

"You're right," Morgan said.

"Besides, it's easy. If McNally finds out it's really lost, you won't waste your time and your client's money, going to court. If it's sealed, immediately get a order prohibiting the report's alteration and then fax the order and petition for the writ of mandamus to *The Daily Sentinel* before there's even a hearing on it. You know how vigilant the paper is about open records. The cops wouldn't lift the cover of that file, much less destroy it, with *The Sentinel* watching and screaming."

"I don't try cases in the newspapers or on TV," Morgan replied. "Imagine what the press would do to Alan Kinman." Morgan paused. "McNally's grown up some. At least we could find out if the report exists. Maybe more."

Morgan called Jeff McNally. An annoyed bureaucratic voice told him to call back in thirty minutes. He was out. Morgan felt like asking for the number of the closest Coney Island joint but didn't. Morgan hung up the phone.

"Sorry about Mrs. Delano's affidavit," Marylin said. "I should have caught it."

"It's my responsibility," Morgan replied.

"It's our responsibility, Boss," she said. "Judge Powers might have understood if you had told him your dopey secretary forgot to prepare it and remind you to sign it."

"I doubt it. Besides I don't put my blame on secretaries. Try not to anyway. Don't always succeed," he said. Morgan thought about Judge Powers' probate docket that afternoon. Had thought about it, too. "Or make them do maybe what they shouldn't."

"Are you thinking about that attorney's legal assistant?" Marylin said, her voice quiet.

Morgan nodded. "I didn't know Massey, James & Peterson ever represented Harrison."

"She didn't act like she wanted to be there," Marylin said.

"When Powers was through with him, I'm not sure Haney wanted to be there either. You would have thought the firm would have sent someone who had been through Eldridge Powers' classroom-courtroom interrogation with an estate that big."

"Or that William Harrison had a trust," Marylin responded.

"That, too. No one was present in opposition, though."

The outer door whooshed open. "Sounds like your four o'clock appointment is here, Chester," Marylin said.

"Yeah."

Morgan met Fred Earl Handy in the attorney's private office. Handy owned Precision Harvest Unlimited, Ltd., a company, according to Handy, that manufactured computers that "told farmers the exact day to harvest their wheat." Precision Harvest had been sued in King County in western Oklahoma by a farmer who had lost his crop by waiting too long to cut. Handy looked like a fire engine with Brylcreamed black hair.

Morgan asked his questions and got his information. Then Handy volunteered, "There may have been a few little bugs in the computer. Hey, you cain't be in business without something like that happening ever once in a while. This guy's just trying to get rich off of us 'cause he had a bad wheat crop."

"A King County jury isn't going to look too favorably on some farmer who thinks he needs a computer to tell when to harvest his wheat and even less so on someone who sells one to him. Get me an eighty-five hundred dollar retainer and I'll do my best for you," Morgan said. "No promises. Just my best."

"Eighty-five hundred dollars? Can't you do it for five? This guy's whole crop ain't worth eighty-five hundred dollars."

"No. It may cost more than that. Eighty-five hundred will get us started and maybe finished. Maybe not."

"Hey, why don't you see what you can do to get it wrapped up and send us a bill for it. Betcha if you just let his attorney know we ain't goin' to trot at his turkey dance, he'd just drop it. Hey, we're talking to some folks in New York, got offices in that World Trade Center, looks just like that bank building over in Tulsa except there are two of 'em up there and both a hell of a lot bigger."

Morgan shook his head. "Get me the retainer and if showing you're fighting does it, I'll refund the retainer less the time I have in it. I don't get in half-way."

"Hey, we ain't nobody. We got a five million dollar contract with the Ukrainians. This guy needs to know he isn't messing around with any small-time operator."

"Then an eighty-five hundred dollar retainer won't be a problem."

Handy left without committing. Instead of whooshing, the outer door clicked.

Marylin said, "I don't want to sound like Shawn, Mister Morgan, but Alan Kinman has a lawn mowing business and he gets pay-as-you-go, Precision Harvest, though, gets an eighty-five hundred dollar retainer."

"If Alan Kinman had told me he had a five million dollar contract with the Ukrainians and was talking to someone in New York, I would have asked him for an eighty-five hundred dollar retainer, too. Let's call McNally again."

An energetic voice talked on the line. "God, Morgan, what kind of cheesy Ninth Avenue dive are you calling me from now?"

"The kind where I just bought your wife a drink," Morgan replied.

"Yeah, and served by your mother."

"Yes, McNally, but unlike your wife, my mother, at least, has clothes on. Hey, Jeff, I need you to check something for me. I've had some problems seeing this file over at The Corral. Tanya Everly's the victim. 90403918.DBAM.CD. See if it's lost, would you?"

"I'll call Hightower over in Police Records," McNally said.

"I don't suggest that. He says it's lost. Maroney, the counter man, says its closed but under seal by order of the chief."

"Shit, Hightower's going to retire and become a librarian. Won't shake his ass for anyone. God, Morgan, you're a lot of trouble. I ought to charge you."

"McNally, do you remember skinny dipping with a hooker at the city reservoir?"

"Yeah. Yeah. Yeah. Sure."

"And, remember who convinced the Civil Service Commission you sincerely believed you were helping a college coed experience nature for an experimental psychology class?"

"Hey, that's what she said."

"Yeah. Yeah. Yeah. Sure. See what you can find out and don't get into any trouble." Morgan paused. "Hey, McNally, I stood by your story."

"I know. I'll get you truth about that file."

"Thanks."

Morgan hung up the phone. McNally—a client first, then friend, now almost a brother—a brother he wanted to protect; a brother he wanted to succeed; a brother, as many of his clients, now like family. Professional? Some would say not, but Morgan remembered the meanest playground fight he got into as a kid. A bully had tormented his sister and made her cry. Morgan had gone home black-eyed and bloodied but so had the bully. Or like family talking straight or listening for the truth. If not with and to family, then with and to whom? If professional meant without feeling or passion, then Morgan was not. If it meant only rules and objectivity, fire the lawyers and send in machines.

Shawn rushed into Morgan's office and showed Chester the file-stamped copy of the affidavit of mailing. "Got it done," she said.

"Thank you."

"And," she said, "I saw the honorable Eldridge himself. I personally gave him his copy. Do you know what he said after he looked at it?"

"No. What's that?"

"He said, 'I knew I would get this today.'"

Morgan had made it to day's end almost. Still a few calls to return and letters to dictate but somehow it still felt like trust.

Chapter Five

The next day, Shawn put the call through to Chester Morgan.

"Boss," the voice said. "I need to talk to you."

McNally.

"Jeff, put your clothes on and think of something besides helping a coed experience nature. You've already used that one."

"No. I'm serious." McNally whispered.

Rarely, Morgan thought. "What do you have?"

"It's here and it's sealed. Chief's orders. Locked up tighter than—"

"A Methodist's billfold," Morgan finished. "I've already heard that one."

"Not that one. Never mind." McNally still whispered. "You aren't going to get the file. I can't even get it."

"Tell me who investigated it. Who got the call?"

"Don't know and can't find out."

"How'd it occur? Where?"

"Dammit, Morgan. You aren't hearing me. It's like it never happened at all."

The attorney was silent. He remembered the high-pitched voice of Alan Kinman saying something about a whole situation that just didn't seem right.

"It's public record, McNally," Morgan said.

"Chester, listen to me. Something's going on here. I don't know what exactly. But stay away from that file. I know that much. Just stay away from it."

Chapter Six

The woman's stained hands held a cigarette burnt to the filter. Silver-gray smoke floated into hazy air. At random, boxes sat half-empty, half-packed around the state-owned office. An oil color painting of a surly-faced clown leaned against a wall below where it once hung.

"How'd ya get in here?" the woman asked, her words slurring and rolling into two syllables or more.

"I didn't tell 'em who I was or what I wanted," Chester Morgan replied.

"Mister Morgan, I don't believe ya," she said. Her dirty-penny tinted hair had been backcombed, teased, and sprayed into a 1964 homecoming queen bouffant. She may have been ten years older than Morgan. Maybe more.

"Some people lie better than I do," Morgan said. "I gave my name to the receptionist and told her I needed to talk with you. She showed me back here as if you were expecting me.

"I wasn't, but I guess I am now," the woman said. She stared at Morgan through brown-framed glasses shaped like the oval television tubes of the 1950s. She smiled and smashed out her cigarette in an ashtray that spilled over with white butts ringed with bright pink lipstick. She ignored the signs Morgan had seen in the straight-lined institutional building. Morgan looked at the stains on her hands again.

"So what can I do for ya, counselor?" she asked.

Most Oklahomans voices carry—sometimes faintly and sometimes distinctly—a sound of origin. For many, it's a Walter Brennan western twang. For others, it's a country music drawl. For some, it is the echo of the Midwestern prairie. For the woman sitting behind the paper-stacked, file-strewn desk, it was none of these. Her voice sounded the way a smooth, rich bourbon tastes on a humid Southern night.

"Doctor," Morgan said, "you remember you testified in a wrongful death case I had several months ago. I represented the dead man's estate. The defense lawyers claimed the man died of a heart attack right before their client's semi ran head-on into the man's car. You did the autopsy."

"I remember the case and I remember you. How'd it come out?" asked Doctor Marcia Nelson, the Deputy Chief State Medical Examiner.

"We prevailed. We got a verdict. It's on appeal." Morgan stared at the woman and remembered McNally's call. He had never before heard alarm and retreat from the young police officer. To dismiss his words would be a mistake. To stop now, though, would be a breach of trust. Or, would it simply be prudent? Morgan hesitated then said, "I need some information about another autopsy I think you did."

"If it was in or around Vivia, I probably did it." She motioned at the half-packed boxes and the bare walls. "Ask me anything. My time here is almost through."

"I noticed," Morgan said, then waited. "I thought if you remember this autopsy, you might be willing to talk with me a bit."

Doctor Nelson relaxed back into her brown leather chair and fingered a single strand gold chain hanging around her neck. "I came to the state twenty years ago from the South, the gothic South. I've heard it called that, haven't you, Mister Morgan? 'Thought I was gettin' away from all that. You know, the Tennessee Williams' decadence, the Huey Long corruption, the brewin' and simmerin' violence. I actually found that I kind of missed it." The doctor's lips stretched into a rubbery smile. "Then, I found out it was all here, too, but without the charm. I'm goin' back home, Mister Morgan."

Morgan listened. By doing that, he always learned and sometimes understood. Doctor Nelson had been an enigmatic witness in the wrongful death case he had tried, yet she seemed honest. Of course, witnesses usually do when their testimony is favorable, even perhaps when they aren't.

"I'm goin' back to Mississippi," the medical examiner said. "Goin' to get me a place not too far from the beach and not too far from the city and have me some fun. Twenty years ago, not much opportunity in the private sector for a lady doctor, that's what they called me—some still do. I don't play golf, and football bores me, so I became a dedicated civil servant, workin' nights and weekends even when I didn't have to because there wasn't anything else to do."

A clerk in a too-tight floral dress started through the door into Doctor Nelson's office. The young woman stopped when she saw Morgan. "I didn't realize you were with someone, Doctor," she said. "I'm really sorry. I really am." She scooted back across the threshold.

"Whadya want?" the doctor asked, her voice now brittle but her words still in extended syllables.

"I can come back later. I really can," the young woman said. "I just needed a signature. Nothing important."

"Well, you're here now. Let me see."

The clerk crossed to the medical examiner's desk and waited. Her weight shifted quickly from one heavy calf to the other, from one raised heel to the other, then back again and again. The young woman bowed her head and shifted her eyes side to side, trying not to look at Morgan but wanting to. With the signed paper in hand, she hurried to leave.

"Close that door good," the doctor commanded. "You know I don't like interruptions when there are visitors." The word "visitors" hung too heavy and deep as with a meaning known to some but intentionally not to all. Marcia Nelson grinned her rubbery smile again and soothed the buttons down the front of her white smock. "What were we talking about, counselor?"

"You were telling me about becoming a dedicated public servant."

"Oh, yes, I was. Lady doctors scare most men, Mister Morgan. Do lady doctors scare you?"

"All doctors scare me except when I need one."

Marcia Nelson ignored his remark. "And, when these men find out you spend your days studyin' dead people's insides, it just plumb gives 'em the run-away willies. I'm gettin' out of here." She smashed her cigarette out, lit another, and slumped back into her leather chair. "It gets lonely, counselor."

"It can. It certainly can," Morgan said. "'Going to join a practice when you get back home?"

"Don't have to. Retirin'. What do you think about that?"

"If you can, and that's what you want," Morgan said.

"That's what I want to do," she said, "and have some fun. You know life isn't exactly life without some fun. You know what I mean, don't you, counselor?"

Morgan did not reply. The room felt too small and her words too intimate. The burnt tobacco now reeked like drug-store perfume.

"But you didn't come to hear me carry on, did you?" the medical examiner said. "What did you want to know about? Like I said, ask me anything." She sat up and straightened files and loose papers, but she stared at Morgan.

"About six weeks ago, you did, or should have done, an autopsy on a twenty-four year old woman named Tanya Everly. I want to know what you found," Morgan said.

The pale woman with the institutional glasses and the institutional hair stood, rested her hips on the side of the desk, and perched a boxy profile as if for Morgan's view. She paused. "I don't recall the name. What else do you have?"

Morgan told her the date of death, then said, "She may have been a hooker in Kiowa Heights. It's classified as an accident."

Doctor Marcia Nelson made no effort to find or request a file. "Maybe I could locate the file or maybe I could remember. Is this important to you, Mister Morgan?"

"It is to my client," he replied.

"It must be important to you, too, or you wouldn't be here," she said.

Morgan nodded, shrugged.

"Tanya Everly. Twenty-four year old hooker from Kiowa Heights. Six weeks ago." The doctor squinted too hard. "Was that the fall and the drowning? A big bruise on the poor girl's head, water in the lungs. Slipped in the bathtub, knocked unconscious, and drowned, I think." The doctor paused. "Or was that another one? I don't seem to remember exactly."

"Maybe you could get the file and we could find out," Morgan said.

"Maybe," she said, but did not move. "You know, if I tell the clerk to find a file, she will, and if I don't, she won't. I wonder. Do you ever think about having some fun, counselor?"

"Sometimes I do," Morgan said.

"Would a soon-to-be-retired civil servant pose any interest to you?"

Morgan pulled at his watch. "This is business, Doc."

"We could make it some fun, too."

"Maybe we could, but I'd regret it and you would, too. Maybe not now, maybe not then, but sometime we both would."

Doctor Marcia Nelson stood, took a heavy drag from her cigarette, returned to her leather chair, and said, "Then subpoena the file, counselor. My clerk will look real hard if there's a subpoena."

Morgan walked to the door. "Doc, I hope you find what you left back home."

Chapter Seven

"Mister Kinman," Chester Morgan said to the young man across the desk, "you need to know something: I've been told—or warned actually—to stay away from Tanya Everly's file. For what reasons, I do not know. You should consider that."

Alan Kinman stared at the lawyer through smeared lens. "Okay....Someone has it. I...I told you something wasn't right."

"You did," Morgan said, "and, yes, I think they have the file. I can't let you know who told me. He couldn't tell me much. He directed me to stay away for my safety. I know that, am sure of that, and I'm telling you for the same reason."

The awkward young man looked into space over the attorney's shoulder. "So we—so we just stop?"

"No, not necessarily," Morgan said. He picked up a pen and scratched on a legal pad. He said quietly, "Your options are limited, Alan. We could file a lawsuit and ask the police to produce the report, but that won't get us anywhere with what we have now, if the cops say they've lost it. The judge won't be able to do anything. We might have better success with the autopsy report since it's a separate office, but we have been warned to stay away and the local medical examiner plays games. If we had the evidence to show why the cops are hiding the report, that might give a judge a reason to force the police to explain what happened. For that, you'd probably want to hire a private investigator. That would be my recommendation. I don't know what else I can do for you without more information."

"You-you want to stop, don't you?" Alan Kinman asked.

"That's not what I'm saying. You might be better served with a professional investigator. He or she could find out what happened and then we could see what could be done legally to make it right."

"I know I'm not your biggest client. But Mister Morgan, I made a vow," the young man said.

"I know you did," Morgan replied.

Marylin looked at her watch and interrupted. "Oh, Mister Morgan, I forgot to tell you. While you were at the medical examiner's office, I got a telephone call. Judge Greene wants you to call him at four forty-five. Mister Kinman, you will need to step out for a minute."

Marylin escorted Alan Kinman to the reception area. When she returned, the attorney had the phone in his hand. Marylin shook her head. "There was no call, Chester."

Morgan frowned and put down the phone.

"Are you tired, boss? Are you scared?" Her voice floated and dropped like a swallow in flight.

"What do you mean?" Morgan asked.

"It sounds like you want to quit. I'm sorry, but it does," she said.

"I don't have enough information to do anything, Marylin. That's just the way it is." Morgan closed the Kinman file and moved it to the side of his desk.

"I know, but who would you get to investigate this?" Marylin asked. "The last time you used Roger Martin, he required a five hundred dollar retainer up front, it took six months to get the report, and you said, and I quote, 'He demonstrated all the ingenuity of a CPA with a box of receipts and a ten key. Ron Carder is okay as long as there is something to videotape or a cheating spouse to photograph, but otherwise you get a survey of public records. Michelle Harned does a great job on accidents and getting statements, but she talks too much. That might be dangerous.' For one good reason or another, you won't use anyone else in town. Besides, most of the others are retired cops or wanna-be-cops."

"What do you think we should do?" Chester asked.

"Keep looking."

Morgan did not reply.

"Boss, you've told me too many times your license doesn't guarantee you anything easy. I don't know anything about that girl. You don't either, but whoever she was, whatever else she did, once in her life she did something kind. Alan Kinman wants to pay her back and I think you do, too."

Morgan stared at the wall, the picture of Cassie on his desk, and at nothing, then said, "Let's get him back in here."

Alan Kinman returned to the office. He walked the way a batter does on the way to the dugout after striking out at the bottom of the ninth. Morgan looked at him.

"Alan, you are what, twenty-four years old?" Morgan said. "If you don't pursue this, you may regret it the rest of your life. If you do, you may find yourself in peril, in danger. You may even find yourself standing in front of a judge or a jury accused of something you never did or ever intended to do. Do you understand?"

The skinny man, not much more than a boy, nodded.

"You don't know what the consequences are, and I don't know what they are. You may find out things you wish to God you had never found out. I can't speak more plainly."

"I-I know. Isn't that—isn't that what you're supposed to do?"

Morgan picked up a stack of phone messages, looked at a pile of unanswered mail, and remembered the visit to Doctor Marcia Nelson's office. "This job isn't like what you see on TV. You pick up pieces from the past and try to make them right. You look into the future and shoot ghosts as they come over the horizon. Some nights you go home and are satisfied. A lot of time you just want to sit in silence until what you had heard and seen that day disappears from your mind, but it never does. Not really, not completely. You want to make things right about your lost friend. If you aren't being straight up, I will be worse than your worst enemy. If you are, we'll find the truth as much as it is and make things as right as they can be."

"The private investigator. What about him?" Kinman asked.

"I said we'll find the truth. Don't go talking that I'm looking into it," Morgan said. "There's no investigator I trust enough to do the job." He opened the file and looked at the obituary. "You need to tell me all about Tanya Everly."

"She was-was my friend. She liked to make people happy. In high school, she was about my only friend. The other kids weren't very nice, not too much."

"I understand," Morgan said. "Did you ever date her or anything? How often did you see her?"

Alan Kinman rubbed his fingers on his acne-infected cheek and said in a tone lost in the past, "Once in a while, I'd see her. It was like we'd talk and it'd be OK. That's all. Yeah, that's all. We'd talk and it'd be OK."

Morgan looked at the picture of Cassie, his wife, now ex-wife, on his desk. "Not anything more?"

The young man shook his head. He twitched and glanced at Marylin. "Sometimes I wished."

"I understand," Morgan said.

"She-she knew how the others treated me, but it was like she knew how it was to be me."

"Did you know her before high school?"

"No. That's when her and her mom moved to town, I guess. We were sophomores then. I didn't know her before then."

"The obituary doesn't say anything about any family except for her mother: Tamar White."

"That's all there was, far as I ever knew."

"Where can I find Tanya's mother?"

"Where you can."

Morgan stared at the young man, took a deep breath, then frowned. "Alan, I don't—"

"I ain't bein' smart. You just kind of find her in Kiowa Heights when you can."

"Like where?" the attorney asked.

The pock-faced young man shook his head. "Where ever she might decide to set up. You just have to ask around there."

Morgan's glance met Marylin's. "Where do you suggest I ask?"

"Where Tanya worked."

"Where was that Alan?" Marylin asked.

Alan Kinman's face turned red. "It was a place called Vixens. On Ninth Avenue just past Murray Road. She-she took her clothes off to make a living or make somebody a living."

"Do you know if she was living at this—" Morgan stopped. He hadn't said the word yet but he knew he would have to. "The last that you knew?"

"Yeah. She rented a little house there. Lived by herself." Kinman straightened up in the chair. "But you won't find anything out there. The landlady—she lives next door to the north, I guess. She won't talk to you."

"How do you know?"

"I just do."

"Was Tanya ever married? Have any kids?"

"You, you don't understand, Mister Morgan. She didn't live a life like other people. Not even before she got out of high school, her mother put her in that place and made her make a living taking off her clothes and ..."

"Taking money for sex?"

The young man nodded. Morgan paused. "What do you know about how she died?"

"I don't know nothing and that's the God's truth. Nobody will tell me nothing except it was an accident. I don't even know where." With eyes wet, he shook his head and looked away.

"What do you think happened or why?"

"I don't know. You know, sometimes you hear something and you think you know what it means but the more you think about it, the more it might mean something else. The last time I saw her, about two weeks before it happened, she said something about some tapes or discs, something about how they'd get her out of here. She seemed so happy. I was, too, and I never asked her nothin' about 'em—about what they were or what kind or who had 'em or nothin'—'cause it just didn't seem right. Not then. It was like it was something so good you shouldn't ought to have to ask. I wish I had now. I wonder if it was something so bad I should have found out more."

"Nothing?" Morgan asked.

"Nothing," Kinman replied.

Morgan sighed. "We'll see what we can do. Remember don't talk about it." The attorney stood to walk Alan Kinman to the door. "Alan," he started, "sometimes these girls at these clubs use stage names. Did Tanya have one?"

"Yeah. They called her Star."

Chapter Eight

Chester Morgan believed in hunches. All good trial attorneys do, or at least used to, until procedural maneuvering and endless discovery made litigation a contest of attrition to be won by wealth and endurance. Morgan had learned to rely on his hunches: to know when a client was not being truthful, to know when to ask—or not—one more question when a witness could destroy your case or your opponent's. Chester trusted his hunches and he had one now, an illogical but a feels-right-in-the-gut belief that one simple inquiry might answer the questions about Tanya Everly's death. He turned his car from the major boulevard into an old residential neighborhood of straight streets and square city blocks.

Ancient oak trees with leaves bitter gold shaded the small frame houses that had been built in the early 1920's. Beat up cars, abandoned with hoods up, doors opened, or plastic sheets covering missing windows lined the curbs and sat in front yards. The original working class residents no longer lived here. White paint cracked and peeled from many of the homes. Over-abundant weeds grew in front of others. Occasionally, a house with a trimmed yard and a sturdy structure would surprise. Morgan turned onto another street and saw the places of lives forgotten except by those who lived them.

He drove further. Children played on the grass and into the street. Two men with stringy hair worked on a pickup truck with a radio beating loud enough to rattle the windows of Morgan's car. He passed an abandoned house, gray with disuse, and then saw an old man and an old woman sitting on rocking chairs on a front porch.

He turned at the next corner, and saw it, and knew it was the right one without checking the address. A small, faded "For Rent" sign stood in a tidy front yard of a white house with eaves pointing to the blue sky like steeples. Had an angel chosen to live in Old Vivia, she would have lived here. Instead, Tanya Everly, a dancer at a strip club called Vixens, had. As Morgan looked at the house and remembered Alan Kinman's quest, it seemed right.

The lawyer parked his car in front of the house next door. It, too, had been well maintained but, perhaps, with a harsher hand. He got out of his car to talk to Tanya Everly's landlord—the one Alan Kinman claimed would not tell him anything. Morgan believed otherwise. The attorney trusted his hunches. He knocked and waited.

A large, solid woman of fifty or fifty-five opened the door. Short straight hair, dark and graying, outlined her ordinary face at forty-five degree angles. She wore no make-up, tight-fitting slacks, and a white ski jacket with too many pockets. Morgan stared up into the woman's face. She looked like a side-by-side refrigerator with both doors open.

"I'm Chester Morgan," he began.

"So?" she yelled as much as talked.

"And you might be?" asked Morgan.

"None of your God damned business," the woman replied.

"Your friends must call you something," Morgan said.

"If you were my friend, you'd know who I was."

Morgan smiled. "You're right. Pardon my lack of manners. I'm interested in learning about the house next door."

The woman just stared.

"'Nice place you have there. This one, too. I wonder if you could tell me—"

"No," she said. If anything, her volume increased.

"It seems like a young woman used to live there. What happened to her?"

"I'm not telling you, or anyone like you, anything!"

Morgan began to feel defeated. "Well, actually I wanted to talk to you about possibly renting it."

"I don't rent to men."

"You can't do that!" the lawyer protested.

"I just did," she said and slammed the door in his face.

Morgan returned to his car, turned the ignition, and started towards home and his next destination.

I've got to work on my style, he thought, and my hunches.

Chapter Nine

Separated from the white collar commerce and community of new Vivia by a different past and soul, Old Vivia spread over what had once been a trading post clearing on the east side of a big bend on the Cottonwood River. The working class, the dispossessed, and the ignored now made Old Vivia their home amid warehouses, factories, refineries, and places few felt safe to go. Morgan knew these people, yet was not one of them.

Morgan drove through this aged city Friday night, his destination further on, but apart, perhaps, only by time. Old red brick store fronts and shabby old hotels crowded Ninth Avenue and streetlights glared and cut stark shadows. Dance halls, once ringing with Western Swing, were now silent. An occasional movie marquee glowed yellow but titles now carried "XXX" below. Only the patrons in the beer joints knew what really happened there.

Ninth Avenue widened. Parking lots began to be seen in front of concrete block buildings. Motels, once modern with hot pink and tropical green neon signs, seemed tawdry with age and neglect. If anything, the lights of the city were now dimmer. The occasional drive-in restaurant or coffee shop of unusual geometric design and faded bright color mocked the post-war optimism of their builders. This was Kiowa Heights, the once-hoped-for center of Old Vivia's renaissance but, instead, a three or four mile corridor along Ninth Avenue of warehouses, bars not good enough to be called honky tonks, strip joints, adult bookstores, and sex for sale.

Morgan wondered why he was driving through Kiowa Heights on a Friday night. He knew—to find a lost girl who had probably already lost years ago. A case without resolution. A case without satisfaction. A case with threat and a client who had to know. Trouble. Morgan felt the loneliness of Kiowa Heights and knew the other reason he cruised Ninth Avenue that night: To escape his own solitude. He looked at the fancy rigged pickup trucks in the parking lots, the flashing lights, the darkness. Was he that different?

Morgan stopped at the light at Murray Road and Ninth Avenue. An old explosives factory stood in darkness to his side. A few more blocks? A few more feet? His car moved onward as if without guidance. An old Key Petroleum gas station sat boarded up by the side of the road. The yellow key and blue lock of its trademark neon sign, forever dark. Graffiti had been painted on the plywood covering the plate glass windows, but weeds had not grown from the cracks in the concrete drive, yet to fracture from neglect.

The image seared and would not fade.

Morgan thought of William Harrison, the man whose company had owned this station and many others like it. With his wealth, style, education, and generosity, the oilman still died alone in a YMCA swimming pool. Morgan still didn't understand. Harrison knew how to swim. Yet, great athletes make mistakes, have accidents. William Harrison died alone. Maybe the image would never fade.

Light from a sign glared: "VIXENS!" Then in smaller print, "Live Adult Entertainment." Morgan turned into the parking lot and parked his car. He wanted to find Tanya Everly's mother, but he didn't know how exactly or what he might encounter. He sat for a few minutes and decided to go in. He knew why, but he didn't know.

A bouncer behind a smoked glass window took his money and pushed a beat-up sign-in sheet towards him. Morgan wrote his own name and walked through a door posted with a sign "If Nudity Offends You, Do Not Enter." Loud music pounded as a woman in a glossy black G-string draped with silver chains danced on a bare stage. The air felt warm and moist with the odor of fermented beer, tobacco smoke, heavy perfumes, and pungent female perspiration. Morgan looked for a place to sit.

The place looked smaller than it had from the outside. And darker. Cheap paneling lined the walls which held up a low ceiling of dingy acoustical tile. A stark platform extended from the center and on the other side of the room, square utilitarian tables and chairs packed the place with men—large, small, grizzled, timid, all types. Some who fit in, and some who didn't, and some who never would here, or anywhere else. Morgan found a table between an overweight Indian kid and two men with pompadours who sold appliances or Jesus on all-night TV.

The music stopped. The woman wearing the shiny G-string crouched on the stage to pick up the clothes she had thrown off. Sharp rib bones pulled against her thin white skin and her long breasts dangled. A factory worker on the front row snickered and whispered to his buddies as if she weren't there. Morgan needed a drink.

"She just audition," the overweight Indian kid said.

Morgan looked for someone to bring him a drink. Near the back, a small bar stood, made eerie with vibrating blue, gold, and red lights. In the shadows, he saw women, not dressed—but not quite undressed either, sipping frothy drinks next to men who looked like they had more money than the rest, or looked more lonely than the rest, or both. Sip a beer and watch them strip, Morgan thought, or pay a few dollars more for a drink and have them sit next to you in outfits not subdued enough for Frederick's of Hollywood. A con, but Morgan understood. The stripper and the house made money, but for a few moments, you weren't alone.

Another woman took the stage and began to dance to a song that sounded like fifty thousand others that might come out of a synthesizer. A waitress brushed against Morgan. He ordered a drink and watched. The woman on stage grabbed her bosom, tossed her hair, and leered at the crowd. Morgan looked around the room to see who might help him find the mother of Tanya Everly, the dead stripper known in Kiowa Heights as Star. Maybe someone would. Maybe no one. He felt someone watching him from behind a beaded curtain to the side of the main platform, but no one was there.

The drink arrived sooner than expected but not soon enough. He leaned against his chair and focused on the woman gyrating on stage. The music ended abruptly and then switched to a tune with a Latin beat. She swayed and moved to melody and beat. A flip of a hand and creamy flesh fell forward exposed. She looked into the crowd and smiled, not leered. Morgan sipped his drink and watched, lost.

"Want some company?" A small, bleached blonde girl, woman, bounced into an empty chair at his table. She sounded like the kid next door selling Girl Scout cookies.

Morgan hesitated and then said, "The seat's yours, if you wish."

She scooted her chair forward, put her elbows on the table, and her chin in her hands. "What's your name?"

He told her. "And yours?" he asked. Morgan looked at the young woman's face. No wrinkles. Her skin, white and soft and unblemished. She smelled like bubble gum and gin.

"Misty," she said. A loud voice behind her distracted her and she turned abruptly. She giggled as she adjusted a fleshy breast back into the sheer negligee she was wearing. "They don't make these things too practical," she said. She smiled at him. He had seen a smile like that before—a face pudgy with baby fat and mussed bleached blonde hair.

"How long have you worked here?" Morgan asked.

The girl woman touched her fingertips to her thumb as if she were counting. "July. Maybe August. It's good money." Morgan looked at the full, puffy body of this woman child sitting next to him.

"Do you want to buy the lady a drink?" A waitress appeared as if cued.

"How old are you?" Morgan asked, looking at the young woman sitting at his table.

"Twenty-one," she said. An automatic response.

Maybe sixteen, Morgan thought. He paused, then said to the waitress, "I don't think so."

The girl woman touched his arm. "I'm going to have to go. They don't like for us to just sit and talk," she said, looking at a square-built man standing in the shadows across the room and glaring in their direction. "Have a good time." She got up to leave, but the square-built man continued to stare.

Another dancer, a stubby redhead who could have ridden rodeo as well as doffed her clothes, took the stage and, as she moved, the platform shook. She tried but her rhythm was off. Her music—screaming teenaged angst and screeching guitars—beat fast. She was a quarter note behind. At least. The dancer knew it, so she yanked a string, her clothes fell off, and she stood there naked and twitched. He should have been bored or disgusted, Morgan knew, but he wasn't. The drink had hit hard; the week had been long. What difference does it make, he thought as he forgot and watched and wondered.

Morgan felt the presence of someone next to him and smelled the rich scent of a European perfume. "This seat taken?" a slender woman asked, her voice deep, sultry, and in an accent without a home.

Morgan pulled the chair out, started to stand, and then nodded. "Thank you," she said, as she slipped onto the seat and folded long legs beneath her.

He learned her name, or at least what she said her name was: Topaz. Although the stage lights had darkened to flashing colored lights, he could see eyes cobalt blue that seemed to glow. She put a long white cigarette to her painted red lips and lit it. "You don't mind, do you?" she said and smiled.

Chester Morgan shook his head. "This is where you work, where you live," he said. "You ought to be able to do whatever you want."

"Should," she replied. "I've been here forever."

"Just seems like it," the attorney said. "You aren't that old." The woman looked more mature than the last, not much perhaps, but legal at least. "When did you start?"

"You don't come here often," Topaz said. She rubbed an empty glass with a long finger and smiled an orthodontic smile. "Otherwise, don't you think you might remember?" In the dim light, he saw her high cheekbones and thick, golden hair. She could have been a European fashion model.

"I suppose," he said. "Or, maybe your beauty shocks me so I can't remember."

"That will work," she said, exhaling gray smoke. "I started a year or so ago." She stared at the stage where the stubby redhead contorted and bumped another strange grinding rotation. "That's pathetic, isn't it?"

Morgan ignored her remark and stared at the woman at his table. She would know, he thought.

"Does Star still work here?" he asked.

It wasn't her cue, but the waitress was there. "Would you like to buy the lady a drink?" she asked.

The dancer with the cobalt blue eyes scowled, smashed out her cigarette, and rose to stand. "No, he doesn't," she answered.

"I'm willing," Chester Morgan said.

"I'm not," she replied and walked away.

The Indian kid at the next table mumbled something to himself. If the words had been in English, Morgan didn't understand but he didn't think they were. Morgan shivered from an unexpected chill. He motioned to the waitress to bring him another drink. He needed it. Maybe his luck would improve. Maybe not.

Several other strippers jiggled, bounced, and shook under the harsh stage light while Morgan sat alone. He wondered if he had been blackballed. After leaving his table, Topaz had gone over and whispered something to the square-built man in the shadows. They had both stared at Morgan for a minute, but then the square-built man shrugged and the movie star stripper walked away. Morgan decided the man must like to glare. The lonely attorney watched the show and ignored the man.

For over a half hour, no one had approached him and intuition told him inquiries of the televangelists/appliance salesmen and the Indian kid would be fruitless. He looked at his watch and decided he wouldn't learn anything tonight. He wouldn't mind coming back, he admitted. For a change, work had not preoccupied him. He understood why others escaped into this other world, underworld dive. A buxom woman of alabaster curves and night black hair had danced wearing a cowboy hat and she had smiled at him ...

Morgan decided to leave. This was fruitless. As he started to stand, a body landed in the empty chair next to his.

"The drinks are water, sugar, and lime, mixed up in a blender, and served in a frozen glass. I can't stand to drink another one of them," the woman said. "If ya get me black coffee and pay the higher price, I'll sip on it here for a long time." She sounded as if she might be from Morgan's hometown.

"Fair enough," Morgan said. He liked her approach.

When the waitress arrived, she began her ritual question: "Would you like to—"

"You can skip that," Morgan said. "The lady needs a cup of coffee."

"The only thing I can serve her is the house drink," the waitress replied.

"I said the lady wants some coffee."

"Sorry," the waitress said, but wasn't.

"Can you bring me a cup?" Morgan asked.

The waitress nodded. "I suppose."

"Okay. Bring it to me—large, black, and hot. Bring the lady a house drink at my expense, except the house can keep it with my compliments," Morgan said. "I'll pay for it."

The waitress shrugged and slinked away.

"Nice job," the woman said. "I didn't even have to show you some tit or rub your leg to get you to do that." She talked matter-of-factly, only a hint of tease and come-on. "God, you're easy."

"Maybe."

The woman leaned back into the chair and took a deep breath. She was new and hadn't been fired yet, or had taken her clothes off for strangers and made money for Vixens so long she could do what she wanted.

"They don't push you around, do they?" Morgan said, as he looked at the square-built man.

"Still try. Got rules for everything," the woman said with a half-shrug. "It's worse with a new police chief in town, and everything that's going on."

"What's that?" Morgan asked.

"Nothin', I suppose," the woman said. "Bruce is forever convinced the cops are going to show up some night and close us down."

"'Bruce, the guy over there who likes to stare?" Morgan asked.

The woman laughed. "What guy in here doesn't?"

"None at the customers, except one," Morgan replied. The bleached-blonde child woman who had been the first to hustle a drink from Morgan started to dance on the main stage. "Bruce doesn't ask too many questions, does he?"

"Never, except when he has to," the woman next to him said. She saw the lights from the stage reflect from Morgan's eyes. "Yeah, when I first came here, I bounced instead of drooped, too."

"She might remind me of someone," Morgan said. "Pardon my manners. I suppose you'll be up there sometime this evening, too."

"Already have. 'Don't recognize me without a cowboy hat pushed down to my eyebrows, do ya?" she said, then smiled.

Morgan grinned. "Let's just say I couldn't see your eyes."

The waitress slid a cup of coffee in front of Morgan, and he paid enough for the whole tree to be imported from Brazil. Even with a good tip, the waitress grumbled and sauntered away. "What's your name?" he said as he pushed the coffee to his tablemate.

"Call me Lucy Roundbottom if you like. Or call me LaToya TaTas," she said. "Whatever happened to your manners?"

"I'm Chester."

"Everybody here calls me Candy," she said.

Morgan said nothing.

"They do," she said. She paused, looked at the silent attorney, then whispered, "My name's Maria. Really." The stage light sparkled from a small geometric earring she wore.

"Let me see," Morgan said, touching his ear.

She pulled back her wavy black hair and tilted her head to show him a sterling silver earring. "It's a star," she said. "I wear it for someone."

Morgan slowly reached his hand to examine the dancer's earring. "Tell me about her," he said.

Maria pulled back, stiffened. Morgan lowered his hand. "What do you mean?" she asked.

"Tell me about Star."

"Tany ... Star isn't here anymore," she said.

"I suppose I know that. I'm interested in what happened to her."

The woman shrugged. "Dancers show up and leave. Sometimes they leave and we never see 'em again. We don't ask questions. It's part of the business."

"Star wasn't a dancer who showed up and left, though," Morgan replied. "You're what—twenty-three, twenty-four? She'd worked here for six or seven years. Maybe longer than you have. Maybe the same. You know her real name. You're wearing that star for her."

"I never said that."

"But you are," Morgan said.

"What's your interest?" she asked, shaking her head and covering the sparkling ring with her full dark hair.

"Let's just say I'm chasing a dream that never came true," Morgan said. "I'm an attorney. I'm going to find out."

Maria sighed. "You know she's dead. And, anymore, we don't ask. We don't want to know. Rumors are the cops did it. When someone disappears in Kiowa Heights now, or there's an unexplained accident, people say the cops did it and laugh this morbid laugh, but it's not funny. A new police chief comes to town, wants to clean up Kiowa Heights. Make your own conclusions. When we don't see someone now, we know there is not going to be any kind of investigation. The attitude is 'One more gone, one less problem.' When somebody is up and gone, we don't ask. We're afraid of what we might find out."

"But you want to know," Morgan said.

"I suppose," she said.

"I told you I do, too, and if I can, I will," Morgan said. "Between us, you'll help me?"

"You straight?" she asked.

Morgan nodded. "Are you?" he asked. He didn't wait for an answer. He didn't need to. "Where can I find her mother, Tamar White?"

Maria swirled the remaining coffee in her cup and stared at it a moment. She looked around the room and then back at Morgan. She said, "When they ran her butt out of here for selling Tanya's ass, she lighted from one place to another on Ninth Avenue. Still does, far as I know. You might try Bennie's. Look for the new white Lincoln."

"You mean—"

"She pimped her own daughter."

Morgan caught his breath. The music continued to play, but he didn't hear it. He only felt the incessant pounding of its bass beat. Maybe Alan Kinman's accusations had been less perverse, angry fantasy and more pathetic reality. Morgan felt sick.

"Tanya hated that," Maria said. Her words faded. For a moment, her eyes looked vacant and sorrowful and her form, smaller and vulnerable. A Madonna without a child, perhaps, or a Mary without a pierced corpse.

Across the room, Topaz and two other women approached the square-built man Morgan now knew as Bruce. Topaz's face moved as if she were talking loudly but Morgan couldn't hear her. The two other women had their hands rolled into fists and placed on their hips. Confederates or adversaries, Morgan couldn't tell.

"That woman, Topaz, sat here a few minutes ago," he said. "When I asked her about Tanya, Star—whoever—she acted like I had spit in her cleavage and left. Even offered to buy her a drink. Still left. What show does she live?"

Maria sat up. "Between us?" she asked. Morgan motioned yes. The dark-haired dancer continued, "A psychotic bitch. That's what Tanya called her. Topaz's prettier but Tanya was popular, real popular, made more money from tips and such. I don't know if that's it or if that's all. The girls think Bruce is cutting Topaz in on something."

"What?" Morgan asked.

"This place. Something else. You know how women talk when they work together."

"I've never been one, so I don't," the attorney replied.

She paused. "It's talk. Forget about it." She sipped her coffee and looked at the door. "If I had a best friend, Tanya was."

"What do you think happened to her?"

"I told you. I don't ask questions."

"You wish someone did or you wouldn't keep telling me that," Morgan said.

"Whether it was some creep her mother set her up with," the stripper said, "or that geeky guy who always seemed to hover around, or really an accident like they all say it was, it makes no difference. Death's final."

"If you recognize it, justice is, too—sometimes." Morgan noticed the woman's cup was empty. "How will I know if I find Tanya's mother?"

"You'll know. Overweight. Blonde. And cheap." The woman pushed her cup away. "I'm going to have to go."

"Between us?" Morgan said.

The woman nodded. "Between us," she said. Then, the woman Maria stood, and Morgan watched her long legs and hips sashay across the room and through the beaded curtain doorway.

Chapter Ten

Chester Morgan drove from Vixen's parking lot onto Ninth Avenue. He thought about what he had learned, what he had to do next, but what he remembered was the brief escape the time had provided. He had done exactly what he had told Alan Kinman not to: Say who you are or what you are doing. A pretty, almost naked, woman next to him and who knows? Morgan shook his head and hoped if he returned to Vixen's, it wouldn't be on this job. He might be back, he told himself, if the case resolved. If it did. Maybe even if it didn't. He thought he owed the dancer Maria that much. The boarded-up Key Petroleum station passed by on Morgan's side unnoticed.

Chester had heard it when she said of her star-shaped earring, "I wear it for someone." He recognized it and knew it. In others—clients, witnesses, or sometimes adversaries, he had seen or heard it: A gesture, a phrase, or a tone which exposed unintended truth in the beat of a second. Maria's truth was his, and Alan Kinman's, and every man's and every woman's who might disappear into the Kiowa Heights' night: A life departed can escape unknown, but a life stolen or taken, haunts. If he learned truth about Tanya Everly's death, he would return and tell Maria. He owed the heart in the brash, sultry stripper at least that much. Maybe more he didn't want to admit.

The clock on the dashboard glowed ten forty-nine. Chester felt warm, but the fall night was cold. The lights of Kiowa Heights seemed less stark and somehow brighter, but he wasn't drunk. He knew that. He had never heard of Bennie's, so he slowed for every bar and honky tonk and looked for a sign, and, if absent, for a new white Lincoln. He stopped at one joint with no sign but with a new white Lincoln parked in front. He stayed long enough to see no one matched Maria's description of Tanya Everly's mother and long enough to know that if he asked, he might wind up at the end of someone's fist. He could smell it. "It doesn't mean they're bad," Morgan recalled his first boss back in Tobusky saying about the hangers-on at a local roadhouse. "It just means they like to fight." Morgan didn't stay to find out.

The longer Chester Morgan drove, the more foreign the landscape of Kiowa Heights became: Asphalt, vapor lights, vacant buildings. Strange urban weeds and chunks of uprooted concrete littered the earth. The chill returned to him and the challenge of meeting Tanya Everly's mother turned, for a moment, to dread. The road narrowed and post oaks darkened the night. Morgan turned around and drove back into town on Ninth Avenue.

He passed Vixen's and the vacant Key gas station and the image returned. William Harrison, dead. He shook it away and vowed to find the woman who prostituted her own daughter. The clock on the dashboard read eleven-eighteen.

Bennie's was a pale wooden building a mile up the road from Vixen's. Morgan had passed it earlier without seeing it. It was that kind of place: a rectangular box with neon beer lights in the windows and a small plastic sign hanging from a pole in front. Its asphalt and gravel parking lot extended to the street. At the corner of the wooden building sat a shiny new white Lincoln with gold-spoked hubcaps.

Morgan parked next to a black, mud-caked GMC pickup truck that had a Confederate flag decaled on the back window. Morgan hesitated. Tamar White's model Lincoln was the gaudy top of the line and new enough to still carry a dealer's tag. The gaudy and the Lincoln fit in with the rest of the cars, but the top of the line and brand new didn't, except maybe for a few pickups. Law school hadn't trained him for this. This time, he couldn't know the answer before he asked the question. He hoped life had prepared him. He got out of his car. He knew it had.

Two large men—one tall, the other tall and obese—walked out the door of the bar. Morgan passed the men. They smelled of beer and tobacco smoke. Morgan didn't see their faces. He didn't figure he needed to and didn't want to.

One man asked, "Ya mind if we cruise down to Vixen's for a while?"

"Nuttin' bothers Bob," the other replied. He talked like one nostril was stopped up.

Morgan heard the gunning of a large engine, turned, and saw the dark GMC pickup truck with the Confederate flag decal back up and pull away. Chester Morgan walked through the door into Bennie's.

Smoke and darkness caused him to squint his eyes. A lady with a beehive hair-do and black jeans that were too tight twenty years ago wiped a table with a rag and tossed a remark over her shoulder to a whiskered-face man sitting by himself. A top twenty country and western song played on a jukebox and a crowd of men played pool in the corner. A large bar—padded at its perimeter in black Naugahyde—stretched across the center of the room. On its counter propped next to the cash register, a small black and white metal sign read "NO GUNS." Morgan took a seat a few feet away and ordered a beer. The dance floor was empty.

Morgan drank long enough to be ignored. At a place like Bennie's, even on a busy Friday night, a stranger is noticed until he is there long enough for everyone in the regular crowd to notice him and decide he doesn't merit further attention, which is usually about the length of time it takes to drink two beers. Morgan had glanced around the room several times and realized more people were packed into the place than he had thought. Working people and people of the night. Morgan's clothes were newer than most and better pressed. His hands weren't as calloused and his women weren't as bawdy. His face had taken some blows but not like some here. He had shot a gun but never owned one. When he saw the obese, middle-aged bleached blonde sitting by herself at a corner in the back, he knew he wasn't the first to sit at this bar and think these thoughts. He picked up his beer and went to do what the others had, too.

Tamar White, the mother of the dead young woman, watched him approach. Something distracted her, and she looked away. She pulled a cigarette from a sequined cigarette case and lit it. Morgan stood at her table, illumined by a burning red candle in a plastic fishnet covered glass.

"You're the one I talk to," Morgan said.

"Maybe," she said. She flicked an ash into the ashtray.

"No, you are," he said. "I know you are."

"About what?" she said. Her voice was raspy as if she had trouble breathing.

"About Star. About getting together with Star," he said. "Can I sit down?"

A big hand landed on the attorney's shoulder. "Why, Chester Morgan. I thought that was you," a husky male voice said. Morgan turned and saw Butch Miller, a client he had represented in an injury case several years earlier. "Gaw dang, it is you," the tall, narrow man continued.

Morgan looked at Miller. He had done a good job for his client, probably better than he deserved. "Hey, Butch," he said.

Butch Miller scooted between Morgan and Tamar White and leaned down to talk. "Hey, Tam, you know who you're speaking to? Chester Morgan, the best shyster in town. I guarantee you that." Miller stood back up and put his arm around his attorney's shoulders.

The woman said nothing. Neither did Morgan.

"Didn't mean to interrupt nothing. Ya'll get on with your business," Miller said, as he pulled a chair out for Morgan. "Good seeing you, Chest. Catch ya later, Tam." He clicked a noise with his cheek and winked at the obese woman.

"You, too," Morgan said, and Butch Miller left.

The woman said nothing and then, "I'm out of the business. And, you can stop the dumb act."

Morgan had been caught. He knew it, and she knew it. If he continued as he started, he'd learn nothing. "Is that all you tell people who still want to get set up with Star?"

"What else is there to tell?" Tamar White said.

"What happened to her," Morgan replied.

The woman tapped long nails polished bright peach on the table. On each finger, she wore a ring. "She's dead. That's simple enough."

"Is it?" Morgan finished his beer. "It's not for me."

Tamar White looked straight at him. "Listen, I don't know who you are or what you want. I don't know what you know or what you think you know. Star died at the Bunkhouse Motel almost two months ago. A tragic accident and I'm out of business. You ought to leave a grieving mother alone."

At one time, the woman across the table might have been pretty. Her skin was a translucent white, spread smooth except for lines around her mouth and bags under her dark blue eyes. Fair, light freckles spread over the bridge of a pixie nose and she had full well-formed lips. She wore too much eye make-up and dark roots showed at the base of her blonde hair. She weighed as much as a Dallas Cowboy lineman without the muscle but that didn't repel Chester Morgan. Her eyes—cold, without life—did.

"A grieving mother doesn't say she's out of business first. She doesn't say it at all," Morgan said. "And, she doesn't say 'tragic accident' like she practiced it all morning to get the sound right."

"Listen, mister, I ain't got nothing to hide," the woman said. "She wanted me to do it. She was goin' to whore herself anyway, and she knew she'd blow the money if she got it herself. What concern of it is yours anyway? You can't understand, can you? I never even seen you before. Who sent you?"

"How do you know somebody did?"

"Cause you lawyers ain't better than any of the rest of us. You'll do anything for dollars, and not much for anything else, so don't be judging me or what I done. I asked you who sent you."

"Maybe somebody who doesn't believe it was a tragic accident."

Tamar White motioned the waitress to bring her another drink. "I don't care who you're here for—and I know you are for someone. If it's that little perverted stalker and you find out it isn't a tragic accident, which it is, you and him will be in a bunch of trouble. He'd be a great witness for you—those smeary black glasses, zits, the stutter and that voice. God, that voice. You ought to get yourself a better class of clients."

"Would you tell me what happened to your daughter? Who she was with? Who found her?"

"I would if I knew, but the coroner said it was so bad, I didn't want to know. I supposed she was right."

"Then how do you know it was an accident?" Morgan asked.

"Oh, get the fuck out of here," Tamar White said. She motioned a large man who had been standing in the shadows.

"I'm going," Morgan said. "You don't have to get your protection after me." He stopped. "Miss White, I hope someday you'll feel some heartache for your daughter and, if not for yours, for someone else's."

"Get out."

Morgan nodded and left. An autumn moon glowed in the sky over old Vivia. Its light had shone on the earth here for millions and millions of years, but the lives in the shadowy corners of Kiowa Heights reminded that darkness was as eternal. Morgan wondered whether his quest to remedy the past was folly. Maybe he didn't really understand. Maybe Alan Kinman's obsession was just that. He hoped not, but he wondered. An attorney always wants to believe his client but knows he never can, not completely. And, they all said *accident* as if scripted.

When Morgan arrived at home, even his movements echoed in the silent house. He pondered and sipped some Kentucky bourbon. He pressed a few buttons on some black boxes connected with wire, then music murmured through the night like hope through light and shadows.

Chapter Eleven

Chester Morgan made the trip every Saturday—almost. The dense, broad-leaf woods and the quick-moving streams of the San Bois Mountains made his lungs feel larger and his blood warmer—usually. The slower drawl, the patient nods, and the stories old men tell at gas stations reminded him life means more than existing—most of the time.

The blue, cinder-block building waited at one edge of town, a convenience store at the other. Between, and never to connect, stood a downtown of vacant brick buildings, an Eisenhower-era post office, and a small bank. During the Depression, Pretty Boy Floyd had made a run through here people still talked about and, more than a century ago, Belle Starr had stayed somewhere back in the mountains when this part of Oklahoma was still the Choctaw Nation. Tobusky. Home. Chester Morgan had made it again—almost.

The room, like all the others, had been painted beige, and it smelled of disinfectants and medicine. A boom box sat on a chest of drawers and grainy pictures on the walls suggested a life lived at a time before and elsewhere. A white-haired woman with thick jowls and blue-eyes that tried to twinkle lay in a big hospital bed under a white sheet and an institutional blanket. Chester Morgan remembered when the woman, his mother, would meet him at the front door when he came home and would stand on the porch and wave good-by until the last dust kicked up by his car from the dirt and rock road settled when he drove away.

There in the room in the blue cinder-block building, Chester kissed his mother and asked her how she was. She pressed a button and the hospital bed moved forward until she sat up.

"You didn't need to come today," she said.

"I'm surprised you're not tired of saying that, Mama," Chester said, "and not really meaning it."

"I do," she said. "You don't need to come down here and see this old lady strung out on a Cadillac bed in a nursing home. You have your own life and things to do. I mean it, but I'm glad you're here."

Chester smiled and patted her arm. "They treating you okay?"

The white-haired woman nodded.

"You feeling all right?" he asked.

"'Suppose."

A heavy-set aide in stretch polyester came into the room and took Molly Morgan's blood pressure. When the aide left, Chester Morgan's mother said, "That girl must weigh over two hundred and fifty pounds, but she's sweet. You know, people are kind of prejudiced against fat people. Shouldn't ought to be but they are."

"Mama, I've said this before, but why don't you let me take you up to Vivia. I could get you the best medical care there, find you a nice place to stay."

The woman shook her head. "I'd just have you. I've got my friends here. My people are here."

"Your people are all gone, Mama," Morgan said.

"They ain't ever gone," she replied. Molly Morgan turned her head away from her son. "Ain't ever gone."

Chester looked through the window and beyond the parking lot and saw an abandoned, two-story clapboard house. Wind blew through a broken window and the front door had fallen off. He remembered when the McCollough kids played in the backyard, now thick with brown weeds.

The woman turned her lined face towards her lawyer son. "You carrying something, son?" she asked.

"An attorney is always carrying something, Mama," he replied.

"Something more?" she asked.

Morgan lied to his mother. For the two-and-a-half hour drive from Vivia, he had pondered over little other than Tanya Everly's demise and his trip into Kiowa Heights the previous evening. "No."

"'Got yourself a steady girl?"

"Not right now," he said. He knew she had started her list.

"Chester, it's not good for people to live by themselves. Heavy burdens for two are lighter when two are together, when two are one."

"I know. You say that," Chester said. "Maybe the right one will come along."

"Well, I suppose that's better than the wrong one." His mother smiled and tried to adjust her pillow. Chester reached out to help her.

"Hear anything from Cassie?"

"No, Mama."

"Maybe that's the best anyway. Are you walking the path?" she asked as her son fluffed up the pillow behind her head.

"I'm trying, Mama. I'm trying."

"'Goin' to church?"

Morgan shook his head. "I'm not in Rotary or Lion's Club either."

The woman closed her eyes and then opened them again. "That would sure disappoint your grandmother, but I guess I know what you're saying. I've always had a wild heart, too. Just don't stop lookin'."

"I won't."

Chester heard a wheelchair squeak down the hall and the voices of old people speaking. His mother lay silent except for the sound of her struggled breathing. With her asleep, he thought of what might have been—twenty, or forty, or sixty years before. She awoke.

"You remember Mabel Napier," she said. "They lived down in Look Out Hollow on past the old Pickerd place."

Morgan nodded and shrugged.

"You know they had that boy that just wandered off one day and then strolled back into town six months later and didn't know where he'd been or what he'd done. Never did remember. Least that's what he said, and I guess I kind of believe him."

"Maybe so," Chester said. "I think I remember."

"Well, that boy's daughter—Mabel's granddaughter—picked up her guitar and took a bus to Nashville. She wants to be a singer."

"Think she'll make it?" Chester asked. He thought of someone else who wanted to be a singer, the someone for whom Alan Kinman sought the truth.

The white-haired woman's eyes sparked animation. "Shoot," she said. "That girl didn't take nothin' with her but her bare ass and guitar. Those Napiers are kind of like we were—so poor, can't afford beans. I hate to think what might happen to her."

"You could have made it. Were you ever that poor—really?"

"Chester, you don't know. Your grandpapa tried and your papa tried. We all did, but it was hard times and good girls just didn't get on the bus and go off to the city, even though it was safer then than it is now. Then the babies came along ..."

"You could have made it, Mama. You know you could."

Molly Morgan looked at the grainy pictures on the wall and then quietly said, "I know. I could have been good."

Chester took his mother's hand. "Not could have. You were. Better than any of 'em on the radio today."

"And what good did it do?" she asked.

"What good does any of it do?" Chester asked. "Maybe somebody just about to give up heard you sing and decided not to. Maybe somebody who had lost a loved one heard and decided to get out of bed the next morning. Maybe that Napier girl heard you at a revival years ago and vowed to be as good as you and maybe will be. Maybe even be a star."

"Maybe," she said.

Chester Morgan looked down at the white-haired woman he would always remember as young. He thought of Tanya Everly who would unwillingly forever be remembered as young and the darkness of Kiowa Heights. "Mama, I need to hear you sing. Do you mind?"

She gently shook her head.

Chester placed a tape in the boom box on the chest of drawers and from its speakers came the wild-hearted voice of an Oklahoma country girl singing of golden bells and a land beyond the river.

Chapter Twelve

Drops of sweat clung to the man's forehead; his skin was puffy and red. He pushed Chester Morgan's business card across the Formica counter and said: "Ain't nothing I can tell you. I just rent rooms."

Morgan left the card on the counter. "I thought maybe you or the manager might know what happened to her."

The beefy man smelled of alcohol, his perspiration and his breath. He said, "I am the manager."

"Or maybe the owner," Morgan said. He stood in the lobby of the Bunkhouse Lodge, a worn down Kiowa Heights motel whose sign burned into the night sky a neon cowboy twirling a flashing yellow lariat. Its marquee read "American Owned." An old country music song played on a small, black radio behind the desk where the man stood.

"He's in New Jersey. Wouldn't know him if he walked in right now and I've been here a while." The man turned from Morgan to signal the conversation was over.

"He'd never know you talked to me," Morgan said.

"Not until you sued him," the man said.

"If I do," Morgan said. "If you talk, I may not sue, probably won't. If you don't talk, I may have no other choice."

"I told you. I don't know nothing. I rent rooms."

"By the hour. The half-day and day," Morgan said. "For years, you rented rooms to, or for, Tanya Everly—some people called her Star—and you know what for. Maybe her mother would take out the room. Maybe Tanya would, but I doubt it. Maybe you did and took a cut."

"Bullshit, not her."

"I don't care if you did, but you let rooms to her and to others like her and you know why," Morgan said.

"They pay the rent. I don't ask questions."

"As long as you get your share and the cops don't put any heat on you. Wonder if your boss in New Jersey knows about that."

"Mister, I ain't got to listen to your lawyer yap. As far as I'm concerned, you can haul your chair-shined butt down the road," the man said. He turned and adjusted the sound on the radio.

"I apologize," Morgan said. He hesitated, then said, "I'll talk straight with you. I haven't been retained by anyone who has the right to sue you or your boss in New Jersey. I don't have anything to do with the government or the police. I just represent a kid who wants to know what happened to his friend. I thought you might help."

"It's none of my business what happens back there," the man replied. "As long as the rent gets paid and the place ain't trashed, I don't care." The man shuffled some index cards on his desk that didn't need shuffling. He rearranged them again. "Why did you think I might help?"

"Don't know," Morgan said. "Unless you're different than most, you've lost someone you cared for and have never been really satisfied with why. Or, perhaps, there is some secret in your soul that won't let you sleep, regardless of how much you try to forget, or how much you drink, as long as that secret's locked up there alone. For some people, it haunts them at three in the morning. For others, it's all the time."

The man looked up at Morgan. "Did you really think I'd talk with you?"

"I hoped." Morgan pushed his card back across the Formica counter. "Keep my card, if you change your mind."

Morgan turned and walked towards the door. As he did, he heard the radio's scratchy broadcast of a singing voice, the sound of which ached with loneliness. The singer asked if you had ever heard a whippoorwill cry or the sound of a midnight train or the silence of a falling star. Morgan knew the voice and he knew the words.

"That's the greatest country and western song ever recorded," he said.

The man mumbled something. Morgan turned back towards the manager of the Bunkhouse Lodge and saw him under the glow of fluorescent light. "What did you say?" Morgan asked.

"I said, 'Ain't either.'"

"Well, what do you think?" Morgan asked.

The man looked at the attorney and hesitated. Then, he said, "Anything by Patsy Cline's better."

"God, she was good," Morgan said, "powerful and so young when she died, but Hank Williams—his voice, his soul, is country and western music."

"Damn night deejay on this station." The man shook his head as if he were going to spit. "He calls him Hank Williams, *Senior.* Like folks could ever confuse him with that longhaired boy of his or his grandson. The radio plays all this shit that sounds like a computer wrote it. Hank Williams, *Senior.* Biggest heartache most of these kids now singing country know is getting their boots dirty."

"There's nothing raw in their voices," Morgan said.

"No edge," the man said. "Nothing real."

Morgan stared at the man and said, "The real country singers have the sound God put in them, made rough and smooth by life."

The phone rang. The man picked it up and mumbled a few words. Through the slanted plate glass windows of the lobby, Morgan saw the lights of cars driving up and down Ninth Avenue. The man hung up the phone. "Yeah, that's the way the music used to be," he said.

"Maybe in some places it still is."

The man shook his head. "I think it's just about gone."

"Only if you forget," Morgan said. "Have you ever been to Thompson's Dance Emporium—up the street? All the greats played there: Hank Williams, Bob Wills, Lefty Frizzell, Kitty Wells. They say their ghosts still sing there at night."

"Maybe so," the man replied. "Maybe so."

Except for the plaintive voice singing on the radio, the room was silent. Morgan looked at the man. "If you change your mind ..." The attorney started for the door.

"Lawyer!" the man said. He rattled some coffee cans next to a stainless steel percolator and pulled a pint bottle of whiskey into view. "I always put her in the last room in the back—L-8." He showed the bottle to Morgan. "You say I told you anything and I'll call you a liar and say I never knew ya."

"You say I ever asked, and I'll do the same," Morgan replied.

The man splashed whiskey over the melting ice in his glass and filled a motel-supply tumbler half-full for Morgan. "We ain't fancy here," he said. "You want something besides ice or water, you'll have to find it yourself." Morgan took a drink and recognized the burnt-candy taste of cheap bourbon.

"She was a good kid with the wrong mom," the man said.

"I met her—the mother—last night," Morgan said. "I wasn't charmed."

"Tanya was that lady's bank account. Did you know that?" the man asked.

"Just what I'd heard."

"The mama's the one who started bringing her in here." The man gulped his drink, fumbled for the bottle, and poured himself more. "Probably should have never let that begin. She was so young."

"Was that—when?" Morgan asked.

"Five or six years ago, I guess. Of course, that woman'd just taken her somewhere else."

"You've been here that long?" Morgan asked.

The man nodded. "Where else can you drink when you want and not have the boss drop in since he's halfway across the country? And it's a cash job—mostly."

"For the police, too?" Morgan asked.

The man shrugged. "Maybe. Sometimes ya got to pay a little."

Morgan stared at the man.

"Judge me if you want," the man continued, "but I never took money off Star. Some of the others? Sure, but it ain't nothin'. Stand back here and maybe you'd understand. The owner is writing this whole place off. Look around. Your tax dollars are buying this dump, and the guy in New Jersey gets richer. What's the difference?" The man laughed.

"That's your business," Morgan said.

"You from New Vivia?" the man asked.

"I live there," Morgan replied.

The man tilted his head back. "Some of you have the guts to take that other man's wife to your four star hotel high rises, but most of you don't. Where do you think you go? You don't want nobody to know you come here. I told you I don't know nothing. I don't ask questions. There's a charge for me not knowing—built in. Except ..." The man turned his face away.

"Except when you know and there wasn't an extra charge and there's no one to talk to and no one even wanting to know," Morgan said.

"Drink some more whiskey," the man said. "I'll tell you about it." The man's face flushed red. "That girl was murdered. You know that, don't you?"

"Suspected," Morgan said. "Don't know. Her mother says it was an accident."

"Fuck her," the man said. "Star was murdered, but I don't know exactly why or how or who." The man rattled some keys in his pocket. "I'll show you."

"Why does Tamar White say it was an accident?" Morgan asked.

"She doesn't know? She doesn't ask questions?" the man said. He mocked himself. He rattled the same keys in his pocket. "I'll show you."

The man walked Morgan to the door and pulled it open. He hesitated and then turned the red-and-white sign over to read "No Vacancy." "Fuck 'em," he mumbled and locked the door behind them.

"You know my name," Morgan said. "What's yours?"

"Frank Carlile," the man replied. He had lowered his voice. Morgan heard the growl of traffic on Ninth Avenue and the on-and-off-again surge of power through the neon cowboy and his lariat above. A car door slammed and Morgan saw a figure walk quickly to a room.

"There's all kinds here," Carlile said. "Big revivals? Are we busy? You bet. Conventions? Yeah. About the only time we're not is when the roads are too icy to drive." They passed what had once been a swimming pool, now filled with river rock. In front of the two men, a macadam parking lot, rough and worn, spread to a two-winged structure of redwood and rough beams. Yellow lights illumined doors that led to the rooms that led to ... "All kinds," Carlile said again. "Fat boys and Orientals—they were kind of partial to Star. Old men, too—at least here lately."

"Keep any records of who they might be?" Morgan asked.

Carlile shook his head. "Not that'd do any good. Her mom, then Tanya here lately sometimes, set the deals up by phone. That's something else I shouldn't have started. Gave me the guy's name, phony as hell most of the time. I'd register him, and Tanya's mom or Tanya would pay at the end of the week. Sometimes both."

"Had she been with someone when she died?"

"Yeah," the man said. "John Smith."

"You make the guy pick up the key?"

Carlile shook his head. "Didn't see him. Tanya and Tamar had their own keys. They just called."

"Always the same room," Morgan asked.

"Rooms," he replied. "Always together, at least 'til about six or seven months ago."

Morgan thought of the obese woman in the shadows he had met the previous night. "That woman turned tricks?" he said.

"Naw," said the beefy man with the slumped shoulders. "It took me a while to figure it out. I'll show you in a minute."

A cold October wind blew whirls of sand and debris in the parking lot. A door slammed shut somewhere and the strong gust carried away the sound of the never-ending traffic on Ninth Avenue. The manager of the Bunkhouse Lodge slowed his walk as he and the lawyer approached the flat and long redwood covered building. The two men stopped at the last room in the back and Carlile said. "It's a room like all the others," he said. "The layout's flipped over in some. The colors, the furniture, some of 'em are different, but the rooms, they're all the same. Still, when I walk in here, I see her."

Chapter Thirteen

Frank Carlile turned the key and opened to door to Room L-8 of the Bunkhouse Lodge. He turned on the light and Chester Morgan followed him in. A double bed with a worn bedspread sat in the middle of the room; its sturdy Western style headboard propped against the wall. A vinyl-covered chair that might have been new in 1954 rested nearby. From a small lamp on a desk, dusty light spread onto an industrial gray-carpeted floor. The room was dark and smelled of bug spray and stained nicotine. It could have been any room at any second-rate motel coast to coast.

"Erma McIntosh found her," Frank Carlile said, his voice quiet. "Left her cleaning cart outside the room, walked to the office, and said 'Little girl's dead,' just like that, but I guess it shook her up pretty good. She left that day and never came back. Oh, she's still around. I've seen her. She just never came back."

Morgan looked over the room to see what scars of death, if any, had been left there. He saw none, only a room like many others. "Where was the body?" he asked and, as he did, hated himself for sounding so clinical, so removed, so detached.

"There," Carlile said, nodding towards the bed. "Her arms were spread open out across the bed and her hands were tied to the corners of the head board, one on each side. She was naked." Carlile stopped. He struggled and said, "There was blood on her hands and feet, too. They was tied together, her feet was, and the rope went under the bed, hooked up to the frame."

Carlile opened his hand wide and then squeezed it into a fist. "You wonder how I remember?" he asked. "You see something like this and you don't forget."

Chester recalled the image of William Harrison floating in the YMCA pool. He shook his head and said, "I know."

"Well, that's the way she was," Carlile said. He looked at the bed, stared at it.

"What else?" Morgan asked.

"Her side was cut. Like an afterthought or something. Not much blood I guess but still too much. Her neck was bruised all the way around and her eyes..." Carlile choked. "Her eyes were open like they were watching whoever it was who killed her."

Morgan shivered. "Strangled?" he asked.

Frank Carlile nodded. "Only thing I can figure. Who knows?"

"The blood on her hands and feet," Morgan said. "They were cut, too?"

"Couldn't tell exactly, not really," Carlile said. "Looked like it had been smeared on 'em, not really cut."

Morgan walked to the window and pulled on the heavy drapery. "With the curtains pulled, it's always the same time in here, isn't it?"Carlile nodded, started to sit on the bed, and then stopped.

"When did it happen?" the attorney asked.

"Erma came over to the office about ten o'clock that morning. Star had called the night before, oh, I guess about ten-thirty or eleven. I didn't see her that night. Didn't see nobody around here."

Morgan said, "I understand some people pay for stuff like getting tied up or tying others up. Do you suppose that's what happened to her except it didn't stop when it should have?"

"You sorry son of a bitch," Carlile said. "Hell, even if they paid for it, she didn't get paid to get killed. You don't even know what you're looking at."

"Then you tell me."

"I called from that telephone right there. A squad car came out—one on its regular rounds, I suppose. I had seen the guys before, didn't know 'em, but had seen 'em. They shut the room off and told me to go back to the office. By the time I got back there, a big black car arrived. An unmarked cop car. The squad car left. A couple of guys in suits got out with a lady—old-fashioned glasses and poofy hairdo. After a while, an unmarked armored-car-looking thing arrived—and left. Black car did, too. All of forty-five minutes and no one ever talked to me. No one. Doesn't that make you wonder? That's why you don't know what you're looking at."

"They ever talk to Erma?" Morgan asked.

"Far as I know they didn't," Carlile said. "Of course, she was up and gone by then."

"She know something she shouldn't have?"

"Not Erma," Carlile said. "She finished her job that day and just never came back."

"What did you find when you came back over here?"

Frank Carlile glanced around the room. "It was strange. Everything was gone—sheets, pillows, bedspread. Tanya's clothes. Everything out of the bathroom. All gone and the room cleaned up. Like nothing had happened here."

"What about the mattress?" Morgan asked.

"Except the mattress. They cut a hole out where she bled," Carlile said.

"Let's see," Morgan said.

"Only if you make the bed back up," Carlile said.

Chester nodded. The heavy-set manager of the Bunkhouse Lodge threw the bedspread up and lifted the mattress so that Morgan could see its cut underside. "See. Like I told you."

Carlile lowered the mattress and the lawyer started tucking the sheet back in. "Hell, I'll get it," Carlile said. "I've done it a lot more than you have." Carlile finished the job, quick and neat.

"Ought to send them a bill for the stuff they took," he said.

"Who?" Morgan asked.

"The cops," Carlile replied.

Morgan walked to the back of the room to a small walk-in closet and the entrance to the bathroom. He turned on the light to the pink-tiled, pink-fixtured room. He looked up and down the walls and at the fixtures. "Pink bathrooms at the Bunkhouse Lodge?" Morgan said.

"Yeah," Carlile called back. "Cowgirls like 'em. Some cowboys do, too."

Morgan pulled the shower curtain back and looked into the bathtub. Then, he looked into the sink. "There's no stopper in the sink and none in the bathtub," he said. "Were there the night Tanya was killed?"

"Probably not," Carlile said. He leaned at the doorframe to the bathroom. "The mechanical ones installed gave out a long time ago. Used to keep rubber ones in here, but they disappear pretty quick."

"Any water on the floor before the cops arrived?"

"This bathroom looked like it hadn't been used since Erma had been in the day before," the man replied. "They still took the towels and wash clothes, though."

"They?"

"The cops."

Morgan turned to go back into the bedroom. "Have you changed anything in this space since it happened?"

"Naw," Carlile replied. "Not really. Turned the mattress over."

Morgan stood at the foot of the bed and imagined the young woman, her last moments, her obscene-in-death corpse. He shuddered. "Frank, I want you to think hard," he said quietly. "Was there a bruise on Tanya's forehead? Was her hair matted like it had been wet?"

"No bruise," he said. "Her skin was shiny like she had sweat and the hair close to her head looked that way, too, but matted down? Like it had all been wet? No."

"You sure?" Morgan asked.

"I told you there were some things you don't forget."

"I know," Morgan said.

The two men walked towards the door. "You were going to show me something about the rooms," Morgan said. "You said Tanya and her mother took out rooms."

"Oh, yeah," Carlile said. He stopped. "It took me a while to figure it out. They always got adjoining rooms. Star in this end one and Tamar White in the next. Before I understood, I thought maybe the mother wanted to be close by, to protect her daughter or something. Or maybe, you know, they were kind of in business together. A lot of stuff in Kiowa Heights doesn't make sense. Of course, they weren't in business together. The mother sold off her own daughter full-time—at least until six or seven months ago. The mother quit showing up every time the daughter did; Tamar still did once in a while. I don't know exactly what happened."

"Always these two rooms?" Morgan asked. He touched the worn bedspread and despaired of the young life wasted here— both in life and in death.

"Got in the habit of putting them in these two rooms until I just gave them their own keys," Carlile replied. "A couple of months before Star died, though, I put her in a different one. We were busy, and the mom wasn't with her, but it didn't work out too good."

"Why not?" Morgan asked.

"The girls next to her complained about the noise," Carlile said. "Said the music was too loud."

"Tanya have a boom box or something?" Morgan asked.

"Hell, if I know," Carlile replied. "She never bothered anybody down here, but there was nobody down here to bother

either. This was kind of her own place, their own place really."
Carlile moved to a door on the wall opposite the bed. "What's
this?" he asked to make a point.

"A door to the adjoining room, if like most motels," Morgan
said.

"If I open this door," Carlile said, "what happens?"

"If the door is open on the other side," Morgan replied, "you
walk into the next room."

"And if it isn't open?" Carlile asked.

"You can't," Morgan said. "There's not a door knob on this
side to the second door that leads to the next room."

"You're right," Carlile said. "The same is true if you are on the
other side. If the door in this room is shut, you can't enter
coming from the adjoining room, right?"

Morgan nodded.

"Look," Carlile said. He opened the door, put his foot against
the closed door to the adjoining room, and gently pushed. The
second door quietly opened. "It works the other way, too. Close
the door behind me and watch." Carlile walked through the
doorway to the next room and Morgan shut the first door behind
him. Then, it slid silently open and Carlile reappeared. "I don't
know if either of them knew these doors worked like that or not.
They were jimmied when I first came here and I never bothered
to fix 'em. Didn't figure it was a big deal but you know what that
means, don't you?"

"What?" Morgan asked.

"It wasn't necessarily someone Tanya herself brought in here
who killed her," Carlile replied.

"Was there someone in the next room that night?" Morgan
asked.

"Only if Tamar let them in," the motel manager replied as he
closed the door to the adjoining room. "Or if it was Tamar
herself. Of course, I didn't see anyone around here that night."

Morgan shook his head. "Do you think—"

"Nothing's too strange in Kiowa Heights," Carlile said. He
took a deep breath as if his words should have been sufficient to
satisfy the attorney's curiosity. He pulled his belt up to reach his
wide girth and started towards the door.

"There was something else you were going to tell me,"
Morgan said.

The puffy red-faced man shook his head. "No, not tell you. Show you, because if I told you without seeing, you wouldn't believe me. Leave the light on. I have to show you the other room to make you understand."

Chester Morgan followed the manager of the motel into the night's darkness, the cold wind, and the sound of moving traffic on Ninth Avenue. Frank Carlile unlocked the door to Room L-7 of the Bunkhouse Lodge, the place Tamar White waited while her daughter was next door. Carlile turned on the light to a dim room almost identical to the other in decor and doom, only flipped over.

"You can send me to god-damned China if you want, but someone should have yanked that child out of Tamar White's arms the hour she was born," Carlile said. "Do you think that a mother who would sell her own daughter would want to be nearby to protect her daughter?" The large man shook his head and acted as if he were going to spit. "Protect her investment maybe. Look here."

Carlile opened the first of the two doors that led to the adjoining room, to Tanya's room, L-8. The second door was closed, but in its middle at eye level was a small hole. "Look!" Carlile commanded as he pushed the lawyer towards the door. Through the tiny opening, Morgan saw the double bed with the sturdy Western style headboard, the vinyl-covered chair, and the dusty light falling onto the industrial gray carpeting.

"She watched," Carlile said.

Chapter Fourteen

The following Monday morning, Chester Morgan talked into his office phone, "McNally, get me the names of the beat cops who worked the forty-seventh hundred block of East Ninth last September the fourth."

"Nice part of town, Morgan," the police officer answered.

"Right around the block from where you live," the attorney replied.

"Yeah. Sure," McNally said. "It may not be that easy. Are you positive you want the names of the beat cops?"

"I suppose. Why do you ask?"

"What do have going on?" McNally asked.

"I'm looking into, uh, an accident."

"Look at the accident report," McNally said. "The officer's name will be on it."

"If I could do that, would I be calling you?"

"I forget you can't read."

"Dammit, McNally, just get the names for me."

"If it's an accident, a run of the mill call, it won't be that hard. If it's something serious—" McNally stopped. He lowered his voice. "This doesn't have to do with what you called me about last week, does it?"

"Assume not."

"I assume it will, then. Chester, stay away from that. I'm serious. Whatever you're doing, stay away."

"You started to tell me something. If it's serious, what?"

"The beat cops don't work it anymore. Beat cops are just that. They work the beat: routine accidents, small-time burglaries and petty everyday crimes. If it's something else, it's likely to be SPIT."

"What?"

"Special Investigative Teams. S-P-I-T. Spit."

"Tell me about 'em."

"Yeah. Kurt Hale brought the idea with him from California when they made him police chief. Sort of uniformed supercops. Roam from beat to beat. Usually two of 'em to a car—a young cop who sees only black and white and is too stupid to be scared of anything and an old cop who's grizzled enough to keep the young one from getting killed."

"You could be both, McNally."

"No, these are the crazy fuckers," the officer answered. "They answer the bad calls, the somebody-might-really-get-hurt calls. They're dispatched separately and by code so the old grandpas who listen to police radios won't show up at a crime in progress and the press won't beat us there."

"Then get me the names of the beat cops and these roamers for the place I told you."

"SPIT cops work a whole zone," McNally said. "You'd have a whole list of those guys and … If you need the SPIT teams, it's something besides a routine accident. Chester, I told you."

"Get me the list."

"Don't be getting into that and…" McNally sighed. "Listen, I didn't sign up to be errand boy for the widow-robber most likely to have his full-page picture on the back of the phone book and the one most likely to—"

Morgan interrupted. "The next time you and your buddies go out and roll a few drunks let me know so I can go videotape. Get me the list."

"Morgan, don't—"

"Assume it's not what I called you about and assume I'm not stupid."

"I'll see. Maybe."

"Thanks."

McNally hung up. Morgan looked across his desk at Marylin. "He said he might," the attorney said.

"Maybe he's trying to keep you from getting hurt, boss," Marylin said. "That's all."

Morgan picked up a rubber band from his desk and stretched it between his fingers. "Maybe."

"If the girl at Vixen's—" Marylin began.

"Maria," Morgan interrupted.

"Maria may have been right," Marylin continued. "The police …"

"Didn't follow standard procedure," Morgan said. "That's all we know. It doesn't make sense."

"Few things ever do, in a big way," Marylin said.

"You'd recognize Tamar White if she came in to retain me," the lawyer said. "Not literally, perhaps, but before you would bring her into my office, you would warn me, 'Something for nothing, boss, and she wants way too much for way too little,' and you'd be right. If Tamar White could have gotten anything out of her daughter's death, she would have."

"Then you aren't ready to petition for the writ of mandamus, are you, Chester?"

Morgan shook his head. "I couldn't prove much more than I could Friday and my only solid witness won't talk. Frank Carlile would lose his cut, and they'd shut him down, and he knows it."

Marylin doodled on her stenographer's pad and said, "Assuming he's telling you the truth."

"Yeah, but he is."

"Your intuition?" Marylin asked. She smiled.

"It works better sometimes than others," Morgan said. "I guess it didn't with the landlord, did it?"

"And you even offered to rent Tanya's house."

"Sort of," Morgan said. He picked up an open book from his desk. "We better go through the calendar to see what we're doing this week."

Marylin looked at her calendar and said, "Eleven o'clock, John Morris is coming in. He wants to talk to you about buying a business. A possible divorce client comes in at three. You have an answer due today in the *Oldham* case, and Shawn pulled the files you wanted to review. Tomorrow, you have the deposition of an expert witness. On Wednesday—"

"Marcia Nelson guessed wrong," Morgan said.

"What's that, Mister C?"

"When I asked to see the autopsy report, Doctor Nelson said she didn't know whether this was the case with the big bruise on the forehead and the water in the lungs. Slipped, fell, and drowned in the bathtub, according to the doctor, but Carlile said there was no bruise on Tanya's forehead and her hair didn't look like it had been wet. Probably no stoppers in the bathtub or the sink either, and definitely no water on the floor. The bathroom looked unused, the way it had when the housekeeper had finished in there the day before."

"Doctor Nelson does most of the autopsies for this part of the state, doesn't she? It's not too surprising she'd forget," Marylin said.

"I don't think she forgot," Morgan said. "I thought...I thought she might have been telling me something." The attorney looked at his calendar again and said, "That deposition on Tuesday may take most of the day. Wednesday, we take Mrs. Delano back to probate court in the afternoon. Thursday's the last day to file those liens for Younger Cabinets. Would you please call Bob and see if he wants us to do that? He said he was trying to get that worked out."

Marylin nodded and scratched a note on her secretarial pad.

"Thursday afternoon I have a motion hearing in Sue Colbert's case. Friday looks clear, so far. Make sure Shawn's calendar corresponds with yours." Morgan looked up. Shawn stood at the doorway, with loose papers in one hand and written telephone notes in the other.

"You forgot to pick up your messages when you came in," Shawn said as she crossed the room and laid the slips of paper on the attorney's desk. She gestured with the other papers in her hand and said, "You've already gotten a lot of time in this Kinman case."

"I'm not worried," Morgan said.

"You should be," she said. "He won't ever pay you and I'm the one who's supposed to make sure you make money."

"You do a good job—most of the time," Morgan said. "Put the time on the books. It may not work out the way you expect, or the way I do either."

Shawn looked at the papers in her hand, then jerked her head up and stared at the attorney. "I know what you did this weekend, you told me, but your billing ought to at least be honest. Instead of 'Interviewing Witnesses,' the statement should read: 'Watched trashy women take their clothes off and strut around naked. Two hours.'"

"Don't call them that."

Shawn shrugged and said, "Whatever." Then she left the room.

Morgan shook his head. He picked up the phone and looked at the first message and said, "Let's see who spent the weekend thinking up questions to ask their lawyer Monday morning."

Marylin stood to leave. "Chester," she said. "I've thought a lot about Tanya Everly. You know, she could have been anyone. She could have been me."

Chapter Fifteen

If I didn't swim, Chester Morgan thought, I'd be a worse lawyer than I am. Morgan leaned against the side of the YMCA pool and caught his breath. He didn't believe in exercise as panacea. He didn't swim to make his heart stronger or his physique firmer or to be able to mindlessly brag about his work-out regimen, although he occasionally did some of the latter and hoped for the former. If he would admit it, Chester Morgan swam to think—no phones, no emergencies, no tasks to accomplish by a certain time or ever. He simply moved and disappeared into the water. In such times, what had been fuzzy or confused often became clear: A better argument to make to a judge on a difficult case; a course of action to recommend to a client facing an unknowable future; clarity—at least until William Harrison died that early September morning.

At the locker-room end of the pool, other businessmen and women talked and made noises that echoed. Morgan looked at the opposite wall and saw a door to places not known, at least to him. He thought of other doors, ones to adjoining rooms that clicked shut but opened with a nudge. He remembered a motel manager who gave a mother and a daughter their own quarters and own keys, but when the daughter alone occupied a different room, others like her complained of noise, of the music being too loud. He wondered about a mother who watched, or let others ... Morgan shook his head and climbed out of the pool. Since William Harrison died, mornings had not brought clarity.

In front of his locker, Chester removed his swimming trunks, grabbed a towel, and started towards the showers. He paused for a moment in front of a mirror. He wasn't an ugly man, but the shiny glass reflected a face older than he remembered and showed dark creases he hadn't before seen. Wrinkles don't just show up, he thought. He looked at the body attached to the face. Swimming had tightened its long muscles, but the flesh in the mirror looked soft and pulled by time. He wondered when and how that had happened. He wondered whether he would spend the rest of his life alone. He remembered Cassie, then thought of

Maria and grinned at the possibility and the wonder and then at the absurdity.

Morgan showered and dressed. As he left the locker room, he threw his towel into a large canvas laundry cart. A young man with dark curly hair sat on a stool behind an uplifted platform surrounded by a gray grill. The young man moved his lips as he counted and made checkmarks on a piece of paper held firm by a clipboard. Morgan walked to the platform where the young man sat.

"Sorry you're leaving," Morgan said.

The young man nodded.

"Do you have somewhere else to go?" the attorney asked.

Mario Pacetti shook his head. His blue eyes looked sad. "Something will come along," he said. "Anyway, this job has changed since ..."

"I know," Morgan said as he saw the image again. He remembered Pacetti running past him at the locker room door and diving into the water where William Harrison's body bobbed. "It hasn't been the same for me either."

"Mister Morgan, have you ever looked on the bronze plaque at the corner of the building?" Mario asked. "His name should be on it. He wouldn't let 'em. 1965. He always got here early. I let him swim, always. The lifeguard would show up pretty soon anyway."

"The way you let me sometimes, and did that morning," Chester said. He remembered thinking he heard footsteps, turning down the corridor from the locker room to the pool and then seeing ...

"Yeah," Mario said. "That's not the proper procedure."

"Did they fire you for that?" Morgan asked.

The young man shook his head. He had large shoulders that framed a lean body, sculpted with firm muscle. Drops of water from an earlier swim still hung from a narrow tangle of hair on his chest. "Didn't fire me. Just let me know I wouldn't go any further than counting towels and signing people in and out. I want to be a trainer, a coach. This is a career for me," Mario said. "I don't feel right about staying anyway."

"He was dead when you pulled him out," the lawyer said. "I don't fault you."

"I knew something was wrong," the young man said. "That was why I was behind you. I could feel it. You know how it is sometimes—you sense something, not know it, but feel it."

Chester nodded. "You got him out fast, faster than I knew possible. It was amazing, Mario. It really was."

The young man shrugged. "Not fast enough," he said. He set the clipboard down, picked up a towel that had been thrown on the floor, and put it in the cart. "I suppose he had a heart attack. If it hadn't happened that morning, it would have happened later but ..."

"But what?" Morgan said.

Mario Pacetti looked at the attorney. "There was a bad bruise across the side of his forehead. I figure he had a heart attack standing by the side of the pool and hit his head as he fell into the water. If I hadn't opened the place to him early, if I'd followed proper procedure, maybe he wouldn't have drowned."

"I thought he had been swimming for some time before we found him."

"He had—ten or fifteen minutes, at least. He must have gotten out; that's the only way I know he got that mark across his head."

"I didn't know about the bruise," Morgan said.

"He drowned. They used bigger words to say it, but that's what they meant. I guess a bruise doesn't mean much to them. Maybe it shouldn't to me either, but I thought I heard footsteps, like somebody was running."

A woman came out the other side of the locker room and tossed a towel into the laundry cart. She smiled at Mario Pacetti and Morgan as she passed.

"Had anyone gone into the women's locker room that morning before—"

"Not that I remember," Pacetti said.

"Where does the door on the opposite side of the pool go?"

"Why do you ask?" Mario replied.

"Curious, I suppose. I hadn't really noticed it until this morning."

"The pump's in there and, actually, all the mechanical for the whole building. God, it'd be a great place if you were a kid. It's like a huge maze. Opens up somewhere on the other side of the building." Mario smiled but it was bittersweet.

"How are your boys? They're two and three now, aren't they?" Morgan asked.

Mario nodded. "They're fine. Good Italian kids."

"How's your wife handling this?"

"It's kind of rough on her. She loves taking care of the kids, but she thinks she should find a paying job to help out. I tell her no. I'll find something quick. Besides, two more night classes and I'll have my degree." Mario Pacetti said it with confidence, with the surety that comes from being twenty-three.

"Don't stop," Morgan said.

"I won't."

Chester Morgan walked away from the locker room and the young man who too carried the image of William Harrison. A different image, perhaps, but still the same. When the attorney reached the front door of the YMCA, he stopped at the security guard's desk.

"Do you have an envelope I could have?" Morgan asked.

The burly security guard opened a drawer and silently handed him a blank envelope without ever looking at him.

"Thanks," Morgan said.

The guard mumbled.

Morgan turned down an empty green and black tiled hall. When he was sure he was alone, he stopped and wrote something on the blank envelope.

Later that day when the locker room attendant stopped at the Director's office to pick up his final YMCA paycheck, the secretary handed him an envelope with the name "Mario Pacetti" written on the outside. "A man stopped by this morning," she said, "and left this. He said he found it on the floor in the hall and thought you might be looking for it."

"Who was it?" the young man asked.

"Didn't say."

When Mario Pacetti opened the envelope, he found a one hundred dollar bill and nothing else.

Chapter Sixteen

Shawn slumped at her desk and stared at a printed listing of clients and accounts receivable. She thumbed the edge, sighed, and stared at it again. Chester Morgan walked through the front door, stopped, and picked up his messages.

"Morgan, you ought to get yourself a real law practice," the muscular young woman said. Her platinum blonde hair had been tied up into a wild ponytail.

"Can't pay the bills?" Morgan asked. He took the listing and looked at it. "We're making money, aren't we?"

"Are you trying to do that? You've got special deals cut with half your clients: a rancher who pays you a side of beef every six months, a photo studio that settles your fee in portrait credits. You're going to die of clogged arteries and leave a credit for ten thousand pictures." She kept talking, faster to crescendo. "And, you have a lady who is paying you ten dollars every two weeks. I'll be retired by the time she pays you off."

"You'll be retired and I'll be here practicing law. Mrs. Winfield will still be sending me ten dollars every two weeks and you'll still be wondering why," Morgan replied.

"Chest, you ought to get three or four big clients. Ones that actually have accounts payable departments where you send your bill, they mark it 'approved,' and mail you a check. It's simple. You'd be better off."

"Shawn, that's not why I do this," Morgan said. "My clients are my people. I take care of them. That's what I've pledged to do. You don't understand?"

"You ought to get married and have a real life."

"This is my life."

Morgan left the young woman at her desk. He stopped at Marylin's office. He reported to her as much as she reported to him but maybe for different reasons.

"This guy could have been our witness," Morgan said, referring to the deposition he had just completed. "The other side's expert answered every question the way I wanted. Maybe I asked the wrong questions."

"Maybe the wrong witness and the wrong case, too," Marylin said. She finished arranging a stack of papers and looked up. "You shot bullets at his feet and made 'im dance. You always do."

He knew he didn't and she knew he didn't, but he liked the statement of confidence and wouldn't dismiss it as flattery. "Did you hear from McNally?" Morgan asked.

"Nothing," she said.

Morgan walked into his office. He looked at his phone messages, the too-consuming other part of practicing law. Cross-examination, in trial or deposition, exhilarated: the fluid evolving strategy; the mastery of facts and witness; the reliance on instinct and feel. The phone calls ground and ground and ground. He organized his messages. No emergencies, but Martin Bollant, an attorney who sometimes referred sometimes good business, had called. Morgan picked up the phone.

"How's life up where you are?" Morgan asked when he heard Bollant's distinct, but casual, diction.

"Thirty-two stories isn't too far up," Bollant said. "I suppose it's the same here in the clouds as it is down there—not enough nonmarginal work."

"You're a good attorney, Martin. You have good clients, good connections. You'll never lack ..." Morgan paused. He couldn't say *non-marginal*. "What can I do for you?"

"Chester, I'm having a few people over this evening to—"

"What this time?" Morgan asked. "Last year, it was a regional theatre company. The year before, was it the prairie dog preserve or was it the Vivia Chamber Orchestra? I forget. Who are you raising money for this year?"

"No one, Chester. This is an opportunity to relate to some people who are truly connected into the reality of this community. Really into another sphere of life and making it better. Of course, if this connection makes you want to give—time, money, whatever—do it, but the purpose isn't to raise—"

"I know, I know. What this year?"

"The Corpus Christi Project. Does that connect with you?"

"What is it?"

"Now, Chester, don't think in old paradigms."

"Martin, just tell me what it is."

"A sanctuary, as in ancient, but not traditional, context. A haven for the marginalized of society but without proselytizing or heartless piety or paternalism. Doing tremendous work in the Old Vivia, Kiowa Heights area. It's a complete expression of compassion, hope, and change without judgment."

"Kiowa Heights?" Morgan repeated. "Who will be there?"

"The man who created the Project, is its heart—Don Hubbard. Maybe a few of his volunteers. He's very cautious about them."

"Martin Bollant raising money for a religious organization?" Morgan said. "Thanks for the variety."

"Old paradigms always fail, Chester. This is different, this is breakout. That's why I want you to come tonight. Five-thirty, my office. We'll have bread, wine, fruit. Maybe a few other things."

He refers me business, Morgan thought. "I'll be there," he said and hung up the phone. He picked up the next message to return. Morgan paused and wondered why he agreed to go to another Martin Bollant shakedown. He refers me business, he thought.

Later, Morgan walked into Marylin's office. "Martin Bollant is having a few people over to his office tonight—" he began.

"What's he raising money for this time?" Marylin asked without shifting her face from her computer screen.

"The Corpus Christi Project," Morgan said. "Do you want to go?"

"Can't tonight, boss," she said. "Other things to do; I must do, but thanks. I need Thursday off, too. Would that be okay with you? Do you mind?" Morgan shook his head. "Shawn and I can make it."

"Don't make it well enough not to miss me, Mister C." Marylin looked at him and winked.

"We won't," Morgan said.

That evening Chester Morgan looked at finger food on silver trays spread over a linen-covered table. He smelled a pleasant aroma but, except for the bread, fresh fruit and cheese, he recognized nothing. Around him in the white-on-white reception area of Martin Bollant's thirty-second story offices, people nibbled from china plates and drank from crystal glasses. Morgan recognized the music playing—a waltz by Strauss. He wondered what the food was.

"Our chef specializes in fusion cuisine," a sharply groomed young man in a white tuxedo said from behind the table.

"What's that?" Morgan asked.

"He melds the essences of different cuisines—Southwest, Caribbean, French, Japanese—and fuses them into his own creations," the man said.

Morgan looked at the finger food on the silver platters and said, "You know, if your chef deep-fat fried all this stuff, you could say he fused it with Oklahoma cuisine."

The young man ignored the comment louder than had he spoken. "Just joking," Morgan said as he took a plate.

Chester looked at the crowd and knew the next thing he was supposed to do—mingle. He also knew why Martin Bollant had succeeded at the most prestigious law firm in town, then had taken several of its best clients and started his own practice, and why he, Chester, had left a smaller, but similar, firm a little over a year after he had started there— social chat and shuffling. Martin delighted in it and had mastered it. He was also a brilliant attorney. Chester condoned the social ritual and performed it, but he preferred time and words real, potent, and interesting. Morgan saw Bollant across the room. He wore casual clothes that cost more than most men's suits.

Morgan moved into the crowd. He talked for a few minutes to another attorney he had seen before but did not really know. He scooted away when the small talk died and reintroduced himself to someone he had met at Martin Bollant's last reception. Morgan didn't hear his own words or the words of the stranger. Morgan wondered whether he made the same small talk before. Then, behind him, he heard:

"The undraped body was tied with rope, the arms outstretched, the wrists strapped to a beam across, the feet pulled down together, and likewise tied. A horrible death by suffocation. The body was pierced after demise to see if life still pulsed ..."

Morgan remembered Frank Carlyle's description of the discovery of Tanya Everly's body. Morgan turned. A square-framed man with wavy brown hair spoke. He wore a clerical collar and he held a large gold crucifix in his hand.

His voice sounded like the lower register of a pipe organ that played paragraphs.

"Scripture often refers to 'hanging from the tree' which was the common method of crucifixion. Death came after fatigue and exposure. You see, the body was affixed in so tortuous manner that breathing was impossible except with constant movement. The victim suffocated," the man said. "This symbol I wear is all the explanation I give unless asked."

A woman with strands of silver in gold hair listened, nodded, and smiled.

"I've told you more than I usually tell them. I apologize," the man in the clerical collar said. "However the people of Kiowa Heights suffer, we are there to accept, to be whatever they need for us to be, to share that same suffering."

"It's wonderful somebody's doing something for those people in that part of town," the woman said. "It's just a shame the way that area has just become such a—"

"They are my people," the man interrupted. "I care for them. That's my pledge."

Morgan shifted to move into the conversation when he felt someone next to him. "Chesterfield!" he heard Martin Bollant exclaim. "Glad you could make it."

Morgan shook Martin's hand and acknowledged the greeting.

"Have you met Don Hubbard?"

"Not yet. Been listening, though," Morgan said.

Bollant nodded and said to the man in the clerical collar, "Meet one of the real attorneys—Chester Morgan."

Morgan extended his hand to the man in the clerical collar. Hubbard's hand felt large, soft, and warm.

"Pleasure meeting you, Father? Brother? Reverend? What do I call you?" Morgan asked.

The man paused and looked at Chester. "Don," he replied, "or brother with a small 'b.'" Gold flecks in the man's deep green eyes seemed to dance and glow.

"I overheard you speaking," Morgan said. "You accept without question?"

"None," he said.

Morgan wondered whether anyone could. He wanted to challenge the statement for its impossibilities, but the man's presence made him want to believe. Instead, Morgan asked, "Do those who most need that acceptance find you?"

"I hope so," Hubbard said. "I began by walking the streets of Kiowa Heights at night and, at dawn, picking up those who remained. I learned the people there. They know me, and many, if not most, find me if I don't find them first."

An old man cut between them and started speaking to Don Hubbard. Hubbard gently stopped him and looked at Morgan. "I hope we can talk some more sometime."

"Maybe we'll need to," Chester said. "Here's my card, if I can ever be of assistance."

The old man started speaking again. Morgan glanced at his watch and said to Bollant, "Hubbard may be okay."

"He is," Bollant replied.

"What brand is he?"

"Pardon?"

"What brand? You know, Catholic, Presbyterian, Lutheran?"

"Not any that I know of," Martin said. "I think he may have been a Episcopal priest, or something like that, and became disillusioned so he started the Project. It doesn't make any difference, Chester. New paradigms. Remember, you have to think in new paradigms."

"I know," Chester said. "I may even have to learn to use a computer one of these days." He looked around the room. "I give you a bad time sometimes, but you seem to have done all right for yourself. Do you ever regret leaving the prestigious Summers and Kirk firm?"

"Only when I pay the bills," Bollant said.

"Did you do any work for William Harrison when you were there?"

"Not for him *per se,* for Key Petroleum, yes. The firm has represented that company for years."

"That's what I thought," Morgan said. "I was surprised last week to see Massey, James, and Peterson handling Harrison's probate."

"That firm that fights every unnecessary fight and resolves every ethical question by declaration of ambiguity, or worse," Martin Bollant said. "If your attorneys treat others that way, they'll treat you as a client the same way, eventually. Harrison's son must be the estate's personal representative."

"Trying to be," Morgan said. "His lawyer didn't quite succeed in proving a lost will in Eldridge Powers' court."

"Randolph Harrison went to school with one of the Massey, James and Peterson partners. I guess I'm not surprised they are in the case. Randolph had used them in some negotiations with Key."

"The lawyer, Thomas Haney, claims he drafted the will William Harrison supposedly signed," Morgan said.

"Really?" Martin Bollant shook his head and looked at Morgan. "That doesn't sound right. Harrison always used Bradford, Evans, and Shell as his personal lawyers. Very intentional about that, too." He shook his head and looked again at Morgan. "Are you sure?"

"I was in the courtroom when Haney said he prepared the will and notarized Harrison's signature. Only reason he didn't get it admitted to probate was because Powers wanted the testimony of the two witnesses."

"I'm sure the honorable Eldridge did," Bollant said. He started to speak but stopped. "William Harrison was a good man, Chester. When the eighties' oil boom busted, Key almost went under several times. Harrison wouldn't let it. The majors could have gobbled up a competitor and gotten Key's reserves, but Harrison wouldn't sell. And, Harrison would have done okay, but he didn't. Instead, he pumped his personal assets back into the company and took on a lot of debt to keep it going. Struggled into the nineties, too. Frankly, I'm not sure his estate would be worth all that much now."

"Maybe not," Morgan said. "I don't know."

"Do you know why he wouldn't sell the company or open the book to Chapter Eleven?"

Morgan shook his head.

"He hated to fire or let people go. If he had sold the company, the buyer undoubtedly would have shut down whole departments and laid a bunch of workers off. Same result if he had filed Chapter Eleven. Harrison knew it was a cyclical business and he rode it as well as he could. Better than most. He felt this obligation to his employees more than just Management 101 blather or talk. It was real, from the heart. Even when Harrison closed down an unprofitable gas station, he would personally go out and do it himself to make sure everyone was taken care of. He hated that. He considered a lay off or a closing a disgrace, a dishonor, a failure."

Morgan set down his plate. "I was at the Y the morning he died. I didn't know him that well."

"Nobody did," Bollant said. "If you were around him much, you began to see how he saw things. Not because he said, you just knew. I'm not sure his dedication to his company ever brought him much satisfaction or profit, though. He always seemed to have this aura of loneliness about him—like you do Chester. I don't know."

A woman in a red evening dress took Martin Bollant by the arm and whispered something. He excused himself and left Morgan alone. From across the room, Chester Morgan saw Don Hubbard and saw his mouth form words. As Hubbard lifted the crucifix from his chest, Morgan knew the words he said. Then, he heard the voice of Frank Carlile say the same ones.

As Chester left the party, he looked back and saw the gold emblem as in shadowy smoke—glimmer and glitter and dim.

Chapter Seventeen

"Anyone present in opposition?"

No one in the oak-paneled courtroom spoke.

"You may proceed, counselor," Eldridge Powers stated from the bench.

Thomas Haney stood, inhaled, and said, "May it please the Court. The hearing on the probate of the last will and testament of William Harrison was continued from last week in order to ..."

"I remember the case," Eldridge Powers interrupted. "Your sworn affidavit states you mailed the known heirs of William Harrison written notice of their right to contest the will and the notice was duly published. No further notice is necessary and, Mister Haney, no recitation of the evidence presented at last week's hearing is required. Proceed."

Chester Morgan leaned back in his chair and watched Thomas Haney, the Massey, James and Peterson attorney who, like Morgan, had been required to return to Eldridge Powers' courtroom in order to satisfy the technical requirements of the Oklahoma Probate Code and the stricter demands of the judge. Morgan thought about reviewing Mrs. Delano's file again, but he knew the school-marmish magistrate would be unable to fault Morgan's preparation or evidence. Morgan waited to see if Thomas Haney would make any mistakes this time.

"I ask that Robert Fulcher be called to the stand," Haney said.

A tall and obese man wearing a black western shirt, blue jeans, and scuffed boots ambled towards the front. When he passed the gate, he stopped and looked. Judge Powers squinted and said, "Come forward, sir." The big man walked to the judge's bench and stopped again.

"Robert Fulcher?" the judge asked.

"Yes, sir." The man's voice squeaked a nasal pitch.

"Raise your right hand. Do you swear to tell the truth, the whole truth, and nothing but the truth, so help you God?"

"Yes, sir. I do."

"Mister Fulcher, would you mind taking the witness stand please," Judge Powers said.

"No sir. Nothin' bothers Bob."

Chester Morgan sat up. He had heard that voice before say the same thing. He looked at the man and tried to remember ...

After a few preliminary questions, Thomas Haney asked, "How were you employed on July twenty-eighth of this year?"

"I worked as a gardener for Mister..." Robert Fulcher paused, "for Mister William Harrison."

"At his residence?" Haney asked.

The large man nodded.

"Answer out loud," Judge Powers instructed.

"At his residence," Fulcher replied. His eyes opened wide and then narrowed as to focus only on the attorney.

"On July twenty-eight, you saw William Harrison sign a will, did you not?"

"I did," Robert Fulcher replied. Thomas Haney walked to the court reporter and retrieved a document. He stepped to the side and handed it to the witness. Fulcher continued to stare at Haney. The attorney extended the papers towards the big man.

"Let me show you what has been marked as Exhibit One," Haney said. "This document is a true and correct copy of the will you saw William Harrison sign on July twenty-eighth of this year, is that correct?"

Fulcher took the document. "It is," he said. He kept watching the attorney and never looked at the will.

"Please tell the court the circumstances under which the execution of the will took place." Thomas Haney paced to the opposite side of the courtroom.

"Kenny Duckworth—he's the assistant gardener—and I were out working in the yard that morning. Mister Harrison came out and asked us to come inside to witness his will. I told him that nuthin' would bother me about that. He was the boss. Kenny and I went up inside to the library—"

"Who was present?" Haney asked, his voice loud, his words rapid.

"Mister Harrison" Fulcher said. "And you."

"In your presence, William Harrison declared that Exhibit One was his last will and testament, is that correct?"

"Yeah."

"That he signed it freely and voluntarily without any threat of duress or coercion, is that correct?"

"Yep."

"That he was over the age of eighteen and that he had asked you to witness his will."

"Exactly what he said. Yes, sir."

"You, Mister Duckworth, and myself were present as he signed the will. You and Mister Duckworth then signed the will as witnesses and I notarized it, is that correct?"

"Sure did."

"No one else was present?"

Fulcher stared at Haney. Then, "No, sir."

Haney stopped and looked at his file, thinking more than seeing. He pushed his shoulders back and stared at the witness.

"Other questions for this witness, counselor?" Judge Powers asked.

"Yes, your honor. Mister Fulcher, you went to work the morning of September fourth of this year at the Harrison residence, did you not?"

"Yes, sir."

"Your usual and normal summer working hours were from five-thirty a.m. to two-thirty p.m., I understand." Haney's words slowed.

"They sure were," Bob Fulcher said. "Up at sunrise, not so many hot hours."

Haney smiled as if it hurt. The volume of his voice turned conversational. "What happened the morning of September fourth?"

Morgan remembered. The image shimmered, burned, and would not fade. A bailiff opened a noisy door, and Morgan looked at the witness again.

Fulcher leaned forward and shifted his weight so he faced the judge. "I got to work out there and started to mess around in the shed and Mister Harrison stopped by a little before six. He always got up early to go to the six-thirty swim at the Y. The locker room attendant usually let him in early so he usually got there at about six-fifteen. I guess that was what he was goin' to do that morning."

"Excuse me, Mister Fulcher," Haney interrupted. "What had William Harrison been doing before he came out to the shed?"

"Well, like I said, he stopped by and thanked me for witnessing his will. He said he had just been looking it over and it did just what he wanted it to do."

The fourth of September—the body in the water. The too-late attempt to save a dead man by Mario Paccetti. Now Morgan heard that the same person, the morning of his death, had reviewed his will, now claimed to be lost. Thomas Haney placed his hand on the lapel of his suit jacket and began to ask his next question. Morgan shook his head.

"You served in the Navy, did you not?" Haney asked quickly.

"Yes, sir. Honorable discharge," Fulcher said.

What is Haney doing? Morgan thought. Not relevant, he began to object, but stopped before his feet pushed him to standing and his mouth began to speak. It wasn't his case; he represented no one involved, but he loathed the improper question.

"Do you know what it means to take an oath?" Haney asked.

"To tell the truth," Fulcher replied.

That's certain to impress Eldridge Powers, Morgan thought, shaking his head again. If Powers ever suspected an attorney of presenting a witness who didn't know what the oath meant, a mild consequence might be contempt of court, even though the judge knew for some people the oath was simply a ritual to be said and ignored. A few attorneys thought the question and the answer about telling the truth impressed juries, not realizing its inherent condescension; before a judge of Eldridge Powers' integrity and intelligence, it was an insult.

"No more questions, your honor."

Judge Powers tapped his pencil on his desk and looked at the large man. "Why was William Harrison looking at his will at six o'clock or so the morning of his death?" the white-haired judge asked.

Bob Fulcher shrugged.

"I've already instructed you to answer out loud," Powers said.

"Don't know," Fulcher responded.

"Where was he when he looked at the will that morning?"

Fulcher started to shrug again. He sat up straight. "Don't know, sir. In his house, I guess."

"Or where did he put the will when finished? You don't know that either, do you?"

"No, sir. Didn't say."

"William Harrison came out to the—" Powers hesitated. "To the shed at six o'clock or thereabouts the morning of his death to thank you for an act you had done over a month before and to tell you he liked what his will said?"

Bob Fulcher turned his face away from the judge and looked at the spectators in the room. "Yes, sir." A crooked grin spread over his face out of sight of the judge. "That, and to tell me to weed the petunia bed." The grin turned into a self-satisfied sneer.

"Why did he tell you he was pleased with his will?"

"Don't know, sir."

"What did you say to him in return?"

"'Yes, sir.'"

Powers waited for an answer and not patiently.

"That's what I said to him, sir: 'Yes, sir.'"

Judge Powers turned back the pages on a legal pad on his desk. "When did you first let someone know about this conversation the morning of Mister Harrison's death?"

"Last week when Mister Haney talked to me." Fulcher looked at his hands.

"Not before?" Powers asked.

"Maybe."

"That's a yes-or-no question, Mister Fulcher."

"Sir, I don't remember."

Eldridge Powers looked straight ahead, his eyes lost in the reflection of the light in his wire-rimmed glasses. Then, he said to Haney, his voice hushed. "Any re-direct on my cross-examination, Mister Haney?"

"Just one question, Judge," the attorney said. "Before I talked with you last week, did you have any reason to tell anyone about the conversation you and William Harrison had the morning of September fourth?"

"No sir. Not that I can remember, Mister Haney. I figured nuthin' was botherin' nobody."

"No further questions."

Judge Powers acknowledged Haney's conclusion. "Anyone now present in opposition to admission of the lost will of William Harrison?"

The faces of the experienced probate attorneys in the courtroom did not change expression, but Chester Morgan knew his colleagues thought his thoughts. Eldridge Powers gave one chance, and only one chance, to oppose the admission of a will. This afternoon he had given two.

The courtroom remained silent except for a young attorney who sat in the gallery tapping his foot as he reviewed his file for his client's hearing.

"Step down, Mister Fulcher. Please step down."

Chester Morgan watched the tall and obese man rise and exit the witness stand. Morgan had heard the witness' voice before and knew it had been recent, but Morgan did not recognize Robert Fulcher. With no hesitancy of step or awkwardness of motion, the witness passed quickly by the counsel table.

Thomas Haney asked that Kenneth Duckworth take the witness stand and the person Bob Fulcher had identified as the assistant gardener came forward. He wore a denim jacket and heavy aviator glasses. His skin had the nighttime pallor of one who never tans and never burns. He could have been easily seen and forgotten except he was taller than almost any other man in the room and his burr haircut hovered over a misanthropic skull. Judge Powers swore the witness in and asked, "You understand you have taken an oath to tell the truth, don't you?"

"Yeah."

"You understand what you just did?" Judge Powers asked.

"Yeah."

"You should also be aware that the penalty for perjury in this state is five years in the state penitentiary."

"Yes, sir."

Judge Powers leaned back in his leather covered chair and touched the fingertips of his hands together. "Mister Haney, I saved you from asking a question or two, didn't I? Proceed."

"Thank you, your honor," the attorney said, his manner unchanged, unshaken.

Haney's collected, Morgan thought. Powers had returned the oath insult with little subtlety and the attorney refused to acknowledge it either in speech or word. Haney asked the witness direct questions to establish a foundation for Duckworth's testimony, non-leading questions that did not suggest an answer by their very form. Then, he made a mistake.

"Were you employed by William Harrison on July twenty-eighth of this year?"

"Yeah," the man responded.

"In what capacity?"

"Maintenance man."

"Maintenance man?" Haney replied. "If Bob Fulcher testified you were the assist—"

Duckworth interrupted. "Maintenance man and assistant gardener. Wasn't enough gardening to keep two people busy all the time and wasn't enough maintenance to keep one person busy all the time either, so I did both."

"Thank you for the clarification, Mister Duckworth. You saw William Harrison sign a will on July twenty-eighth of this year, did you not?"

"Yeah."

Haney showed him the copy of the will which had been marked Exhibit One. Duckworth said it was what William Harrison had signed.

"Please tell the court the circumstances under which the execution, the signing of the will, took place," Thomas Haney asked.

"Bob Fulcher—he's the full-time gardener—and I were out working in the yard that morning. Mister Harrison came out and asked us to come inside to witness his will. We told him we had no problem with that. He was the boss. Bob and I went inside the house to the library ..."

The same answer, Morgan thought. Almost the same words and certainly the same pattern.

Haney concluded Duckworth's testimony by leading him, as he had Fulcher, through the formalities of the execution and witnessing of the will. When finished, the attorney formally requested the lost will be admitted to probate and Randolph Harrison be appointed personal representative of the estate.

Judge Powers thumbed through the court file. "Did you notify William Harrison's daughter of her right to object to the admission of this will?"

"Written notice of this hearing was mailed to her at her last known address as required by statute," Haney said. "My affidavit on file with the court establishes that fact."

"She did not respond?"

"No sir."

"What is the value of the estate?" the judge asked.

"It's undetermined at this time," Haney said. "The primary asset will be the decedent's shares of stock in Key Petroleum."

"I'm surprised he didn't use a trust to dispose of that."

"I advised him to but, like so many, he thought he could do it later. He failed to follow my recommendation."

Eldridge Powers took off his glasses and wiped his eyes with a neatly folded handkerchief. He put his glasses back on and looked at his notes. "Mister Haney, as you should know, the court has the discretion to admit or deny the admission of a lost will based on the evidence presented."

"Yes, sir."

"Would you agree, Mister Haney, that my choice, based on the record before me, is to admit Exhibit One into probate or to decide that William Harrison died without a valid last will and testament with the result that his estate would be split equally between his son and his daughter?"

"I agree, your honor. That is your only choice."

"In order to decide William Harrison died without a valid last will and testament, in the absence of any objection or evidence in opposition, I would have to find that five witnesses: you, your legal assistant, Randolph Harrison, and the two men this afternoon, all lacked sufficient credibility to establish that Exhibit One is a true and correct copy of William Harrison's properly executed last will, would I not?"

"You would, and such decision would have to be based exclusively on the appearance and demeanor of the witnesses."

Judge Powers slowly turned the pages of the copy of the lost will. He looked at Thomas Haney and the citizens in back. In a barely audible voice, the old judge said, "Based on the record before it, the Court has no choice but to certify Exhibit One as the last will and testament of William Harrison and to appoint Randolph Harrison as the Personal Representative as set forth in the will."

Chapter Eighteen

Two old hippies—a friend and a cousin—arrived early Thursday morning at the woman's house. She had been renting it from her mother, but her brother with his wife and two children were returning to Vivia. The brother had lost his job again, and he had no money. The woman's mother had not required her daughter to leave the house; the daughter had made the decision herself with the surety impelled from the notion of helping family. Besides, she had learned of another place to live and going might help another come to peace in his soul.

The two old hippies made their decision to help her move the same way. They owed her nothing. They would accept no payment. She had asked for help. For them, the only questions were how and when. The boxes had been packed and marked when the friend and cousin arrived Thursday morning.

The decision had been made quickly; the destination determined by chance. The woman had learned of the rent house from her boss at work on Monday. That night, she had seen the home, met the landlord, and signed a lease. After work and into the night the next two evenings, she had arranged and stored her belongings in cardboard crates. She had learned to live light because life itself could be heavy enough. By the weekend, her brother and his family could be home and living in the house she had rented from her mother.

The two old hippies and the woman had driven around Vivia Thursday morning, laughing and talking and looking for a rental truck of proper dimension and price. When finally located, the monster machine blew black smoke and growled like a foul beast. One of the old hippies joked about the springs in the seat goosing him and the woman joked about enjoying it.

She drank some wine and the hippies drank some beer. Then, piece by piece, they loaded furniture and appliances into the truck. Then, box by box, they loaded the cardboard crates. By mid-afternoon, her mother's rent house was empty and the truck ready. Dark autumn clouds had settled low and huddled in the trees. The truck growled and blew black smoke, and she began her journey across the river. Then, box by box and piece by piece, the three had unloaded the truck into a house on a corner in a neighborhood forgotten by most.

Now, she stood alone in the house and looked at cardboard boxes, bare walls, and misplaced furniture. For the first time, the woman, a Vivia legal secretary named Marylin, wondered what she had done and down the dark street a half block away, a man sat in a pickup truck and watched.

A white-eaved house where an angel might have lived.

Chapter Nineteen

The white stucco building stood next to a narrow sidewalk on an Old Vivia side street. Drapes hung over the two arched plate-glass windows of this place where ex-GI's and their new wives had, in years past, peered at the latest model Studebakers. A few blocks away, the neon of Kiowa Heights was dim and the nighttime sounds quiet. The white façade of the building gleamed in the bright autumn sun but cut shadows sharp and lonely.

Chester Morgan crossed the street. After that morning's swim, he had gone directly to court and from there, to here. Morgan didn't know why, not exactly. Perhaps because nothing had happened on the Kinman case in the last week. Maybe because, instead of thinking about his argument in court that morning, he had thought about a dead strip dancer—found and forgotten at the Bunkhouse Lodge. Morgan had other sources about life in Kiowa Heights besides Don Hubbard but ... The small sign on the door to the white stucco building read: "The Corpus Christi Project."

An elderly woman whose earrings jangled when she walked led Morgan past a wild-haired man who silently played an invisible electric guitar. She led Morgan down a fluorescent lit hall to a large, dark office where Don Hubbard waited. On the wall behind his desk, a heavy gold crucifix hung.

"I am pleased you have come to see us," Hubbard said, standing to shake Morgan's hand. He sounded as if he meant it.

Morgan took a seat and looked at the man, much as he would a witness before cross-examination. Hubbard's manner and method, voice and eyes seemed serene and sincere. Still, Hubbard was like a grand piano with a rich sound and an out-of-tune B flat.

"Mister Hubbard," Morgan said. "If I believe our chief of police, there is nothing to salvage in Kiowa Heights. Yet here you are."

The minister smiled. "The same was said two thousand years ago and I can assure you that the stable and prosperous, though beloved, weren't the ones who followed that itinerant rabbi over the hills of Galilee."

"I'm interested in what you do," Morgan said, "but more interested in life itself in Kiowa Heights."

The minister held his hand up as if in benediction. "More can be learned from the prophets on the streets than from the bishops in their pulpits."

"My grandfather preached tent revivals in Mississippi, Arkansas, Louisiana, and Southern Oklahoma. I am confident he would have agreed except he would have added 'on the farms' and 'back in the hollers,' too," Morgan said. He paused. "I've heard that Kurt Hale's campaign against what he calls vice has turned into a war on the people in this part of town."

"Our new chief of police," Hubbard said. He looked away and rubbed his chin, then said, "Mister Morgan, I see victims here, not victims of other people necessarily, but victims of life, of life without meaning and of too few resources: economical, educational, social, emotional, spiritual. Kurt Hale's campaign can't change anything except the dynamic, creating different problems, instituted by different means. And, Hale knows it."

"I've read, heard, what he has said," Morgan replied. "For one who knows he can't change things here, Hale certainly sounds convinced, almost dangerous."

"He may really believe what he says, but his campaign is for the press and the public. There's not the political will to do what he wants or to support it. Too much money involved in Kiowa Heights and too few questions asked about where cash contributions to politicians come from. So, Hale'll go after streetwalkers and the really bad actors and close them down, all the time receiving publicity. May try to play up some drug busts, too, but it's to create the public impression he's shutting down Kiowa Heights. That's all it will be."

"Don, I'll be more specific. I've heard that instead of using police to eliminate crime, Hale is using the police to eliminate people, those I've heard you call 'your people.'"

"What's easier? Getting a conviction of a drug seller or shooting him?" Hubbard didn't wait for an answer. "Does it happen? Of course, but most police officers are good men and women who try awfully hard in a world of grays. With a new tough-sounding police chief, those rumors of excess police violence begin anew. They always do. It's akin to urban myth."

"You haven't directly responded," Morgan said. "Are the police killing people to clean up Kiowa Heights?"

Hubbard looked across the room where a small statute of the Virgin Mary stood on a pedestal. He was silent for a moment, and then said, "I've heard the same reports you have."

"You think they are, don't you?"

"Statistics," Hubbard said. He sat up and folded his hands together on top of his desk. "The suburban voter across the river doesn't know crime. The people here do. If you control the numbers for the official crime rate, you can tell those voters that crime has gone down and they'll believe it and feel better. That's enough for them, but the people of Kiowa Heights remain victims. I'm not here to judge those voters, the police, or my people. We're here to help, to demonstrate a greater compassion can make lives whole, no matter how wounded or fearful. That's all we can do."

Morgan looked around the office. Near Hubbard's desk on a pedestal sat a porcelain replica of the Pieta, the Virgin holding the broken body of Christ.

"Why don't you show me around," Morgan said.

The minister locked the door to his office and led the attorney down a hallway. They passed a series of offices, the doors open and the spaces spartan. "I try to teach the benevolence of random life," Hubbard said. "Too often for the people of Kiowa Heights that unpredictability is frightening and harsh. Yet, in it, there is goodness and sometimes justice."

"And, I suppose," Morgan said, "justice never seen or fully understood."

"That's right," Hubbard replied. "It is not ours to determine; it is simply ours to give by living lives of compassion. My people don't need forms or formulas or criteria or minimization by rule and regulation. Therefore, little we do at the Project seems other than chaos."

Hubbard stopped at the door of one of the open offices. "I arrange for volunteers to come in as they are inspired: Psychologists, vocational counselors, nurses, attorneys. They use these offices to meet with whoever might need them. College students often are good at helping however they can."

"Martin Bollant said you were very selective," Morgan said.

"I am," the minister replied. "Too many want to save or to change the people here. We don't have that power. One can only be a conduit for grace."

They stopped at a large room cluttered with beat-up gray folding chairs. "This is our meeting room. Teachers talk here. If I'm inspired to speak on some topic of practical life or psychology, I post a sign with time and topic. More often than not, the place is full. Alcoholics Anonymous meets here as does Narcotics Anonymous. A group of ex-cons trying to live straight uses the room, too."

With Hubbard showing the way, the two men progressed towards the center of the building. Hubbard walked slowly, each step secure and balanced. When he talked about his people or the Project, Morgan had noticed, light shone from his eyes. His voice was deep and peaceful. He spoke as one with authority.

"I keep this stocked as well as I can," Hubbard said when they arrived at the kitchen. A woman in faded denim pants and a scuffed leather jacket poured a glass of milk for a small girl. "I get up at four several mornings a week and drive to the fruit and vegetable markets. Ah, the farmers and the wholesalers! Some of their hearts are blessed with a such a spirit of generosity." He tussled the hair of the small girl. "We cook meals three times a day and share what we can. We have a locked pantry and refrigerator for emergencies."

Morgan looked around the kitchen. It was small and inefficient and lacked the sterility of institutional design. Someone had worked hard to keep it clean, shiny. "What can one expect if they come to the Project?" he asked.

"What they need, to the extent we have. A safe place, a place of peace," the minister replied. "Of material things, I give what I have, but the Project is not a cornucopia. For that, most people know to go to the big shelters where funds and food seem unlimited. This is more for respite and renewal and back to the rest of life again."

"How many employees do you have?"

"Just one," Hubbard said. "Me. Everything else is done by volunteers, when they are so inspired."

They walked through a large sitting room. A pastel mural of flowery prairie and multiple horizons covered one wall. On an institutional blue couch, a young man with a thin, black beard lay passed out. Nearby in a straight back chair, a man, an old sailor perhaps, sat, his hands shaking. A TV buzzed in the background and tears quietly rolled from the eyes of a young woman, her face smeared with heavy makeup. She chewed on her lower lip and sobbed alone. Hubbard stopped, then walked to the woman, and knelt on one knee in front of her. He lifted his hands and wiped the tears from her face. He patted her arm, then continued Morgan's tour.

"Friday mornings are usually quiet like this," Hubbard said. "I have no complaint."

The cleric led Chester to a short, dark hall with a door at each side. Hubbard opened the left one. "There are seven bedrooms down this hall. Not fancy—a bed, a chair, a lavatory. A common bathroom at the end there. All the rooms are occupied almost every night. Zoning and city ordinances limit the stays to three nights. Of course, we aren't a shelter or a warehouse for the homeless; we are a sanctuary, a temporary space for peace. I'm not unhappy with the time constraint."

Chester Morgan turned to open the door to the right. It was locked. "What's this?" he asked.

"My quarters."

"You live here?"

Don Hubbard nodded.

"Are you married?" Chester asked. "Do you have a family?"

"In an earlier life, I was. My spouse now is divine, my marriage is to the Project and her people, and those you passed are members of my family." Hubbard stopped. "Does that sound strange to you?"

Morgan shook his head. "One of the best attorneys I've ever known claimed the law was his mistress."

"I have one more place to show you. Come this way."

The cleric touched Morgan's back and nodded. He led Morgan back past the sleeping man, the sobbing woman, and the shaking man and through an open door to a windowless room, a space where it could always be either day or night. From the high ceiling, lights beamed onto a simple altar. Above it in stark shadows hung a massive sculpture of Christ, nailed to a cross, his side pierced, blood running down his face, his feet, his hands, and his eyes opened but not seeing. Morgan remembered Don Hubbard's explicit description of crucifixion and, from the memory of the words of the manager of the Bunkhouse Lodge, he saw the corpse of Tanya Everly. Morgan shook from a chill.

"The chapel is always open," the minister said. "On Sundays, I lead a liturgy. On other days, prayers of intercession. I usually say a few words, too, depending on the inspiration. I'm still credentialed to marry, to do funerals, to perform the sacraments." He looked around the dark room. "This is the most important space at the Project."

"But you don't proselytize," the lawyer said.

"I don't," Hubbard replied. His voice echoed in the room. "This is the body of Christ. If we are successful showing his compassion, his acceptance, his humanity, people are led here with no words from us. Mister Morgan, you may have heard that Christ died for your sins. I'd rather think God took the form of a man and conceded to cruel death so the people would know that however they might suffer, God too had suffered and understands their pain. That compassion has to lead here."

Morgan looked again at the anguished dying Christ on the cross. Then he saw at the corner of the altar another figure: Mary, the mother of Christ, with her hands outspread, her face serene. He turned to leave.

In a quiet, intimate voice, Hubbard said, "In ways I consider this religion incomplete. If God took the form of a man to know suffering, should he have not also, at some time through the ages, taken the form of a woman and likewise suffered?"

Chapter Twenty

Marylin set the bag of groceries on the white-tiled kitchen cabinet. She knew she shouldn't have carried them in from the car, but what choice did she have? Besides, she felt better than she had Friday, the day following her move. She had woken up that morning and her hip hurt so badly she didn't try to get out of bed. Instead, she had called the office and told Shawn to let Chester know she wouldn't be in.

Marylin hoped Morgan wouldn't be mad. He didn't know about the old injury. If Chester would learn of it, he would worry or try to make her go see a doctor, both equally futile. She hated the doctors. Going to one made her feel like Martusé, the carnival's two thousand pound woman on exhibit at a hands-on museum. And she didn't want Chester to worry, as do all attorneys, even those with the most braggadocio. By experience, they worried too much: about righting what had gone wrong in the past and trying to prevent wrongs from happening in the future. Chester didn't need more to fret about. She always figured old attorneys never actually retired. They just wake up one morning too anxious about what might go awry to ever leave home again.

When Marylin hurt at the office, she ate aspirin and tried to walk so no one would notice the limp. She considered her forthright posture and graceful walk badges of strength, though they probably resulted from the velvet boot-camp training of childhood charm school interments. She laughed now when she thought about learning to balance books on her head while she walked and how the middle-aged maiden teacher taught the proper ways for a lady to sit.

Marylin knew what caused the pain in her hip—a motorcycle ride with a cool-looking guy twenty-two years before. It wasn't the ride exactly. It was the cool-looking guy on the motorcycle. He drove like a monkey on acid. The accident fractured no bones, and most of the time, her hip didn't bother her. She didn't even notice. But when she woke in the night with pain burning in the joint or when she stood at day's end with hip locked, she remembered a three night hospital stay and a four week dance with two awkward crutches. She still liked motorcycles and cool-looking guys. She just avoided the ones who resembled non-human primates.

Marylin unpacked the groceries and looked out the window at her landlord's house. Murle Mueller, or Miz Mueller—too many decibels, too much structure to appear other than intimidating, and too few words. What a trip! Marylin knew what she would do: Make Flaming Chocolate Bursts!

She turned on the oven, heard the burner light, and smelled the first whiff of ignited natural gas, a smell that took her home and back to her grandmother's warm kitchen. She found two glass bowls and mixed eggs, sugar, white and brown, and butter, not margarine. She stirred in a generous portion of vanilla extract. In the other bowl, she sifted bleached flour and salt and baking soda and added in an equal part of floured whole wheat. Gently stirring, she combined the contents of the two bowls into a doughy mix. She smiled and looked around as if to protect the secret and poured in twice as many chocolate chips as ever called for in conventional recipes and put in an extravagant dose of cinnamon. As she began to dollop the lumpy dough onto a lightly greased cookie sheet, she hummed a song she knew from twenty years before. Soon, the spoonfuls of dough fell to the pan in rhythm to the music. Her hip felt better.

Later, she stood on the porch of Miz Mueller's house with a plateful of freshly baked cookies. She knocked on the door and the square-built, loud-speaking woman opened the door.

"Go down to the Goddamned basement and beat hell out of the pipe with a hammer!" She yelled as much as talked.

"What?"

"I said ..." Murle Mueller saw the plate of cookies.

"These are for you," Marylin said. "A place isn't home until you make something there. I won't be able to eat them all."

Murle Mueller took the plate and chomped into one of the cookies. She kept talking, yelling. "Forgot to tell you about the plumbing. Make noise?"

"No."

"It will." Mueller set the plate of cookies inside and zipped up her windbreaker. Crumbs had gathered at the corners of her mouth. "Show you."

Murle stomped down the porch stairs and plowed towards her rental house. Marylin turned and tried to catch up. "Would you mind slowing down a little?" she asked. "I'd like to walk with you."

The landlord turned. "Hmph." She waited with expressionless face as Marylin joined her.

"When I move into a new place, I always try to cook or bake something first thing," she said. "Have you ever gone to someone's house or apartment and they've lived there three or four months and it still doesn't feel like a home? I figure they haven't cooked or made anything there yet."

"Hmph."

As the refrigerator-big woman and the lithe legal secretary walked into Marylin's house, an unnoticed man sat in an old pickup truck a half-block away and watched.

Mueller looked around the living room. A few unpacked boxes still sat on the polished hardwood floor. "Gotta hammer?"

"That's one thing I think I can find," Marylin said. She moved as quickly as she could to the bedroom where she had left it to hang pictures. She met her landlord at a door off the kitchen.

"Don't break your Goddamned neck goin' down into this basement!" Murle yelled. "Turn on the water."

Marylin did so and started down the narrow wooden stairs into the cellar where Miz Mueller waited by an exposed black pipe. She held the hammer in her uplifted hand.

"When it sounds like this ..." Murle Mueller pounded the pipe with the hammer until the plumbing clunked and clanked. "Turn that stupid water off."

Marylin went back up the stairs and turned it off. When she returned, the landlord said, "When it sounds like that, you just beat hell out of that pipe. Just beat hell out of it." She took the hammer and pounded the exposed pipe with flourish and fury. "Turn the Goddamned water back on."

As Marylin did so, the clunks and clanks returned. She started down the stairs.

"Stay up there! Sometimes you got to pound it with the water going and sometimes not."

Bang!

Bang!

Bang!

Bang!

Bang!

BANG!

BANG!

"Turn it off! Now turn it on slowly!"

The house settled into silence as Marylin turned the faucet off. As she turned it back on, the jumble of knocks and clanks returned louder. She listened to her landlord downstairs.

Bang!

Bang!

Bang!

Bang!

"GODDAMNED MOTHERFUCKING SON OF A BITCH!"

BANG!

BANG!

BANG!

BANG!

Marylin quietly stepped down the stairs and watched her landlord pound hell out of the bare black pipe. Miz Mueller stopped and looked up. As she did, the cacophony of clunks and clanks murmured to flowing silence. She put the hammer in her baggy pants pocket and wiped her hands together. "Just do that," she said. Marylin followed her up the stairs.

When they returned to the kitchen, Murle Mueller said, "I suppose I ought to get this house replumbed." Her voice was softer than Marylin had yet heard.

"You'd hate to do that. You don't know what the repairmen might mess up," Marylin said. "Besides, you can't find craftsmanship like this anymore, the plaster walls and all. I can already tell this house is special, as if it has its own soul."

Murle Mueller stood there and for the first time, Marylin saw something fragile in her landlord's pale blue eyes.

"I shouldn't eat all these cookies," Marylin said. "Why don't you take some more with you?"

The large woman waited for a moment, grabbed a fistful, and left.

Chapter Twenty-One

"Where is Marylin? She's always here before I am." Chester Morgan sat down at his desk the following Monday morning. "You haven't heard from her?"

"Some people, Chest, don't do the same thing every day of their lives." Shawn followed him into the room and landed in a chair.

"But it's not like her," he said.

"Breathe deep and don't worry. Guess what?" Shawn said. "I waited for the perfect time and I nailed that ex-roommate."

"What are you talking about?" Morgan said.

"The one who copied my term paper last semester."

"You don't know that she did that."

"I swear, Chester, she did. I finished mine before she even started. She used different words, but it was the same paper. Same thoughts, same points, same arguments. And the bibliography was identical, precisely identical."

"And, she made the better grade, didn't she?" Morgan said.

"That's irrelevant. I made a mistake on my bibliography and guess what? The same mistake was on hers."

"Maybe neither of you knew how to do the citation."

"It was a typo."

"Could have been from the source." Morgan shook his head and looked across the room. "Anyway, what did you do this time?"

Shawn rose from her chair, walked to the window, and pulled back the drape. Ugly gray clouds poured heavy rain as they had through the night. "Nice weather we're having, aren't we? Particularly if you are running late, like you always do, and you discover the air out of all your tires."

"I can't believe that, Shawn."

"No crime, counselor. Nothing was destroyed and she was deprived of nothing of monetary value. It will drive her crazy."

"When I hear stuff like this, Shawn, I want to tell you to just pack up your desk and go."

"Yeah, but you won't. Your clients all love me. You give me something and it gets done even if it can't be done, and I keep your cash flowing."

Morgan chewed the inside of his cheek. He knew she was right. One afternoon, due to Morgan's error, Shawn had arrived at the court clerk's office two minutes after it had closed. The brief had to be filed that day, and, if not, Morgan's client could, and probably would, have lost his case. Shawn knew that and got the document filed. She later told Morgan, who did not want to know, something about how she'd had a mysterious onset of a strange seizure in front of the clerk's office and how a sympathetic bureaucrat believed her mussed clothes and hair resulted from the convulsions Shawn said she had been having for the previous ten minutes. Morgan's clients liked her, too, even the old bachelor Schupert who despised everyone and everything post-1963. And, Shawn had the cold ability to isolate money and finances from everything personal and living, which made her a good business manager, the best one Morgan had found, but ...

"Besides, Chest, that woman was so hypocritical," Shawn continued. "I got so sick of her and all her goody-goody spectaculars. Amnesty International. Save the Whales. The Vivia Project for Empowerment. Like anything she might do could ever make a difference. And, she'd bring home all these Iranians and Africans. I don't know where she came up with all these guys and—"

"Sorry I'm late," Marylin said as she walked into Morgan's office, intense but composed. "I moved last week and it takes longer to get here than I thought."

"I hope there was air in your tires," Morgan said.

"What's that?" Marylin replied.

"Never mind. You moved?" Morgan asked.

"Had to. My brother came home. His family needed a place to stay. What else could I do?"

"Give me your new address and phone number in case I need it sometime," Morgan said.

"It's across the river."

The attorney raised his eyebrows. "That's okay. What's the address?"

Marylin told him.

"Sounds familiar. Do we have a client who lives on that street or something?"

"It's Murle Mueller's rental house," Marylin said. "The one where Tanya Everly used to live. I thought I might learn something, boss."

"Marylin, I don't know if that was a good—"

Shawn interrupted. "Oh, God, this has gone from the bizarre to the surreal. Morgan's working for some pimpled-faced loser, going out and watching trashy women take off their clothes, running up a huge uncollectible bill, and his secretary is moving into the house of some fifty-cent whore. Oh, this is just great."

"At least she's trying to do something, Shawn," Morgan said. "Something better than letting the air out of someone's tires in the middle of the night."

"There's no relationship," Shawn said. "You've never even known these low-lifers. Why bother except to waste—"

"You can tell me, and you can tell Marylin, we are wasting our time but that doesn't impress me. You were raised in a nice home by two nice parents in a nice neighborhood with trimmed green grass and a new car in every driveway every couple of years. You work here for your resume and a letter of recommendation, not because you need the money. You don't. You've never wanted and you've never lacked. You've never struggled. You've never been defeated and you've never had to worry about the next meal or how you were going to live from one day to the next. You can shrug some things off, but some of us can't and won't—ever."

"That's not the point, Morgan. This whole episode is pointless. You aren't going to be able to make a difference anyway."

"You're right. A thousand years from now nobody is going to know that you or I ever lived. The cynic is right, but lazy. He says 'You live, you die and nothing you do will ever make a difference.' But as long as I live, I'm going to be like Beethoven and shake my fist at fate and try to do something for those who live here now and who knows how far into the future that will go. If I accomplish nothing more than making my arm sore, at least I will be satisfied that I have lived."

"Well, whatever." Shawn stood and left. Quietly.

"She got you going this morning, boss," Marylin said.

"Dammit, she's too young—"

"Chester, it's a show, it's an act. At her age, it's not cool to be anything but a skeptic."

"I suppose you're right," he said. "But low-lifes? Losers? Fifty-cent whores? Someone raised in the last twenty-two or three years with words and base judgments like that? Is this what we've become? How can it be?"

"Maybe the advantages she has had don't include the ones you might expect," Marylin said.

Chester Morgan looked at her. She had been with him ten years. Devoted, her to him and him to her. He had taught her the law. She had, once more, taught him something else. He felt urgent compassion for her, his secretary who now in the forced office light seemed vulnerable and frail. "Marylin, be cautious with this Tanya Everly case. We don't know enough not to be."

"You aren't mad?"

"What can I say now?" He stopped, then grinned.

"Have you heard from McNally? Anything about those roaming secret cops?" Marylin asked.

Morgan shook his head.

"Would you like me to call him, Mister Morgan?"

"Not yet. It's always easier to say no than yes. Don't want to force Jeff to say either. He was hesitant when we talked with him." Morgan tapped his fingers on the desk. "Friday, I went to the Corpus Christi Project and talked to that preacher I met at Martin Bollant's reception."

"Don Hubbard?"

"Yeah. He says the tougher the police talk, the more rumors there are. He's heard what is being said on the streets, but he acts like he doesn't believe it."

"Still have the same impression of him?"

"He works hard. His whole life seems to be that project. Seems sincere but ..."

"Maybe you just don't trust preachers," Marylin replied.

"He says the right things, the way he should, when he should. Makes me feel like something's missing. Always does. It's too neat otherwise. Then he talks about death and the images and the icons surround him."

"What do you mean?"

"In his office, there is a large gold crucifix, a statute of the Virgin Mary, and a replica of the Pieta. There's a small dark chapel with a huge, ghastly sculpture of Christ on a cross and a statute of the Madonna. He said something about how God never took the form of a woman and suffered. I remember how he described crucifixion and I remember how Tanya Everly was found. I don't know ..." He scooted back in his chair. "Let's get the calendar and see what we have to do this week."

After they had reviewed the week's schedule, Marylin said, "Chester, don't you think you need to make a decision on the Rufus Daupin case?"

"You're right. I do." Daupin had invested a large portion of his savings in shares of oil and gas limited partnerships promoted by a local brokerage firm. The bountiful tax write-off he had been promised resulted instead in a devastating tax liability and the oil and gas properties had never produced. It was the wrong investment for a professor near retirement. Morgan thought he might be successful with the case but ... "Let's call Martin right now. He'd do a good job with it."

After Bollant answered the phone and heard a summary of the facts, Morgan said, "I'd like to keep it, Martin. It's kind of a miniature Red Strike Affair, but the promoters' law firms would bury me with paper. I'm afraid I'd need to hire another attorney to keep up with it. You interested?"

"Why don't you send the file over? I'll look at it and make an appointment with Mr. Daupin."

"I stay involved in the case."

"You don't trust us, Chesterfield?"

"Marty, what do you know about trying lawsuits?"

"We have some excellent litigators here."

"I know you do. I just stay involved with my people, my clients. Call Marylin after you look at the paperwork. She can set up an appointment for the three of us." Morgan got ready to hang up the telephone, then, "Martin, what do you know about Don Hubbard?"

Bollant started to repeat what Morgan had heard the week before.

"Not that," Morgan said. "Personally. His history, background, his story. What does he do besides run that mission?"

"Hubbard's mission is his mission. Otherwise, I don't know much, I suppose. Some watershed experience made him walk the streets. He keeps it close. His past, too. Why do you ask?"

"Curious, I guess."

"Hey, Chester, did you hear that my old law firm, Summers and Kirk, laid off seven attorneys. Lost the Key Petroleum account. Rumors are that another ten to fifteen lawyers will be gone."

"Really?"

"The first act of Randolph Harrison as Personal Representative of his father's estate. Fired Summers and Kirk—by telephone. Bradford, Evans, and Shell, the firm that used to do the elder Harrison's personal business, is going to take Key's transactional work. The regulatory and litigation matters will be handled by Massey, James, and Peterson, Randolph's firm."

"Odd to split the company's work like that, isn't it? But Key never had that many lawsuits, did it?"

"With Randolph running things and Massey, James, and Peterson representing the company, there will be now."

Morgan did not reply. The image seared and would not fade.

"Chester, are you still there?"

"Yeah. I was just thinking."

"What?"

"I don't like it."

"Pardon? What did you say?"

"Nothing. I'll get the Rufus Daupin file to you. Give Marylin a call when you're ready."

Morgan hung up the phone. Marylin had waited. "The house, Murle Mueller. Did you learn anything?" he asked, but he was thinking of something else.

"To bang hell out of the pipes," she said, "and I found some guitar strings in the bedroom."

Morgan sat in silence, staring at something no one else saw.

"Something bothering you, boss?"

"Powers didn't want to admit Harrison's lost will into probate," he finally said. "If he had had any choice, he wouldn't have. The first thing the son did was fire the old man's law firm. I don't like it."

Marylin held up the calendar. "You have enough to do. Your own clients can make you brood. Don't take on more who are not."

"I still don't like it."

Chapter Twenty-Two

It was a jazz night. It had been that kind of day. Morgan wanted to hear the sound of clear Brubeck-cool jazz. That's all. The telephone had rung most of the morning and afternoon. He had been in court, had two or three real emergencies, and had had convinced three or four clients they hadn't. Now at home, he changed his clothes and put on the music.

The phone rang.

"Is this Chester Morgan, the attorney who leaves his name wherever he goes?"

Morgan recognized the voice: something sweet, something saintly. He stood straighter. "Should I call you Candy or Maria?" he asked "What did you do to find me?"

"If you go to a strip bar, don't sign your real name when you pay the cover," she said. "Your name and number's in the phone book."

Morgan paused and thought. She hadn't told him everything that night. He knew it then; he knew it now. "What can I do for you?" he asked.

"You might offer to buy supper. I'm not workin' tonight and I'm hungry. The Hot 'N' Hearty on Eisenhower Parkway, in your part of town, by the expressway. Meet you there in thirty minutes? You don't have to buy."

He didn't need anything else today. He didn't feel like searching for Tanya Everly's ghost tonight but ... He remembered how Maria looked and smiled and how her spirit intrigued. "I'll meet you there."

Hidden spotlights shone on the wood and river-rocked façade of The Hot 'N' Hearty. Morgan stopped his car and wondered whether he should go in, whether his intuition about this woman was wrong, and whether ignorance of what she hadn't told him might be safer than knowledge. A good lawyer doesn't prejudge, he rationalized. He got out of his car. He knew another reason for his hesitation he didn't want to admit: If a man—even a good paying client—had called for dinner at an all-night franchise diner, he would have not considered it, not this night. He straightened his hair with his fingers and walked in.

* * *

Morgan didn't see her. He saw people, though. A lot of them. People you might meet, blink, and never remember. People sitting at faded yellow counters and in orange Naugahyde booths, and people shuffling along on stained avocado colored carpet. Globes hung from the angled ceiling and burned twenty-four-hour light. The place looked like suburban America 1972, except aged.

The attorney told the hostess he was meeting someone. She nodded at a corner booth in the smoking section where a woman sat at a round table—a woman Morgan had seen, but not recognized. He took a menu from the hostess and walked to the table.

"Didn't recognize me in the light or in clothes?" Maria asked as Morgan sat.

"I lose however I answer that, don't I?"

"'Didn't expect me in just a cowboy hat, did ya?" She smiled. "A lot of dancers don't like this kind of light. I don't mind. All I do is light and shadows anyway."

She wore a brown leather jacket and a low-cut blue lamé dress. Over tobacco smoke and coffee shop aromas, she smelled like Old Spice, only sweeter, stronger. Morgan looked at her: smaller than he remembered and her skin, fairer. Star-shaped earrings glittered silver against her wavy black hair.

"I haven't been here in a long time," Morgan said. "I didn't know The Hot 'N' Hearty was ever busy except at three o'clock in the morning."

"I didn't want to bankrupt you," she said.

"Thanks for the consideration. We can wash dishes together."

A hard-life waitress stopped to take their order. She wore a brown uniform that matched the walnut paneling on the walls. Her face showed no expression and her hands looked old.

"Bring me a cup of hot coffee, two eggs scrambled, bacon, a side of hash browns, and biscuits," Marie said.

"They say that's bad for your heart," Morgan said.

Maria sat back and stared at the attorney. She grinned. "Fuck 'em."

The waitress scratched on her pad. "What would you like, sir?"

"The same thing," Morgan replied. The waitress nodded and walked away.

The hostess seated a lone scruffy-bearded man at a nearby table. He pulled a book from his raincoat and began to read through black-framed glasses. Others waited, then were seated. Maria took a cigarette from a sequined purse and lit it.

"You look nice," Morgan said.

The dancer blew smoke and seemed to ignore the comment. "You haven't been back to the club," she said.

"I haven't needed to."

"You haven't?" She smiled and touched the edge of her low-cut gown where it met the curve and flesh of her cleavage. Then, she laughed.

The expressionless waitress slid cups of hot coffee and sweating glasses of ice water in front of the attorney and the dancer. The waitress turned and walked away.

"I liked the way you got me coffee the night you came in," Maria said. "'Figured that scheme pretty quick."

"You were straight, didn't play games, told me what you wanted. I liked that. Respect it." He wondered whether time and thought had given her opportunity to do the opposite.

Muzak oozed from hidden speakers. Customers' voices buzzed and, from the kitchen, dishes clanked and silverware rattled. Pieces of conversation dropped and evaporated, but from across the table, silence loomed. The hardest thing Morgan, as a lawyer, had had to learn was to wait for the silence to stop, to play the inquisitor by being mute, to let the other speak, to learn the other's design, and not for the other to learn by yours.

"D'ya find Star's mama?"

Morgan looked at the woman. He knew he should make her dump her purse onto the table and turn her cigarette case inside out. He knew he should check her coat, her dress, her body for a wire. The lawyer knew he should, but Chester nodded.

"Good description you gave me," he said.

"You find out anything?"

"Not much other than what you told me."

Maria stirred her coffee with a spoon. "You know I could have told you other stuff the night you came in," she said. "I'd never seen you, didn't know nothin' about you."

"Still don't, do you?"

"No, but I could find you and that means somethin', doesn't it? I suppose I knew you weren't workin' a con that night." She stubbed out her cigarette. "Tanya could make you feel good by just listenin' to ya."

"Some people can," Morgan said.

"When you lose someone like that, it's like a thief stole somethin' you can't ever get back. Sometimes I still hear her voice. Then, in a flash, it's gone."

"I know," Chester said. Some people hear, he thought, some people see.

"And, you never knew her. She could walk in here, sit down at this booth, rub up against you, and you'd never even know it was her."

"No, I wouldn't—not to touch, see, smell, or hear. But is any life so isolated that it lives only in the past and not in the present and future, too?"

Maria glanced over her shoulder. "'Suppose not," she said.

A busboy cleared a nearby table, his movements precise, mechanical. Across the room, a ladies' prayer group was seated for pie and coffee. Morgan heard someone talking about sales quotas. Maria sipped her coffee.

She said, "Tanya wasn't no crusader, but Bruce is so far out of it, he wouldn't know."

"'Bruce—the manager at the club?"

She nodded. "He imagines, and the more he does, the more paranoid he gets. What have you found out?"

"Not much."

The dancer stared at the attorney.

"Tanya died at a place called the Bunkhouse Lodge," Morgan said. "It wasn't an accident and the investigation was minimal."

"There's more. You know that, don't you?"

He nodded.

"Who's your client?" she asked.

"'Can't tell you. The person I represent wants what you want. Isn't that enough?"

The black-haired woman played with her star-shaped earring. The white globe hanging over the table reflected off the window and back. "This is between us, for Tanya," she said.

Chester nodded. "I'll protect you as much as I can, but I don't know where this is going."

"'Never do, do we?"

The expressionless waitress refilled their cups and glasses, quickly, with the surety of experience and routine. "Food will be out in a minute," she said.

Maria pulled another cigarette from her purse. Chester moved next to her, took her lighter, and lit her cigarette. "Thanks," she said. He started to move back, but didn't. "I've worked at Vixens for six years, goin' on seven. Too long, I guess. Place has never been busted or shut down. Kinda amazing, isn't it?"

"I suppose."

"About a year ago, rumors bounced around that we were goin' to be. Bruce wigged, but it never happened. Then, what? Five months ago the new police chief comes to town and Bruce wigs again. Worse. Knows we're goin' to get shut down, I suppose, or we're goin' be in the papers, or somethin'. And Topaz plays it."

"Remind me."

"The one Tanya calls a psychotic bitch. Looks like a model with tits."

Morgan remembered—the one who left his table when he mentioned Star's name. "Go ahead," the lawyer said.

"You've seen the dancers out there. With Tanya gone, I'm the old lady and I'm twenty-three. Girls, that's what they are. Fifteen, sixteen, seventeen, most of 'em. Bruce thinks they're better for business so he just asks, 'You legal?' and if they say 'no,' he figures they're too dumb to hire anyway."

The brown-uniformed waitress placed their meals in front of them. Around the lawyer and the stripper, people ate, talked of their own lives, and left. Waitresses, busboys, and cooks worked like a machine. Chester Morgan took a biscuit and broke it in two. "One of those women, girls, sat next to me the night I was there and tried to get me to buy her a drink."

"Yeah, it's the only way Vixen's would get busted. Bruce doesn't tolerate drugs, hookin', or wild-ass boyfriends. Anybody vulgar on stage—" The dancer laughed. "I guess we all are, dependin' on who you ask. Anybody too gross *and* vulgar on stage, gets warned once, twice, and then they're out. But the young girls, that's how he'd get busted. Probably the only way."

"But Bruce isn't stable," Morgan said.

"He's not, but the money's good. Operation as clean as any of 'em and he treats his girls better than most, I hear."

Morgan put the broken biscuit down. His meal lay in front of him as it had been brought to him from the kitchen.

"You better eat," she said. "Your food will get cold."

"That's okay. I'm listening."

"Well, I'm eating." The woman took two or three bites of food and sipped some coffee. "When Bruce started weirdin' about bein' shut down or busted, Topaz figured she could get two things she wanted: Star gone and more money. She started feeding Bruce that Tanya was goin' to do somethin' to get him busted. He started slippin' that psychotic bitch money and the more money she got, the more extravagant the stories got."

"How do you know this?" the lawyer asked.

"He was givin' Topaz money for something and Star was always Bruce's darlin' until then. Then he was crazy about what she was doin'. Anything. He had to know everything, but he didn't."

Morgan hesitated before asking the next question. He thought he knew the answer, but the lawyer asked. "Was Tanya going to get him shut down or get something published in the newspapers?"

"Never. She didn't like it kids were dancing there because that was the way she started out. But she knew that some were runaways or didn't have any other way to make a livin' or survive. Or had no choice, like her. She wouldn't have tried to close him. Ever. Could have never gotten another job on Ninth Avenue and her mom would have been livid. Star wasn't no crusader."

"You sure?"

Maria nodded.

"Then it doesn't make any sense," Morgan said.

"Neither does wall-shrinkin', noise-amplifyin' paranoia. And cash money to pay whoever needs to be paid."

"What's Topaz's real name?"

"Don't know and don't care."

Maria had stopped eating. Morgan picked up his fork and set it down again. "What do you make of it?"

"Then Tanya's dead. Worked at a place that could have been busted at any time and wasn't, even though everyone in Kiowa Heights, police, hookers, everyone knows it could be. Why do you suppose it's not? The death's called an accident. Not investigated, not much. The rumors say the police did it. Who else could get rid of someone with so little asked? Whoever is taking the payoff?"

"Why do you keep working for Bruce?"

"I suppose I hope you prove me wrong."

Morgan looked at his plate. The all-night special. What those who work until twelve or two or three eat when night is at its darkest. "You better start, Maria," he said. "Your food will get cold."

They were silent for a moment. Then, Marie picked up her fork once more and began to eat. Morgan did the same. They didn't talk about Tanya Everly anymore or about nightclubs where women, no more than girls, took off their clothes for leers and money or about paranoid managers and payoffs. She asked him about him and he told her more than he thought he would or should. When he asked about her, he heard a vague story of a childhood of different towns and different people, about arriving in Vivia at sixteen married to a wild cowboy and at sixteen and a half, being left here alone. He knew the rest of the story so he didn't ask, but when she talked about the future, her husky voice got quiet as if something in it wanted to hide something like hope. He noticed her skin, smooth and white. He wanted to touch her cheek to just to see how if felt. She started touching his arm when she talked. When she realized what she was doing, she stopped. They were both in The Hot 'N' Hearty because a young woman had died.

"If I learn anything else," Maria said, "I'll let you know." She picked up her purse to go.

"If I need to talk with you?" Morgan asked.

"You know where to find me."

"But if I could telephone ..."

"Maybe I'd like to see you there out in the audience at Vixens," she said. Then, quietly like the future, "Maybe it's better that way."

"If you like."

She stood and looked once more at the middle-aged attorney. Her lips curved up and fell. Then, she turned and left.

Chapter Twenty-Three

Marylin took off her heels and looked through her bedroom window into her backyard. Survivors of another season, the old trees' faded greens endured, not yet shocked to rapid, beautiful death by autumn's frost. She smiled. In the twilight's hues and forms, her landlord raked scrawny piles of fallen leaves next door. Marylin wondered, why not?

Minutes later, the legal secretary joined the landlord, separated by the yards' chain link fence. Across the street and down, a pickup truck, unobserved, had stopped as if to watch. The evening air felt heavy and sensual, especially when the day at the office had ended, seeming static, routine, even though it wasn't. Never was, not for Marylin, not willingly. Scratching the rake over the earth, feeling arms and shoulders move, made life real in the turquoise-hued evening.

She grinned. Hardly enough leaves on the ground to bother, she thought. Must be the same way in Murle Mueller's yard, but the big woman kept working. When Marylin had walked out of her house into the backyard, she had silently acknowledged the woman's presence. The landlord had nodded. Kind of. Marylin liked her and suspected there was truth in Murle Mueller. Bedrock truth. Chester had been right to start his inquiry with Tanya Everly's landlord. His execution had just failed.

Marylin's rake hit the edge of the flower bed. She looked and sighed. A straight cut, no weeds, little debris. At the corner of the yard, a redbud grew, pruned perfectly round. The turf beneath Marylin's feet stood smooth, even. She felt someone looking at her. When she turned, she saw Murle Mueller look away and heard the landlord's rake pull quickly against the grass.

"Beautiful yard," Marylin said, "especially for a rent house."

"Not a rent house." Murle Mueller didn't look up.

"It's a beautiful yard."

"I take care of it," the large woman said. "Now."

Marylin waited. "Miz Mueller, what did you mean it's not a rent house?"

The landlady kept raking. "I lease to two people and the place is seventy years old. It's not a rent house."

A breeze shook the leaves of the oak and sycamore that shaded the two yards. A mourning dove and a mockingbird flew away.

"No offense meant," Marylin said. "It's a wonderful home."

Murle Mueller stopped raking. "I've tried to be careful." Her voice was quiet now. The first time Marylin had heard it that way.

"I'm only the second renter? I'm honored."

The landlady mumbled something. "Miss Mary took good care of that yard." She bent down and pulled a weed out of a flower bed. She stared at it a moment and tossed it away. "Little girl before you not inclined that way—yardwise. If you aren't, I'll do it."

"I may not always have the time."

"I'll do it. Put away the rake."

Marylin stood not knowing what to do. She twirled the rake in her hand, then stopped. "Who was Miss Mary?"

Murle Mueller acted like she didn't hear. She made her pile of leaves bigger and reached down to pick them up. "Little girl before you lived there six months. Before that, Miss Mary. Her whole life—with her parents, then alone."

"What was she like?"

"I told you I tried to be careful." Murle Mueller stood and looked over her yard. Silence passed. "Little girl before you was like Miss Mary. You, too. Not look like her, but have ways like her."

"You miss her, don't you?"

Murle Mueller nodded and started raking again. Marylin saw tiny splashes of tears in the eyes of her landlord.

Chapter Twenty-Four

Marylin laid the one-page fax on Chester Morgan's desk. "Looks like McNally finally got a list of those SPIT cops, the ones that roam," she said. Morgan looked up from a contract he had been reviewing and took the document.

"No transmittal page?" he asked.

Marylin shook her head. "I don't think Jeff wanted anyone to trace it back. Look at the top: All zeroes for the number of transmittal. All x's for the location."

"Maybe their machine is programmed that way."

"Don't think so, boss. Other faxes we've gotten from him have VPD and a phone number at the top. He didn't initial or sign it either."

"If it came from McNally," Morgan said, argued. The statement was a bluff, and Morgan knew it. Lawyers, he thought, always offering the contrary even to the obvious. He hoped McNally hadn't compromised himself and the police officer's intentional anonymity reminded him of his friend and client's caution: "Just stay away from it."

The list identified five officially designated zones with nine teams of cops each. Eighteen officers a zone, identified only by last name and car number. "I didn't think there would be so many," Morgan said.

"Do you think it will help?" Marylin asked.

"I don't know. Frank Carlile at the Bunkhouse Lodge said he'd never seen the patrol cops who arrived on the scene first. Doubt he'd remember names or car numbers."

"Should we call Jeff McNally?"

Morgan stared at the empty space in front of his desk as if all answers were contained there. "No," he finally said, "Don't want to involve him more than we have. Not yet anyway."

"Chester, wouldn't you have to be willing to talk with every cop on that list to learn who went out there that day? And, it's a secret squadron. Do you think any of them would tell you what you really need to know?"

Chester Morgan shrugged. He walked to the window. A plains-bellowed wind had blown since early morning. The high-

rise office buildings of downtown Vivia stood sculpted against the
blue-matte sky. "I'll call Frank Carlile at the motel."

The phone rang four times. On the fifth, the attorney
recognized the worn, heavy voice.

"Frank. This is Chester Morgan. We visited the other night
about Tanya Everly."

There was a pause. "Yeah."

"Can you talk?"

"Yeah, and say too much again?"

"If you'd like, I'll come out there and talk with you."

"Don't need to." Over the receiver, Morgan heard glass touch
glass and the gurgle of liquid falling from a bottle. "My butt's
already fried if you ain't straight. If you are, both of ours might be
anyway. Wadya want?"

"I've got a list of names I want to read to you. Cops. Some
might have been there that morning."

"I told ya I didn't know these guys—"

"Just listen. It might trigger something."

Morgan read the list, pausing after each name. When he
finished, Carlile said, "Rumpelstiltskin. J. Paul Getty. Ernest
Tubb. Don Ameche."

"What?"

"I don't know any of them, counselor."

"Afraid of that," Morgan said.

"Me, too, when you started. Just a second." Morgan heard
Carlile speak to someone else, the receiver pulled away. "About
half-way down the building. On this side. It's like in a closet. You
know what a closet is? There's a big sign that says Ice. I-C-E."
Morgan heard a door close and Carlile mutter "Jesus Christ" and
put the receiver back into speaking range. "We were talking
about cops, huh?"

"I guess we were."

"Ain't been a decent beat cop out here since Middlebrooks
retired last year. He knew what mattered and what didn't. He
liked being appreciated, but didn't act like it was his due."

"Money?"

"Appreciation," the motel manager said. "Wish he would have
taught some of these other guys how to cop."

"Your precinct goes past Vixen's on Ninth Avenue, doesn't
it?"

"Guess so." Morgan heard Carlile sip his drink. "Everybody in Kiowa Heights knew ol' Jack Middlebrooks. Why do ya ask?"

"No reason. Frank, watch for me, for Tanya. If you see the patrol officers who came out that day, get their car number at least."

"I ain't expecting to find no more dead bodies out here."

Morgan let the silence draw.

"Sure," Carlile said. "She was a good kid."

Morgan hung up the phone. He stared at it. Marylin had tried to tell him it would be waste of time. Carlile had, too. But sometimes a word, a sound, triggers an image or recollection of something forgotten. *A search for the truth* sounds romantic, a thoughtful quest. As often as not, it is as mind numbing as reading a list of names or looking through scores of obtuse documents in the hope of finding a clear pattern, divined by not much more that intuition and observation. A shrugged-off remark can lead to more truth than studied responses to severe cross-examination And, when there is nothing much else ...

"What are you going to do now, boss?" Marylin asked.

"Don't know. Maybe I'll think of something when I get out of the city and go see Mama."

"How's she doing?"

"About the same, I suppose." Morgan picked up McNally's anonymous fax. "You know, I realized the other day she'll never sing again, not like before."

"I'm sorry, Chester."

He handed the fax back to Marylin. "Why don't you call Alan Kinman and tell him we're still working. And double check with Mrs. Delano and see how the inventory for her husband's estate is coming along."

Marylin picked up her note pad and stood to leave. "We got a call this morning from one of the laid-off secretaries at Key looking for work. She'd been with them for over seventeen years, time enough to conceive, have a child, send him to school, and teach him to drive."

"A lay-off at Key? That doesn't happen."

"She didn't think we'd have anything, but the market is pretty tight, Chester. Ten percent of the company's 'non-essential' employees are being laid off."

"The only employee old man Harrison would have fired would have been the one who came up with the idea of calling anyone 'non-essential.' Unless he had absolutely no other choice. You knew what to tell her?"

"If we could hire everyone who needed a job ..."

Morgan nodded, and Marylin left the room. He glanced at the photograph of Cassie, his lost wife, but he didn't think of her. He took up the contract he had been reviewing, but his thoughts weren't there.

Later, Chester Morgan walked past Shawn's desk to leave the office for a four o'clock appointment. He opened the door to the hallway and ...

"Hey, Chest," Shawn said, "why don't you buy me a membership to my spa?"

Morgan turned and looked at the young, strong woman. He liked her. She said what she thought and she had no fear. He hoped age never took that from her. "Hasn't the university dropped more dollars than sense on a work-out facility for the students?"

"Yeah, but everyone goes there."

Morgan shook his head.

"You could write it off, " Shawn said.

"I'll get you a visitor's pass at the Y anytime you want," Chester said. Shawn frowned. "I have a job for you, Shawn. There's a retired Vivia policeman named Jack Middlebrooks. Find out where he is. Everything you can about him."

"That's easy enough," she said, reaching for the phone. "I'll call Jeff McNally. He thinks I'm cute."

"Don't challenge him to Indian wrestle. You'd probably beat him."

"Could you."

"I'm smart enough not to take you up on the challenge. And, if you call McNally, don't tell him you want to know about Middlebrooks for work or for me."

Shawn's face brightened and her eyes shined. "He'll never even know he told me. I promise."

"And," Morgan said, "don't ever tell me what you did to find out. I don't want to know."

As Morgan left the office and walked down towards the elevator, he wondered, as he often had before, what wisdom the ancient DeSoto Building could teach if he could hear all the stories of the lives lived there. When he pressed the bell to call the elevator, though, he thought he might throw away all experience for youth.

Chapter Twenty-Five

The phone rang. Marylin picked it up.

"I need my hammer!" The voice screamed as much as talked.

"I'm sorry, Murle. I meant..."

"Sorry doesn't get me my hammer!"

"I'll bring it over."

"I'll get it."

"No, stay," Marylin said. "I'll be there."

Silence.

"OK."

The phone clicked. Marylin looked around the kitchen and then remembered she put it in the utility room. Marylin remembered it was her hammer, not Murle's. Whatever. She picked up the hammer and went to her landlord's house.

Murle Mueller met her at the front door. "I've been calling you all day!"

"I've been at work."

"Ought to get a goddamned answering machine."

"You don't need to yell at me." Marylin bit her lip.

"Oh." Mueller blinked a couple of times. "Just get off work?"

Marylin nodded.

"Come drink some tea."

Murle reached out and placed her hand on Marylin's shoulder. An awkward push-pull brought Marylin over the door jam and into her landlord's home. "I'll make some tea," Mueller said.

The house smelled of furniture oil and detergent. An overstuffed leather couch and a matching maple-shaded recliner sat in front of a large, new black-framed television set—the living room, spacious and empty. Through an archway, a delicate table stood, surrounded by delicate chairs that looked hand-carved. Although Marylin recognized the beauty of the table, she said nothing. Murle clomped through the dining room and Marylin followed silently.

Mueller pulled a white chair away from the kitchen table, and although the large woman did not speak, Marylin knew it was an invitation to sit. Mueller lit a gas flame beneath a kettle and took two china cups from a cabinet. "They got a ceremony for this in Japan."

"That's what I understand."

"Green tea," Murle said. "Cures everything."

Marylin said nothing.

"Except getting old." Murle turned for a response. There was none. "Don't let me get you. I don't mean ..."

"It's all right. I'm just a little..oh, never mind," Marylin said. Her words echoed as if to taunt her. Then, "It's kind of comforting to be here."

"Hmph." Murle pulled out a canister and put bright green tea leaves in the cups. "Y'aren't acting like you."

Marylin did not reply. The kitchen remained silent until the teakettle whistled.

"Murle, I think someone followed me home from work."

The landlord dropped the teakettle back on the stove with a loud bang. "Scumbags and perverts!" Murle Mueller stomped into the dining room and peeked through a lace-curtained front window. "Nobody out there."

But a half block away, an old pickup truck waited, half-hidden by a tall hedge.

Murle Mueller came back into the kitchen. "They mess with you, they mess with me. What they'd look like?"

"I didn't really see anyone."

"What kind of car they driving?"

"I didn't see one. You know, I just felt like someone was following me and—"

"I know! I know! Every time I go to the market. Push that cart down the aisle and somebody's behind me. But turn around and nobody there! Little son of a bitch is gone!"

Marylin grinned.

"Scumbags and perverts!" The landlord poured steaming water into the cups and put the teakettle back on the stove. She picked up the cups, stopped, and placed them back on the counter. She opened a cabinet door and took down two saucers. She stared at the top one, then rubbed her finger across the top. She wiped the saucer across her hip and placed one of the teacups on it. Her eyes shifted back and forth towards Marylin. She picked up a towel to dust the other. "Don't worry," she said as she brought the tea to the table. "They haven't caught me yet. They won't catch you either." Murle's chair made a loud noise against the linoleum floor as she sat. "'Gotta let it soak for a while," she said, pointing at the tea cups.

Marylin started to say steep, but didn't. She smiled. "Thanks."

Murle Mueller made an indecipherable sound and nodded.

Marylin picked up her cup and looked at the tea leaves floating at the bottom. "Did your friend Miss Mary play the guitar?"

"Nope! Why did you ask that!"

Marylin looked out the kitchen window towards her home. "The house was empty, completely empty, when I moved in, but I found some guitar strings. I was curious. The envelope was a little dusty, but the strings had never been used."

"Oh. Little girl before you played the guitar. Wanted to go to Nashville. Be a big star."

"Could she have been?" Marylin asked.

Murle shrugged. "Like that kind of music, I suppose. Pretty voice. Yeah, pretty voice." Mueller picked up her teacup. It looked awkward in her big hand. "Too young," she mumbled as she twirled the cup, jarring and stirring the tea leaves until they resettled. "She's passed, you know."

Marylin raised her eyebrows.

"Oh, not there in the house or anything," the landlord said. "Don't worry!"

"If you say not, I won't," Marylin said. "What was she like?"

"Tanya—that was her name, Tanya. A mess. That's what she was. Never at home at night. Slept all day."

"Sounds like my brother."

"Never paid her rent on time. First of the month, always had to remind her. She'd say 'Have to talk with Billie.' Then she'd show up with six one hundred dollar bills. Had a little boyfriend named Billie, I guess. Think he paid for her."

"Billie?"

The landlord nodded. "Never met him. Never came around. Nobody did. She was good about that. Always real quiet." Murle stopped. "I'd hear her sing sometimes." The large woman looked away.

Marylin sipped on her tea. Its warmth calmed her; its taste puzzled. "You liked her music."

Murle nodded. "Suppose I did," she said, her voice quiet. "Thought I might meet him. At the service or here. Afterwards. Never came around. Not even for the deposit."

Marylin touched the hard, but fragile, edge of her teacup and the large woman across the table sat straight, solid, but her voice betrayed. "A mess," she said quietly. "A real mess."

The refrigerator's motor kicked on. Its hum murmured through the house as if to fill silent corners and empty lives. Marylin waited and wondered how life alone here boded.

Murle Mueller jerked back and set down her cup, took a quick, deep breath, and roared, "'Still need a goddamned answering machine!" She pushed her chair back, stood, and walked in one motion. "Come along."

Marylin followed her landlord out a side door and up a concrete driveway to a door at the side of a white detached garage. Mueller reached her hand into her pocket and mumbled, "Think I'm wacko." Then, she shrugged and pulled out a ring of keys. She turned to Marylin and said, "Little girl's mother didn't want her stuff. Took what she could sell quick, what she needed. Left the rest. I ought to do something with it but ..." Murle's voice trailed off. Marylin followed her into the one-room garage apartment.

A make-shift clothes rack stood at one side of the door. Shiny sheer negligees and diaphanous gowns and strange lingerie hung next to pretty but common dresses, blouses, and jackets. Stacks of boxes sat scattered around the room. A beaten-up vanity with an oval mirror leaned against a wall and a burnt orange rocker with ripped upholstery looked like it would collapse. The garage apartment smelled like a perfumed love letter too long left in a dusty alcove.

"Little girl didn't even get a good service!" The voice screamed as much as talked. "Some street preacher. Started out crying, 'I'm sorry! I'm sorry!' Talked a bunch of gooblygook and then smiled and said 'It's all fulfilled in my lifetime.'" The big woman shook her head. "Little girl deserved better."

Murle Mueller tore into a stack of boxes, opening and looking, and closing again.

"Who was it?" Marylin asked.

"Some goofy son of a bitch!" Murle kept looking through boxes. She kept digging. "Here it is. Doesn't exactly work right. She said the tape sticks and sometimes doesn't erase. Guess that's why the mother didn't take it, too. Or forgot."

Murle Mueller handed the legal secretary an answering machine, scuffed, heavy, and old.

Chapter Twenty-Six

The answering machine sat on Chester Morgan's desk.

"Watch this," Marylin said. She pressed the rewind button and the tiny cassette spun its tape. It stopped. She pressed the play button.

Silence.

The tape wound at regular speed.

Silence.

"I see, but ..." Morgan said. He knew she must have a reason.

"Remember when we thought we lost the Echohawk brief you dictated, but we really hadn't?" she asked. "I've had to make machines work for me my entire career." She pressed the rewind button and allowed the tape to spin back. She took it out of the machine, played with the recording head, and placed the tape back in the small black box. "Listen," she said as she jiggled the play button and pressed it down.

"Tanya. Hope this will be a peaceful day for you. Call me when you are able," the male voice said. Then, the talking recorder: "Wednesday. September Third. Ten twenty-three a.m."

Beeeeeeeeep.

"Tanya. I know you're there." The same deep voice in embarrassing sing-song. "Please call me." Click. "Wednesday. September Third. Eleven forty-six a.m."

Beeeeeeeeep.

"Babe, pick up the receiver and talk to me. I just want to chat with you. Just want to hear your voice. It wouldn't hurt to talk for a minute, would it? You know what the number is." Same voice, pleading, resigned. Click. "Wednesday. September Third. Twelve o-four p.m."

Beeeeeeeeep.

"I have to talk with you. I really have to talk with you! Come on! I ... I really do!" Again the voice, this time panicked, desperate. "Pick up the phone ... Call me then or come see me. You know where I am, where I always am. We have to talk—both of us." Click "Wednesday. September Third. Two-thirteen p.m."

Beeeeeeeeep.

"Stop playing games! Be an adult and pick up the phone. I said pick it up." The bass voice squeaked to tenor in anger. "This is childish! Work your dumb little blond broad charade on your sleazy dumb tricks but not me. That's due me! You're a woman. Have some character, or are you afraid? I'll make you have talk to me!" Click. "Wednesday. September Third. Two-fifty-two p.m."

Beeeeeeeeep.

"TANYA! STAR! TANYA! I don't want to do this. I don't! Tanya, I was the pestle that put life into your vessel, made you more than the shell you were before. It all came together in you, for you. Should I kiss your cheek? And you...you...you..." Click. "Wednesday. September Third. Three-o-one p.m."

Beeeeeeeeep.

"You little slut." A female voice, raspy with too much cigarette smoke and nightclub air. "Make sure your fat little cheeks are at the Lodge tonight. Ten-thirty. You got business there tonight. Important business." Click. "Wednesday. September Third. Three-o-six p.m."

Beeeeeeeeep.

Marylin pushed the stop button. "Nothing else for that day except a couple of hang-ups. By the next, Tanya was dead."

Morgan stared at his framed diplomas and certificates on the wall, but he wasn't looking at black-and-white words.

"Chester, you always say a good trial attorney should be able to get kicked hard and never have it show by the look on his face," Marylin said. "What's wrong?"

"That was the preacher, Don Hubbard," Chester Morgan said. "And the woman, Tanya's mother."

Chapter Twenty-Seven

The six-lane expressway cut through Vivia flat and straight, with mown rights-of-way, solid shoulders, and concrete barriers. Saturday morning—a chance to drive, a chance to think. The car's engine hummed and Morgan felt the steering wheel vibrate beneath the palms of his hands.

The expressway, built to Federal spec and regulation, led away. Morgan drove the concrete expressway straight, level, and even. No reason to turn the steering wheel more than a fraction nor to accelerate suddenly nor to brake. A chance to think: The straight, the facts, the logical constructs that make the law engineering with words.

The expressway led away from phones that always rang, from tempestuous judges, from clients who demanded. Alan Kinman had not demanded—not yet. He had an earnest request: Learn the truth. Kinman had no case—not yet, and Morgan had more hours invested than rationality would suggest prudent, all to require by law that the police answer for the absence of the record of Tanya Everly's demise. And, more than one witness had suggested his client's devotion stemmed from irrational obsession. Irrational enough to brutalize the object of that same obsession? Morgan drove.

The expressway led away from crowded streets and scared people frightened of scared people. Morgan heard the refrain "I don't ask questions," the landlady's door slamming in his face, and Jeff McNally's ominous warning to "just stay away." Morgan saw the dancer with European-model looks leave his table abruptly, and he heard imagined whispers with the nightclub's manager. Morgan drove.

The expressway led away from dull-eyed clerks in orange smocks selling mass-merchandise in mass-merchandised malls and box stores. Morgan saw the well-dressed people in the fashionably furnished reception space of Martin Bollant's law office. He remembered the young uniformed cop in police records intimidated into false statement by a uniformed superior. He remembered the come-on of the lonely medical examiner and the whiskey-drinking motel clerk just doing business then showing him the scene of a young woman's final degradation, the sight of her mother's perverse vantage, and locked doors that opened. Morgan shuddered and drove.

The expressway led away from skyscrapers and old money. The image returned: the lifeless body floating in the YMCA swimming pool at dawn. Other images, too. The odd probate hearing, the two improbable witnesses to an improbable signing of an improbable lost will, the young YMCA attendant attempting to be a hero forced out of a job he wanted and did well.

The image shimmered, then burned, and would not fade.

Morgan drove and drove.

The road led away from straight-lined houses and straight-lined streets. Morgan heard the answering machine tape play again, the voices Marylin had discovered. The casual friend turning to despondent lover then to monster murderer? He remembered Don Hubbard's peaceful voice, the right words said the right way, the odd tone when he discussed a two thousand year old method of execution and women. Battered wives in divorces learn that the ogre who blackens the eye or splits the lip, or worse, often knows the right words and how to say them. The clue was to listen for that tone, that off-key coda that told you something was wrong. But had Hubbard's odd timbre been that or strange inspiration or divine madness?

The suburbs surrounded Chester Morgan, the houses all straight cut. No sidewalks, no front porches. Isolated developers' dreams in indistinct subdivisions with Disneyesque names. Morgan drove and wanted to escape.

Miles clicked over on the odometer and golden fields, yet to be touched by bulldozer and surveyor pins, replaced tract homes. Traffic lightened. The expressway curved abruptly and then narrowed to two lanes. Tobusky, and what was left of home, ahead.

The road led away from Vivia and from neon lights and naked skin in a place just called "across the river." Morgan drove.

The road turned rough. Ancient post oaks and cottonwoods threw heavy shadows over the faded macadam. A gray clapboard filling station sat in a gravel parking lot as it had since before the Depression. The ride took course, up and over, down and up, slower and faster, a certain sign of passage into the heart of the old Indian nations.

Morgan organized facts and theories. Would it not be probable ...? If X happened, then Y must have ... A sudden curve jarred him. A large hill loomed to the side of the road. Morgan traveled. He preferred these small two-lane highways that would finally take him home. The ones with narrow lanes, sudden curves and inclines, the low shoulders, the rapid drop offs. He liked their danger, their intimacy, their peculiar beauty.

The attorney's calculus began to lose its linear consistency. Don Hubbard seemed as probable as anyone, but what about the strange events the morning Tanya Everly's body was discovered? The imagination of an alcoholic motel clerk? The games at police records and of the medical examiner? Did Don Hubbard have that pull? The thoughts blurred. He saw Maria's face and smelled her scent. He remembered her touch. Morgan traveled. The road curved and wandered. The undergrowth wrapped itself around trunks of trees and grew and spread in verdant wildness.

Morgan recalled Maria's story: The underaged strippers, the paranoid manager, the suggestion of payoff, and Tanya's jealous, insane competitor. A mother with no remorse driving a new Lincoln Towncar. Not a complete story, but what if? What if? The thoughts blurred. He felt as he had the first time he saw Maria, her splendor, her beauty. He remembered her attitude, her humor. Morgan traveled. He passed a white steepled church and an old schoolhouse of native stone. The hills spread out on either side, their woodlands crowned with the golds and reds of early fall.

Morgan's hands loosened; his thoughts of law practice and his unsolvable case gathered and dissipated into another sphere. He saw the dark-haired woman, heard her husky voice, and imagined the touch of her white satin curves. Morgan traveled. He passed through old, dark towns with one stoplight and through the hills and the woods that threw mysterious shadows on roads that made strange turns and then—sudden light.

Morgan journeyed, not lost, but homeward, his weekly pilgrimage. A journey to wholeness, a journey to duty as well.

Later, when Chester Morgan walked into his mother's room, she looked at him and said, "You oughtn't 'a come, but glad you did." He kissed his mother and pulled a chair closer to her hospital bed.

"Are they treating you OK?"

Molly Morgan nodded and pressed a button that moved the bed upward. "Chester, do you remember old man Speelman?"

He shook his head.

"Used to live down here just on the other side of Black Bog Creek. You know, had that dog that did magic tricks. Never saw it, that's just what people said. Well, the old man lives here now, two or three doors down. Comes in here all the time." She stopped and caught her breath. "He comes in here and talks his talk like I'm supposed to be godawful impressed. Here I am stuck in this bed. I told him to stop and that my son's a lawyer, but he doesn't." She took a breath. "I think he's a lunatic."

A bird-skinny black woman in a loose white uniform stopped at the door. "You need anything, Miss Morgan?"

"Would you get my boy here a Coca-Cola please?"

"He don't look like no boy to me," the aide replied.

"You don't know him as well as I do," Molly said. She sat forward and pulled the pillow up behind her neck. "You haven't known him as long as I have."

"I can get one from the machine," Chester said.

"Don't mind at all," the aide said and left.

"Mama, I could have gotten that myself," Chester said.

"They do that for family—make 'em think they're takin' good care of us."

Molly Morgan took a few struggled breaths and her eyes closed. Chester Morgan looked at his mother and wondered how long. This cinder block building wasn't where he knew her. This wasn't where she lived. He wondered how long until she went to the place she had sung about so often in her gospel songs. Morgan sat by her bedside and heard her struggled breathing and the echoes of lives receding.

The old woman snorted, woke up, and opened her eyes. "I get so tired anymore."

"That's okay, Mama."

"You don't look as peaked, son. You not workin' as hard?"

"As hard as ever."

She turned her head and looked at him. "You on the path?"

"Mama, let's not start this again."

"You found yourself a steady girl," she asked, said.

Chester hesitated.

"You did, didn't you?" she said.

Chester looked through the window and then at his mother. "I met someone interesting."

"What's her name?" Molly asked.

"Don't you think this is premature? I said I met someone."

"What does she do, Chester?"

"Let's just say she's in entertainment."

"Entertainment?"

"Mama, let's talk about something else."

The aide returned and handed the attorney a soda poured over institutional ice in an institutional plastic glass. "Anything you need, you let me know."

Morgan thanked her and she left.

"They think you're goin' to take me out of here," his mother said. With worn hand, she smoothed her bedding. "That Napier girl came home. The one that went bare-assed on the bus to Nashville to sing."

"Really? She wasn't gone long."

"I guess she got there, ran out of money. No one to give her a break, got scared, and came home."

"That's too bad. You thought she had some talent?"

Molly shrugged. "Reality's harder than the dream, 'specially if you're poor and ignorant and from nowhere. You almost gotta to have someone to help and if you get the wrong one ..."

"I was hoping she'd make it," Chester said. "I didn't know her, but I was hoping."

Molly Morgan nodded. "Son, you lay around these places, you just start feeling worthless. All these old people around, just waitin'."

"Don't say that."

"I said feeling, not am."

Chester took his mother's hand and smiled. "You're feeling better today, aren't you?"

She patted his hand. "Tell me about your work. Have any interesting cases?"

"A lot of them are starting to seem the same. You hear the first part. It's like watching the first of a movie and thinking you've seen it before, but the stories are never exactly the same. You have to watch out, not be complacent, not assume the characters are identical or that the plot will work out the same way." Morgan walked across the room. "I've got one like I've never had before."

"What's it about?"

"I can't really tell you. I can't figure it out." He stuck his hand in his pocket, looked out the door.

"'Eatin' at ya, ain't it, son?"

Chester nodded.

"You can't put it in logical order, you can't make it neat and tidy and have it all make sense like they taught you to do in law school?"

"That's right."

The aged woman breathed deep. A fall wind blew through the trees outside. "The older you get," she said, "the more you find out it isn't that way much at all. Kinda like Nina Throckmorton's house. Always the neatest and cleanest in town but she never understood nothin' about people. Is your heart right?"

"What do you mean?"

"Do you let it understand? You could stand there and do math problems all afternoon and not learn anything. You see, it's the heart that really learns and if your heart isn't open, you won't learn anything, anything that's important anyway. But, be careful. The heart that's open also's the one more'n likely to be wounded, the one more'n likely to be destroyed."

"Mama, I've learned a lot of things I wish I didn't know."

Chapter Twenty-Eight

Chester Morgan drove to the DeSoto Building when he returned from Tobusky that Saturday. Work. He had his work. He always had his work, and what else? The late afternoon sunlight reflected off the black marble and silver-chromed building—the lone and decaying Art Deco monument amidst the bland. He had returned.

Morgan walked down the fourth floor hall to his office. He knew the offices on either side were unoccupied—not unusual for a late Saturday afternoon, but he would have known anyway. The lack of pulse, the lack of energy—the same lack that made old buildings crumble and collapse when vacant. His footsteps echoed in the hall. He looked over his shoulder, but no one was there.

He stopped in front of his office door. He pulled out his keys and paused. He listened, shook his head, and cracked open the door.

Something slammed shut.

Morgan pulled open the door. Light hit his face. A person sat at the vintage World War II reception desk.

"Hey, Chest." Shawn tapped a pencil between her fingers and smiled.

Morgan exhaled a sigh and pushed the door closed behind him. "Working Saturday afternoon? I'm impressed." He stared at her and her cleared desk.

"Keeping you solvent isn't easy," she replied.

"Paying you what you think you're worth isn't either."

Morgan started for his office, but stopped. Nothing was on Shawn's desk. He turned and looked at his receptionist-business manager. She stared at him and smiled again. She wore a lavender and pink nylon sweat suit. She sat still, but looked as if she wanted to come out of her chair.

"Anything I need to know about my accounts receivable or billing?" Morgan led her.

"Joey Schwartz hasn't made a payment in over ninety days. Did you know that?" Shawn asked.

"Really? Did he lose his job?"

Shawn shrugged.

"Give him a call," Morgan said. "I've represented his family for years. Must be having a problem. Find out what's going on. Do you think he's getting the bill?"

Shawn shrugged, but then shook her head and stood up. "Chester, cash up front." She tapped her open palm with the fingers of her other hand. "It's not difficult. Every other attorney in Vivia has grasped the concept."

"I'm not every other attorney. Won't ever be."

"Won't ever be rich either," Shawn said. She tried to sound disgusted, but didn't, not convincingly.

Morgan looked at the young woman with the muscle and wild platinum tresses. She hadn't missed a beat when he questioned her. She hadn't been working on his billing, but what? Her blue eyes glinted cold, but Morgan saw vulnerability in their depths. He had seen the same look and had felt the same restless energy cross-examining witnesses when questions veered too close to embarrassing or devastating truth.

"I'm glad you're here," the middle-aged attorney said.

Morgan walked into his office and sat down behind his desk. Cassie smiled from the frozen-in-time photograph. A stack of files towered perilously to his left. A bunch of loose papers sat in a pile in front of him and random phone messages were strewn on the desk. Some attorneys created order by arranging things neatly before they left. Others cleared their desks completely. Not Chester Morgan. He had heard that neat desks made for neat minds. He didn't believe it exactly. He would have added: neat minds often miss what appears only in the shadows or in the subtlety of a sigh. To him, the jumbled papers represented the life the law tempts to control, and not the mundane paper churning the law often becomes. On some days, though, Morgan would admit a cleared desk caused him fear, the fear that every solo practitioner feels—that there might not be more work to do. On those same days, Chester Morgan would admit he always knew every file on his desk, every name on each old phone message, and the importance of each loose paper in the thick pile. He picked up the Anderson contract to review in silence.

Morgan heard a file cabinet drawer slam shut and then he sensed a presence at his door. He looked up. Shawn stood there.

"Do you still want to know about Jack Middlebrooks?" she asked.

The last good cop in Kiowa Heights, according to the manager of the Bunk House Lodge, Morgan remembered. "When you can get to it," he said. He looked down at the contract.

"Guess you don't want to know about him this afternoon," Shawn said.

Morgan raised his eyebrows and glanced up. "You find something out?"

She smirked to tell him, "Of course."

Chester Morgan set the Anderson contract down and looked hard at his receptionist-business manager. Her eyes still twinkled; she had the kinetic energy of her youth. It had been less than two days and she probably knew more about Jack Middlebrooks than Middlebrooks' best friend. And, on a case Shawn had no use for, on a file she wouldn't even open. He wanted to tell her she was good, but couldn't.

"How'd you find out so quickly?" he asked.

"You said you didn't want to know."

"You're right. What did you learn?"

"Middlebrooks was on the force for twenty-three years. Retired March of last year. He spent his entire career as a beat cop, most of it in Kiowa Heights. He had several chances to be promoted downtown and inside or into a less dangerous assignment. He never took the opportunity."

"What else?"

"Middlebrooks had the smarts to work a tough beat without getting hurt. His friends in the police force wondered why he stuck with it, but they knew not to ask. More than any place in town, Kiowa Heights presents the best chances for 'tips.' You know what I mean? Like pay-offs. Nothing was ever pinned on him, of course. As a matter of fact, the other officers knew they were safe with Middlebrooks. They describe him as 'solid.' He even got a couple of awards from the mayor."

"How did you get this information, Shawn?"

"Did you know that Middlebrooks has a daughter who goes to school with me?"

Morgan shook his head.

"By a divorced wife?"

"Really?"

"And did you know this daughter never really knew her father?"

Again, Morgan shook his head.

"And the daughter is planning a 'This Is Your Life' birthday party for him after this long separation?"

"I didn't know that, Shawn."

"Neither did Jeff McNally when I told him. You would be invited to the party, Chest, but you'd be the only one there." She stood and waited for Morgan to voice his approval. "I'm good, Morgan. I'm good."

The lawyer picked up a paperclip and played with it between his fingers. "You are," he said, "but you have no sense of propriety."

"Morgan! You give me the impossible to do, and then you question my technique!" Shawn growled.

"You do the impossible work, Shawn. You collect the fees and you pay the bills. And, you're good." Morgan stood up and Shawn knew the lawyer spoke his truth. She looked at her watch.

"I've got a hot date tonight. Gotta go!" The high-energy receptionist left the room.

"Have fun," Morgan said, but thought, that poor son of a bitch, I wonder if he knows ...

The attorney called out, "One more thing, Shawn!"

She bounced back into the room.

"Where is Middlebrooks now?"

"I knew you'd ask that. He has a cabin in a little community along Nathan's Creek in Keetoowah County. He just fishes and collects a government check. I'll write down the directions."

Shawn took a pad and began writing.

"You found all that out, too?"

She looked up with a smirk on her face, but kept writing. She tore her scribblings from the pad and stuck the paper in Chester Morgan's hand.

"I'm good, Chest. I'm good." With that, she rushed from the room.

Morgan sat down and pushed the Anderson contract to the side. As he did with each development in a case, he dictated a memorandum to the Alan Kinman file about Shawn's discoveries. He looked through the stack of case files towering perilously to his left. The Kinman file wasn't there. He looked again. Still, no Kinman file, even though it had been there Friday night when he had been the last to leave. Maybe Marylin had come to work in the interim and left the file on her desk. Morgan shook his head. Marylin would have returned it. He looked again. Then Morgan remembered the loud noise when he opened the outer office door, and, later, the sound of a file cabinet drawer shutting.

As the attorney walked across the hall into his office's workroom, he glanced at the receptionist's clunky desk with its loud-shutting drawers. He located the Alan Kinman file where one would logically expect it to be—in the K's in the file cabinet. Morgan took the folder to his office and when he opened it, he found amongst its pages a single wild platinum blonde hair.

Chapter Twenty-Nine

When Chester Morgan knocked on the screen door, dust flew and the sound echoed in the country air. An oak tree lay fractured shadows over the concrete stoop and unseen life rattled under piled leaves. Morgan pounded again on the door. From crooked pine limbs, blue jays screamed and awaited their distant replies. The sound of a pickup truck rumbling over a river rock road rose from the wooded valley below.

Morgan looked at his watch and waited for Jack Middlebrooks. Too late for respectable fishing, the attorney knew, but not too late to talk to a cop who knew Kiowa Heights—if Morgan could find him. Respectable or not, Chester intended to spend this autumn Sunday with a fishing rod on the banks of Nathan's Creek in the old mountains of Keetowah County.

Chester Morgan pulled Shawn's map from his pocket. She had underlined "redwood frame house" and he stood on the bare porch of a redwood frame house. It had been too easy. Had Shawn's suburban heart softened or was devotion unchallenged simply a word? Morgan crumpled the map back into his pocket and heard Maria's molasses voice: "wall-shrinkin', noise-amplifyin' paranoia and cash money to pay whoever needs to be paid." Chester had a tape recording and an explanation. Maybe he should give these to Alan Kinman and close his file on Tanya Everly and the shadows of Kiowa Heights.

The door opened. Through the screen, a man looked. He had soft gray curls and watery blue eyes. "What can I do for you?" he asked. A television blared someplace deeper in the house.

"I'm from Vivia," Chester Morgan said. He looked down and brushed an acorn off the porch with his foot. "I'd like to fish Nathan's Creek. 'Need somebody to show me the spots."

"I'm kinda busy right now," the man said. He looked over his shoulder back into the house.

"'Know someone who could? Or, if you're interested, I wouldn't mind waiting a while here, or down at the creek. Your pleasure," Morgan said.

"'Ain't bitin' today."

Morgan held up a fifty-dollar bill tucked between two fingers. "It ain't the catchin'. It's the goin'."

The man saw the bill, but glanced back into the house. He looked again at Morgan and sighed. "Hell, if you've seen one rerun of *Gunsmoke*, you've seen 'em all. That fuckin' Chester's an imbecile, anyway. Been thinkin' about goin' back down to the water anyway. Got your own rig?"

Morgan nodded.

"Might have some luck with channel cat today. Ever fish for channel cat?"

"Did a lot—when I was a boy. Not much recently—"

The man kept talking. "Best bait's raw chicken liver. Ya got an aversion to that? You'll stink like holy shit for a few days."

"I don't have anyone to complain except me," Morgan said.

The man stepped to the side of the porch and spat. "If it were spring or summertime, we'd just take this road." He motioned at the one in front of his house. "That'd get us to Nathan's and some places we could toss bait at those little fuckers. Being that's its fall, we'd have better luck goin' over the mountain and fishin' a little farther down stream." The man stopped. "The name's Jack Middlebrooks." He stuck his hand out.

The attorney introduced himself and shook Middlebrooks' hand.

"How'd ya know I fish?" Middlebrooks grinned. "You just stopped here and took your chances? Hell, I might not know nothin' about good fishin'."

"Maybe I'm a better hunter than fisherman," Morgan replied. "Let's go."

"Let me shut things down here. You can just follow me. The road's pretty rough, but you won't have any problems. It ain't washed out or nothin'."

A few moments later, Chester Morgan followed Jack Middlebrooks' shiny new Chevy pickup down a rough Keetoowah County road. Some more rain and the road would have been washed down the mountain. In the valley below, haze lifted in eerie silver wisps from pastures cut from the timber-rich—but topsoil poor—hills of the old Cherokee Nation.

Morgan's car bounced and jarred as the lawyer followed Middlebrooks around the mountain and then down the hill to a white cinderblock store. Middlebrooks got out of his pickup and waited by a lone gas pump. Morgan stopped his car and swore. Middlebrooks opened Morgan's door.

"That road wasn't too bad now, was it?" Middlebrooks asked.

Morgan got out of his car. "No, but there ought to be signs so you know the names of the craters you're visiting."

Middlebrooks wiped his thigh with his hand and said, "The locals know the politics by the condition of the roads."

Morgan looked at him and gambled. "You would think a little money on the side to a county commissioner would take care of it."

"You'd think," Middlebrooks said. He brushed something off the arm of his jacket. "That's what you would think, wouldn't ya? I guess it's not always that easy." Middlebrooks motioned and Morgan followed him into the cinderblock store. A lone neon beer sign glowed in the window.

A bell rattled when Jack Middlebrooks pushed open the door. From behind a worn Formica counter, a fat teenaged boy looked up from a hotrod magazine and nodded. He pushed his glasses up and turned the page. Four pairs of old fluorescent lights glared harsh light, but the merchandise-crammed store felt dark and dank. Middlebrooks walked to a refrigerated display, lifted two cartons of chicken livers, dropped them back, and waited for Morgan to join him.

"Those two would be just fine," Middlebrooks said, nodding at the containers he had just set down.

Morgan picked them up and walked to the counter. Middlebrooks slid a pack of Juicy Fruit off a nearby rack and put it next to the bait. Silently, Morgan handed the boy a five-dollar bill.

"'Ain't bitin' today," the kid said.

"It ain't the catchin'," Morgan said. "It's the goin'."

The boy shrugged and carefully counted out Morgan's change. "I'd rather be gettin' down the road myself," the boy said, tapping his hotrod magazine.

"I thought that one time, too," Morgan replied. The attorney pushed his change across the counter towards the boy. "Use it to buy some gas."

From the little store, a descent down another primitive road led to the rocky banks of Nathan's Creek. Morgan got out of his car and walked silently with the former Vivia cop until they reached a large, brown boulder.

"This ought to do," the man with gray curls said. "Just fix up your line to fish off bottom." He held out a lanky hand and pointed to white water running over rocks. "Sometimes you can get pretty good luck over there."

Morgan opened his tackle box, got out a knife, a treble hook, and a sinker. He glanced at Middlebrooks. A middle-aged retired cop who spent his days fishing and watching westerns on TV. Morgan shook his head and wondered what Kiowa Heights had taken from Middlebrooks. Morgan knew what Middlebrooks had taken from Kiowa Heights: money. But what else?

"'Had your place out here long?" Morgan asked as he finished tying his rig.

"About a year. A little over," Middlebrooks replied. He cut a piece of chicken liver and put it on a gold hook. "Ya know the fish bite better if ya get up early."

"It's a long way from Vivia," Morgan said. He cast his line into the water to a quiet kerplunk.

"Sure is," Middlebrooks said as he flicked his bait and hook out into the stream.

The men spotted the places where their lines pulled out of the water and spooled them tight. The two men waited. The rapids murmured peaceful and quiet. The sun warmed the skin. Morgan took a deep breath of the air. A breeze stirred the red, gold, and brown leaves on the bushes and trees surrounding them. Time passed. The water flowed. The men fished, but no bites. Morgan sighed and relaxed; really relaxed. Nothing seemed separate, nothing felt unordered, nothing seemed wrong. He looked at the retired street cop, and knew the ruse was.

"Middlebrooks," Morgan said. "I knew who you were when I knocked on your door."

The lanky man pulled his fishing rod back a bit and tightened his line. "You think I hadn't figured that out? You know I was a cop for twenty-three years?"

Morgan nodded. "And you spent all those twenty-three years working the streets in Kiowa Heights. That's why I wanted to talk with you. Frank Carlile said you were the last good cop who worked that beat."

Middlebrooks squinted, then looked at Morgan. "I'm here. Talk, but if one of those little fuckers bite, I'll have to interrupt ya." Middlebrooks rubbed his palm on his thigh and said: "And, I might not talk at all."

Morgan turned the handle on his reel. "A young woman died in Kiowa Heights. I'm looking into it. No charges have been filed. Doubt any ever will. I represent someone who just wants to know, and that's all."

"When'd she die?"

"The first part of September, this year."

"Ain't mine. I sure didn't work it. I'd be an open book if I had. Been retired for over a year now. Yes, sir."

Morgan nodded. "The young woman worked at a place called Vixens. A guy named Bruce manages it and has for well over a year. Main attraction is girls, children in women's bodies, taking off their clothes."

"A bunch of that in Kiowa Heights. Vixens ain't the only sex joint where that happens. I'll tell ya, it's not."

"I'm sure you're right, but this place has never been busted. Not once, at least not in twenty-three years. How do you account for that?"

Middlebrooks kept fishing. He stretched open his hand and began to brush his thigh with the palm of his hand, but he stopped. He remained silent.

"I figure a little cash is paid to the beat cop," Morgan said. "The one who knows what really happens on the street; the one who can tip the vice squad whichever way he wants. Or doesn't want. The street cop lets vice know the place is clean, doesn't cause trouble, and they stay away, don't ask too many questions. What happens when that street cop retires?"

Morgan felt the urge to push the answer. He didn't. Middlebrooks stared at the flowing water and let the silence pass.

"I grew up over in the next valley," Middlebrooks said. "My daddy was already an old man when I was born. Retired off the Fort Smith police department and moved up here, where my mama's folks were. There was a little spring house back of our place. Old man used to just sit back there, drink cheap whiskey, and watch that spring well up from the earth. I used to wonder why. Growin' up, the only thing I wanted to do was to get to the big city and fight the bad criminals like my old man had."

Middlebrooks crouched down. A noise in the woods across the creek caught his attention. He looked up. Morgan waited.

"Now you've got yourself a nice, neat, little theory, Mr. Lawyer. When I worked that beat, I made a couple a' thousand bucks a year more than a garbage man on the same route. The garbage man, though, ain't a target for any damned goon who wants to knock down a cop to get his picture on the color TV. You lawyers make a livin' provin' we messed up. Civil rights folks always yellin' about somethin', but who gets the call when somebody's kid is missing or their house is broken into or their son's killed. You know who sees things nobody else sees, that nobody else ever ought to have to see."

Middlebrooks grew quiet. He stared at the moving and humming water. A lark sang from a nearby tree. Morgan waited for a strike, but there was none. The silence urged a question, but Morgan knew silence prompted stronger.

Finally, Middlebrooks continued, "The owners of the donut places never charge us. The managers of the coffee shops let us eat and drink all we want, anytime we want. Free food and coffee every day. A gratuity as much as paying cash. It all adds up. Bruce over there at Vixens might have paid a gratuity, but you got the rest fuckin' wrong."

"How's that?"

"Those children you talk about, aren't. Not all of 'em. The underaged ones are runaways almost always, usually. Do ya know where most of 'em end up otherwise?" Middlebrooks asked. "Hooked on drugs their brains turned to shit, or molested and hurt in ways that make ya sick, or killed, or left for dead in alleys or on the highways. That Bruce is crazier than a three day Mexican drunk, but he don't let 'em get hurt. At least, not if he can help it. Could be worse." Middlebrooks paused and tugged on his line. "Could be a lot worse. Ya wonder why God in heaven lets some things happen."

Middlebrooks reeled in his line to discover his bait had been stolen. He cut another piece of chicken liver and stuck the three-pronged hook through the fresh meat. Morgan watched the man's careful actions. The wrinkles on Middlebrooks face seemed deeper, his hair whiter.

"Vixens never got busted, not because no country-boy street cop picked up a little gratuity. Go look in the records."

Middlebrooks tossed his line in a smooth arc out into the water. "If you look a little bit, you're goin' to find some corporation owns Vixens. If you look a little bit harder, you'll find out who really owns that company. A smart lawyer would keep lookin', wouldn't he? Like maybe at those records that lists money given to folks runnin' for office and he'd see some names.

They'll look real familiar, 'cause the names of the people who give the most money to the most candidates are the same ones that own the corporation that owns Vixens. You go do a little looking and then you tell me if a little gratuity to a street cop keeps 'em open." Middlebrooks spat. "Vixens won't ever get closed."

"This Bruce must not think so," Morgan said. He swatted at a bug circling his face. "You left the force and he's convinced somebody's going to shut him down."

"Do ya ever see these vice hotdogs ever bustin' the big guys?" Middlebrooks shook his head. "They bust the minimum-wage clerk who sells the dirty magazine. They bust the loser who blows up his home-cookin' meth lab. They don't go after the money— the big guys. Bruce knows if something goes bad, it'll be him who gets knocked down. Him, they'll make an example of. Then the corporation that owns the joint will get some other poor fucker to run the place. Won't ever touch the owners. Won't ever stop their nice, little profit. Won't ever see their names in the paper."

Morgan reeled his line in. The shriveled bait hung by a sinew. Morgan took it off and threw it in the water. He cut another piece of chicken liver and rebaited his hook. Middlebrooks was right. The odor would last.

"Would Bruce murder one of his girls, or cause someone else to?" Morgan asked.

"Not likely," Middlebrooks said. "Maybe if he cracked. Nothin' planned or anything like that. Fear's too big of a threat to that man."

"Do you know Don Hubbard? Morgan asked. "He runs a mission in Kiowa Heights."

Middlebrooks nodded.

"What do you say? Would he murder someone?" Morgan asked.

"Hard to say," Middlebrooks replied. "Let's give it five or ten more minutes here and if we don't get a strike, let's move on down to the other side of that boulder and see if we can do any better there. What do ya know about Hubbard?"

"Not much. Met him a few times. I've heard his story."

Middlebrooks sighed. "Ya can't really tell what nobody might do. What triggers 'em deep down. Preachers might be worse. They know they have to act a certain way, even if their impulses inside is another. Hubbard, he's OK, I suppose. He'll go off on a crusade every once in a while, but at least he's trying to help and not just a yellin'. I think he's pretty lonely, really."

"I can understand that," Morgan said.

"Me, too. Kinda miss people up here," Middlebrooks said. "Didn't think I'd ever say it, but some days I kinda miss being on the force."

"Would you want to go back?" Morgan asked. He yanked his fishing rod back and reeled fast. Then, stopped.

"Get a strike?"

"Thought so. Maybe it was just hope." Morgan loosened his line and let it float. "Kurt Hale says he wants to wipe out all vice, wants to close it out of Kiowa Heights."

"And he likes to get his picture on the color TV and in the newspapers, too," Middlebrooks said. "Older cops are droppin' out. Ambitious sonabitch like Kurt Hale can be dangerous. Something goes wrong and he's not going to be behind ya. My friend Hennessey—four years from retirement and a smart officer—just dropped out."

"Why?"

"Wouldn't exactly tell me. Somethin' about a homicide. A hooker in Kiowa Heights."

"Where can I find him?" Morgan asked.

"Do you think he'll talk to you for fifty bucks, when he wouldn't tell his best friend?"

"You didn't answer my question. Where is he?"

"He's cowboyin' on a thirty thousand acre ranch up in South Dakota, out on the range. No phone and no way to get in contact with him. He wouldn't talk anyway."

"I'll go to South Dakota and subpoena him," Morgan said.

Jack Middlebrooks chuckled a heh-heh-heh laugh. "Mister Lawyer, you ever see that old show on TV about the German prison camp? Gots this fat guard who says, 'I know nothink!' Well, cops learn to say that pretty good. That's what Hennessey'll say and what I'll say if anyone ever asks me if I talked to ya." The curly-haired man lowered his voice. "Ya might be onta somethin', but be careful, damned careful." Middlebrooks reeled in his line. "Let's go onto the other side of the boulder. We might do better there."

The attorney and the watery-eyed retired policeman moved to the other side of the boulder and fished. Two hours and no bites. They drove the primitive road further down the creek and fished some more. Hours passed and no bites. Later at the curly-haired man's house, the lawyer pulled the fifty-dollar bill out of his pocket and extended it to his guide. The watery-eyed man waved his hand to say "no need." The attorney said "It's the goin', not the catchin'" and Jack Middlebrooks took the fifty dollar bill.

Later, Chester Morgan would remember the image of an old man in a spring house drinking cheap whiskey and watching the water welling forth, and his son, years later, staring at the clean, clear water of Nathan's Creek.

Chapter Thirty

An old answering machine sat on Don Hubbard's desk in the gray artificial light of his office at the Corpus Christi Project.

"I want you to hear something," Chester Morgan said.

Don Hubbard lifted his hand from his desk to show his assent. Marylin jiggled the play button on the answering machine and then pushed it down. Hubbard's recorded voice spoke from the speaker:

"Tanya. Hope this will be a peaceful day for you. Call me when you are able."

Then, the talking recorder said: "Wednesday. September Third. Ten twenty-three a.m."

Don Hubbard's face wrinkled into a frown. "How did you—"

"Listen!" Morgan commanded.

Beeeeeeeeeeeep.

The preacher's voice continued from the answering machine. "Tanya. I know you're there. Please call me." Click. "Wednesday. September Third. Eleven forty-six a.m."

Morgan looked at Don Hubbard from across the desk. Always watch, an attorney learns in the courtroom. A witness's subtle gesture, the look on a face, or the distress hidden in cloudy eyes often signal deeper truths than words. Hubbard glanced around the room, but his eyes stopped on Marylin.

Beeeeeeeeeep.

The recorder played: "Babe, pick up the receiver and talk to me. I just want to chat with you. Just want to hear your voice ... It wouldn't hurt to talk a minute, would it? You know what the number is." Click. "Wednesday, September Third. Twelve o-four p.m."

Hubbard tightened his fingers around the arms of his chair and stared at the small black box playing his voice. Morgan couldn't look at the preacher any longer. Morgan had seen the people of the Corpus Christi Project, had seen how Hubbard calmed their hearts. If this man confessed, or worse, denied without credence, what then? What would happen to these people? As an officer of the court Morgan knew his duty: the evidence would have to be disclosed to the authorities. And, to what purpose? What would become of this sanctuary? Morgan silently cursed the demons of loneliness and truth. He stared again at the minister.

Beeeeeeeeeep.

"You don't have to play anymore!" Hubbard said over the sound of his recorded voice. "You know the rest of it. Why do this?"

Marylin reached for the button on the answering machine. Morgan shook his head. "Do we know, pastor?"

The tape continued: "Stop playing games! Be an adult and pick up the phone. I said pick it up. This is childish! Work your dumb little blonde charade on your sleazy—"

"We don't need to hear this," Hubbard said. He looked away.

The machine continued, "I'll make you have to talk to me!" Click. "Wednesday. September Third. Two fifty-two p.m."

A pause. Silence.

Beeeeeeeeeep.

"TANYA! STAR! TANYA! I don't want to do this. I don't! Tanya, I was the pestle that put life into your vessel, made you more than the shell you were before. It all came together in you, for you. Should I kiss your cheek? And you—you—you—" Click. "Wednesday. September Third. Three-o-one p.m."

Marylin stopped the tape. Silence waited for disturbing sound. The gold crucifix on the wall behind Don Hubbard hung over him like a perverse golden diadem. Finally, Hubbard said, "Counselor, you choose to unveil my weakness this way, in front of a stranger?"

"A stranger?" Morgan said.

Hubbard nodded towards Marylin.

"I don't mind—" Marylin began as she started to stand.

"She stays," Morgan said. "You've heard the tape, Don. Tell us what we know."

Hubbard stood and folded his hand behind his back. "I regret ..." Hubbard's voice trailed off.

"You regret we found the tape?" Morgan said.

Hubbard nodded. Something glistened from the corner of his eye. "I regret those might have been the last words she heard me speak to her." He looked away and wiped his cheek.

"Tell us about Tanya," Marylin said.

The street preacher sat down. Tears fell from his eyes and hit the wooden desktop. "I'm sorry," he said. "I'm sorry." He wept.

Marylin pulled a tissue from her purse and extended it across the desk. Hubbard waved his hand to decline and wiped his face with his hands.

"Tell us about Tanya," Marylin said.

"Have you ever felt so dead inside you wonder if you were ever alive?" Hubbard said. "Have you ever felt the opposite?" He stared at the statue of the Virgin Mary across the room. "I had a church once of pretty stones and green lawns. The major spiritual crisis? Who got the Mercedes in the divorce. That's not what I wanted, so I came here. I walked the streets. With God's grace, I opened this shelter. I gave everything I had, until one day I realized I had nothing left. What would happen to my people and where did my God go? I kept working and feeling nothing except this raw barrenness."

Morgan shifted in his chair and avoided looking at the minister. A rumble sounded and forced air began to wheeze through a vent overhead. Morgan looked up, started to speak, and then stopped.

"Then one day, you laugh or smile," Hubbard continued, "and you realize one little part of you is still alive. Tanya came in one hot July day—problems with her mother. Tanya needed a place to stay for a few days. Perhaps you never grow so old or dead that you forget the scent of a young woman in the summer." Hubbard hesitated and looked at Marylin. "Or, of a young man, perhaps."

"Maybe you can finish the rest," Hubbard said. "But I lied to her on that tape. I didn't give her life." He paused. "She gave me life. And, the tape—my cry, my sin of idolatry. I'm sorry. I'm sorry."

Morgan waited. "What did you say to Tanya's mother when you called her after that last message?"

"What do you mean?" Hubbard asked. He sat up in this chair and put his hands outstretched on his desk.

"You know what I mean," Morgan said. "Marylin, play the rest of the tape."

The legal secretary pushed the button on the answering machine. A raspy female voice said, "You little slut. Make sure your fat little cheeks are at the Lodge tonight. Ten-thirty. You got business there tonight. Important business." Click. "Wednesday. September Third. Three-o-six p.m."

"Five minutes after you left your last message, preacher," Morgan said. "What did you say to Tanya's mother, Tamar White?"

"I never talked to that woman that day," Hubbard said, his words crisp, definitive.

"And you never went to the Bunkhouse Lodge that night either," Morgan said.

"What are you saying?"

"I'm asking," Morgan replied. "My client has hired me to learn the truth about Tanya Everly's death. That's why we're here."

Hubbard stood up, but the lawyer and his secretary didn't move. "The truth is I made an ass of myself on that tape and then caught a plane to Kansas City with your friend Martin Bollant. We went to a conference together, even shared a room." Hubbard picked up the telephone and lifted the receiver. He pushed it towards Morgan. "Call and ask. Martin Bollant speaks the truth, doesn't he?"

Don Hubbard pushed the button pad on the telephone as Chester Morgan called off Bollant's number. Morgan took the receiver and placed it to his ear. When he got through to the attorney, Morgan said, "I have one question for you today, Marty. When were you in Kansas City last?"

"What?"

"Martin, it's a simple question: when have you been in Kansas City recently?"

"Easy enough, Chesterfield. Around Labor Day—the Third, Fourth, and Fifth of September, I believe. Went up there with Don Hubbard for this meeting, to find out what is evolving with other services for the dispossessed. You remember Don. The Corpus Christi Project? Have you been out there to his place? You really ought to go." Bollant paused. "Who do I bill for this call? Why did you call and ask me this?"

"Let's just say I'm playing a game of truth or dare and I just lost. I thought your friend Don Hubbard was some place other than Kansas City."

"No, it was Kansas City. He was with me practically the entire time. Is that of help?"

"Yeah. You share a room with him?"

"Yes."

"Was Hubbard with you the night of September Third and the morning of September Fourth?"

"I went to get some Rolaids at the newsstand. I don't think Hubbard sleep walks. What's this about?"

"Reverend Hubbard can tell you later."

"Chesterfield, we need to get together on that Rufus Daupin case sometime."

"Later, Martin. Thanks."

Morgan handed the telephone back to Hubbard. "Tanya was murdered the night of September Third or the morning of the Fourth. I apologize. I had to ask, though."

Hubbard relaxed back into his worn leather chair. "I wonder what happened to Tanya, too," Hubbard said. "Beautiful Tanya." He folded his hands together as if to pray. "If I'm forgiven, you are, too."

Morgan adjusted his suit jacket and began to stand. Marylin reached for the answering machine and frowned at her boss. Morgan eased back and waited.

"Don, you didn't tell us the rest of the story," Marylin said quietly, as she touched her ankles together and leaned forward. "Something else happened, didn't it? Something that made you feel that Tanya no longer needed you?"

Hubbard hesitated.

"It might help us," Marylin said.

"Do you think you will find out what happened to Tanya?"

"That's my pledge, pastor," Morgan said.

The street preacher stared as if recalling an event from long ago and in another life. He waited, then said, "About six or seven months ago, she started talking about a young man—I assume a young man—named Billy. He had some money apparently. He rented a place for her. She grew distant and ..." Hubbard shrugged.

"What's his last name?" Morgan asked.

"I don't know."

"Where can I find him?" Morgan said.

"I do not know. I thought I might discover his identity at the funeral, but I had no indication he was there."

"Anything else?" Marylin asked softly.

"His name was Billy. That's all I know."

Chapter Thirty-One

Chester Morgan eased his car into a narrow parking place. He turned off the ignition and waited. For what? Pink and gold neon light flashed from the sign above and made the black night a carnival of strange color. Morgan told himself he had come to this place because he had not learned the truth about Tanya Everly's death. He had more information, of course, but no explaining cause. Without that, what had he accomplished? He had other cases to work on, but this one compelled. Morgan had confronted Don Hubbard with his most incriminating evidence and Hubbard had as easily exculpated himself. He had followed Jack Middlebrooks, the old street cop who had worked this beat, into the mountains of eastern Oklahoma, only to become convinced of the improbability of Tanya's employer causing her death. Morgan told himself he had come to this place to talk with his last secure source, to find out who Billy was—this boyfriend spoken of by Don Hubbard and Murle Mueller. Morgan told himself these things, but he knew he had come to see the beautiful black-haired woman who reminded him of life. He got out of his car and walked towards the front door of Vixens.

Chester Morgan glanced across the street and saw the boarded-up Key Petroleum gas station. Weeds had grown tall in the concrete cracks and the building looked forlorn. He remembered what Martin Bollant had told him about William Harrison: The owner of the oil company considered it a disgrace to lay off employees and a dishonor to close a gas station. Harrison himself went to any Key Petroleum site that had to be shut down to make sure his workers had means to continue their lives.

The image seared and would not fade.

Chester stopped. Had Harrison visited this service station in months past? A humid night breeze blew and rustled far off into the dark. The lawyer shook his head, told himself he had to find his witness, and walked through the front door of Vixens.

Morgan faced the smoky-glassed window where the bouncer took money for cover and made patrons sign in. The attorney started to ask whether Candy, his witness and his intrigue, worked this evening, but didn't, remembering the paranoid stare of the manager and the "fuck you" reaction of the fashion-model-perfect dancer when he had asked about Star, Tanya. Morgan slid cash to the bouncer who pushed a beat-up notebook towards the attorney. He looked at the sign-in sheet and saw illegible scribbles. To hell with them, he thought as he signed his name in big, clear letters.

Morgan walked into the club. He passed empty tables and sat down. On the stage in front of him, a baby-faced stripper with soft curves and small pointed breasts tried to dance a seductive take, but vacant seats outnumbered the occupied, and her efforts became self-parody. Morgan nodded and grinned. He had argued losing cases, too. He ordered a drink and glanced around the room. He didn't see his witness, his Maria, or as she was known here—Candy. He could wait. Perhaps she was in the dressing room or making small talk in a dark corner with someone as lonely as he.

Morgan watched the women strip. Some he recognized from before; others were new; several appeared ambiguously present, triggering neither memories of the past nor new memories for the future. After several drinks and no sight of Maria, he thought about leaving, but didn't. He wondered why he stayed, but he knew.

A man, shorter than tall and skinnier than fat, walked quickly into the bar. He wore faded jeans and a tan corduroy jacket, smooth at the elbows. A red-haired stripper from across the room waved and smiled at him. He gave her a thumbs-up. Another dancer reached out and patted his arm as he passed. Another thumbs up. The man sat down at the table in front of Morgan, adjacent to the stage. As the man draped his jacket over his chair, Morgan read the words "Vixens Vexed" ironed on with crooked letters across the front of his pale blue t-shirt.

As soon as the man sat, a waitress placed a pitcher of beer on his table and gave the man a groping hug. The stripper on stage wiggled two or three fingers at him and smiled. He sloshed beer into a glass and moved it and the pitcher directly in front of his right hand. He pulled the cellophane and the tin foil corner off a pack of cigarettes and placed it, a stainless steel Zippo lighter, and an ashtray immediately in front of him. He unfolded a wad of dollar bills and arranged them in a neat stack to his left. The man stretched his arms and gave the naked woman on stage a thumbs up.

When the music stopped, the stripper leaned over the man's table and cuddled the man's face into her cleavage. He fumbled for a couple of bills and pushed them into her g-string. She jiggled and let him go. She smiled and waved two or three fingers as she left the stage. The man gulped beer and brushed back his thinning brown gray hair. He looked at the other tables next to the stage, all empty except for his. He turned and said to Morgan.

"Hey, you get a better show up here on perverts row." The man had a bass voice and a crooked smile. He pulled out a chair next to him. "Come on up!"

Morgan shook his head and said, "I'm fine where I am."

"They won't bite, you know," the man said.

"Your head would be gone if they did," Morgan replied.

"Wow! What a great headline! 'Man's Head Devoured by Ravenous Titties.' What would the funeral director tell my mother?" The man took a drink of his beer and noticed Morgan hadn't moved. "Suit yourself, but the view's better." He turned towards the stage once more.

The man lit another cigarette and placed the pack precisely where it had lain. A tall skinny black woman stood at the back of the platform and waited for the music to start. The man gave her a thumbs up and she grinned a phony bedroom smile. The music started, a beat vibrated, and the dancer moved without enthusiasm. She slid in front of the man, yanked her top off, and dropped it on the man's head. "Yes!" the man exclaimed as he stuck a dollar bill between the woman's chocolate skin and her lime colored thong. The dancer pivoted and the man slid another bill under the thin garment on the other side. She turned backside to the audience, shook her narrow hips at the man, and collected a third green bill. She sauntered to the other side of the stage and turned. The man took a slug of beer and gave her a triumphant thumbs up.

Morgan looked at the dressing room door and wondered how many dollar bills the man had placed against Maria's bare skin. He remembered her laugh and a sound in her voice that reminded him of something like hope. He remembered her sweet spice scent and her full curves. Morgan looked at the man with the pile of money. Morgan's jaw tightened, and then loosened. That was her job: dancing nude and collecting stares and tips.

Maybe the man had put thousands of dollars in Maria's flimsy lingerie. Morgan wanted to hope so, but didn't. Maria had told him to come here to find her. Was he different than the man with the pile of bills and the "Vixens Vexed" t-shirt? He rolled his empty beer glass from one hand to the other and then stood up to join him.

"You must be one of their best customers," Morgan said as he took a seat next to the man.

"Not one of the best," the man said, smiled. "*The* best! Yes!" He held his right hand out inviting a high five. Morgan shook it instead and introduced himself.

The man looked at his hand and then said, "I'm Mark Stevens." He fished a beat-up business card out of his billfold and slid it to Morgan. "You're going to enjoy being on perverts row. Betcha five!" He nodded at the black woman on the stage and tossed her lime green bikini top from the crown of his head. "Her name's Zoe. She's been here about two months." He leaned towards the attorney and whispered, "She's not going to make it. She's bored, and if a dancer is bored, the audience is bored."

"Unless the stripper's a good actress?" Morgan asked.

The man frowned and his deep black eyes looked pained. "You don't call them 'strippers.' They're dancers. 'Strippers' sounds cheesy and amateurish. These women are professionals." The man sipped his beer and glanced at Zoe. "And, you don't call them booger bars or strip joints, for the same reason."

Morgan glanced around the room. "I'll be damned if I call it a 'gentlemen's club.'"

"Yeah. Yeah," the man said. "I know. I always try to be."

"Is that why you slipped three bills to that last dancer?" Morgan said. "You didn't find her—what? Inspiring?"

"It's money." Mark Stevens shrugged. "I'd rather give it to curvy young women struggling to make it, than to the Cyclopes of the global economy. Wouldn't you?" Stevens leaned towards Morgan and made an indistinguishable sound, then said, "Besides, I have a reputation to keep up." He pounded the ironed-on letters of his t-shirt with his thumb.

"I know," Morgan replied. "You're their best customer."

The man motioned to the waitress. "I'm ordering you another beer," he said. "You need to get out of the Dragnet mode and have some fun. That's why there's a perverts row! It means to forget about things and to have a good time! Slip the girls a few dollars." He picked up some bills from his stack and put them on the table in front of Morgan. "It might give them, and you, some life."

Morgan looked at the bills in front of him and at the man in the sky-blue t-shirt. He had learned never to deprive another of a blessing by refusing a gift. A few bills in a strip bar a blessing? He had been in enough pool halls and honkytonks to know that practical safety and barroom etiquette required the same thing— acceptance. Still ...

"You don't need to," Morgan said, pushing the three dollars back towards Stevens.

"That's yours," the man said, refusing the bills. He raised his arm to catch the eye of the waitress and pointed his finger repeatedly at Morgan's head. "I'm getting you the beer, too." When the waitress nodded, Mark Stevens gave her a thumbs up.

A guitar rift and a two-step beat introduced a chart-topping country music tune. Computerized, too clean, and without heart, Morgan thought when he heard the sound. He looked up. A bleached blonde, her face pudgy with baby fat, looked at the ceiling, concentrating on the rhythm of the song as she began to move across the stage. Morgan had guessed her to be sixteen on his last visit. She looked down and smiled a tender smile, but it was to no one, simply a gesture in the dark night.

"Misty!" Mark Stevens called out. "Wild child!" He flipped back some of his grayish brown hair and picked up a dollar from his pile. The young woman moved in front of him and tugged at her blue bikini bottom allowing him to lay the bill against her fleshy hip. She paused in front of him and shook her finger at him. "Do you know you're beautiful?" he moaned as she danced away from him.

Morgan looked at the money Stevens had given him. Perverts row, he thought. Across the room, Morgan saw the manager—the man Maria called Bruce—standing next to the bar, his arms crossed. He stared into space, not at Morgan. No inquisitive glare tonight. A few feet away, Misty moved and shook in the rose-tinted light of the stage, a girl-woman who might be the next Tanya. What the hell, Morgan thought. He placed one of Stevens' greenbacks on the stage. The dancer stepped in front of the attorney and grinned. She turned and let her royal blue fabric of her top fall to the floor.

"You aren't disappointed, are you?" she asked, looking at Morgan over her fleshy bosom.

Morgan shook his head. "No."

Mark Stevens leaned over and tugged at Morgan's shirt. He whispered, "Heck, you don't even know how to do it."

"What?"

"You don't just put the dollar bill on the stage like you don't give a fuck. You hold it up with some panache, some grace, and the dancer, she'll let you know where she wants you to put it." Stevens knocked a cigarette from its pack and lit it.

"I bet," Morgan said.

Stevens exhaled gray smoke. "Well, Misty likes you anyway. She's world class, isn't she? Life's grand on perverts row." He made a thumbs up gesture and poured beer into his glass. "Isn't it grand?"

Morgan shrugged, nodded. He wondered about the young bleached-blonde girl. A runaway supporting a worthless boyfriend, perhaps. A parent's dinner ticket, maybe. A baby at home? How long before she would be another casualty of Kiowa Heights? Is this who Tanya had been? Chester Morgan sipped his beer and wondered. Two of Stevens' bills lay on the table in front of him.

The music stopped and applause echoed. Stevens whistled and clapped. Misty threw gentle kisses from the stage.

"Bravo!" yelled the man in the pale blue Vixens Vexed t-shirt. "Encore!" He raised his beer glass in a toast. A powerful bass beat pounded from large black speakers looming on both sides of the stage and Misty moved and danced more.

Morgan took another draw on his beer and felt that boozy feeling of separating and watching himself drunk, although he knew he didn't and couldn't. He looked at the full soft body of the woman moving on the stage and longed and wanted. Next to him, Mark Stevens held up a dollar bill. Misty took it in her hand and dropped it to the floor behind her. Am I any different than him? Morgan wondered. He held up one of the dollars. The dancer moved in front of him, leaned over, and placed his hand between her breasts, gently squeezing the dollar from his fingers.

"Ooooh, feels good," she murmured. She turned and shimmied down stage.

Morgan took a deep breath and sighed. The last of Stevens' bills lay on the table in front of him.

"See, I told you she likes you," Stevens said. He had two cigarettes burning in the ashtray.

The music kept playing. Morgan felt the room get fuzzy. He pushed away his glass of beer and saw Stevens give the naked young woman another dollar. Morgan held up his last bill. Would she turn away? he wondered. The bleached blonde woman child stopped in front of him and gingerly pulled open the front of her blue bikini bottom. Morgan questioned her with his eyes. She nodded and as he tucked the dollar in, she held his fingers against her soft, moist skin.

"Thank ya, darlin'," she whispered, then smiled at the middle-aged man before letting go of his hand.

The music faded. With a high-heeled shoe, Misty kicked the dollar bills fallen to the floor into a pile and then gathered them with her blue top and left the stage.

"Do you feel alive?" Stevens asked. "Do you? Huh?"

"I suppose," Morgan said and then remembered why he had come to Vixens tonight. He shook his head for clarity, but even so knew why he had stayed.

"Mark," Morgan said, "does Candy work tonight?"

"Naw, she always takes Tuesday off when she can, but I'll tell you something. The guy at the Orpheum Theatre, down at Third and Renfrow, has just about all these girls—and some who aren't even here anymore—on tape for viewing. Can you believe that? Just tell him that Mark Stevens sent you. He might give you a discount."

Morgan motioned for the waitress. "Bring me a cup of coffee and a glass of ice," he told her. He handed her a twenty. "And bring all the change in ones."

"In ones?"

"Yeah."

Stevens handed her his empty pitcher and motioned her to fill it up. "You see why I wear this t-shirt and sit on the first row right next to the stage?" he asked Morgan.

"I understand," Morgan said. He started to speak, then stopped. "Even a stranger's touch can be imagined kind."

Morgan kept sixteen ones after paying and tipping the waitress. He spooned ice into the black coffee and let it melt. He then took a business card out of his pocket and scribbled his home phone number on the back. He drunk the coffee swiftly as another unknown woman of the Kiowa Heights' night began to bare herself on stage. When the cup was empty, he handed the business card to Mark Stevens.

"The next time you see Candy, give her my card and ask her to please call me. Tell her I was here looking for her. You're my witness."

As Stevens looked at the card, Chester Morgan placed sixteen dollars in ones on Stevens' neat stack of bills. "Have a good time," Morgan said.

When the lawyer reached the door, he paused, looked at the man in the pale blue t-shirt with the words "Vixens Vexed" crudely ironed on and gave him a thumbs up. Across the room, young Misty tried to seduce a man into buying her a drink, just as Tanya had perhaps years ago.

Had this been Tanya, the woman whose death compelled him to find truth?

Chester Morgan turned and walked out into the black damp night.

Chapter Thirty-Two

Ten minutes later, Chester Morgan stood outside the Orpheum Nu-Art Theater in the hazy night of old Vivia. Small dim lights glowed overhead leaving the entranceway a dusky yellow. The glass in the doors and the ticket booth had been painted an opaque gold and a frame which had once held movie posters was empty. A sign read: "Erotic Escapades! Featuring Vivia's Finest! Adult Videos. All Shows XXX Each Time. Every Time." Tanya had made some kind of recordings in the months before her death, Chester remembered, tapes or disks to get her out of Kiowa Heights for good. She had told that to Alan Kinman. In the shadowed light, the lawyer shook his head and saw large gold horseshoes embedded in the terrazzo leading to the theater's heavy glass door. A string of bells jingled as he pulled open the door and walked in.

A short, stocky man with a full moon belly, greasy black hair, and a pointed silver-streaked beard stood behind what had once been a concession stand. Two three-ringed binders lay on the counter, one open and one closed. Morgan smelled popcorn and insecticide and heard muffled groans and artificial sighs from the back of the stark, stripped and black lobby.

"Ya gotta sign in," the man said. He pushed the open notebook towards the attorney. "Oh, yeah. Good evening." The accent was from someplace north of the Mason-Dixon line and someplace east of Newark.

"Everybody wants my signature tonight," Morgan said. "Do I get a prize if I win the drawing?"

"Maybe," the man said as he patted the cover of the other notebook.

Morgan took a pen from the counter and saw scribbled signatures in the notebook. In clear, bold letters, he wrote: CHESTER MORGAN. "How does this place work?" he asked, snapping the cap onto the pen.

"Ya ain't been here before, huh?"

Morgan shook his head.

"Ya look in the book. Pick what you want. We got individual showing booths or ones for groups. We set it up. You watch. Guess ya won't want one for a group."

"No, I won't."

Morgan started to open the other notebook and the man slammed it shut.

"Five dollars for a view," the man said, staring at Morgan. "Keeps away cheap vice cops." He grinned, but his eyes were cold and gray and watery.

"A man by the name of Mark Stevens down at Vixens told me about this place. Said you had almost all the girls who work there—and some who don't anymore—on tape."

The man rubbed his hand against his greasy hair. "Fuck. Fuckin' cheap Okies," he said. "Awright, ya can look at it for three."

Morgan handed him a five-dollar bill. "There are no chains on you."

The man slipped the bill into the cash drawer and closed it. "You can go ahead and look." He motioned towards the closed book.

"My change. You said three bucks."

The man opened the cash drawer, and with thick fingers, pulled out two bills and dropped them on the counter.

Morgan opened the book. Cheesecake photos of bosomy women and beefy men lined the pages. Columns in the middle listed titles and prices. "Black Venus and Peter Pan ...$10.00." "Sexcetera and Friends ...$8.00." At the bottom of each page was a copyright notice, and the year, and the name Olsen Productions.

"Organized by actor's name and what your into, and vice versa," the man said. "So if there is anyone you want to look at in particular, you ought to go to her, or his, page."

"There used to be a dancer down at Vixens. Her name was Star. Where would I find her?" Morgan looked down. "Where would I find her?"

"Try the cemetery."

"You'd charge me for looking there, too, if you could," Morgan said. "I meant—where in this book would I find her listing?"

"Alphabetical order," the man said.

Morgan thumbed through the acetate pages and looked at the home computer-generated lists of videos. He saw pictures of women he had seen at Vixen's. He saw others, too: Women and men who shopped at deep discount stores, who rode Harleys, and who walked alone in the dark Kiowa Heights night. He wondered whether Candy appeared in a video here, but he flipped quickly through the C and K pages. He didn't want to know. At the bottom of each, he saw the same copyright symbol and the words "Olsen Productions."

"How would I locate Olsen Productions?" Morgan asked.

"Depends," the man said. "We ain't interested unless you have a monster, nine inches at least."

"You made the book? You make the tapes, too?"

The man grinned. "It's art." He tapped on the open pages of the book. "It's art."

"Show me Star. I want to see Star."

"Always popular," the man said. He turned the pages in the notebook and stopped on a well-worn one. At the top, "Star!" appeared in gold and blue. "Here."

Morgan looked. He had seen the high school yearbook picture of Tanya Everly with the light, hopeful eyes and the bleached blonde hair, mussed cheap. He had imagined, too. He looked at the naked image of the acetate page. The bright colored make-up and creamy skin. Generous breasts and hips and pudgy baby fat. The narrow legs with tight, black windowpane stockings. He sighed, then shook his head and mumbled, "Who was she?" Morgan stared at the image.

"She liked what she did," Olsen said. "Some of 'em come in here and never get over being naked. Takes all my directorial skill to get 'em to be more than corpses that fake orgasm. But Star? She was an artist. She could say 'hello' and make ya feel like you'd gotten a hand job. And, she liked the action. That helps."

"What happened to her?"

"On this side of the river? Who really knows?" Olsen stepped back. "Look as long as you want. Let me know if you want to look at a tape."

"Did she just walk in and say, 'Make a movie of me?'"

"Yeah, pretty much. The girls down at Vixens, they know my money's good. They come looking for me. Most of my talent now—men and women—does. I take good care of 'em."

Morgan looked at the old, cheap stockings Star wore. "I'm sure you do." He took a wad of bills from his pocket. "Show me the last tape she made for you. She made some about six months ago, didn't she?"

"Nah. Longer than that. More like a year," Olsen said. "Yeah, about a year, a year and a half."

Olsen pulled a ring of keys from his pocket and unlocked a large drawer full of black cassettes. "Fifteen bucks," he said, "and I don't care if ya know the pope. It's fifteen bucks."

Morgan separated his bills and put perfect change on the counter. "You could put all this on the Internet and save yourself a lot of overhead."

"Yeah, until some born-again prosecutor in Goobertown, Arkansas sees something he don't like and calls the F. B. and I and I'm defending a fuckin' interstate charge in God knows where." Olsen took a tape from the drawer and set it on the counter. "Here, I've got it all under control."

"How do you know I'm not a vice cop?" Morgan asked.

"You're not," Olsen said. He motioned Morgan to follow him into the black lobby to a bank of closed doors, each outlined in gold. "Naw, you write your name too clear and, besides, you've got the look." He opened one of the doors. "There's Kleenex in there. Don't make me start charging a cleaning deposit."

Morgan walked into the viewing booth and Olsen closed the door behind him. Olsen opened another door and walked down a back hallway to push the tape into a machine and to start the big screen projection in Morgan's booth. Olsen went to the lobby and back to his post behind the counter. He rubbed his eyes and looked at his watch.

Time passed, then Olsen heard the lawyer's voice yell:

"TURN IT OFF! TURN THE GODDAMNED THING OFF!"

The door to the booth opened and Chester Morgan bulled his way out into the lobby. "How much for the goddamned tapes? Every damn one of them." He peeled off bills from his wad of cash and threw them on the counter.

"I don't sell copies," Olsen said.

"I don't mean copies. I mean every tape you have of her. The list in the book. The one showing in the machine. Everything of Star's you have. How much?" He kept throwing bills on the counter.

"Heh. Heh. Heh. Same thing happened three or four months ago, except the guy was older. Silver-haired and taller than you. Threw bigger bills at me and had a little more class, too. Same tape. I told you I was good."

"You goddamned worthless sorry son-of-a-bitch."

"I'll tell you what I told him: They ain't for sale." Olsen pushed the cash back towards Morgan. "Keep your money. Stick it in a teenager's g-string down at Vixens."

Morgan slid four ones across the counter and slipped the rest of the bills into his pocket. "Here, mail a copy of the tape you showed me to your mother in Brooklyn. She'll be proud of you out here in Oklahoma."

Morgan turned to walk out.

"Well, ain't this *déjà vu* all over again," Olsen said, then yelled, "That bitch loved the action!"

Morgan didn't look back.

At home, he poured a shot of bourbon and pressed the power button on his sound system. He picked up a compact disc of a Beethoven symphony. He shook his head and set it down. He did the same with a Verdi opera. He fingered a disc of Hank Thompson and then one of Lefty Frizzell. He took a cassette tape of his mother's singing and started to put it in the tape player of his machine, but he stopped.

The music would not carry him away tonight.

Chapter Thirty-Three

"You did come and look for me," the voice on the phone said. Chester Morgan leaned back in his chair and flipped a paperclip across his desk.

"Are you bragging or complaining?" Morgan asked. "If you aren't complaining, you're the first person who's called this law office today who hasn't."

"If you just came to look, then I'm complaining."

It had been two days since Morgan had gone searching for his dancer with the candy-coated drawl. Mark Stevens had done his job.

"I would have looked, but that wasn't the only reason I tried to find you," Morgan said. He heard and saw movement outside his office door. He sat up straight. "I needed to talk with you. Still do, about Star."

"You really did come looking for me," Maria said. Her voice was tentative, unsure for a moment.

"Of course. If I'd known where you might have been, I would have gone there, too." he said. Marylin's bright laugh echoed from her work area in the lawyer's office suite. "I'd like to talk with you. Could you come in for an appointment, during the daytime?"

"Tuesday's my day off next week, too. The place is closed on Sundays and we try to rotate so everybody gets the same exact amount of slow and busy nights."

"Do you want to come in next Tuesday?"

"Well ..."

Silence.

Morgan eyes wandered to the stack of files on his desk and his mail to go through like every other day. "Do you want to go to dinner Tuesday night? Have you ever been to Abernathy's Steak House?"

Maria said, "You know this girl likes to eat and Abernathy's is a fine place, I'm sure, but it'd make me feel bought and I'm not for sale. Just appears that way most nights. I'd rather go someplace intellectual, like a museum or the planetarium ..." She stopped for a moment, then giggled. "Or the roller skatin' rink!"

"And do what? Study the mating habits of six graders?"

"A little roller skatin'. That'd untighten your ass a little. What'd ya think?"

"I didn't know it needed—"

"I got me a new, blue pickup truck. Is your address the one in the phone book?" She didn't wait for him to answer. "I'll pick you up around seven."

"Dinner?" he asked.

"Skatin'," she said and hung up the telephone.

Morgan tapped his desk with two fingers and smiled. He made a note on his calendar for Tuesday night, but knew he wouldn't forget. Skatin'.

Shawn walked in carrying an empty file box. "So, you've voted for life," she said and set the empty box on the empty chair in front of Morgan's desk. "And, you're making dates on company time."

Morgan ignored her. He picked up a court filing he had been reviewing.

"So Chest, who is she?" Shawn folded her arms across her chest and tapped her foot.

"Your mother," Morgan said without looking up.

"Funny." She said it in three syllables.

Morgan kept reading the pleading.

"I'm waiting," she said.

"Your sister?"

"Morgan, you make me crazy."

"Make you?" He looked at the empty box. "You have work to do."

"That's exactly what I want to talk about," Shawn said. She slipped into the other vacant chair in front of Morgan's desk.

"I'm not going to tell you who she is, what she does, or where she lives. I'm not going to draw you pictures or take photographs, draw diagrams or take videotapes and I'm not going to give you the play-by-play the next day," Morgan said. "Now, what do you want to talk about?"

"Do you know they have data retrieval services you can call? They come to your office, pack your closed files, and haul them away—leaving your receptionist/business manager available to do her job. If you need a closed file, you call them, they retrieve it, and deliver it here. It's simple."

"I'm sure it is. Now, what do you want to talk about?"

"It would be a much more cost effective way of dealing with your old papers than having your valued office staff pack up the stupid closed files and then take them to the idiotic mini-storage. Correct?"

"Shawn, you have a sports utility vehicle that costs more than what some people pay for a home. There might be three places in this county steep enough to even need an SUV. You work out every day. You exercise muscles my body doesn't know it has. Taking closed files to storage gives you an opportunity to use your SUV and your muscles."

"A service would save you money."

"The owner of the Downtown Mini-Storage is a client. He gives me a discounted rate—"

"I bet he tells every lawyer that."

"He might, but I bill him for work and he pays within thirty days, never late. Since you're my business manager, you know he pays me more than I pay him. You also know he refers new business and—"

"And new business always creates more new business," Shawn said, bouncing her head from side to side.

"You're scared to go to the mini-storage," Morgan said.

"Never!" She glared at him.

"I suppose not," Morgan said. "What's the problem?"

Shawn sighed. "The whole place is painted crimson and cream. The University of Oklahoma schooner is stenciled on the door of every unit. When you key in the access code so the gate opens, it plays 'Boomer Sooner.' It's so queer!"

"Thank you for your honesty, Miss Frederick. Now go pack up the closed files and take them to storage."

Shawn pouted, picked up the empty file box, and left the room. Morgan began reading the pleading again. A few minutes later, Shawn came back into the room.

"Chest," she said. "On that Kinman file, you need to go after those videotapes or discs hard."

Morgan raised his eyebrows and started to ask Shawn when she became interested in the Kinman case, but stopped. Instead, "Why do you think that?"

"Every time somebody gets ahead a little, somebody pulls 'em back. If those tapes were Tanya's key to get out of Kiowa Heights as your wonder client says, then you need to find who wanted to keep her there. Someone goes up, someone else yanks the string and pulls 'em back down. It's human nature."

"I hope not," Morgan said. He heard Marylin's computer gin up to print out another legal document. "What else do you think about the case?"

"You've got to find the boyfriend. And," Shawn paused, "you've got to stop billing so much time on a case that you'll never get paid on."

"Go back to work, Shawn."

"Do you know what my mother says?"

"What does your mother say?"

"Men are like mother bears, except instead of using that fierce instinct to protect their young, they use it to hunt and gather women."

"So you think Tanya's boyfriend—"

"Who said anything about Tanya's boyfriend? I'm talking about you and your mystery date!"

"Shawn, go pack up the closed files and take them to storage."

She walked towards the door and pivoted back. "I didn't tell you the worst part. It's opening the door to the storage unit and trying to figure out where to put the new closed files. The place is jammed crammed packed. Chest, most lawyers set a time limit on how long they keep old papers. The past is past."

"The past isn't even over, Shawn," Morgan said. He looked at the pile of files on his desk. "It keeps happening, sometimes with different characters and settings." Chester knew he remembered every case those old papers represented. "Do you want me to help you close the files?"

"No!" She turned and left his office.

Morgan smiled, then picked up the court filing and began reading. The phone buzzed. He picked it up.

"Boss, you have a deposition at two at Bradford, Evans, and Shell. Is there anything you need?" Marylin said.

Morgan set down the document. "Thanks for reminding me. I have the file here somewhere." He pulled a stuffed manila folder from the pile at his left and hoped it wouldn't teeter and collapse.

A good deposition—a sworn statement taken before a trial—narrows controverted issues and leads to new facts relevant to the case. The deposition at Bradford, Evans and Shell that afternoon did neither. It only increased attorney fees.

Golden Spur Exploration, Limited, had an Andarako Basin gas well that failed before it ever produced. The company's attorney, Jack O'Dowell, a Bradford, Evans and Shell partner, sued every company that had any involvement in the failed drilling attempt, including one of Morgan's clients, a small outfit which supplied drilling mud.

O'Dowell interrogated an oil field worker for an hour and a half. The questions had been mean-spirited enough to make O'Dowell's client think his attorney was tough, but the opposing lawyers recognized his approach as superficial and unskillful. Morgan had spent most of the deposition staring at the brush strokes in the oil paintings which hung on the wooden-paneled walls of the conference room.

After the testimony was over, Morgan waited for the court reporter and the other attorneys to leave. When they had, he said to O'Dowell, "If I want to represent my client well, I have to attend every one of these depositions you set."

"That's right," O'Dowell said, sliding a document to his paralegal who placed it in a large black notebook.

"Your lawsuit would be better without Collier and all these little guys in it," Chester said. "Golden Spur is in a high risk business. It loses on one well and takes it out on everybody else with lawsuit? A jury won't like that."

"If I let your client out, one of the other Defendants will point at your empty chair and say Golden Spur didn't sue the real culprit," O'Dowell said. He hadn't looked at Morgan yet.

"I understand, but most attorneys don't sue someone until they have some evidence that the defendant did something wrong."

O'Dowell stopped playing with his papers and stared at Morgan. "Why don't you go back to the DeSoto Building and handle some DUI's?" A young lawyer who had sat silently at O'Dowell's side during the deposition snickered.

Morgan picked up his file. "I was surprised to see Massey, James and Peterson handling William Harrison's probate. I thought your firm did all his work. Probably a nice fee on that estate."

O'Dowell shrugged. "Won't hurt us. We worked on an estate plan for him all summer. He died before he could get the final drafts signed." He shrugged again. "Some turn out the way you want. Some don't."

"I know." The image of William Harrison's body floating in the YMCA pool returned. "I know."

As Morgan left the conference room, he saw a man in a gray and white striped uniform approach the law firm's receptionist. Chester overheard the man speak:

"We're here from Data Retrieval Services International to close files and take them to storage. Is the office manager available?"

Chapter Thirty-Four

"Fuckin' Okies!"

Phillip Olsen wiped the counter, balled the rag up in his fat hand, and threw it under the counter. He set the two three-ringed binders back in place and waited for his first customer of the day. His watch read three-thirty and the sun outside burned with clear October heat. A Friday afternoon. Damn Okies, he thought. When you think you've figured them out, you haven't. A day like this usually brought out the jerks. God knows why.

He never had gotten square on these people, not since his first night in town twenty years ago maybe on his way back to Queens from Los Angeles. He had checked into the five-star Prairie View Hotel on the Eisenhower Expressway and had gone to the hotel lounge for a drink. It was the damnedest thing: You paid a dollar for a fuckin' membership to buy water-downed hard liquor, sold for about five times its cost. An evangelist wept crocodile tears on the big-screen TV and Southern Baptist girls worked the bar like hookers, except you didn't have to pay. It was, is the damnedest thing. Made him want to stay, though, but he should have known: He would never figure these people out.

Phillip Olsen looked around the Orpheum Nu-Art Theatre lobby. You'd think the place would be packed on gloomy, cloudy days which it wasn't, unless it was. He looked at his watch and shook his head. Fuckin' Okies. He'd never figure them out.

The bells on the front door jingled, and a white-haired blonde walked up to the counter. She wore a silver-sequined blouse, cut low to a beauty mark, a bull's eye right between the boobs. A deep blue skirt hugged her hips and spread loose over her thighs. She had thick, sinewy legs. Like the chicks from Paris, Olsen thought. He wondered if she shaved. She walked up the steps and leaned on the counter. His day was getting better.

"I'm looking for a guy named Olsen," she said. She chewed a wad of gum and adjusted a lingerie strap through her blouse.

"It's your day," he said, acting like he was looking away, but he wasn't. "You've found him, kid."

She pushed a strand of her hair behind her ear. "I'm sort of short on cash, you know. The car broke and the mechanic says it's gonna take a couple of grand, you know, to fix it. And, I'm like 'Yeah, I'll just write a check.'"

"Do I look like a fuckin' mechanic?" Olsen said. Spreading his arms, "Does this look like a fuckin' garage?"

She rubbed her tongue over her front teeth. "Naw, your finger nails are cleaner." She stood up straight and stared at him. A mechanical click-click-click sounded somewhere towards the back of the lobby.

"So, whadya want?" Olsen asked.

"The girls down at Vixens said you made, you know, movies and stuff and sometimes you needed, like, actresses? They said you paid good." She paused. "And are good."

Olsen squinted his eyes and tilted his head up. "I ain't never seen ya."

"I started just this week and I don't have, like, watermelon-sized kazoombas, so I haven't made, you know, exactly a fortune. I mean, I did pretty good, but didn't land enough, you know, to get my car built all over again. I need the job cause I need the money and I gotta have a car to get to the job to get to the money." She gulped and her eyes welled up.

"You've got some size on ya," Olsen said, looking at her broad shoulders and muscled-sculpted forearms. "That sometimes brings in some extra bucks at those strip joints—"

"Gentlemen's clubs," the white-haired blonde interrupted.

"—but not here. Ain't too noticeable on camera unless you get yourself a following. You worked any other flesh factories?"

She shook her head and looked down. "My first."

"Who sent ya?"

Rolling her eyes at the ceiling, the woman hesitated, then said, "Misty and Heather told me. Nobody *sent* me, baby. They just said you'd pay me to get naked in the movies and like maybe have to do some other stuff."

"What's your name, kid?" Olsen asked.

"Olympia."

"Ain't got one of those. Good." He paused and fingered his greasy silver-black beard. "How much do ya need? Olympia."

Her silver ringed fingers and thumb pulled a crumpled piece of green paper from her silver sequined purse. "Two thousand four hundred thirty-five dollars and three cents," she read, then folded the paper into her purse.

Phillip Olsen nodded towards the side of the lobby. "Let's go up to my office and talk. Olympia." He said her name as if he were teaching his tongue a new word. From a shelf beneath the black counter, he took an old department store counter service bell and a little sign that read "Ring Me Hard," and put them in front of the two three-ringed binders. He checked the drawers and walked to a set of black-carpeted set of stairs. "You first," he said and motioned and then followed her svelte hips pumping side to side up the staircase. His day was definitely getting better.

Olsen's office occupied the theatre's old projection booth without the projectors or the class. A black metal desk sat on black shag carpet and a black leather couch leaned against a wall covered by cheap imitation walnut paneling. A door opened from a darkened closet. Olsen held his hand out to the couch, pulled a printed form from an open desk drawer, and stuck it onto a clipboard.

"Fill this out," he said, "and I need two forms of identification."

Olympia sat down on the couch, touched her knees and ankles together, and opened her purse. "A driver's license and ... will a credit card work?"

"If ya got a fuckin' credit card, why do you need my money?"

"Cause I'm tapped and Frederick's of Hollywood doesn't, like, fix like whatever the fuck is wrong with my car."

Olsen took the driver's license and credit card to a desktop copy machine and switched it on. "Put your real information on the release and application. I'll put it as Olympia in the book downstairs. Don't worry. I ain't going to let your mama or your daddy know you're showin' your twat winkin' at the world unless you want 'em to know." He pointed to the form on the clipboard. "This is just in case the F-fucking-Be-up-your-ass-and-I show up and decide to inspect my little movie arts project."

"You're going to pay me in cash, aren't ya?" the white-haired blonde said, looking up from the clipboard.

"Always worried about the goddamned money," Olsen mumbled as he pushed the button on the copy machine and the light shone up through the glass. "Look," he said, "I ain't even checked you out yet, much less much less auditioned ya, much less offered you a frickin' job. If ya do the work, ya get paid. Don't get your crack frosted."

"It's not." She pulled at her skirt and started writing on the form again.

Olsen sat down behind the desk and tapped the credit card and driver's license against an old brown blotter. "Olympia," he said. He looked at the cards and then started playing with them again. She set the clipboard on the desk and leaned back against the couch. Olsen looked the form over and mumbled to himself.

"You clean?" he asked.

"I took a shower this morning," she said with a clipped college girl staccato. "More recently than you, I bet."

"To hell with you, bitch," and a meaty thumb pointed to the door. "You need me a crappin' lot more than I need you. I don't care if ya put dusting powder up your crawl this morning."

Olympia leaned forward and stared. "Well, let me ask you: Are you clean?" She rolled her tongue over her red lips. "There may be a reason I want to know." She stood up and, with a sultry lilt, had her hips against the desk and close enough Olsen could smell her. He took a breath and leaned back to look into her face.

"No drugs," he said. "No AIDS. No gonorrhea. No syphilis. No herpes. No genital warts. One hundred percent clean. Honest to god."

"Me, too," she said. Olsen took her right arm and looked at the veins textured against the muscle and did the same with the left.

"OK," he said, checking a box. "Tell me what you won't do or what you won't show on camera."

"Nothing where I get bruised or cut and nothing up my ass." She crossed her legs. "And, what about you?"

"Hey, I'm production, not a flesh monster. The questions are for you. You're the one come looking for me, not me looking for you."

"Maybe," she said. The white-haired blonde fingered the bull's eye beauty mark between her breasts. "I promise I won't stick anything up your ass," she whispered.

Olsen picked up the clipboard and looked closely at it. His hand tremored. "No problem interracial or same sex?"

Olympia shrugged. "I mean, like, the FBI really cares about all this shit? The guy who invented it, you know, wore dresses."

"Ya sure got a mouth on you," Olsen said.

"Some people say it's my best quality," Olympia replied. She touched her wet tongue to her cherry red lips. She leaned over

towards Olsen and grabbed his shirt at the collar. He took hold of
her arms but by then he was standing up in front of the great
maw of the darkened closet.

"It's OK, baby," she said and caressed his face with her
fingers. "You'll like this," she said, easing his arms to his sides.

One button by one, she unbuttoned his shirt, pausing a
moment and breathing between each. She unclasped his belt and
unfastened his pants, his beer belly dropping, expanding. Her
fingers touched his fly and pulled his pants down with a jerk.

"Oh yeah, mama," he moaned. "Come to daddy."

The big white-haired blonde kneed Phillip Olsen in the groin.
As he shrieked and collapsed, Olympia knocked him back into
the darkened closet and slammed the closet door shut.

"OOOOOOH! GODDAMN SON OF A AAAAAAWHH GOD
DAMN UHH UNCTUOUS BITCH!"

"I knew you would enjoy it," the young woman said, toppling
the file cabinet over to block the closet door

"OOOOOH SHIT! WHAT IN THE HELL—OOOOOOH
SHIT!"

Olympia grabbed the form she had filled out, stuffed it in her
purse, and ran down the stairs. She pulled at the drawers behind
the counter and then saw the shiny keyholes. Upstairs, Olsen
pounded on the closet door and his muffled bellows could be
heard in the lobby.

"Dammit," she mumbled.

The strand of bells on the Orpheum Arts Theatre's glass door
jingled and a middle-aged man with burnished blonde hair and
black Cherokee eyes came up the stairs to the counter.

"Shit!" she said to herself. She stood up straight and grinned
at the man.

"Eh, we've got a live one today, eh?" the man said. He smiled
a toothy smile and winked.

"You wish," she said. "We're closed."

"What? The sign says 'Open'. Hey, I've got cash. Why'd ya got
the sign out and the bell out if you aren't open?"

Olympia crossed her arms over her chest. "We're closed for
the season."

"What season is that?"

"Bowling season. The owner is a big bowler. He just found
out he likes bowling and has decided to close until the season's
over."

"Bowling?"

"Yeah, it's queer, I know, but it's true. Now scoot along." She put her arm on his shoulder and turned him towards the door. From up the stairs, the pounding on the closet door and muted screaming got louder.

"Ey, what's that?" the man asked.

"You know, some people think our films are fake," Olympia said, her face twisting with a phony smile.

"Yeah?"

"Well, they aren't. This one is almost a wrap. It's called 'Bellybusters'. They're just about to finish shooting now. You ought to come back and see it when we reopen."

"Ey, yeah. Bellybusters. Yeah." The man turned and looked at Olympia. "Hey, you want some action. I've got cash."

"Get out."

The muscular young woman let the bells on the front door of the old movie theatre remain silent for a few minutes. Then Shawn picked the two three-ringed binders up off the counter and rushed out into the Kiowa Heights afternoon.

Chapter Thirty-Five

"I'm not paying you time and a half. I'm not paying you anything at all." Chester Morgan stood at his office desk with a piece of paper in his hand.

Shawn put her strong hands on the curves of her hips, pursed her lips, and stared. "Ever hear of the Thirteenth Amendment?"

"What?"

"It abolished slavery. Maybe that wasn't required curriculum at your law school. A simple concept: I work for you. You pay me."

Morgan shook his head. "Whatever you did, and I don't want to know, you did on your own time, at your own instigation." He tapped his fingers on his desk. "Shawn, you pushed it too far this time."

"Oh, great! I risk my life for you, and for your near-sighted client, and for your idiotic quest, and the reward? Nada! Nothing! Zip! Well, just great!" Shawn swung into one of the client chairs and said in staccato, "Tell me: What is my job? To keep money coming in, right? To pay the bills, right? To make sure you have dollars to keep the doors open, right?" She leaned forward. "You're obsessed. Bless Tanya Everly's little trashy heart, but IOU's from Alan Kinman aren't valid currency, not now and, Chester, they never will be. They won't pay my wages, or Marylin's, and they really won't make the landlord very happy. You'll end up meeting your clients at McDonald's during the daytime and putting Monopoly money in strippers' g-strings at night. I risk my life for the big break just to save your practice, and I don't get paid. It's my job!" Shawn leaned back and glared.

Morgan sat down at his desk and looked at Shawn's invoice. "Time and a half *and* a performance bonus?"

"You should have seen me." Shawn stood up and twirled completely around. "It *was* a great performance. That slug wanted to yank his zipper down within thirty seconds. Me, a nudie dancer! Can you believe it? He had no idea, not until I—"

"I don't want to hear it," Morgan said.

"There's no extra charge for the slut dress I had to buy either."

The middle-aged attorney shook his head and stared into that familiar empty space in the center of the room.

"You got a great deal, Chester. You'd pay a private investigator. You'd yell, 'Shawn, bring me a check!' Look, I brought back the only evidence you can put your hands on. Don't go there, Morgan! Try saying it: 'Shawn, bring me a check.'"

"I don't pay for stolen evidence."

"Like what's going to happen? Phillip Olsen is going to call the F-Fucking Be Idiots and say this blonde bimbo wacked me in the nuts instead of giving me a blowjob and then took my sign-in sheets and my show books. Give me a break! It's all on computer. He can duplicate anything he needs, and the sign-in register? That's just his little way to blackmail perverts who wear suits."

Shawn's eyes twinkled and she waited, waited.

"I'll make a deal with you, Shawn. If anything you did helps resolve this case, you and a friend can spend the afternoon at the spa of your choice at my expense. Whatever you want there."

She stood up and extended her hand. "Deal. Look, I know I didn't get the tapes, but, Jesus, what would you have discovered with them anyway? They're the literary equivalent of people screwing in light bulbs with sound, but these binders have the secret. I know it."

"Don't leave Olsen's register or catalogue in this office. Keep them anywhere you want, but not here."

"Sure, Chest." Shawn left the attorney's office and, with her, took the prairie storm energy of undefeated youth.

"You amaze me," Chester said.

He looked at the stack of papers and files piled on the left side of his desk. The basic substance of the practice of law, words and paper, left undone. Too many meetings, court hearings, telephone calls, and—Shawn was right, almost—too much time spent on the Tanya Everly case. Maybe today would be different, he thought. His clients deserved prompt work; his clients deserved that respect. Maybe today.

The telephone rang. An enraged client in a perpetual fight with a neighbor over a new fence and the property's true boundary line. Twenty-five minutes later, Morgan hung up the phone. It rang again. Ralph Abercrombie, a retired parts inventory clerk at a local car dealership, didn't understand a perfunctory pleading filed in his late mother's probate case. Morgan explained it as simply as he could. The client still didn't understand. The attorney explained it again a different way. That confused Mr. Abercrombie more. To clarify, Morgan provided hypothetical examples which prompted question and question and question. Forty minutes later, Chester Morgan placed the telephone in its cradle and he knew his client still did not know why the court document had been filed or why his bill would be so large. The telephone buzzed and Shawn's voice spoke from the speaker.

"Better call Bill Bartholomew back, Chest. He's irate."

Morgan found the number on his Rolodex and punched the numbers. By force and determined action, Bartholomew had made more money than anyone with the wrong parents from the wrong side of the river could have ever reasonably expected. On good days, Bartholomew tolerated lawyers. On bad ones, he hated them, even his own.

"Where's that goddamned contract?" Bartholomew growled.

"I received the information you sent at the end of last week. I haven't looked at it yet."

"It's not the end of last week, is it? I need that fucking contract."

"Bartholomew, there are at least thirty-seven hundred lawyers in this city. Three thousand six hundred and ninety-nine will jump when you bark, but I won't. Three months ago, I asked you to provide the specifics. You mailed them four or five days ago and now wonder why the work isn't completed today. Which do you want: the contract done right or do you want it done right now? Which do you want?"

Bartholomew was silent.

"You'll have a draft by the end of the week," the lawyer said. "Call me with any modifications. We can kick something out today if you absolutely have to have it, but I won't be satisfied with it and neither should you."

"Look over that stuff I sent you, and let's get it done," Bartholomew said.

Morgan hung up the phone and Marylin tapped at the door frame to his office. She wore a sleek gold dress and held an open file in her slender hands. She lifted her eyebrows, but her face had forced a smile from a frown.

"Boss, I woke up this morning and thought about *Herrol versus Maxum Pipe Fittings*. I just knew I should look at it when I got here. Sometimes your mind organizes things and you aren't even aware of it. I forgot about it again until just now. Somehow we didn't get the date on the calendar to answer the plaintiff's petition."

"What! How did that happen?" Morgan asked, his words sharp, loud. "When were we supposed to file it? Are we in default?"

"It's due today, Mister C. Sorry about the mistake."

"More mine than yours," he said, taking the file from her. "I'm glad you woke up this morning."

Judy Robertson, a tough-talking, cowboy-boot-wearing, snuff-dipping thirty-year old woman had purchased Maxum Pipe Fittings, Inc. for its assets, but not its debt. With it, she had acquired the conmen, liars, and incompetents who had made the previous owner go broke. Despite her swagger, Judy hadn't been prepared for the swampland of dishonest Oklahoma commerce and this lawsuit was one of the results.

"We've got to take care of Judy," Morgan said as he left his office and went into the library to research a defense he intended to raise in the answer. "Shawn, hold my calls until I get this finished."

Chester found the statute he needed and started to search for Oklahoma Supreme Court cases interpreting how that particular law applied to specific cases. The library telephone buzzed and Shawn's voice sounded from the speaker.

"Morgan—"

"I told you to hold my calls."

"Judge Posey's office is on the line. Do you want me to tell them you're in a crappy mood and you refuse to talk with 'em?"

"I'll take it."

His honor's minute clerk instructed the attorney to be in the judge's courtroom at one-thirty that afternoon for a hearing originally scheduled for the following week. Although Morgan knew it served no purpose, he still asked why. The minute clerk informed him the court had an irreconcilable conflict which had developed. In other words, Morgan thought, Judge Posey was clearing his docket in order to take off to the Oklahoma panhandle and go pheasant hunting.

"Be on time and be prepared, counsel," the minute clerk said.

He would be, with effort, but the work on his desk was more important than his honor's hunting trip. Now, the middle third of this day would be gone and no progress made. Morgan found the

Supreme Court cases needed to prepare Maxum's answer, returned to his office, and dictated the pleading. It wasn't good enough, but time demanded. He gave the tape to Marylin to transcribe and yelled at Shawn to put calls through once more.

Morgan picked up the first file at the top of the pile. The telephone rang. I'm going to yank the damn thing out by the wires and publish an announcement I only communicate by letter or face-to-face meeting, he thought. He picked up the receiver.

"Morgan," he growled.

"Chester? Even after all these years and miles away," the old woman's voice said, "a mother still knows when her son is having a bad day."

"Oh, Mama. A funnel cloud might make it worse."

"Am I botherin' you? You too busy to talk with me?"

"It's just a crazy, hectic day."

"'Makin' a bunch of money, I bet. Nothing's all bad."

"I probably got twenty-six dollars in the bank, give or take thirteen cents. What a hell of a way to make a living."

"Son, don't you be talkin' like that. You could be working for Mister Paul haulin' hogs." She coughed. "I just sensed—I just thought you needed to hear from someone who cares for you."

"Sorry, Mama, and thanks, too." Morgan paused. "You know you can call whenever you want." He heard the tap, tap, tap of Marylin's fingers hitting her computer's keyboard outside his office door.

"That case is eating at ya, isn't it? That one ya kinda told me about."

"A lot of time and energy spent, no resolution, and it's not bringing in any money. I'm getting tired of it. The case will break—they all do—but when and how, I don't know."

"Stay after it, son." The old woman's struggled breathing could be heard over the telephone line. "Maybe spendin' some extra time with that little entertainer girl would be good for you."

Morgan wondered, then remembered Maria. "Little isn't exactly the word you'd use for her and she's much more than a girl. She's someone I've met, a surprise I suppose."

"I want to be introduced to her, when you're ready, when she's ready." Molly Morgan's voice quieted to sanctuary whisperings. "Chester, I dreamt about Cassie last night. She was doin' just fine; the dream, well, it was like she wanted you to know that. That she was okay."

The middle-aged attorney did not respond.

"She was so lovely the day you two got married. That was the way she looked last night. Her eyes twinklin', her big smile, as radiant as woman ever made."

"It's still hard, Mama. Suppose it always will be."

"Oh, Chester, I'd give anything to have her back."

Morgan bit his lip and, after empty silence, said, "There's something else I'd give up everything for, too."

"What's that, honey?"

"To hear you sing again, like you used to."

"I know, Chester, I know.

When the call was over, he hunted down the file needed for the one-thirty hearing before Judge Posey. Today, as too many others, lunch would be a time to review, to outline arguments, to anticipate the incisive and the ludicrous. Today, it would be a cold sandwich and estoppel by deed.

As Morgan walked file in hand towards the outer hallway door, Shawn said, "Hey, Morgan, I need to take Thursday afternoon off. You got a problem with that?"

He turned and sighed. "What for now?"

"Amber and I have a project due for Business Structures on Friday. You know, a presentation. We need to get together and figure out what we are going to say."

"I've never known you to be at a loss. What's Business Structures?"

"It's why you made a lousy deal not paying my invoice and promising to treat me and Amber to an afternoon at the spa. You look at the risk, the cost, the probable return, and figure out the most profitable way to structure a deal or business."

"Check with Marylin. If she doesn't have a problem with you being off, I don't either." He walked to the door and then turned around. "What are you doing for your project?"

"We've figured out how the recording industry can bring a new star to market with minimal investment. Do you have any idea how much it costs an entertainment company to market a new artist? Two million bucks minimum and your odds are better at the crap tables in Vegas. One singer we read about had everything: A voice, stage presence, experience before live audiences, a good belly button. The recording company spent two point six million dollars to promote her and get her first CD cut. Guess how many records she sold? Guess. Six hundred and seventy-eight."

"Glad it wasn't my money." Morgan looked at his watch. "So what's your idea?"

"Limited partnerships, like in the oil and gas business. Individual investors buy into an unknown's career. If the singer doesn't make, the investors take a loss and write it off on their taxes. If the singer hits, the investors take a little of the future success. A promoter or a record company calls the shots, acts as general partner, and significantly reduces their costs and risk. *Voila!*"

"Now if you could figure out how to make this place profitable." He turned the doorknob. "Good luck Friday."

"Morgan, you're hopeless!" Shawn pulled a large black notebook from under her desk. "Chest, there's something else. When you go to places like the Orpheum Nu-Art Theatre, don't sign your name so others can read it."

"I told you not to keep those notebooks in this office."

"Yeah. Yeah. I'll take them when I leave tonight. Hey, what's the name of that guy you found sucking water at the YMCA?"

"Shawn, it's been a long day already. Don't push me. Show a little respect."

The image seared and would not fade.

"Chill, Morgan. I'm just trying to help you. If the name's right, that guy is the only other person who signed off in this whole notebook so you could read it."

Morgan walked to her desk and looked at the page opened to May fifth. There, written in clear, bold letters, read the name William Harrison.

Chapter Thirty-Six

Fluorescent lights glowed and skates sounded, rolling on the buffed wooden floor. Maria caught up to Chester Morgan and pinched his tight rear end.

"Ya gotta keep your butt loose," she said, "or you're gonna fall and break yore head."

"You're saying I'm tight-assed?"

"No. Petrified-assed." Maria squeezed again and chuckled. "Just stay loose and roll."

Chester jerked forward and then yanked back. The walls and track flipped upside down and Morgan's skates went ceiling bound.

FUWHOP!

Chester landed flat on his back; every vertebrae popped. A swarm of fifth-graders swerved to miss rolling over him. He twitched his shoulders and realized nothing hurt, not now anyway. Instead, he felt a strange exhilaration.

"Hey, sleep somewhere else old man," one kid called as the other grade school boys snickered and skated around the lying form.

Maria slowed and returned to Morgan's side. "Ya ain't goin' to get very far tryin' to skate on your backside," she said.

The middle-aged lawyer crawled to stand up. "Some people would pay a chiropractor fifty bucks for that." He took a deep breath and sighed. "It's been a long time, but I've always been a good skater."

"I can tell," she said, then winked. "Just stay loose."

Morgan stood and wobbled. "Only six blocks with concrete sidewalks in all Tobusky and I lived out in the country." He started to move forward unsure. "But I liked to skate."

"Remember, when you're fixin' to fall forward, don't jerk back like you're reining in a stallion," Maria said. "Ya just kinda got to trust the motion and ease into it. It'll come back."

Chester skate walked and then let the wheels roll. "Over in Wilburton, there was a huge rink. At least it seemed pretty big to a nine year old kid. When I'd go see my cousins, if we weren't swimming or playing around back in the woods, we'd go skating.

Same idea there and back then as here: You pay money and go in circles, letting the world be just a whirl of passing images and sound."

"How long ago was that?" Maria asked.

"Too long," Morgan said, looking at the young woman, "but I've always been pretty good at it."

The sweet, salty, buttery smells of popcorn, soda-fountain Coca-Cola, and floor wax mixed and hung in the air. An old Marty Robbins' song pounded scratchy vibrations from over-used speakers. The skate floor spread into a straight-away, sparse with skaters even for a Tuesday night at Ruby's Regal Roller Ranch, a Vivia landmark with painted cowboys and lariats and pastel sunsets on the walls.

Maria moved ahead like the wind—effort, then breeze, and effort again. Chester watched, amazed at her ease, delighted with her presence. What was he doing? Here, with her. He, an attorney; she, a stripper. He, off-balance and slow; she, a ballerina on steel. His eyes dulled from cynical experience; hers still glowing with what? Hope? Maria swept into the curve ahead and Morgan smiled.

The wheels of his skates ground against the polished wood, and he tentatively pushed out with his right leg, his left following. He moved and didn't fall, but it didn't feel right. He tried to balance, couldn't exactly, swerved his arms in awkward circles, and then straightened up. He glanced over his shoulder and smiled. He thrust his left leg out and followed with the other. He thought he would tumble, but moved and didn't. Not yet. He kept trying, kept going forward, but with no fluidity and no grace. What had happened since his feet glided over the red and blue tiled floor of the Wilburton Skating World rink?

Chester rolled around the curve, feeling as if he might do the upside-down-backwards cheerleader splits if he even breathed too hard. He noticed a fragrance of spice and tobacco and someone breezed up next to him.

"Ya know ya ain't really skatin' together if one person pulls out ahead and leaves the other behind," Maria said.

"Well, what I'm doing right now isn't exactly skating period," Chester said. "You're really good, and fast. Don't slow down for me. It'll just take a minute or two for me to remember how all this works."

"Maybe skatin' wasn't such a good idea."

FUWHOP!

Morgan crawled to stand up. "No, it was a great idea. It's like trying a lawsuit. You get hit. You get knocked down. You get up and keep going like nothing happened." He surveyed the western adorned snack bar and mumbled, "And sometimes the next morning you wake up feeling like you've been wrestling a nine hundred pound gorilla in a cage too small."

Maria brushed a handful of thick black hair behind her ear and slowed to cut a small circle to line up next to Chester. He started skating again, awkward with cement legs and limbs.

"I'm embarrassing the hell out of you, aren't I?" he said.

"Embarrassed?" She laughed. "I bounce around naked five or six nights a week, let strangers rub my ta-tas and touch my bottom and ya think I am embarrassed? Maybe you ought to be, hangin' around someone like me."

"Never."

A small child with a white helmet and polka-dotted knee pads cut in front of them.

"You skate so well. You must skate a lot," Chester said.

"Aw, it kinda blows out the cobwebs and ya can't take it seriously." She looked up and smiled at him. "I figured it'd be good for somebody who has to work his brain so hard and his tail end so little."

She pinched him again

FUWHOP!

"Jesus Christ!" Chester said from the shiny track.

Maria giggled and as he struggled to get up, Chester laughed, too.

"I guess I forgot to ease into it," he said. He reached over and pinched her, too. Maria lost her balance and grabbed at Chester.

FIWHIP!

FUWHOP!

And they were both on the skate floor in each other's arms, laughing, and tickling, and pinching at each other.

A voice echoed, echoed over the loud speaker: "SKATERS MUST AT ALL TIMES SKATE IN A COUNTERCLOCKWISE DIRECTION. HORSEPLAY ANYWHERE ON OR OFF THE TRACK IS STRICTLY PROHIBITED."

"I guess we'll have to go someplace else," Maria said and they both laughed again.

"Whatever you say," Chester said. "Before we leave, though, I'm going to skate. I'm going to fly. Stand up and show me how."

"Ya don't need showin'; ya just need doin'."

"Those are true words," Morgan said as he got up from the floor.

Maria nudged him with her elbow. "Now, let's talk about skatin'. First, ya gotta quit thinkin'. Ya gotta quit wonderin' whether you're doin' it right or whether you're embarrassin' me or yourself or who might be watchin' or laughin' at ya. Then, ya gotta let go of all that stuff that's stacked up and piled around in your head. We're here, with each other, what difference does anything else make? D'ya understand, babe?"

Morgan nodded.

"This whole world is spinnin' round and round. Ya just have to feel that energy and know it'll take you on. It'll be in your ankles first, and then it'll move up your legs and into your hips. Then, let go, let loose, and fly!"

The sounds of a Bob Wills' rag sang from the overworked speakers of Ruby's Regal Roller Ranch. Chester looked at the woman, her voluptuous curves, her white satin skin, and the optimism of youth in her eyes. She was right. He started to move and she joined; first to the right, then to the left.

It started in his ankles and moved up his legs to his hips and beyond. Chester reached for Maria's hand and they flew in circles, just letting the world be a whirl of passing images and sound.

* * *

"I'm going to feel like hell in the morning," Chester Morgan said as he climbed into Maria's Chevy pickup truck.

"Ya will if you think you will," she said, slamming her heavy door. She gunned up the engine and put it in gear. "Hey, you ended up looking pretty good out there."

"I told you I'm a good skater, always have been," he said.

"Mister Morgan, you best not press that or I'm going to have to tell you I can argue a law case in court better'n you and I can do brain surgery in my kitchen with a butter knife." She reached over and patted his hand. "You men."

"You looked tremendous," he said.

Maria turned the big blue pickup truck onto Hurley Parkway. "Tell me I'm beautiful and I'll tip ya a one."

"You're beautiful, too."

"Maybe the tip'll come later," she said and winked.

They rode on in silence, still feeling the vibration of steel wheels and the airy breezes of the skating rink. Centuries-old oak and cottonwood trees hung over the boulevard making jigsaw puzzle shadows under the street lights. A flash of light reflected from Maria's star-shaped earring.

"I looked for you to talk about the Tanya Everly case," Morgan said. "Wanted to be with you again, too, really." He crossed his legs easily in the roomy cab. "I thought I knew who murdered her. A street preacher named Don Hubbard who runs a mission on Seay Street near Ninth Avenue. I guess Tanya hid out there sometimes to get away from her mother and there was some kind of magic—at least in the preacher's mind. The guy was, is, obsessively devoted, whether to Tanya, his mission people, or his god, but he has an alibi—one I can't challenge. The night Tanya died, he was with a lawyer, a friend of mine."

"Man or woman?" Maria asked.

"Man," Morgan said. "They were at a convention together. That's all, I suspect."

"Is your friend upright?"

Morgan shrugged. "Always has been with me. In my business, you can always find somebody who thinks some lawyer screwed him out of something."

"Even you?" she asked.

"I could probably give you a list, and not even get a tenth of 'em. Most lawyers who do their job can. With Martin Bollant, you might get a longer list and the money might be bigger, but if he tells me, I believe." Morgan paused. "You want to stop somewhere and get some coffee? Something to eat? A drink maybe?"

"Just coffee," she said. "I like the way ya order that."

"There's coffee house down by the river called Crazy Snake's. Ever been there?"

Maria shook her head. "Where's it at exactly?"

"Well, you take Hurley, except the other way."

Maria glanced at the truck's mirrors, tapped the brakes, and cut a squealing u-turn across the center median divide. Chester shifted his weight back to upright center, looked at the woman behind the steering wheel, and chuckled.

"Ain't this fun!" Maria tilted her head and smiled at Morgan. "Ya do that with a Daewoo and people just think you're a pissant.

Do it with a big ol' pickup and they think you're a wild-assed cowgirl."

"No doubt which you are, huh?" Chester looked back over both shoulders and then straight ahead. "Crazy Snake's will be down here about three or four miles, right on the water. I'll let you know."

"Tell me more about Tanya," Maria said, turning down the radio.

"The lady who lived next door to her. Murle Mueller. A little odd, but harmless I think."

"God, yeah. Star told me it was like havin' your own bodyguard living next door. That landlord wouldn't have done nothin' to Tanya."

"Something's not right about Tanya's mother," Morgan continued. "Driving a new Lincoln Town Car and not showing any regret her meal ticket—or any grief—her daughter is dead. Something isn't right about that. There's a connection, maybe, but not life insurance. Tamar White isn't one who'd put a check in the mail every month to some financial conglomerate in Des Moines."

"Ya gotta wonder how somebody so good and generous would ever come outa a bitch like that," Maria said. She pulled a cigarette from her purse, placed it between her red lips, and lit it.

"Those will kill you, you know," Chester said.

"So will sittin' in an office, takin' on everyone's problems, and not doin' nothing for fun," she replied. She stopped for a traffic light. "Great thing about a big truck: You can see people in their cars, watch what they're doin', and they don't even know it."

"Speaking of watching: Vixens stays open because of political connections. Is money paid? Yeah, but probably not to street cops, probably not to the cops at all. The graft's higher up and more sophisticated. Probably nothing that can be traced or proven. Maybe what's been going on at Vixens isn't connected. I just don't know." Morgan cracked the pickup truck's window. "What have you learned?"

"Chester, you takin' me out in the country to rapture me?" She said rapture as if she were licking ice cream.

"I hope. Or you, me." He grinned at her and then looked through the windshield at the city lights and the shadowed structures nearby. "Crazy Snake's just a little farther, not even out of the town limits, on some Indian land. Saves taxes, I guess."

Maria sighed and tapped her fingernails against the steering wheel. "It's still ain't playin' right over in Kiowa Heights, just as worse. The whole place, and Bruce is wiggin' pretty good nearly every day. Topaz's ... Well, Topaz enjoys misery and fear." They drove in silence. She half-shrugged her shoulders. "Fuck if I know. Chester, I'm afraid to get into it. I am."

"Then don't, sweetheart. Listen, but don't ask. The police force now has stealth cops. Old-timers are quitting fast. These stealth cops—SPIT cops or roamers are what they're called—are completely off the screen, doing God knows what. We've got a twenty-three, twenty-four year old woman dead, brutalized, and there's no record. You were her friend. Just listen. That's all and no more. Just listen."

The pickup truck's tires bounced against the cement joints in the boulevard's pavement. "Turn left at that blacktop drive."

Maria drove the blue Chevy pickup onto the macadam road and followed it under a canopy of gnarly riverbank trees and underbrush until it reached a dimly lit parking lot. A one-story wooden building with a low pitched roof, heavy overhanging eaves, and narrow ground-to-ceiling windows stood nearby. A big woodblock sign in front read "Crazy Snake's Coffee Beans and Beverages." Maria stopped the truck and turned off the engine.

"Ya mind if I finish this cigarette?" she asked.

"If you want," Chester said. They waited in silence. Through the tobacco smoke, he could still smell her scent, still feel the touch of her moist white hand. He remembered a picture of a young woman in a high school yearbook and an inscription surrounded by bold stars. "Who's Billy? Where can I find Tanya's Billy?"

A wisp of a smile came across Maria's face. She shook her head. "About nine months ago, a year, maybe, Tanya got herself a real boyfriend and she was just crazy about him. Not jack rabbit naked and coyote howling crazy, but sugar 'n' butter, soft 'n' sweet crazy. He came into the club a few times. I guess that's where they met, but I can't say I ever got introduced to him or nothin'. Has tons of money. That's about all I know."

"Where does he live? What does he do? Old money or new? Where can I find him?"

Maria shrugged. "Tanya kept that all real secret, like it was sacred or somethin'. Didn't tell nobody nothin' much about him. Wonder how's he doin'."

"Everyone knows *about* Billy, but nobody seems to *know* him," Morgan said. "He didn't show up at the funeral. He paid her rent, but never came back for the deposit. It's strange. You'd think ..."

Maria smashed out her cigarette in the ashtray. "Some people deal with death that way, Chester. It hurts so bad, they cain't look back. They just go forward."

"And they die with stiff necks." Chester took the handle to open the door. "Let's get some coffee."

The outside air smelled of dusty autumn leaves and decaying underbrush. Pieces of light reflected through the trees off the slow-moving waters of the Cottonwood River. Chester Morgan placed his hand on the small of Maria's back and felt the gentle incline of hips.

"Crazy Snake was a full-blood Muscogee Creek. His English name was Chitto Harjo. When the do-gooders and the swindlers decided to divide up Indian land at the turn of the last century and take the rest, Crazy Snake led a rebellion. It might have changed things, but Chitto Harjo just disappeared one day. Some say the government murdered him. Others say he ran off to Mexico. By tradition, he still roams the hills of the old Creek Nation."

"D'ya think Tanya might walk with him?"

An owl made a soft, low-pitched sound from the dark riverbank woods.

"Maybe."

Chapter Thirty-Seven

Maria sipped from a stout sandstone mug, its steam curling, twirling in the muted light of Crazy Snake's. "Pretty good coffee," she said.

"As good as the Hot 'n' Hearty's?" Chester asked.

"The Hot 'n' Hearty is for chowin'. This place is for sippin'." She took another and looked up at him through the vapor.

"And for being with you," Chester said, "being together."

"Yeah, that's right," she said.

In the corner of the coffee house, a duet performed. An African American woman played a Native American flute; a gray-bearded white man sang a haunting ballad. Nearby, six or seven nonconforming conforming college students with books and backpacks sat in a broken circle, intense, listening, discussing. The earth smell of brewing coffee meandered through the room and in the faint light, people sat alone, together, distanced apart, at thick oaken tables and overstuffed sofas and armchairs.

"Oh, Chester, I get these crazy thoughts," Maria said. She stretched her neck, surveyed the room, and then giggled. "What if everyone here got naked and danced right now?"

Chester raised his eyebrows; Maria's blue eyes darted, twinkled. "And you taking the lead?" he asked.

"Well, it's not exactly anything you can do and take yourself too seriously. Might make everybody just feel a little better." Maria grinned and winked at a young man sitting several tables away. A slender woman in elegant white, and gold jewelry and hair, leaned and pressed against him.

"Kind of like when I go somewhere and want to give every lady a rose and every man a cigar?" Chester commented.

"Yeah, same kind of thing." Maria glanced at the table with the man and the lithe blonde.

"In the daytime, there's a beautiful view of the river," Chester said, pointing a thumb at the picture windows. "People on the hiking trail stop in."

Maria touched white skin where her shirt separated at the neck and descended to hinting cleavage. She stared at the man several tables away and rolled the tip of her tongue over her lips.

"The artwork is all original, all by Native Americans," Chester said. "The Southeastern tribes, the ones settled in eastern Oklahoma, believed the rabbit was an ornery trickster." He nodded towards a painting across the room. "Rabbit is being outsmarted by the terrapin. It's my favorite. I'll show it to you close up before we leave."

"Yeah. That's right." Maria drank from her mug and continued to stare at the young man and woman. "The coffee's really good." She moved her hand in a subtle wave.

"My big date, and she's flirting with a guy out of an L.L. Bean catalogue," Chester said. "What are you doing?"

"I'm fuckin' with that guy."

"Really?"

"He's a regular—a real regular—at Vixens, just about cain't keep his pants yanked up and he's actin' like he cain't even see me. What a wienie!"

Morgan chuckled, took a business card out of his pocket, and wrote: "My date wants to switch dates with you. Interested?" He pushed the card across the table. "I think I'll give this to the skinny blonde. What do you think?"

"Heck no." She made an exaggerated frown and placed her soft hand on Chester's arm. "Ain't goin' trade a man for a boy, least not one like him."

The song finished. The gray-bearded man set down his guitar, made stage musician small talk, and reached behind for a bodhran. As he rubbed the Irish drum to vibrating pitch, the African-American woman sang a Woody Guthrie tune, slow and deep and optimistic.

"Tanya sure could sing," Maria said. "If she'd lived long enough to get her break, she'd be on TV. We'd be standin' in line to buy her CD's. I sure miss her."

"If we can only find the reason, the people involved ..." Chester stopped, remembering the stark room at the Bunkhouse Lodge, the young woman's final terror, the ultimate loneliness of death.

"Do you think she's at peace?" Maria sighed. "I mean, do you think she can be, really be, if we don't find out?"

"We may never know who, or exactly why, but somehow, someday I'm going to make those sons of bitches downtown show her some respect. If I can do no more than that, I'll be satisfied." He pulled at his shirt collar and looked away. "She had enough troubles here; she isn't being tormented now."

Maria ran her finger over her mug's rim. "Sometimes I'll just hear her voice so clear, somethin' she used to say, or I'll be at home by myself and know she's there somehow. That sounds crazy, don't it?"

Morgan shook his head. "Maybe I hear her voice or feel her presence, too, and simply don't recognize it."

The music played.

"You're a beautiful young woman. You're a professional at what you do. And, you're wonderful at it, you're great, but is it what you really want for your life?"

She leaned forward, at once determined, at once vulnerable. "Other choices ain't too good for girls like me. Cashierin' at Wal-Marts or being some rich man's plaything, or worse, being hooked up with some pretty boy who promises ya the moon and gives you a mop instead. No sir, no thanks! I take home three to five hundred dollars cash a night. Tally all that up. It's more'n your secretary gets, I bet, but without the headaches or the wardrobe." Maria stopped. She pulled at her silver necklace and adjusted a small geometric crucifix that lay perched at the rise of her breast. "We all have dreams, though."

"I wondered," Chester said. "What's yours?"

She lifted the cross by its chain. Its rectangles, squares, triangles sparkled. "Ya see this?"

Morgan nodded.

"Guess who designed it? Made it?"

Chester shrugged.

"I did. The earrings, too. All my jewelry I make. Someday I'm goin' to have me a chain of boutiques, every nice place you can think of. Fantasia by Maria, or something like that. You'll be able to get my creations all over the country and there won't be nothin' like it nowhere else in the whole world. All high-class and high-quality. You wait and see."

Morgan tapped on the table with his fingers and nodded. "Your dreams won't come true unless you dream 'em. Learn all you can. Imagine all you can. Don't give up. Don't let anyone make you think you aren't good enough, or smart enough, or anything else. Most of all, don't ever let some man detour you or kill your dream. Make it real."

The woman with the coal black hair and strawberry lips looked down. The corners of her mouth lifted to a half-grin. "How do you know I'm not married or have me a serious, big boyfriend now?"

"You've been single-woman spoonin' me all evening, even when you didn't intend to," Morgan said. He stared at her and said: "I'm not complaining; I'm bragging." He picked up her mug. "I'll get us some more coffee."

At the shiny glass counter, Chester waited behind an SUV mother as her two small sons chose pastries, changed their minds, and changed them back again. After the wait, he returned to his table.

"Thanks," Maria said, as he placed the fresh cup in front of her. Her voice was quiet, pensive.

"It costs more at Crazy Snake's than at the Hot'n'Hearty because they give you a clean mug for refills," Chester said as he sat down.

Maria nodded and stared nowhere. The lawyer started to speak, but didn't. He blew at his steaming mug, tasted the smooth, pungent beverage, and let the silence be. A minute passed.

"I bet you think it's pretty damn silly sitting here with a strip dancer who's talking to ya about opening up her own coast-to-coast jewelry boutiques, don't ya?" she said, looking to the black darkness through the windows.

"No, it would be pretty damn silly if you told me the only thing you thought you could do was to marry a rich man and have babies," Morgan said. "In ten years, I plan to walk down Rodeo Drive and into your Beverly Hills store and get a discount because I'm a friend of the owner. Learn the business well, Maria."

She moved forward and closer; Chester smelled her scent of spice and tobacco. "Do you really, really think I could do it? I mean my own line of jewelry, my own stores?"

"I know you could."

Maria looked up, her sapphire eyes wet. "You really do, don't you?"

Morgan nodded. "Why the hell not?"

"Goddamit," she muttered quietly, leaning back against her chair. "I've got something to show ya."

* * *

A stark yellow bulb glowed onto the wooden porch of Maria's white clapboard house and an autumn breeze off the prairie rustled overgrown cedars in the yard. Maria stuck a key into the stubborn door lock, pulled, turned, pushed, and opened. The stoop's wooden planks squeaked beneath Chester Morgan's shifting weight. A light switch flipped inside .

"Come on in," she said.

"It's quiet out here," Chester said as he walked into the old ranch house and smelled sandalwood, cedar, and tobacco. "It must make for some nice morning sleeping."

"Yeah," Maria said as she grabbed a pile of clothes off a blue corduroy divan and threw them into a laundry basket. "Except for the peacocks."

"The peacocks?"

"'Didn't get the clothes folded before I left," she replied, carrying the basket down the hall. "Have a seat. I'll be right back."

Morgan sunk into the couch. A big screen TV and a music system with large black speakers stood against the opposite wall. "Tell me about the peacocks," he called.

"The guy down the road has some." Maria came back into the living room. "'Can be about the noisiest damn critters I ever heard."

"What does he do with 'em?"

"Well, he doesn't ever tell 'em to shut up."

"I mean, does he raise 'em for the feathers or what?"

"'Guess so. 'Ain't ever seen no peacock filet at the meat counter in the grocery store, have you?" Maria turned a light on in the adjoining dining room. "Hey, this is what I wanted to show you." She opened a gray wooden door and motioned Chester to follow.

The room was painted bright white. Near the door, a work table held molds, a burner, crucibles, a polishing machine, magnifying glasses, and tiny hand tools. A large wooden cabinet had been built into the side of the room and adjoining it, a stainless steel sink. A rock tumbler murmured on the counter.

"This is my studio," she said. "That sounds kinda highfalutin', doesn't it, but that's what it is. This is where I make my jewelry."

"Tell me how you take an idea and make it into an object?"

"'Ya really want to know?"

Chester nodded.

Maria opened one of the large cabinet doors and took out a three-ringed binder. "First, ya got to see the piece in your own mind." She opened the notebook to pages and pages of pencil-sketched drawings. "I got so many ideas, I don't know if I'll ever get 'em all made. There are some days, I just sit out on that back porch and inspiration just seems to pour out of the sky. I cain't hardly scribble fast enough." She thumbed through the pages and stopped. "This here is this cross I'm wearing."

Chester looked at the sketching.

"They don't ever come out exactly like they look here. You imagine 'em, draw 'em, and make 'em. The drawing's the least reliable thing. What I see in my own mind, that's what I end up gettin'. Most of the time anyways."

"I would have recognized it," Chester said. "Do you mind if I look at your drawings?" And he saw light pencil lines of rings, studs, brooches, and bracelets. Some delicate, some bold. Some with stones and gems. Some with silver and gold. Others bold or frilly in design. All unique. "After you get the idea, what do you do?"

"Well, it all depends on what it is. Ya gotta figure out how you're goin' do it. Make it, I mean. That's kinda the hard part. Let's take a simple ring." She moved to the work table. "I'll shape it outa wax and then pour this stuff like plaster of Paris around it in a can. Then you fire the plaster in the kiln and you have a mold. Heat up whatever metal you're goin' to use and pour it in. Ya let it set, ya take it out, get off the rough edges, and hand tool it until it looks like what you want. Then, polish it up. If I like it, I keep the mold, make more maybe. If I don't, I put it back in the pot, melt it, and start all over again." She smiled. "I do a lot of pourin' and remeltin'." Maria put her hand on the small of Chester's back. "God, I didn't even offer you a drink. 'Want somethin'?"

"Sure," he said.

"Now, if you're usin' stones or gems, ya gotta figure out how the piece is going to hold 'em," she said, showing him a rose quartz ring. "Right now, I'm pretty much stickin' to stones if I use anything at all. I got some turquoise shinin' up in the tumbler. Let's get those drinks."

Morgan followed the woman in the plaid western shirt and tight blue jeans through the dining area into the kitchen, stacked with dirty dishes and glasses. "What do you do with the jewelry you make?"

"Right now, not a whole lot. I'm savin' up, learnin'," Maria said, as she opened cabinet doors and pulled out a two-liter bottle of tequila. "I sometimes sell stuff to the girls at work. Until Exotica poisoned Bruce's mind, I used to bring some of it there and sell it at Christmas time and Valentine's to the guys. Talk about a good mark up, jees! You could sell gravel at a hundred dollars an ounce to some of those guys if ya flash 'em your boobs and talk sweet, but I ain't sure it's such a good idea to sell my darlin's in a tittie bar. I mean I want people to buy my stuff and know it's high class." She shook the bottle of Jose Cuervo and poured two or three drops into the sink. "Oh, hell! Caffeine and tequila make ya so fun crazy. Oh, well."

"Do you have some bourbon?" Morgan asked.

"Not bourbon," she said, frowning. "It just makes ya sad and sentimental. With all that coffee, you'd just be awake all night bawlin'."

Maria opened the refrigerator door and funky, fruity cool air escaped. "How about some—" She shifted some plastic containers and bowls around, then paused. "Wonder what the hell that is?" She peeked inside a faded plastic butter container and shrugged. "Still don't know." Maria fumbled around some more and pulled out a large-bottomed green bottle. "Some sangria wine?"

"I haven't had sangria wine since—" Morgan stopped.

"Makes you silly and crazy," she said. She took a couple of mismatched wine glasses from a cabinet shelf and jutted her hip. "I promise."

"Pour it, sweetheart."

The piquant citrus burn reminded him of high school nights and summers of parked cars on deserted country roads. He smiled and lifted his glass to a toast. He leaned against the counter and heard the clatter of dishes falling, jarring and settling into the sink. They laughed and Maria touched her glass to his.

"Hey mister, go sit on the couch," she said. "I've got more to show you."

As Chester sipped the sangria in the living room, he heard from the workshop the click-click-clicking of a safe's tumbler, the opening of a heavy door, and it closing. Maria returned carrying a small, velvet lined tray, and a long, narrow box. She fell into him as she sat on the couch.

"I left my wine out there," she said, getting back up. Silver stars glittered on the black velvet of the tray. Chester picked up the smallest one, held it in the light, and admired its tiny detail.

"That's to wear if ya got anything pierced." She settled back onto the couch. "Surprise me," she said.

Chester shook his head. "Don't care for needles much."

"Me neither," she admitted, "just about had to morphine me to get my ears pierced."

Morgan's hands touched the small silver pieces and he remembered how he was here. A gruesome murder, a cover-up if there was any investigation, and the people of Kiowa Heights always insisting they asked no questions.

"You figured it the first night we met," Maria said. "You said I wore these earrings for Tanya, and I do, and I'm goin' to keep wearing 'em for her, too. For as long as it takes. This whole line is because of Star." She took the tray and set it on the coffee table. "Here, open the box. It's for you."

Chester lifted the lid and saw a silver-clasped bolo tie, a star to match the design of Maria's earrings in its center. "How kind," he said, lifting it from the box. "It's beautiful."

Maria smiled and blushed.

Chester admired the western tie. "You shouldn't give such fine gifts. It's worth a lot of money, I'm sure."

"You're the only one who's steppin' over the line to do right by my little blondie, my best friend. I made it for ya, but I didn't know if I'd ever be able to give it to ya."

Chester saw Maria's reflection in the shiny medallion, distorted by the outline of the star.

"If it was me who was gone," she said, "and Tanya who stayed, she'd sing a song for ya."

Chester leaned over and kissed her on the cheek.

"You can do better than that," she said.

Chester kissed her wet, full lips and lost himself for a moment in their softness. Maria put her hands on his shoulders, pulled away, and shook her head. "Knew you could do better," she said, smiled. Her hand reached for her glass of sangria and before she took a big swig, she mumbled, "Goddamit!"

Chester fingered his bolo tie and said: "This really is a great gift, especially the reason you gave it."

"I've got something else to show you," she said, taking him by the hand, and helping him off the sofa. She giggled and stopped. "'Cain't forget our crazy wine."

They walked arm in arm to the sliding glass doors. "This is why I rent this little old house and drive twenty-five miles to work every day." Maria opened the door and they walked out onto a concrete patio. Silver-dusted stars lit the rolling hills of the Oklahoma prairie. "Fuck the peacocks. Look at that sky!"

Chester let her arm drop and crossed the grass to a barbed wire fence. Maria rushed to catch up with him. A night wind rattled the dying prairie bluestem.

"Look out into the universe," he said. "We're seeing things that have already happened. That little twinkling light might be a star, burned out, and gone twenty-five million years ago, but its image reaches us just now, tonight. The light from this planet earth is reflecting into space as we stand here. As that light travels, it becomes the measurable past—not just seconds or minutes—but days, weeks, months, and years. You know what that means? It means the past is still happening out there somewhere, maybe not in a way that can be discerned, but as real as our light and images."

"And somewhere Tanya's still singing," Maria said, her voice still. "Maybe the past is still happenin', but not out there. Here." She shivered. "Chester, I'm cold."

He put his arm around her, felt her flesh, felt her youth, and sighed.

In the prairie darkness, a coyote howled.

Chapter Thirty-Eight

An empty large-bottomed wine bottle sat on the dresser of Maria's cramped bedroom. Chester Morgan and the young woman perched against the edge of the mattress of an old, high four-poster bed. His hands were on the flesh of the upper rise of her hips; hers, on his bare swimmer's shoulders. Their lips touched, kissed, pulled, played. Her jeans, unbuttoned; his pants, entwined around his feet.

"Hey," Maria said, drawing back, "I almost forgot I's supposed to tip ya." She slipped off her jeans, dropped off the bed, and wobbled, rolling to the door where her purse hung on the knob. Morgan focused, watching as she bent to get money out of her billfold.

"I know I've got one," she said. "They must think I own a bill changer when I go to the bank."

Chester sensed the air against his flesh and looked at his pants and feet. He drawled, "This is ridiculous." He lifted one foot to put over his knee and the other foot pulled up behind it. "Guess that won't work," he said, unfolding his legs and struggling to unknot and slip off his pants. "There's gotta be more dignified ways to get undressed."

"What kind of stripper would I be if I cain't even dig up a single dollar bill?" Maria said, rooting around in her purse with this and that falling out unnoticed to the floor. "Ah, found one." She swayed back over to the bed and pushed herself up onto the mattress. She stuffed the cash in the shiny fabric of her bra.

"Now stand up here and look at me," she said. "Ya don't have to dance or nuthin'. Just imagine there's loud 'lectronic music playin', it's smoky, and there's black lights 'n' mirrors in here."

Chester stood without shoes, pants, shirt. He laughed and Maria took the one dollar bill from her décolletage, slipped it into his plaid boxers, and lingered.

"Either you're happy to see me," she said and touched, "or we've just found Elvis." She kissed him with sloppy, wet lips.

Chester reached to embrace her, but instead let his arms drop. He sighed, silent for a moment. "I'm old enough to be—"

Maria grabbed his hips and eased him to her. "Besides you, who the fuck cares?" He felt her cool, moist skin and he held her against his chest and beating heart. She sighed, turned her head away, and muttered quietly, "Godamit!"

They rolled onto the four poster bed, frenzied and tearing off the rest of each other's clothes. Lips locked to lips. Hands, fingers roaming, fondling, caressing sinew and flesh, moving into the soft white waves of the sheets.

Urging, aching, pulsing.

Yearning, wild, inviting, melting.

Rolling, moving, shaking.

Naked bodies dancing under thin cotton sheets and a worn quilt.

"Hust m mmmonit," Maria said, almost biting off her tongue, or his. Loosening her lips and catching breath, she said, "Just a minute." She put her hand at the top of the covers spread over Chester's chest. "Ya mind if I take a good long look? Promise ya won't get mad?"

"Why not?"

Maria threw back the sheets and the hand-stitched quilt and stared at his nude body. "Oooohohooo!" And then laughed, really laughed.

Chester felt himself sinking. "What? What? I know I'm—"

She put her finger to his lip to shush him, but kept laughing. "You men!" she snorted. "Ya got names for 'em; ya give 'em lives of their own; but, just see, it's crazy lookin'. Always are, always have been, I guess."

The attorney chuckled and shook his head.

"Hey, it ain't your fault cause God made men look ridiculous naked," she said, propping her head up and looking at him. She giggled and laughed some more. "Cause you look ridiculous, and sweet, and magnificent. Come here." She kissed and mouthed his neck, pressed her heavy breasts against him, and lightning touched the thick flesh at the juncture of his thighs. Chester laughed.

He touched the corner of Maria's eye and brushed her mussed hair away from her face. "Let me admire you," he whispered. He ran his finger over her cheek, neck, and circled a tiny beauty spot on her shoulder. He raised her hand over her head and floated his lips, tongue along the underside of her arm.

One, then the other. She shivered, resisted, relaxed, murmuring soothing sound.

He nibbled at her neck and then down, down to rose bud blooms on rises of white satin; ripe strawberries sinking into soft ice cream. He touched, caressed, teased. She quivered and gasped.

"Please," she said, entwining her fingers through his hair and squeezing him tightly to her chest. He nuzzled and kissed—one, the other, both—and felt her pleasure. Moments, slow and rich, passed and her fingers pushed down his muscled back. Chester's body loosened and a deep primitive sound uttered from his lips.

His hands slid to her narrow waist, then to widening hips. His lips lingered over her tight stomach. She giggled, muscles rippling, shaking. His fingers danced to black damp forest and to her spreading center.

"Let's ride 'em, cowboy!" she said, twisting to turn off the lamp, and easing him onto his back and straddling. With each opening, she moaned. With each descent, she laughed.

"Oh, my God," he groaned, hands enclosing, kneading, feeling.

Hips rode on hips. Breasts touched at the hair of masculine chest, then spacious nipple rubbed nipple, and at each beat, Maria giggled or moaned. More and more and more. Garbled words, sounds, gasps. Chester smelled her scent, felt heat within him flow and contract, rendering control powerless. Her laughter stopped, turned to deep sighs and dark sound, then hot, rapid breath against Chester's neck, her thick black hair across his face. Her movement jolted to rhythmic jerks; over, over and over until a panther shriek, bursting release, and collapse onto Chester's expanding, contracting chest.

Not yet, he thought, please, pressing her hips solidly to him, and biting his lip. Not yet, not yet. He gasped, held.

Maria let her arms sink around him and they breathed and breathed.

"It's been a long time," she mumbled, kissing him lightly on his cheek and neck.

"*You* think it's been a long time," he said. His hips bucked, aching, wanting, yearning.

Maria slipped off and straddled his chest. She turned to look behind her and patted. In a breathy voice, she said "Hold on, buster. The night's just started." Her hands massaged Chester's face and head. Her fingers reached into the tight muscles of his neck, shoulders, touching deep and forgotten places. Then further into his arms, hands, chest, hips.

"Maria ... Maria ..." A mantra as touch, smell, sight, taste, and sound merged. "Maria ... Maria ... Maria ..." He reached for her, all of her, touching her glowing skin, at once cool and warm, soft and firm. Maria turned abruptly, pressing her hands down the muscle of his thighs and calves. Chester mindlessly played with the globe of her hips and traced the curves down her long silky legs.

"How can this be?" he mumbled. "How can this be?"

She touched and teased deep between his legs. A warming peace murmured through him, then a sudden surge as her hands enclosed his veined branch. He thrust and thrashed, alive and vital, commanding control.

"Now," he said, pulling her to him. "Now."

"Not yet, honey," she whispered.

"The night's just started."

* * *

Slatted, amber light awakened Chester. The smooth sheets and soft mattress weren't his own. He opened his eyes to a small, feminine bedroom and wondered where he was. He closed his eyes and realized the wonder of the night hadn't been a dream. He grinned, amazed and pleased. Sharp fumes of burning tobacco drifted in the air and Chester heard a sniffle. Maria sat propped against pillows, the worn hand-stitched quilt pulled tightly across her chest. Tears trickled down her face.

Chester kissed her cheek and tasted salt. "Was it that bad?" he asked.

She shook her head and bit her lip.

Morgan rolled onto his back and looked at the ceiling. No court this morning, no office appointments. I'm here. I should call the office. Too late already for the morning work-out at the YMCA pool.

"Just happens sometimes," Maria said, her voice muffled and cracking.

"I can call a cab and get out of here, if that would be better," Chester said.

The woman with the midnight hair and sapphire eyes slid her hand under the cover and played with the hair on his swimmer's chest. "That'd be the last thing I'd want this mornin'," she said, punching out her cigarette.

Chester pulled her to him and felt her wet tears on his shoulder. Maria's narrow rib cage expanded and relaxed in his arms. He kissed her head and stroked her thick hair.

"Chester, even if ya find out cold who did it," she said, "Tanya's still goin' to be gone."

"I know."

"I'd like to call her, talk with her," she said. "Tell her about last night." She giggled through her stopped-up nose. "All the details, not just the extra good parts."

Chester rubbed her back. "I would have loved to have heard her sing," he said.

Maria lifted her head and sniffed. "You mean you've never heard her sing?"

"How could I? She was gone before I knew her."

"Come with me," she said, wiping her eyes, and crawling out from under the covers. "It's colder in the winter out here, but cooler in the summer." She eased into a blue terrycloth robe.

Morgan watched.

"Come on," she said. "The mornin' bite'll get the blood flowin'." She looked in the dresser mirror. "This is crazy." She pressed a tissue to her eyes, her nose. "I look like hell."

Chester got out of bed and wrapped himself in the worn quilt. He held her hand as they walked quietly down the hall to the living room.

"If ya get me some hot, black coffee," he said, "I'll stay with ya all day." He flopped onto the corduroy couch. He could see that Maria's eyes were red.

"Just hold on a minute." She crouched down and dug through a box on the floor next to the stereo. "About three or four months ago, Star got herself a demo made. Oh, she was good. She wanted to go to Nashville so bad and you ain't never heard her."

"No."

Maria placed a compact disc in the player. From the black speakers came the wild-hearted voice of an Oklahoma country girl lost in the city and singing of loneliness and forgotten dreams.

Morgan wept.

Chapter Thirty-Nine

Marylin stopped her car in her garage's driveway. Looking across the yard to her house, she could see russet and gold leaves scattered and piled up again. Morgan won't mind if I take an early lunch, she thought. The doctor's appointment had taken more time than planned. Besides, her boss hadn't gotten to the office yet that day anyway. Or even phoned. That's what Shawn had said when she called as she left the medical complex and Shawn wasn't joking. Not this time. Morgan not at work? And, no telephone call, no court appearance, and no outside appointment? Marylin didn't like that. Chester Morgan had warned her to be careful. Had he ignored his own admonition? She got out of her car.

A man stood there.

Marylin shrieked.

"Shhhhhhhhh!" he whispered, a callused stained finger at his lips. He reached to cover her mouth, but hesitated. "It's—it's OK. I-I been watching you," he said, his voice no more than a meager breath. "So you'd be O-OK. Shhhhhh!"

Marylin exhaled. "Alan."

"I didn't mean to scare you," Kinman whispered. "Never. I-I wouldn't hurt you. W-wouldn't let nobody hurt or scare y-y-you. S-s-something's not right over there." He nodded towards the house next door. Marylin's landlord's place.

"What do you mean? Murle's seeing her sister in Burns Flat until at least Friday."

"Then something's really not right," he said. "I-I'll show you, but please, keep quiet and keep out of sight." He made an awkward jerk with his hand, a direction to follow him into the alley that ran alongside her garage.

"You've been following me, haven't you, Alan?"

He stopped, looked down, and chewed on his lips.

"I-I may not be so smart, but I'll be damned if I let anyone hurt you or Mr. Morgan 'cause you're—took Tanya's case. Somebody's breakin' in next door. If'n you're scared, get in your car and go. If'n you're not, follow me. Either way I'm takin' care of you first."

"Damn it, Alan. I felt you there, behind me, not knowing who. Do you have any idea—" Marylin remembered his timid appearance in Morgan's office that first day, his reluctance to even speak in her presence, his shy looking away, but wanting to look. The newspaper clipping. The yearbook.

"I-I'm s-sorry. I-I-I didn't know ..." His eyes were shiny and sad behind his smudged glasses.

"Oh, Alan, if you're going to help someone like that, let them know." Marylin saw the roof of her neighbor's house through the trees and tightened the purse strap at her shoulder. "Nobody messes with my friends: You or Murle. Let's go."

Alan Kinman gingerly took the legal secretary's hand and led her down the rocky alley. Overgrown honeysuckle wound in and out of the chain link fence, barricading the yards from clear view. Alan and Marylin passed her garage, then crouched and crept along the green-vined barrier until Kinman motioned them to stop. Marylin's hose were ruined; she didn't trip on her heels, but worried about balance and her skirt. Next time I'm coming back as a man, she thought. Kinman pointed to a sparsely grown area in the mass of vines and Marylin peered through.

A black, mud-caked GMC pickup with a Confederate decal shiny on its back window had its tailgate down, parked a few feet away from the out-building in Murle Mueller's backyard. The garage apartment door stood open to the place where Marylin's landlord had retrieved Tanya Everly's answering machine and where the rest of her belongings had been abandoned, except to Murle Mueller. Two large men—one tall, the other tall and obese—carried boxes and threw them carelessly onto the bed of the truck.

"Why'd 'ya think he wants all this shit," the tall man said.

"Hell if I know," said the tall and obese man, his voice high-pitched and sounding as if one nostril were stopped up. "Rich folks are different, I guess. Why, he could take himself down to the flea market down on Murray Road 'n get stuff better than this."

"You fuck brain. He could go to Paris, France and get whatever he wants," the taller man replied. He brushed one hand against the other.

"He could, but he wants this." The tall and obese man shrugged and lumbered back towards the garage apartment. "Nuthin' bothers Bob."

The men disappeared through the door.

Marylin took her cell phone from her purse and pushed nine-one-one. Alan Kinman stumbled around the alley and gathered fist-sized rocks as Marylin reported the burglary: Urgent! In progress.

THUD!

Something dropped to the bed of the truck.

THUD!

Marylin looked through the vines and saw the two men walk back into the garage apartment. She looked at her watch, took a notebook and a pen from her purse, and scribbled a few notes.

"They don't do this to make a livin'," Kinman whispered.

Marylin looked at him and raised her eyebrows.

"They're too slow," he said. "If'n they knew what they were doin', they'd be outta here so fast we'd never know they was there. Not 'till Mule got home anyways."

Marylin smiled, but said nothing. Then, "I wish the police would hurry up and get here. I should have told 'em the cameras had just gotten here from Channel Seven." She heard the men in the yard and looked through the honeysuckle leaves.

The tall man closed the tailgate. Marylin wrote down the tag number. The other man stood at the garage apartment door.

"What about this other stuff?" he squeaked in a nasal pitch.

"It's all a bunch of crap," the tall man said.

"Why not take it? Nuthin' would bother Bob about that."

"Let's get the fuck out of here."

The tall and obese man started towards the driver's door of the pickup and then stopped. "Let's make it worth our while," he sneered, and walked towards the back door of Murle Mueller's house.

Marylin started to stand up.

"No," she gasped.

Alan Kinman grabbed her arm and pulled her down. "G-go start your car now and open the passenger door and be ready to drive like hell," he said.

"What?" Marylin hesitated.

"Go!" he said, swatting her on her backside. "I'll be OK."

Marylin dashed towards her car.

The tall and obese man opened the screen door to Mueller's house.

"Leave it!" the other man said.

"It's ours, man. They ain't goin' to get us no way," the tall and obese man said, lifting a foot to kick the door in.

A volley of rocks bombarded the pickup, the tall man, the tall and obese man. The rear window and the shiny Confederate Flag decal fractured into tiny silver slivers.

Alan Kinman raced up the alley and hopped into Marylin's car. "Get outta here fast as ya can!"

Marylin shifted the car into reverse, pushed it into drive, and raced, raced into the anonymous traffic of Kiowa Heights.

Fifteen minutes later, Marylin and Alan Kinman drove into the driveway of Murle Mueller's house. The GMC pickup truck was gone. The back door secure. Shards of fractured glass glittered in the driveway. When Marylin and Kinman looked into the garage apartment, the make-shift clothes rack was empty. The shiny sheer negligees and diaphanous gowns and strange lingerie, gone. The stacks of boxes, gone. The touchstones of Tanya's life, vanished. What remained belonged to a different generation, to a different life.

Stepping back out into the autumn sunlight, Marylin said: "Alan, I wish you wouldn't have done that. I'm scared. I'm really scared. What if they come back?"

"I'll be here. I won't let nobody hurt you."

A half-hour later, the police arrived.

Chapter Forty

Chester Morgan wiped the crumbs from his chin and waited for Marylin to finish. A dusty northwest breeze stirred and Morgan imagined high plains farmers planting winter wheat.

Marylin had packed gourmet sack lunches, and she and Morgan had eaten them on a bench in the Community Sculpture Garden, a small park in downtown Vivia next to the Key Petroleum Building. Marylin had waited several days to tell her boss about the burglary at Murle Mueller's house. Why, she didn't know. To get things in order? To avoid criticism? She had made exotic sandwiches and cut fresh fruit and brewed black tea for this outdoor meal.

Local artists had furnished the garden. A stainless steel star burst reminiscent of a 1950's Las Vegas coffee shop; a glob of something that looked like welded chicken wire; a giant copper sombrero whirling with a child's tug; the Little People of the Cherokees formed in terra cotta figurines; and other three dimensional art spread over grassy knolls and in front of park benches. The Vivia Arts Foundation had ripped up an asphalt parking lot and replaced it with this place of peaceful gathering through an anonymous gift. Chester Morgan looked at the Key Petroleum high rise. He knew who the anonymous donor was.

The image shimmered then burned and would not fade.

The lawyer folded his paper bag and listened to Marylin tell of the two men and the garage apartment and Alan Kinman. When she finished, he waited in silence and then said, "We need to move you from there. You need to be somewhere safe."

"I never run away," Marylin replied. "I'm careful, but not scared. I don't flee."

Morgan grimaced, then grinned. "How about this? I wish you hadn't called the police."

"Chester, these guys could have wiped Murle out! What was I supposed to do?"

"There were two men with a truck at someone else's direction at the place where Tanya's things were stored—"

"And feet away from my friend's house," Marylin interrupted. "Antiques, heirlooms. Who knows what else? Even for an insurance claim, there has to be a police report. It was happening while we were there!"

"I'm not criticizing you," Morgan said. "You did what the circumstances required. I just wish you hadn't."

"I just wish those rednecks hadn't been there at all." Marylin swept her lap with her hand sharply and stood up, not speaking further.

"Thanks for the lunch," Chester said.

She didn't reply.

They walked back towards the office in silence. A pack of men in golf shirts and khakis passed by. Sweet bitter smells escaped a Vietnamese carry-out and evaporated into the diesel belch of a city bus. A car with vibrating speakers disturbed the murmuring hum of traffic.

"Tell me more about the two men," Morgan said.

"They were both tall. Wal-Mart and gun show dressed. One was tall and fat. Honky-tonk white trash, if you pardon."

"Any distinguishing features?"

Marylin thought. "I didn't see—wouldn't want to see—any tattoos, but I'm sure they both had them."

Two short women in floral dresses and thick tennis shoes marched past them. Marylin's heels clicked against the sidewalk.

"The one who was fat," she continued. "He had this high-pitched, nasal voice. Almost like a teenaged boy after his first pimples, waiting for his next growth spurt."

A huge man in a shiny brown suit stood at the next street corner, a thick book open in his ebony hands. "These are the final days!" he bellowed. "You steal from the poor and build your idols for own self-gratification. You prostitute yourselves and sacrifice your own victims. Repent, my friends, for the day of the Lord is at hand!" He shuffled from foot to foot, moved from side to side, and a moaning song came from his lips.

Chester and Marylin kept walking.

"What did the police tell you?" Morgan asked.

"'We get a burglary call on the average of every thirty minutes. We don't have the manpower to fully investigate every one we get. They are difficult cases to prove even with the evidence. Blah, blah, blah.'"

"Yeah, but you got a license plate number."

"The officer took that and said he would see what he could find out."

"Did you hear from him?"

"Yes. I've got something to show you."

The two of them entered the art-deco lobby of the DeSoto Building and rode the elevator to the fifth floor with Madge, the elevator operator, ever listening to talk radio on her boom box. Once back in the office, they went to Marylin's desk. On her credenza, a multitude of children's faces smiled, frowned, squinted, looked goofy, grinned. Pictures. All given by clients, family, friends, and others.

"The officer called me here at the office that afternoon and told me the pickup had been reported stolen."

Marylin pushed a paper across her desk to Morgan. A fax from the Oklahoma Tax Commission reporting vehicle registration. The attorney looked at it:

GMC Pickup. VIN: 2G1XF62D739403569. License Plate: VVZ-642 The Owners: Robert and/or Darlene Fulcher.

"The dude with the high voice," Marylin said. "He had this phrase he mindlessly repeated: 'Nuthin' bothers Bob.' That truck wasn't stolen."

"Did you get the name of the officer who investigated the burglary?"

Marylin took a business card from her purse and gave it to Morgan.

"Make a copy of that card and put it in Tanya Everly's file. Type up a memo about what happened and put a copy of the vehicle registration in there, too."

Morgan went into his office and began thumbing through Tanya Everly's file. "This officer an old guy? And his partner, a young one?"

Marylin came into his office. "Yeah. Why do you ask?"

Chester held the file open to the untraceable Vivia Police Department fax received weeks before.

"Why do you suppose they needed a Special Investigative Team to check out a run-of-the-mill burglary?"

Chapter Forty-One

"You want to sue Randolph Harrison? William Harrison's son?"

Two women sat across the desk from Chester Morgan. The younger woman wore a sheath of teal and gray geometric patterns. The other, a faded navy suit. The younger one was tall and slender. The other, short and solid. They both had the same eyes but the younger's flashed lightning energy. The other's glowed dim with experience and disappointment. A heavy geranium scent of perfume spread and lingered in the sterile office air.

The older woman nodded.

"Attorney Morgan, you must understand how important this is to my Aunt," Tiawanna Jones, the younger woman, said.

Although Morgan had represented her for over ten years, Tiawanna declined to call him anything other than "Attorney Morgan." This was the first time he had met Althea Willis, the older woman in the faded navy suit.

"You see," the younger woman continued, "people of Aunt Althea's age were not brought up to demand respect. This is the first time she's had a mind to."

Randolph Harrison, Morgan thought. He remembered the probate hearings concerning the elder Harrison's lost will. He remembered the well built man with the wavy charcoal hair, the casual but elegant suit, and the too-even tan. Morgan knew the stories about the lay-offs and the restructuring at Key Petroleum since William Harrison's death. Now Althea Willis wanted to sue Randolph Harrison, the man running the company.

"So tell me why you want to file a lawsuit against Randolph Harrison," Morgan said.

"I worked as the Harrisons' housekeeper, cook, and maid for a number of years. There at the home in Oak Hills," Althea Willis said.

"Thirty-five years to be precise, Attorney Morgan," Tiawanna Jones interrupted.

"Yes, Mister William Harrison. I worked for him for over thirty-five years. You could not find a finer man. Of course, you know ..."

You could not find a better or safer swimmer either, the attorney thought.

The image seared and would not fade.

"I know," Morgan said. "I know."

"It would not dignify myself to talk about Harrison family matters." Althea Willis paused. "Now that Mister Harrison is dead and Mister Randolph has done what he has done, I have to do what I have to do."

Marylin looked up from her stenographer's pad and subtlety winked at Chester Morgan. Marylin knew and appreciated strong resolve. The attorney folded his hands on his desk and stared into the dim eyes of Althea Willis.

"Well, Mister Morgan, they's should have just left that Randolph at the hospital the day he was born. That boy done nothin' but grieve Mister Harrison his whole life. Everything he done was just to get money out of his father. Just like he thought it was always all his when it weren't."

"Aunt Althea, Mister Morgan is a busy, busy man. You just need to tell him what Randolph Harrison did to you."

"That's okay, Tiawanna," the lawyer said. "Let her tell her own story. We have plenty of time."

"Of course, that boy's mother, she was a wild one. She just got up one day and left Mister Harrison. Took that baby girl, Jocelyn, and was just gone. She didn't want nothing of his, just to be gone. Poor Mister Harrison never recovered, no sir."

Morgan remembered Cassie and the day she left. Where had her last postcard come from? Vermont? South Carolina? Wyoming? How long had it been? Two years? Three? He told himself he didn't remember, but he did.

"'I thought they—the daughter at least—might have come back for the service if nothing else," Morgan said.

Althea Willis shrugged. "I ain't seen her since she was just a little girl. Mister Harrison neither. He had himself a private investigating service track her down last year, but he didn't write or phone Miss Jocelyn, so far as I knows."

"William Harrison never remarried, did he?" Morgan asked. "Did he have a live-in, a woman friend, perhaps?"

Althea shook her head. "He had a lady about this past year, yes sir, but she didn't never come around. The happiest Mister Harrison had been for a long time."

"What did she do? What was her name?"

"All's I know is that she was an entertainer." Althea Willis stopped.

"I don't see why these personal things make any difference to what I'm here about."

"I found Mister Harrison's body in the water at the YMCA. It's really bothered me. He was a good man, great swimmer. Would you excuse me for a minute?" he said, getting up and leaving the room.

Chester Morgan walked to Shawn's desk. She had *The New York Times* crossword puzzle spread out in front of her and a pink pencil at the edge of her glossy lips.

"Shawn, in a probate case, you have to notify the heirs in writing of their right to object to the admission of a will. All you have to do is swear you mailed the notice. Call the court clerk's office, have them pull the probate file for William Harrison's estate, and get the address where Randolph Harrison said he mailed the notice to his sister Jocelyn."

"Do you know a seven letter word for *pointless*?"

"Shawn, do it now."

"Why?"

"Sometimes you just know and you act." Morgan walked towards his office and turned. "Have them fax a copy of that notice, too. Do it now."

He heard laughter as he opened his door to his office. Marylin had charmed another new client. He nodded, sat at his desk and recognized the familiar strong scent of Tiawanna Jones' perfume.

"Pardon me for the interruption." Morgan picked up a pen and put it to his legal pad. "Tell me, Mrs. Willis, why you believe you have a lawsuit against Randolph Harrison?"

The sturdy, short woman sat straight up in her chair. "If Mister Harrison lived, I had a check for the rest of my life. Mister Harrison died and Mister Randolph just up and fired me."

Chester Morgan looked at the woman. Sixty years old at the youngest and maybe even seventy. An eighth grade education, perhaps. Dignity learned, intrinsic dignity in who she was. William Harrison *would* have provided for her for the rest of her life.

"There are some things we know that the law makes us prove," the lawyer said. "Did you have a written contract with either William Harrison or Randolph Harrison?"

"No, sir. I didn't needs one. I knew."

"Did William Harrison ever give you anything in writing stating that he would pay you a salary for the rest of your life if you did something in return? Or, did Randolph Harrison?"

"I told you. You didn't have to have nothin' with Mister Harrison; you just knew."

"I understand. What you know is not always enough. Did William Harrison or Randolph Harrison ever tell you that you would receive a check for the rest of your life?"

The older woman sighed. "Not in words, no sir."

Tiawanna interrupted. "Didn't they make you think you were going to be taken care of if you stayed with them?"

"If you worked for Mister Harrison, you knews you was gonna be taken care of."

Morgan laid his open hand on his desk. "When you go to court, the question is: What can you prove? He paid you? Every two weeks? And, you could have quit at anytime you wanted?"

Althea Willis nodded. "But why would I wanna do that?"

The telephone buzzed. The attorney picked up the receiver.

"Here it is, Chest: Sixteen B Street, Seattle, Washington 98301. The fax is coming through."

"Thanks, Shawn." Morgan got up from his desk. "Pardon me, again." He walked to Shawn's desk, took the note she had written, and went into the library.

He looked at the gold volumes lined neatly on the shelves and took a deep breath. The dusty old books, the smell of the law. Would the lawyers who knew precedents only from computer screens remember the tradition and recognize the past? He found his law school alumni directory and looked up the telephone number of Bill Winters, Seattle.

The receptionist told Chester Morgan the attorney was not available.

"Interrupt him and tell him Chester Morgan is on the telephone. Tell him I still have the pictures of him with the goat."

A few minutes later, a cheerful tenor bass came through. "Hey, Morgan, what's going on?"

"I don't have much time. I'm going to fax you a document. Take it to Sixteen B Street there in Seattle and give it to a woman named Jocelyn. Ask her if she has ever seen it before and if she has, tell her: 'Thanks and have a good day.' If she hasn't, tell her to get an attorney in Vivia, Oklahoma, as quickly as possible."

"What's going on?"

"I have clients waiting. I'll let you know later. Please, just do this for me."

There was silence. Then, "Sixteen B Street, huh? I can get someone to track that down, I guess."

Morgan stood straight. "I need for you to do it right now."

"Gosh. I'm right in the middle of something here. Can it wait two or three hours?"

"Bill, who did you rely on to get through Property I in law school?"

Winters sighed. "That was fifteen, eighteen years ago, Chester. You don't forget anything, do you? That's the primeval past."

"Who said the past is past? Do what you can, as soon as you can."

Morgan stopped at Shawn's desk. "One of the beneficiaries in William Harrison's estate was a charity. Get the name and address and find out everything you can about it."

Shawn rolled her big green eyes.

"Now."

When Morgan returned to his interview with Althea Willis and Tiawanna Jones, the lawyer asked, "Do you remember where Jocelyn Harrison lived when that private investigator found her? Was it Seattle?"

"It was someplace that started with an *S*," Mrs. Willis said. She put her finger to chin and looked around the room. "It definitely started with *S* and it was someplace up north." She stopped. "Spokane." She smiled big. "It was Spokane. Mister Harrison said two or three times he just ought to fly up to Spokane and see her."

"Are you sure about that?"

"Just as sure as the Cottonwood River is wet."

"I apologize for the disruptions," Morgan said. "Mrs. Willis, the law doesn't provide a remedy for every wrong. A person can be mistreated but there may not be any recourse. I don't see that you have a breach of contract lawsuit against—"

"Attorney Morgan, she ain't interested in no breach of contract. This is discrimination. That's what this is," Tiawanna Jones said.

Morgan looked at his longtime client and bit his lower lip. Like him, Tiawanna Jones watched out for the people in her life. Her family. Her friends. She had an advocate's spirit and meant the words she said.

"We are going to talk about discrimination. It's an easy claim to make but harder to prove," the attorney said. "Why did Randolph Harrison terminate your employment?"

"He says he's going to remodel the place and he don't need nobody to be under his feet when he moves in."

"Did he replace—"

"They didn't replace her, Attorney Morgan," Tiawanna said. "They just brought in some trailers and started tearing stuff out of there."

Marylin took her legal pad, put it into both hands, and leaned forward. "Mister Morgan is asking whether someone of a different religion, ethnic background, race, age, sex, or whatever, took over your job."

Both women shook their heads.

Morgan pulled at his ear lobe and then said, "The Oklahoma Human Rights Commission investigates complaints of discrimination, but even so, certain requirements must be met. Were you an employee of Key Petroleum?"

Mrs. Willis shook her head.

"When you were paid, did your check have the name of a company on it or did it simply say William Harrison?"

"It says 'William Harrison, Household Account'. He just pay the bills round the place with that."

"How many other employees did William Harrison have at his home?"

"None."

"None?"

Chester Morgan remembered the gardener and gardener's assistant who testified they had witnessed William Harrison's will last July, the one supposedly lost. He remembered a tall man and a tall and obese man with a pitched nasal voice. Both stated under oath they worked for William Harrison and one of them said he had talked to William Harrison the morning of his death, had talked about that lost will. "What do you mean?"

"I means I was the only one who worked for him."

"Didn't he have a couple of men—a gardener or maintenance man and an assistant?"

"A long time ago. Maybe fifteen or twenty years, but he used a service for the yard. They came out once a week and did what they had to do and goes."

"Was anyone from the lands keeping service there at the house that morning, before William Harrison went to the Y and drowned?"

"They never there that early."

Tiawanna Jones looked at her watch. Marylin nodded at her and motioned it would just be a minute.

"Mrs. Willis, think, did you ever see two tall white men. One is really fat. Both in their mid-thirties. Did you ever see men like that on the work crew?"

"Oh, heavens no! They were all Mexicans. Had been at least for the last two or three years. Now what does this got to do with my case?"

"Nothing, really. The Human Rights Commission won't investigate a discrimination claim unless there are fifteen employees or more. It would probably not do you much good to file a complaint with them."

"Attorney Morgan, she wants to sue Randolph Harrison."

"Plenty of other people want to as well, I'm sure, but there has to be a legal basis for a lawsuit. Based on what I've heard, I'm afraid there is just no recourse. I'm confident William Harrison would have made financial arrangements for you, but he's dead and I see no obligation on the part of his estate or on the part of Randolph Harrison. You can consult another attorney if you like. Another attorney might have a different view. Might see something I don't."

"But I hear on TV all the time where peoples sue for all these millions of dollars," Althea Willis said.

Chester knew the woman would be lucky to find a minimum wage job, would be fortunate not to do backbreaking manual labor. He hated this part of his work, telling someone for whom events had destroyed hope that the law provided no hope. Still, he spoke the truth.

"Mrs. Willis, old defense lawyers say, 'The only thing it takes to file a lawsuit is one hundred fifty dollars—the court costs— some paper, and a typewriter'—I guess they say computer now—

'that can type a lot of zeroes.' Do you understand? I'm sorry for you, Mrs. Willis. I'm sorry for what has happened to you and what you will now face, but a lawsuit would simply lead to more disappointment."

After Althea Willis and Tiawanna Jones left, Morgan worked through the papers on his desk. Letters, court pleadings, contracts, the words and documents that are the practice of law. When it worked, Morgan read and knew incisively, intuitively how and if to respond. This afternoon, though, his work was shallow and distracted. Something was happening in the case that had become indistinct from the shadows and light of his own life. He did not know what, but he knew as a mother would who wakes in the middle of the night to check an infant for no other reason than she knows.

The telephone rang.

"Hey, Morgan," the cheerful tenor voice said. "Thanks for interrupting me with the impossible."

"What do you mean?"

"I got your fax and checked the map to find out where the hell B Street is. Guess what? The Seattle map shows no B Street."

Morgan moved to the edge of his chair. "It makes it hard to deliver to Jocelyn Harrison that notice of right to object, doesn't it?"

"Yeah. Just to be sure, I called the local title company I use, and guess what?"

"There is no B Street in Seattle."

"That's right. Hey, Chester, what's this about?"

"A brother not wanting his sister to make a claim to an oilman's estate and a girl whose voice could make God weep."

"Sorry I couldn't help," Bill Winters said. "You know those years in Oklahoma for law school were the best of my life."

"The prairie skies can always make you see more than what you believe," Morgan said. "Thanks, Bill, this is one of those cases that remind you why you first went to law school. Let me know when I can help you in Vivia."

Chester hung up the phone. He remembered Randolph Harrison's attorney seeking to have the lost Last Will and Testament of William Harrison admitted into probate. Morgan remembered the legal assistant whose body movements told the truth and her words that did not. He remembered the two witnesses to the lost Will, confused whether one was a maintenance engineer or gardener but the other knowing that he was the assistant. Two men, both tall. One tall and obese who talked with a nasal voice. He remembered Judge Powers had asked the sharp question: "Did you notify William Harrison's daughter of her right to object to the admission of this will?"

The response: "Notice had been mailed to Jocelyn Harrison at her last known address."

Morgan had tested the latter and learned truth. He looked at the certificate hanging on the wall that recited his oath as an attorney: "...to do no falsehood or consent that any be done in court and upon knowing of any to give knowledge thereof to the judges of the court or some one of them, that it may be reformed ..."

It was no mistake, and he would give knowledge, but when?

Marylin tapped-tapped at his door. She wore a silky scarlet dress. Her head was tilted with question. Her look, tentative.

"Boss, do you have just a minute?"

"For you, always."

Marylin sat in the chair across his desk and smoothed her dress across her lap.

"Boss—" She hesitated. "You always look so sharp. You wear nice suits. Your ties accent them just right. Your hair combed. A smooth shave. You always look as an attorney ought to look. It makes me so proud."

"Thanks. I have to complement you, the best dressed legal secretary in Vivia."

Marylin looked down. "Well, Boss ... I don't know ... well, it's very pretty and everything, but Boss, a bolo tie just doesn't go with a Brooks Brothers suit!"

Morgan put his fingers on the tie's shining star and knew a single dollar bill rested in a matching money clip in his pocket. "It's a gift. What's that you always say, Marylin? A gift's power comes from the spirit with which it is received, not just from the spirit with which it is given? It's a gift." He turned and looked out the window. "I've about decided that Brooks Brothers suits don't go with Oklahoma anyway."

Shawn's voice came through the speaker on the telephone: "Chest, that charity you wanted to know about is called United Oklahomans for American Values and its mailing address is Kurt Hale's home. Oh, and by the way, Wally Jackson of *The Vivia Daily Sentinel* is on line one."

Morgan picked up the phone and Marylin left the room.

The reporter said, "Wilbanks has gotten, he says, 'an exclusive' on the Red Strike affair and he's given it to me to work. He wants a story."

"Tell Wilbanks to write his own story, or is he the guy who goes to all of the society affairs to convince the Vivia establishment that you all aren't a bunch of rabid Democrats?"

"He's the Executive Editor. He doesn't have to write anything. I do. Let's talk about Theodore Lauren."

The Red Strike Affair had made national news a few years after Morgan started practice in Vivia. Theodore Lauren, a geophysicist who wore European-cut suits and gold jewelry, had set up a number of oil and gas limited partnerships that returned large profits and provided investors substantial tax breaks. Lauren had persuaded the young and too rich from California to New York to put their money into the Red Strike drilling programs. Red Strike collapsed when it was discovered the huge profits came from the other investors' monies and the oil properties were, at best, marginal. When Lauren tried to pay off a government regulator, every large accounting and legal firm in Vivia became embroiled in litigation.

"This is what I've got, Morgan. Our source says you were the first attorney to approve of Lauren's drilling programs, and, had you not made that first approval, your law firm would have refused the Red Strike legal work and the whole scheme would have been derailed at the outset."

"Who's Wilbanks' source?" Morgan asked.

"I can't tell you. You know that. I can't do that. We have to protect our sources and the law won't make us tell you."

"That's all bullshit, Wally, whoever your source is, and you know it. I was right out of law school when my firm did that work. I had nothing to do with it. You can figure out the date of the first Red Strike drilling program and the date I left that firm. I wasn't even there when the first partnerships were sold. I met Theodore Lauren once and didn't like him or his type. It was a case of someone's sense of smell being overpowered by greed."

"There are a lot people who don't think greed is particularly bad, Chester, and they are pretty self-righteous when deprived. We have a copy of the first bill your law firm sent to Red Strike and your name is all over it."

Morgan knew the advice he gave clients: Never answer a question about a document until you see it. Still, he said, "That law firm had one of the first comprehensive computer billing systems in the region. A senior partner thought he was an accounting/software guru, tried to create his own program, and the clients rarely got an accurate invoice. Created all kinds of hell. The fact that my name is on that statement is not surprising. If any bill from that law firm during that time was correct, *that* would be a surprise."

"Wilbanks thinks this is a good story, and he swings a pretty big dick around here. He's going to do what he can to publish it," Jackson said.

"Ten law firms and five accounting firms have been sued over the Red Strike Affair," Morgan replied. "One or two of the cases are still going on and this scandal took place twelve or thirteen years ago. There's a whole room at the federal courthouse where the Red Strike documents are kept. Hundreds of depositions have been taken. I have never been sued, never given a deposition. I've never even been served with a subpoena. You can be assured if there was any culpability on my part, my name would have shown up on a lawsuit years ago. Who's your source?"

"Honestly I can't tell you."

Morgan stood up and said loudly, "Listen, you tell Wilbanks and every other editor down there I will fight until the day I die to protect the newspaper's right to print what it wants, but you can also tell them I know the law of defamation; I have a hundred and fifty bucks, some paper, and I own a typewriter that can type a lot of zeroes." Morgan slammed down the phone. The young and too rich twelve or thirteen years ago; that's what Randolph Harrison would have been then. Chester Morgan picked up the phone, pressed a button and called Shawn and Marylin to his office.

When they gathered around his desk, Morgan said, "It's time to file Alan Kinman's lawsuit for the writ of mandamus, for compliance with the Oklahoma Open Records Act, to see what our police chief has to say about Tanya Everly's missing incident report."

Chapter Forty-Two

Several weeks later, Chester Morgan sat at the table in his office library. A few books lay open. In front of him were two stacks of papers and a legal pad. The night was black, and the telephone had quit ringing.

Morgan had filed *Alan Kinman, Plaintiff, versus Kurt Hale, Chief of Police of the Vivia City Police Department, Defendant,* after his client, too, had requested the incident report regarding Tanya Everly's death. Same story, except different ending. This time, Orin Hightower, the officer in charge of police records, explained the file's absence by saying an investigation was pending.

Kinman's lawsuit demanded compliance with the Oklahoma Open Records Act and the production of the official record.

A judge would decide the case, not a jury. Morgan preferred juries even though juries sometimes disregarded the law and evidence, and sometimes he preferred them because they did. Twelve citizens provide experience and perspective—the ears, eyes, and heart that judges, cursed with lawyers minds, can lack. In Oklahoma, though, only a judge can issue an order to compel, a mandate requiring someone to perform a certain act. Thus, one elected official—a judge—would decide whether a popular appointed official—the chief of police—would be required to produce or explain Tanya Everly's missing incident report.

Fourteen pieces of paper lay in the stack on Morgan's left. Two in the stack on his right. The light in the library was golden.

Nine district judges sat in Viva County. Three handled criminal trials; five heard civil and divorce cases; and one presided over probate matters. Judicial assignments were made at random, except for probate, to insure equal distribution of work and to minimize chances of impropriety.

Every trial attorney imagines a perfect jury and the perfect jury depends on the particular facts of the case and the client. In lawsuits heard only by a judge, attorneys imagine what they do not want: a political hack; or one who does not understand that power comes from the law and not the black robe; or one who is intemperate or dense. Morgan knew what he did not want: a judge who lacked courage and integrity, who paid more attention to the law than to the witnesses and the exhibits, or who never recovered from grade school and still showed fawning deference to law enforcement officers.

Morgan thumbed through the thicker pile of papers.

The first judge assigned to *Kinman versus Hale* recused himself by written order. The first document in the bigger stack. The presiding judge of Vivia County then assigned another judge to the case. The second order. The next judge recused herself, another piece of paper, and the presiding judge made another assignment, another sheet of paper, then another withdrawal from the case, and until every district judge had recused except one: The Honorable Eldridge Powers.

Judge Powers' integrity and intelligence could not be impeached, but he was a narrow-minded slave to his peculiar interpretation of the law. As the only probate judge in Vivia County, it had been years since he had heard a civil case. Powers hadn't even been a possibility Morgan had considered. The attorney straightened the fourteen pages, the fourteen orders.

If Morgan had been the presiding judge, Eldridge Powers would have been the last judge assigned, too.

Two documents lay in the smaller stack, both orders granted by Eldridge Powers in Alan Kinman's lawsuit without the benefit of oral argument. The City Attorney had sought to limit discovery, the law sanctioned method of investigating a civil case before actual trial. Allowing Kinman the opportunity to obtain documents or statements under oath, the City Attorney had pleaded in her brief, would compromise public safety. Discovery should be limited to the simple question of whether the incident report had been made public. A greater threat to the public, Morgan had argued in written reply, was the police effort to keep the public from knowing.

Alan Kinman's attorney picked up the first piece of paper in the smaller pile. An order signed by Judge Eldridge Powers: The police chief's motion to limit discovery is granted because the sole question for determination is whether the police report in question has been made open to for inspection, copying, and/or mechanical reproduction.

That order blocked any meaningful investigation of the City records and personnel.

Morgan believed, no, he knew William Harrison's will had not been lost and that Harrison's true intention would be found in the files of Bradford, Evans and Shell, the law firm that had for years handled Harrison's personal affairs. Jack O'Dowell had said that Harrison had worked on an estate plan all summer, but had died before signing the papers. Morgan knew, too, that those papers connected Tanya Everly's death to the silver-haired oilman so Alan Kinman's attorney had subpoenaed Harrison's file from that law firm and from its storage company.

Bradford, Evans & Shell objected and claimed the attorney/client privilege kept the law firm from turning those records over to Kinman and his attorney. Morgan had argued the law firm's records would demonstrate why the Vivia Police failed, and continued to fail, to produce the incident report.

Alan Kinman's attorney looked at the second sheet of paper, the second order from Eldridge Powers in *Kinman versus Hale*. The pertinent language read:

"Inasmuch as this Court has limited discovery to issues directly relating to the production or lack of production by the Vivia Police Department of Incident Report Number 90403918DBAM.CD, Bradford, Evans, and Shell's Motion to Quash filed on behalf of itself and Data Retrieval Services International is sustained and neither the law firm or its storage service are required to produce the estate planning file of William Harrison or to give any testimony in regard thereto.

IT IS SO ORDERED, ADJUDGED, AND DECREED."

For some reason, Powers hadn't granted Bradford, Evans and Shell's motion on the basis of the attorney/client privilege. It made no difference, though. The two orders would keep Morgan from presenting the evidence which showed truth and neither order could be appealed before trial without the judge's permission and a long delay.

Morgan looked at the two stacks of paper on his library table.

Son of a bitch.

Chapter Forty-Three

The courtroom was humid and the radiators clanged. Outside the sky was deep purple with a strange winter storm threatening tornadoes and sheets of ice.

Chester Morgan sat beneath the sharp fluorescent light of Eldridge Powers' courtroom. He arranged his trial exhibits again. Despite the people shuffling and whispering in the spectators' section, the room was silent to him. The advocate tapped his foot, squeezed his hand into a fist. He glanced around the room.

At the other counsel table, Tom Gardner, an Assistant City Attorney, dug through loose papers from a disheveled file. Deep dimples pierced the man's pudgy cheeks and he wore square horned-rimmed glasses and a scraggly pageboy haircut. He sat alone, not like Morgan. Alan Kinman wore a smug grin.

Towards the back of the room, a man worked his way around those already seated and took a place in the corner. Not far away, Morgan saw Shawn Frederick with her elbows on her knees and her chin in her hands. Morgan checked the man in the corner again. Wally Jackson of *The Vivia Daily Sentinel*. Morgan scribbled on a legal pad, whispered to his client, then strode to the railing behind which his receptionist sat.

"What in the hell are you doing calling the newspaper?" he whispered.

"Chest, this case will get you publicity and publicity means business and I'm your business manager. It's my job!" she said and shrugged.

"Shawn, I've told you: We don't try our cases in the newspaper. We don't try our lawsuits on television. We don't argue the law and the facts on the radio. Period."

"Chill, Chester. Newspapers go ape shit over public access, open records, and all that. You watch."

"I ought to—" Morgan saw a woman with dark hair, alabaster skin, and sterling silver jewelry walk in. "Who's answering the telephone at the office?" he asked. "You know Marylin is here."

There was a loud knock at the front of the courtroom. "All rise!"

"The District Court of Vivia County, Oklahoma is now in session. The Honorable Eldridge Powers presiding."

"Amber," Shawn whispered. "You know, the one who's going to the spa with me when you win this case."

"You may be seated," Judge Powers said. He opened a court file. "The plaintiff has filed a verified application for a writ of mandamus and other equitable relief. The defendant has filed his answer. Thus, the matter of Kinman versus Hale comes on for trial today on the merits."

"The plaintiff is present and ready, your honor," Morgan boomed.

Tom Gardner stood up and said with little certainty, "Kurt Hale is being sued in his official capacity as the Chief of Police. The City Attorney's office appears on his behalf and announces ready. My name is Tom W. Gardner."

Judge Powers hunched his shoulders and asked, "Are there any preliminary matters that need to be taken up? I assume opening statements are waived."

"Your Honor," the Assistant City Attorney said as he walked towards the Judge's bench with a paper in his hand.

Eldridge Powers stared at the young attorney until he stopped. "Mister Morgan?"

"Three of the Mister Kinman's witnesses—Tamar White, Kenneth Duckworth, and Robert Fulcher—were served with subpoenas requiring their presence here this morning and they are not here," Chester Morgan said.

The judge checked the court file and replied, "We'll have the Sheriff's office bring those three people in so they can tell the court why they disregard my orders. Mister Gardner?"

The skittish young lawyer placed a document on Morgan's counsel table and handed one to the judge. "The City Attorney's office acting on behalf of Kurt Hale in his official—"

"The Court knows who you are representing and in what capacity. The Court Reporter doesn't need extra words."

The red-haired woman who tapped the words into her black stenographer's box showed no emotion.

"Of course, your Honor." Gardner looked up. "We filed a motion for summary judgment this morning and believe it resolves this case, completely resolves the case."

Powers and Morgan both scanned through the written motion that requested the case be dismissed without a trial. Orin

Hightower, Vivia's Supervisor of Police Records, had signed a sworn statement reciting that the incident report relating to Tanya Everly's death had been lost and all good faith efforts to locate it had failed. Morgan remembered Orin Hightower lying to him about this same report weeks before. The motion, but not the affidavit, was a surprise.

"Mister Morgan, what does Oklahoma District Court Rule Thirteen provide?" Judge Powers asked.

Morgan stood up. "A motion for summary judgment must be filed more than fifteen days before trial to preserve judicial economy and to prevent the expense and inconvenience of preparing for a trial only for it to be resolved without a hearing or for the trial to be continued."

"You are correct," Judge Powers said. He leaned back in his chair and grinned. "Now, Tom W. Gardner, why should the Court even look at Hale's motion?"

"The plaintiff seeks a writ of mandamus, an order requiring the Chief of Police to provide a copy of the incident report regarding this young lady's..." The Assistant City Attorney fumbled through the papers in his hand. "Tanya Everly's death. In a lawsuit for this type of writ, the burden of proof shifts from the plaintiff to the public official. The uncontroverted evidence establishes that the incident report is lost. A judge may not order the impossible to be done. Therefore, the plaintiff has no remedy as a matter of law. That's not going to change today, ten days from now, fifteen days from now, or ever. There is no use to try this case."

The white-haired judge tapped his pencil on his desk. "Interesting. Mister Morgan?"

"It is no surprise the Police Department claims this incident report is lost and Mister Gardner is correct about the burden of proof. The Assistant City Attorney can put Officer Hightower on the witness stand to testify the report is missing. Mister Kinman can cross-examine and then present his rebuttal evidence. If, after hearing the witnesses and examining the exhibits the Court is convinced the incident report is truly lost, the Court simply does not have to issue the writ of mandamus and the case is over. If, however, the Court is not convinced the report is actually lost or believes the report has been destroyed, the Court should order Chief Hale to produce it or to come into this courtroom and explain why the Oklahoma Open Records Act has been ignored.

That's the way this process works. It's fair not only to Alan Kinman but to the citizens of this city." Morgan stopped and stared at the judge. "We are prepared to prove the incident report was either destroyed or has been intentionally withheld to cover-up the murder of Tanya Everly."

Gardner replied quickly. "The Open Records Act has a number of exceptions. In a civil case, it only allows a district judge to order the production of a record or to declare the record is not covered by the act. That's all. The City makes initial incident reports available to comply with the Act and the Chief of Police admits the requested incident report is a public record, but the report is still gone. It's still lost. There is simply no remedy this Court can give the plaintiff. Therefore, there is no use in wasting the Court's time today with a trial."

Eldridge Powers raised his eyebrows and started reading the police chief's motion for summary judgment.

"May I respond?" Morgan asked, demanded.

Powers looked over his glasses. "You may respond when and if I tell you, counselor."

The elderly judge turned the pages of the written motion then took a green book and looked at it carefully. "I've studied the Open Records Act and I believe the Assistant City Attorney is correct. The statutes don't say that I can enter the Order you request, Mister Morgan."

"Judge, the law governing mandamus authorizes the order we seek if you believe the Open Records Act doesn't. The statutes and the cases we cite in our trial brief clearly allow the court to enforce public access to public records. Furthermore, officials can be criminally prosecuted for violating the law. If this Court determines Tanya Everly's incident report has been destroyed or is buried in the offices of the police department, then you can refer this to the District Attorney for prosecution or to the State Attorney General for a grand jury investigation. Mister Kinman, as a citizen, has the right to have access to the report, to a trial, and to a hearing before an impartial judge for determination after the presentation of all the evidence. The people have that right."

The white-haired old man looked down from the bench. "The law doesn't give me that authority, however much you wish for it to, Mister Morgan. If the law did, every public official would be subjected to political witch hunts."

Gardner's shaggy head bobbed up and down in agreement.

Morgan squeezed his hand into a fist. "Then the Open Records Act means nothing. The City's interpretation of the law protects only those public servants who fear truth. Judge Powers, half the judges in this state were under federal indictment for taking kickbacks when you were first appointed to the bench. Your appointment meant neither truth nor justice would be defeated in the open courts of this state. If you do not permit a trial today, you honor the ghosts of those men who took money in dark hallways. Don't you remember?"

Eldridge Powers took off his glasses, rubbed his eyes, and then said quietly, "Chester, you have practiced in my court for a long time. I respect your advocacy, but I'll be damned if I have forgotten why I was appointed and why I have been re-elected and re-elected. I don't make the law. Take this case to the Supreme Court and if they tell me the law is what you say it is, your client will have his day in court before a fair and impartial tribunal, and not before. That's why there are appeals."

Morgan picked up the affidavit and held it out in his hand. "Officer Hightower, the supervisor of police records, now has three stories why the incident report regarding Tanya Everly's murder is gone. Police records identify this report with these letters: DAM.cd. That is code for death by accidental means and the case is closed; the police investigation is finished. Officer Hightower told me the report had been lost, but later told Alan Kinman an investigation was pending and that was why it wasn't available to the public. Officer Hightower now tells the Court the report is gone. Which version of the truth is true? That's why there are trials, to determine the truth. If the Court grants the motion for summary judgment, the right to even challenge Hightower's affidavit is lost. The public is entitled to a hearing before a fair and impartial tribunal today, not two or three years from now."

Eldridge Powers leaned forward and squinted. "Do you have any direct evidence this incident report is in existence?"

"No, sir. There is circumstantial evidence, however, and the Oklahoma Evidence Code makes no distinction."

"No direct evidence, though. Correct?"

"That's correct, your honor. This court's order limiting our investigation precluded direct evidence from ever being located."

Judge Powers picked up a pen, started writing and speaking. "The motion for summary judgment of Kurt Hale in his official capacity as Chief of Police of the City of Vivia is hereby granted for the reason that the uncontroverted evidence establishes as a matter of law that no remedy is available to the plaintiff."

"Your Honor, before you enter that order, I want to point out District Court Rule Thirteen also allows the party opposing a motion for summary judgment fifteen days within which to respond," Morgan said. "The motion was filed today. Mister Kinman is entitled to fifteen days to provide you with additional legal authority to overrule the motion."

"There's no need for that, Counselor. There's no remedy available to Mister Kinman."

"The plaintiff demands a three week continuance of this trial."

"Denied."

"Judge Powers, every party to a lawsuit is entitled to make an offer of proof of the evidence he or she would present if the court's ruling threatens to prevent the presentation of that evidence in trial. With all due respect, your Honor, allowing this offer of proof is not discretionary. If it is requested, you must allow it and Mister Kinman so requests."

Eldridge Powers looked at the clock on the wall, then at Tom W. Gardner and Chester Morgan. "Make your offer of proof, but I'm not going to spend my time listening to it. Present it, have the court reporter transcribe it if you wish, and submit it. Mister Gardner, you should consider the motion for summary judgment sustained after Mister Morgan's offer of proof. All witnesses who are present as a result of being served with subpoenas are released and are free to leave."

"I demand a record of the offer," Morgan said.

The elderly judge said to the court reporter, "Maggie write down everything Mister Morgan says—"

"And transcribe it," Morgan said, "so Judge Powers may consider it."

"The Court has made up its mind," the white-haired jurist said as he left the bench and walked through the door to his darkened chambers.

Tom Gardner looked across the heavy counsel tables at Morgan, shrugged and began putting his papers away. The bailiff and minute clerk glanced at each other and then marched out of the courtroom. The witnesses began to leave: Officer Maroney, the young police records clerk; Erma McIntosh, the Bunkhouse Lodge housekeeper who had discovered Tanya's tortured body; Frank Carlile, the motel manager the police never interviewed; Mario Pacetti, the former YMCA locker room attendant who pulled William Harrison's body from the pool; and the Reverend Don Hubbard, the street preacher who ran the Corpus Christi project and knew of Tanya Everly's life. Murle Mueller grumped out a sigh and swatted Marylin on the shoulder before stomping to the glass double doors of the courtroom. Althea Willis, the former housekeeper at the Harrison home, waited and looked at Morgan. He nodded and she left.

Chester Morgan had persuaded these people to do their duty and to speak truth. He had assured them no harm, not with Eldridge Powers presiding over the case. Would these people be willing to witness again to truth or would fear dominate feeble human courage and memory into silence? What would happen to his witnesses now? Official vengeance? Would they believe Alan Kinman's attorney again? A noise snapped from the front of the room as the court reporter began to disassemble her stenographic machine. Morgan walked to her desk.

"Maggie, the judge didn't adjourn court. Please keep recording the proceedings. I want the entire hearing transcribed, but this offer of proof I want typed tonight and on Eldridge Powers' pillow before he goes to bed and, if not then, on his desk no later than when he walks in tomorrow morning. My secretary will give you a check before we leave today for an expedited transcript. Whatever you want. Here are the exhibits for the offer of proof and a list of the witnesses who would testify to the facts."

The court reporter nodded and clicked her machine back together. Tom Gardner exited the courtroom on rubber-soled shoes. Alan Kinman stared into nothingness. Wally Jackson, the newspaper reporter, fidgeted in the corner, but remained. Marylin tried to smile, but failed, and Shawn rolled her eyes. Maria waited on the back row, her sterling silver earrings sparkling against her hair like stars in the black night.

Morgan returned to his counsel table, sat for a moment and then stood. To the vacant bench, Morgan said, his voice echoing: "May it please the Court.

"Tanya Everly, a twenty-four year old dancer and sometimes hooker, was murdered the late night of September Third or the early morning of September Fourth in Room L-8 of the Bunkhouse Lodge in Kiowa Heights.

"The official police record does not suggest murder. The report is identified as 90403918DBAM.CD. Death by accidental means, case closed. The official death certificate, dated September Fifth and signed by the now affluently retired state medical examiner Marcia Nelson, M.D., states the cause of death was asphyxiation. The autopsy itself remains shrouded, the result of this court's well-intentioned but misguided orders.

"Another Kiowa Heights hooker. So what? Except for Alan Kinman's quest, Tanya Everly's death would have passed unnoticed. Not even her mother cared. Oh, perhaps her mother did. Tamar White abused the gift of her daughter, prospering from her daughter's looks and dependence instead of her own abilities and efforts. This mother brokered and arranged meetings with the men Tanya Everly performed sex with for money. Kept the money for herself mostly, this mother did.

"On September Third—the late afternoon, Tamar White called her daughter, threatened and ordered her to go that evening to the Bunk House Lodge, the usual place of the daughter's assignations and the mother's observation. Perhaps Tamar White cared that Tanya's death go by unobserved because the prospect offered and accepted by Tamar White was too lucrative to pass, even if it meant her own daughter's demise—a daughter who otherwise would soon be free of seedy motels, strip joints, and a woman called 'mother' only by biological accident. Tamar White knew the time approached soon when her threats would be meaningless and her brokered arrangements futile. Tamar White cared all right. She cared that the truth and her pay-off not ever be discovered.

"She refuses to tell you otherwise today. She ignored your subpoena. Where is she? Look for the new white Lincoln Towncar parked in front of the dives of Kiowa Heights. Look for her in a faraway state with a changed name, dyed hair, and no one here in Vivia mourning her departure.

"Erma McIntosh discovered Tanya's wounded body, stripped and sailored-tied to a double bed in room L-8 of the Bunkhouse Lodge that September morning. Erma immediately told Frank Carlile, the motel manager. Mister Carlile called the police. A marked police car arrived, officers entered the room, and left. A short time later, an unmarked car and a vehicle to carry away the body arrived. Less than two hours later, they were gone, leaving no evidence, no indication a crime had been committed in that room. To this day, the police have not interviewed Erma McIntosh or Frank Carlile and likely no one else either.

"Listen to what the motel manager saw that morning and no conclusion can be made other than Tanya Everly's death resulted from an intentional killing, probably by two men with one posing as her customer and the other pushing his way through the jimmied door from the adjoining room, a fact well-known to Tamar White.

"The death of a Kiowa Heights hooker and dancer." Morgan paused. "Our school children are taught that no human life is of such meager value that it is not entitled to the protection of the law. Why wasn't Tanya Everly's murder investigated? A crusading police chief who seeks to eliminate vice in Kiowa Heights by any means? A factor perhaps, but not the reason. Why wasn't Tanya Everly's murder investigated?"

Morgan stopped, then, "Money and two family members who feared the truth of their own inadequacy and who believed what belonged to others belonged to them.

"Nine months before Tanya's death, William Harrison, as was his practice, went to a Key Petroleum gas station slated to be closed to make sure his soon to be ex-employees had other work and were provided for. The station was directly across the street from Vixens, the nightclub where the young woman, Tanya Everly, danced unclothed for money. For some reason, Mister Harrison decided to step into the club. To have a beer with the station's employees? Curiosity? Loneliness? We don't know for sure, but he did. There in the flashing light, loud music, and smoke he met 'Star,' also known as Tanya Everly, the spot's most popular entertainer."

Morgan turned and looked to the back of the courtroom. He saw Maria, the woman with white satin skin and the soul that reminded him of life. He bit his lip, then continued speaking: "William Harrison and Tanya Everly became compatriots, friends, then lovers. Harrison listened to Star's music and separated her from her mother. She found a home where she was free and protected. William Harrison provided her with the money to rent it from Murle Mueller. The young woman called him 'Billy.' Tanya's Billy didn't ridicule her dream to become a country music star. Instead, he recognized her talent as perhaps legendary and financed the recording of a demo, proof that even in the dark Kiowa Height night, hope is not always futile. He intended to take her to Nashville and make her a real star.

"The wealthy, respected oilman and compassionate young woman who traded her body for money became emblems of each other's freedom. He represented release from the mother who controlled Star's life, and she, release from the strictures of responsibility and the lonely ways of an honorable man.

"Last summer, William Harrison engaged the law firm of Evans, Shell and Bradford to develop a plan for the transfer of his assets at his death. What he specifically intended is not known. Had this court allowed a reasonable investigation in this case, Eldridge Powers, the probate judge of Vivia County, would now know the lost will the court admitted into probate last fall wasn't Mister Harrison's last will and didn't state his intentions at all. You remember two men—Kenneth Duckworth and Robert Fulcher—testified they worked at William Harrison's home and they witnessed the signing of his last will there last summer. Based on the sworn testimony of these two men, the court had no choice but to admit this 'lost' will into probate leaving William Harrison's fortune to his son, Randolph. The will had been drafted, so you were told, by Massey, James and Peterson, a law firm with no prior history of representing the elder Harrison, but known to be the long-time attorneys of the son.

"You remember Duckworth and Fulcher got confused. Were they maintenance men or gardeners? They didn't know. They contradicted each other, but they knew exactly what to say to prove the supposedly 'lost' will had been signed and witnessed as required by Oklahoma law. Memorized, perhaps? Coached by an attorney from a prestigious law firm? One of the men, incidentally, was a former sailor. A significant reference perhaps, but neither man had been hired by Harrison—William Harrison, that is. Althea Willis, the family housekeeper for the last thirty-five years, was the only person employed in the Harrison home last summer. No gardener. No maintenance man. No assistant. No Duckworth. No Fulcher. And, no lost will.

"On November Seventh of last year, Marylin Jenkins and Alan Kinman witnessed two men breaking into Murle Mueller's garage apartment where Tanya Everly's remaining possessions had been stored. The burglary was directed by a third man, one not present that day. The thieves took only that which had belonged to the exotic dancer, although other items of more value in Mueller's home and garage apartment were easily accessible. Had this court forced the testimony of Kenneth Duckworth and Robert Fulcher today, the court would have seen not only the two men who falsely testified they witnessed William Harrison's will but also the two men who broke into Murle Mueller's apartment to steal the remaining physical evidence of Tanya's existence. At whose direction?

"Randolph Harrison becomes a powerful, wealthy man if truth remains shrouded, if the public record remains secret. Judge Powers, you asked Randolph Harrison's attorney if his sister had been provided written notice of her right to object to the admission of William Harrison's lost will. The Massey, James and Peterson lawyer told you the notice had been mailed to the sister's last known address. It wasn't. It was sent to an address that doesn't exist, even though her whereabouts could easily have been ascertained. This 'lost' will, incidentally, had another beneficiary: United Oklahomans for American Values, a non-profit corporation whose mailing address is the same as our police chief, Kurt Hale.

"The morning of September Fourth—the same day Tanya Everly's body was discovered in Kiowa Heights—William Harrison drowned at the Downtown YMCA swimming pool. His death certificate is dated September Fifth, the same date and in the same handwriting as Tanya Everly's, and signed by the same newly affluent retired state medical examiner. William Harrison's cause of death? Asphyxiation, not a fortune imagined for a good and safe swimmer. Mario Pacetti, the locker room attendant who pulled William Harrison's lifeless body from the water heard footsteps that morning. I did, too.

"The lives of William Harrison and Tanya Everly demand compassion. The past and the future demand truth. This is our offer of proof. The motion for summary judgment should be overruled and the trial of Kinman versus Hale should proceed."

Morgan sat down at his counsel table. The image did not appear, not at all and never again.

Chapter Forty-Four

Chester Morgan hadn't stopped to change out of his suit. After the failed trial of *Kinman versus Hale*, he had gone to his office to check his messages and mail, then drove with, ahead, and away from the threatening winter storm to the Cherokee mountains of Keetoowah County.

He hadn't stopped to get his fishing gear or to persuade Jack Middlebrooks to come with him. Morgan got out of his car by the creek and felt the ancient flint stones beneath his feet.

He could and intended to seek reversal of Eldridge Powers' ruling but an appeal threatened years. Powers had committed gross error, but Morgan had told himself that before in other cases only to have the Oklahoma Supreme Court tell him otherwise. If reversed, Powers would follow the directions of the appellate court, but would likely reach the same conclusion—Powers simply would be more careful making his rulings next time.

Morgan felt the cold wind on his face. He cursed Eldridge Powers; he cursed the law; he cursed all the stupid little rules that hid truth and minimized people. Morgan wondered whether the judge had taken money, too. Not Eldridge Powers whose appointment had been the symbol of integrity in corrupt days. Not Eldridge Powers who always judged by the rules, but who just never quite ever understood the purpose behind them. Not Eldridge Powers who had never been intimidated by anyone.

The dusty smell of fallen leaves, the feel of uneven rocks and stones beneath his leather-soled shoes, and the bitter cold air against his skin reminded Morgan he lived. From a tree overhead, a crow squawked.

The best trial attorney Morgan had ever known had cautioned him that it was more important to learn how to lose a case than how to win one. Those words taunted Chester now. He walked to the bank of Nathan's Creek and stared at the clean, clear water flowing, flowing away.

The next morning Chester Morgan got out of bed early to swim once more at the YMCA. He poured himself a cup of coffee and looked at the morning addition of *The Vivia Daily Sentinel*. On the City-State page, he saw this headline:

JUDGE SLAMS DOOR ON OPEN RECORDS

Attorney Claims Police Cover-up in Deaths of Oilman, Stripper.

Chapter Forty-Five

Eldridge Powers did not change his mind after reading Chester Morgan's offer of proof and the following day's story in *The Vivia Daily Sentinel*. He did, however, personally walk a copy of the transcript to the District Attorney's office and laid it on his desk. After his trip to the District Attorney's office, Judge Powers appointed Chester Morgan to represent the unknown and unrepresented beneficiaries and heirs of William Harrison.

The attorney who had not prevailed in *Kinman versus Hale* immediately contested the "lost" will and notified William Harrison's daughter Jocelyn in Spokane, Washington of her rights. Morgan again subpoenaed William Harrison's records from Evans, Bradford, and Shell, the oilman's personal attorneys. This time Judge Powers ordered the law firm and its document retrieval service to produce those files in whatever form they had been maintained.

The Daily Sentinel pounded hard at official corruption and cover-up always. The newspaper picked up the story of the missing incident report and ran articles, pictures, and features day after day, week after week. Kurt Hale resigned as Chief of Police upon the news of his secret police division and the never written or destroyed incident report. So did his top assistants. The department fractured, and the mayor promised new leadership, integrity, oversight, and everything else embarrassed politicians promise.

The murders of Tanya Everly and William Harrison remained unresolved, but Tamar White's new Lincoln Town Car had disappeared from the parking lots of juke joints of Kiowa Heights. Robert Duckworth and Kenneth Fulcher were missing.

William Harrison's file from the law firm of Bradford, Evans, and Shell showed that the late oilman had, in fact, been working on an estate plan at the time of his death, one that remained incomplete at the time of his death. Had it been completed, Tanya Everly would have received a monthly stipend in such an amount she would have never had to work again. Randolph Harrison and his sister would have received smaller monthly sums, but none of the three would have inherited William

Harrison's assets. He had established a non-profit foundation to promote the performing arts, to benefit of artists seeking careers in entertainment, to provide them grants and scholarships. The foundation would have owned the bulk of the oilman's fortune, and Key Petroleum would have been managed and controlled by professionals, not family members, lovers, or conmen.

The contest of William Harrison's "lost will" remained unresolved. Jocelyn Harrison had retained her own attorney, and Randolph Harrison had his. Judge Eldridge Powers didn't care for the attention the case brought and pushed the lawyers to settle the case. When that didn't happen, he set the case for trial.

That's when Thomas Haney called Chester Morgan to arrange a meeting.

Chapter Forty-Six

Chester Morgan and Maria sat at a black lacquered table next to a picture window at Club Forty-Six, the most exclusive dining and drinking establishment in Vivia. Members only. A Cordon Bleu trained chef. An annual membership fee higher than the per capita income of most Oklahomans and the state's most extensive wine list. Club Forty-Six revolved on top of Progress Plaza, a skyscraper built by oil money, a building that looked like a massive quartz crystal with a trampoline affixed to its top. They waited for Randolph Harrison's attorney to appear.

Maria ordered a Harvey Wallbanger when the black-suited cocktail waitress stopped at their table. Morgan, a bourbon and water. Below they could see Vivia in the deep reds and oranges of the late Oklahoma winter. Spring would arrive soon with its wild winds and storms, and the prairie trees and shrubs would turn green like emeralds glittering on the city hills.

"Can ya could see the river up here?" Maria said, stretching to look out the window.

"We're too close from this angle. We'll move some in a minute and you will," Morgan said. "Look, you can see all of Old Vivia. Maybe if we look hard enough, we can even see Kiowa Heights."

Maria smoothed down the front of her white cotton blouse, tugged at her navy skirt, and then played with the silver star hanging on her necklace. "Chester, this is all real nice," she said, "but if you're trying to impress me and all, I'd rather go to the roller rink or go eat me some bar-b-que."

He shook his head and smelled her scent of tobacco and spice. A blood red rose in a crystalline vase stood in the middle of the table. Footsteps echoed as patrons walked across the parquet floor.

"I want you to listen very carefully to everything Thomas Haney says. You are my witness," he said as he ran his finger over the clear condensation on the outside of his glass. "Don't lie, but he won't ask. He'll think you're my paralegal."

Maria raised her eyebrows.

"My brilliantly attractive paralegal who can skate better than a fifth-grader and eat more bar-b-que than a cowboy."

"Chester, you're a mess."

"You see the McIntosh Hotel over there in Old Vivia? On the bluff?" Morgan said.

Maria nodded.

"That's where the Dawes Commission met when they allocated individual parcels of land to the Creek Indians—"

"Sorry I'm late," Thomas Haney said as he took a seat and reached to shake Chester Morgan's hand. "Good to see you."

Morgan shook his head in a slight nod. "I was just pointing out to Maria where the Dawes Commission met when they divvied up the Indian land on the other side of the Cottonwood."

"Of course, of course," Randolph Harrison's attorney said. "Sorry to interrupt there, friend."

Morgan paused for a moment and looked at Thomas Haney. Chester continued, "Back in the 1890's, the government decided the Indians in eastern Oklahoma ought to divide up their lands and get rid of their tribal governments so Congress passed a law that did just that. Up until then, all the land was owned in common; every tribe member owned a part of the whole. Any Indian could use what they wanted, but the land belonged to everyone. The Dawes Commission took names and deeded out individual lots. For a lot of tribe members, owning pieces of the earth was like putting air in a box and saying 'It's yours.' Within a few decades, most of the Indians had lost their land, their oil rights, and everything that went with it to those not hesitant to take the opportunity."

Thomas Haney sighed. "Well, they wouldn't have made good use of what they had anyway."

"We'll never know, will we?" Chester asked.

Thomas Haney looked back towards the bar and snapped his fingers for the waitress. "Vodka martini here!" He tightened his silk tie and leaned forward. "It surprised me you don't have a membership here. It impresses the hell out of most clients. Great food, tremendous view. I'd be happy to sponsor you if you're interested."

"Don't think so," Chester said.

"It must be a challenge to practice solo. I'm not sure I could do it as well as you do, friend," Harrison said. He raised his glass. "Cheers."

"You could," Morgan replied, ignoring Harrison's toast.

"Another piece of history: Did you know that the first deals that opened up the Anadarko Basin and that oil and gas boom were made right in this room? You wouldn't believe the fortunes made and lost right here." Haney grabbed a handful of cocktail nuts from a crystal bowl on the table and started popping them into his mouth one by one. "The next big area, they say, is going to be the Arkoma down in southeastern Oklahoma."

"The former lands of the Choctaw Nation," Morgan said, looking at the golden shadows of dusk on the streets of Old Vivia.

Haney put more nuts in his mouth and said, "A tip: if you have a chance to pick up any minerals down there on the cheap, it might make you a fortune."

Glass clinked against glass from behind the bar. The air felt humid like it had been circulating and recirculating since the club opened in 1973.

"You want to talk about the Harrison Estate," Morgan said.

"That's right, friend."

"Then talk, Mister Haney."

Randolph Harrison's attorney tapped the shiny black table with his fingers. "I wouldn't be here except at my client's instruction. He wants this nightmare over and he wants to know what he has to do to gain your cooperation."

Morgan waited, then said, "You should have invited Randolph's sister's attorney to this meeting. I represent William Harrison's unknown heirs and beneficiaries. That's all, and now that Jocelyn has her own attorney, the only unknown beneficiary or heir is the charitable foundation William Harrison set up to own Key's stock and to support young performing artists. Your client's sister's lawyer needs to be in on this talk."

Thomas Haney stared at Chester Morgan. "It won't hurt for us to explore some big picture options. If we need to get Jocelyn and her attorney in on this later, we can."

"Get another vodka martini, Mister Haney," Morgan said.

"What's that?"

"Your glass is almost empty."

Haney motioned for the cocktail waitress and lifted his glass. He squinted as he looked out the window. "You can almost see the yard at Bluepipe Supply & Service from here. You know, Bluepipe is one of the biggest privately held oilfield service companies in the country. It competes head-to-head with Halliburton and the big boys."

He lifted the crystal bowl of peanuts to Maria. She shook her head.

"Bluepipe is one of our clients. The company needs a new general counsel. It's a cush job, friend. You would have a small staff of attorneys you supervise. They do the day-to-day work. You farm out the big problems to us; you attend some meetings. You're paid as much or more than one of our firm's senior partners. You get paid vacation, good health benefits, profit sharing. It's a cush job, Morgan. You do the job halfway well, you retire in good health with a fortune. I'd put a good word in for you, if you're interested."

"I'm not."

"What do you want, Morgan?" Haney asked. "Something outside of the oil business? We represent a number of very good companies where you wouldn't have to worry about making payroll. Randolph Harrison has connections all across the country in any number of industries. Of course, if the firm is involved in extensive litigation or if Randolph Harrison is in the penitentiary—"

"Or on death row," Morgan said.

"That's uncalled for, counselor," Haney said.

"You want to speak about the Harrison Estate? Then speak."

He straightened up and continued talking with the same professional calm Morgan had heard in Judge Power's courtroom months ago. "In any event, it would be impossible for us to make any kind of recommendation on your behalf if we're involved in any extensive litigation with you. Randolph needs this nightmare to be over on every level."

"This discussion insults me," Morgan said, squeezing his hand into a fist and loosening it again. "Why do you think I'd be interested in a corporate job? Was I reading the classified ads when you came in? No. I've never thought my license to practice law was a license to wealth. I get up every morning and take care of my people. I'm good at what I do and I respect my oath."

"No offense meant, friend," Haney said. "None at all. You are a good lawyer. I've discovered that and that's the only reason I'm discussing these big picture options with you. Good work, good money. Just thought you might be interested." Haney waved a two-finger salute at someone across the room. "Randolph Harrison just wants this to be over."

"And, what does he expect me to do? Go back and undo the past? And, if so, where would I start and where would I end?" Morgan asked. "Do I pick up the phone and call the OSBI or the FBI and say, 'Your investigation of Randolph Harrison needs to stop. I've got a cush job and what happened really didn't happen.' No, Mister Haney, I'm not interested. Forget your big picture issues. We can talk about the William Harrison Estate or about your own culpability. Your choice."

Haney ignored the insult. "You've simply impressed me with your abilities, friend. Determined advocates always have my respect, but you have no reasonable concept of what you're dealing with."

"Tell me your reasonable concept of what we're dealing with," Morgan said.

"Eldridge Powers has only two choices. He can uphold William Harrison's lost will, as I believe he will, or he can decide William Harrison died without a will, leaving the estate to be split half and half between Randolph and his sister."

"You have a lost will," Morgan replied. "The two witnesses to that will have disappeared. William Harrison was murdered as well as his lover, Tanya Everly, with the bulk of Harrison's fortune going to his son and a chunk of it going to the chief of police through a phony nonprofit. The same chief of police who did his best to keep those murders secret. Eldridge Powers will never be complicit in that scheme. Now you tell me what we're dealing with because otherwise Maria would rather be eating bar-b-que. Now."

Haney shrugged. "If Powers throws out the will, Randolph takes one-half of the estate by inheritance."

"Not if he murdered his father. The law doesn't allow that even in Oklahoma."

Club Forty-Six had rotated a full quarter. The edge of the city to the north had blurred into the plains and inky purples through the gold and reds of the Oklahoma dusk.

"What do you suggest, friend?"

An overhead light reflected off Maria's silver starred earring. For a moment, Morgan saw the barren motel room where Tanya Everly died. He remembered the sound of footsteps at the YMCA swimming pool.

"Judge Powers has two other options you haven't mentioned," Morgan said. "Two options you know and the reason you're meeting with me. He can put off deciding this case until Randolph is convicted of murdering his father. Or, Judge Powers will figure out a way to make sure Randolph never takes a dime. I'm betting on the latter."

Haney opened his hands and spread his arms. "Neither of those will happen."

"Does Randolph Harrison want to take that risk?" Morgan asked. "I'm prepared to present the case. William Harrison's instructions to his attorney leaving his fortune to his foundation is a valid handwritten will."

"What are you suggesting?" Haney asked.

"Neither he nor his sister—Harrison's estranged daughter—take anything outright from the estate. All the Key Petroleum stock goes to the foundation. The monthly stipend Harrison wanted paid to his children would be paid except in Randolph's case, if he's convicted of murder or of any crimes related to the deaths of William Harrison or Tanya Everly, the money stops."

"Is that it?" Haney asked.

Morgan shook his head. "A monthly stipend to Althea Willis for so long as she lives—"

"Who's that again?"

"Harrison's housekeeper. My attorney fees and costs paid for my work in the case of *Kinman versus Hale* and in this estate. No side deals. No promises not to cooperate with law enforcement. No under-the-table promises not to testify in any criminal or civil case. All straight up. That's it."

Haney fidgeted in his chair. "Why would Randolph agree to this?"

"He knows why."

"I'll talk to him," Haney said. He wiped a finger on his forehead, took a deep breath, and then said, "Chester, I could imagine circumstances arising that could imperil my license to practice law. Meritless, of course. I'll pass your idea on to Randolph and see what he wants to do, but I would want your commitment on a personal level, to help me if the Bar Association starts any disciplinary action against me."

"Why would you be concerned?" Morgan asked, although he knew.

Haney half-shrugged.

"That's the other reason Randolph will do this deal. You testified that Harrison's bogus lost will was properly executed by two guys who are probably now in Mexico with no plans to return, their hair dyed blond and going by the names of Juan and Jose. You didn't just speak as an officer of the court. You raised your hand and took an oath. If you had not done so, you might have a defense to a perjury charge, but you don't now. That's the other reason Randolph will settle this case."

Haney adjusted a large gold ring on his hand.

"Talk to Randolph," Chester Morgan said. "Talk to Jocelyn's attorney and let me know." He looked to the purple sky. "I will speak the truth. Nothing more and nothing less. I'll respect my lawyer's oath. That's my promise to you."

"That's all?" Haney said, his voice as quiet as a prairie breeze. "What else is there?"

Haney sipped at his empty martini glass and Morgan waited. Maria slowly stood and walked to the picture window and the sight of the golden sun setting on the western horizon. "Do ya suppose this building would ever just tump over?"

Morgan joined her at the window and then Thomas Haney did, too.

"Of course not," Randolph Harrison's attorney said. "When they built this Progress Plaza, they went down to bedrock. This skyscraper stands on rock."

"When the wind blows real hard, I betcha folks feel it move," Maria said. "Just a little, but I betcha they do."

"Sure, there's always a little movement in these tall buildings. Every one of them," Haney said. "It's simply the law of physics."

"Around here a twister can pop out of the sky at anytime or blow in from the God knows where. You could be up here, doing something, not paying no attention, and the building get hit and you'd never know hardly what happened."

"There would be warnings and sirens. The building is safe," Haney said. "You could get out in plenty of time."

"If you could find your way," Maria said. "If you could find your way."

Morgan took her arm to leave.

"Chester, you didn't introduce me to your assistant."

"Mister Haney, this is Maria. She's a jewelry designer and a dancer at Vixens. Tanya Everly was her best friend."

Thomas Haney shuddered.

Chapter Forty-Seven

A month later, Chester Morgan walked from a hallway of the DeSoto Building into the reception area of his office. He locked the door behind him.

"Finish what you're doing, Shawn. We're closing the office," he said.

"What?"

"Not forever, just today. Early."

"Gee, we're lucky even to get Christmas off." She dropped a stack of computer-generated papers on top of another and pushed back a wisp of white blonde hair.

"One of these days you're going to have to get a real job," he said, picking up his phone messages, thumbing through them, and then putting the slips back in their holder. "We're going on a field trip."

"Oh God, Chest. You start with such promise and then send us back to third grade. Great."

The attorney paused at Marylin's desk as he walked to his office.

"How'd it go?" she asked.

He nodded. "Wrap up what you're doing. We've got somewhere to go." He closed his office door behind him.

Chester went into his office, sat down behind his desk, and looked at the picture of Cassie. He picked up the framed photograph from years before, opened a bottom desk drawer, and slid the picture in. He looked at her face one more time before pushing the drawer shut.

* * *

"So, Chest, where we are going?" Shawn asked from the back seat of the lawyer's car as they drove over the Cottonwood River Bridge to Old Vivia.

"Thompson's Dance Emporium," he replied.

"A normal attorney would take his staff to Club Forty-Six to celebrate a big settlement."

"Why do what every—" Morgan began.

"Shawn," Marylin interrupted, "no one's ever accused Mister Morgan of being normal! For a college girl, you sure don't see the obvious." Shawn scooted closer between the two front seats. "Okay, Morgan, what about your fee, huh? How'd we do, huh?"

Chester looked at the hazy June sky and the verdant trees along the riverbank. He saw the red brick of Old Vivia appearing in front of him. "We'll get all our fees and costs paid in the *Kinman* case and I'll get paid my standard rate for the time I have in the Harrison estate case."

"And?" Shawn said.

"And that's it," Morgan said.

"That's it? The biggest contested probate case in Vivia County history, and that's it? A normal attorney would have drug it out for ten years, made a career out of the case, and collected a huge fee. At least figured out how to negotiate a huge bonus for himself."

"Didn't you hear what Marylin said?" he replied.

Shawn folded her arms and dropped back against the seat. "Maybe we can stop, pick up a Happy Meal, and have a big time this afternoon. So, what are we going to do at Thompson's? What?"

Morgan kept driving.

"Is it what you wanted, Boss?" Marylin asked. "The settlement, that is?"

"The foundation will get all the Key Petroleum stock and stipends will be paid by a special trust to Randolph, Jocelyn, and Althea Willis just as I wanted. Jocelyn will get any remaining assets. It's not perfect. I had hoped everything would go to the foundation, but Jocelyn had a legitimate claim to estate by law. Maybe she'll find some way to reconcile with her dad in the salvage of his house and belongings. The settlement's fair, not perfect."

"It's over," Shawn said from the backseat. "Again, what are we going to do at Thompson's?"

"I tried to call Alan Kinman to get him to meet us there," he said.

"Boss?" Marylin said, raising her eyebrows and nodding towards Shawn.

"It was the strangest thing," he continued, ignoring Shawn's question and Marylin's prompt. "I dialed Alan's number and nothing happened. No ring. No recorded message. Just silence. He has a cell phone. That's all he uses, isn't it?"

"That's right," Marylin said. "Home and business, the same number."

"Here," Morgan said, taking a slip of paper from his pocket. "Try him again."

Marylin took her cell phone from her purse, dialed the handwritten number, and waited. She disconnected, pressed the buttons, and waited.

"Nothing," she said.

"I checked the file, my Rolodex card, your Rolodex card. It's the right one," Chester said

Marylin redialed, waited, turned off her phone and slipped it into her purse. "Nothing this time either."

Morgan looked in the rear-view mirror to see in the back seat. "Shawn, you got something wrong. You told me in the Kinman case, I'd never get paid for all that work—"

"For all that ogling at cheap naked women in low class dives, is what I think I said."

"Well, I am getting paid, but you are right about something else. I didn't use my court appointment in the Harrison Estate as an opportunity to get rich. Maybe a poor country girl like my mother was, or a trapped city girl like Tanya was, will now have a chance to test her dream. Justice isn't about fixing the past; it's about healing the past's future."

"You're hopeless, Morgan," Shawn said.

"You're right," he replied, "and it will never change."

Morgan stopped at a light at the intersection of two of the main streets of Old Vivia. Summer sunlight and shadows fell onto the old redbrick buildings.

"So, Chest, what do you think really happened? Who do you say exactly killed Tanya Everly and William Harrison?" Shawn asked.

"I said what I could prove in the *Kinman versus Hale* case."

"'What you can prove is not always what the truth is,' quoting the only licensed attorney in this car," Marylin retorted. A horn honked behind them and Morgan accelerated.

"Then, I'll tell you the truth which connects the verifiable facts. The truth as I know it, believe it to be, as it will turn out to be." Chester tapped on the steering wheel and took a breath. "William Harrison's life changed when he met Tanya Everly. He was a lonely, honorable man. Tanya reminded him of all that was past and all that was never to be regained. Randolph thought she was a gold-digger who threatened what Randolph had deluded himself to believe was his absolute right: His father's wealth.

"This son had some resources of his own. The younger Harrison cut a deal with Kurt Hale. The former police chief assumed it would simply be a matter of looking the other way. With the Special Investigative Teams organized, it wouldn't be a big problem for the police force. Hale assumed professional hits. Instead, Randolph hired a couple of cheap Kiowa Heights thugs— Duckworth and Fulcher."

Bells rang and red lights flashed as a railroad crossing guard lowered itself in front of Morgan's car as he approached a warehouse district. He stopped and waited.

"Randolph made another mistake," the attorney continued. "He thought his father was about to leave his entire estate to Tanya, which really makes no sense when you think about it. Randoph paid off Tanya's mother for her acquiescence and silence. When the two deaths occurred, Kurt Hale was into more than he had anticipated. Randolph made some deal with his old attorney friend at Massey, James and Peterson who then suborned perjury to get the Key Petroleum legal work.

"When I showed up and asked Tamar White questions, she used my inquiry to squeeze more money out of Randolph. He got paranoid and decided he had to destroy any other evidence that might connect Tanya to his father. That's why Fulcher and Duckworth broke into Murle Mueller's garage apartment to steal Tanya's things. Once more, the police provided cover, but Marylin was an eyewitness and the investigating officer learned she worked for me. That was fed back to Randolph who then tried to plant the story about the Red Strike affair and me with *The Daily Sentinel*. Of course, there wasn't anything there which just stoked Reporter Jackson's curiosity about his source's motive."

After a gray and red engine backed across the street, the clang clanging and flashing red lights stopped. The guard lifted and Morgan pressed the gas.

"In the meantime, thanks to Althea Willis, we learned Fulcher and Duckworth never worked for the elder Harrison and never witnessed a lost will. Perjury after murder probably seems pretty inconsequential. Duckworth and Fulcher committed both murders at Randolph's behest and pay. That's what I think. It was messy and stupid with too many players. Somebody will break and the criminal case will too, then."

"You'll still be paying Randolph his monthly stipend, though," Shawn said.

"Not for long," Morgan said. "Not for long. The money stops when he's indicted or convicted for anything—and he will be."

"There you go again, Morgan," Shawn said. "You forgot the part that almost cost me my life and virtue and won me and Amber a day at the spa," Shawn said. "The proof of romance between wealthy Willie and tart Tanya?"

"Amber and I," corrected Marylin. "And what virtue, girl?"

Morgan stopped his car at a stoplight. "Why was William Harrison at the Orpheum Nu-Art Theatre? Who else would have raised as much hell as I did after watching Tanya's video? Or offered cash for all the masters? Star's Billy had a lot of money, didn't show up for the funeral, never claimed his security deposit from Murle Mueller, never appeared again after September Fourth." He blushed and remembered the real and parallel reason he knew the connection. "We're meeting Maria at Thompson's."

* * *

Chester, Maria, Marylin, and Shawn sat in the middle-seats of the middle section of Thompson's Dance Emporium, an old auditorium with a wooden dance floor in front of the stage. The faded green sign outside the building flashed a dancing neon couple, but the structure's interiors of hard dark wood and the uncomfortable 1920's theatre seats still provided the best acoustics for music anywhere in Oklahoma.

"This is the Ryman Auditorium of the Southwest," Chester said. "All the greats of country and western music played here. The Carter Family, Jimmie Rodgers, Roy Acuff. Bob Wills and the Texas Playboys? Just a cowboy house band out of Tulsa, until they played Thompson's. Kay Star, Patsy Cline, and Tammy Wynette all sang here for Vivia. Roger Miller, Johnny Cash. To the folks back home, Reba McIntyre was a just a barrel racer from over in Chokie, but once she sang at Thompson's, she was a star."

Except for the four, the auditorium was empty, silent and empty. A smell of wood polish and ancient cigar smoke hung in the air.

"Are you all ready?" Morgan asked. Maria squeezed his hand. Marylin nodded. Shawn, too. "OK, Scotty!"

The houselights dimmed. As the red velvet stage curtains parted, an announcer's voice boomed:

"And now, Thompson's Dance Emporium is proud to present today for the very first time ever Vivia's own Tanya Everly!"

A spotlight hit an empty stool on the stage and from the large speakers came the big-hearted voice of an Oklahoma country girl finding life in the dark city and singing of hope.

Chester slipped his arm around Maria and felt her sob. Then they, the four witnesses, heard Tanya's voice joining all those of the past and all those yet to come.

Epilogue

After work the next day, Chester Morgan stopped at a liquor store and purchased a large bottle of Kentucky bourbon to thank Henry Voss for referring Alan Kinman.

When he arrived at Henry's Oak Street Garage and Mechanic Shop, Morgan parked the car and told himself it wouldn't take long. Henry Voss never said much.

The big gray-haired man was working on an old yellow Ford high on a rack in one of two service bays.

"Henry!" Morgan said, carrying the wrinkled-bagged bottle of whiskey.

Voss had a streak of grease on his cheek and squinted at Morgan through brown horn-rimmed glasses. "Hey," he said. He picked up a different wrench and continued working on the underside of the engine.

"Chester Morgan," the lawyer said. "It's been a while."

"I ain't forgot ya," the mechanic said, still at work.

"I brought you something. You referred Alan Kinman to me. This token isn't for the referral, but for the compliment. Alan said you told him I was the best attorney in town."

"Who?"

"Alan Kinman. He's the guy who indirectly got me into the William Harrison estate."

Henry Voss stopped working on the car and looked at his attorney with a puzzled expression. He kind of shook his head.

"Well, you heard about the police chief resigning and the police force being reorganized and all that," Morgan said.

"Reckon I have some."

"Well, Alan Kinman pursued the lawsuit which resulted—" the attorney stopped. "He has a lawn mowing service. Twenty-three, twenty-four years old. Real skinny. A little taller than me. Light brown hair, kind of sun-burned skin year round. Wears glasses that looked smeared all the time."

Henry Voss squinted again. "What's he drive?"

"A pickup of some sort and a trailer, I imagine."

The mechanic shook his head again. "What did you say his name was?"

"Alan Kinman."

"'Don't know who the hell you're talking about." He glanced back up at the engine.

Morgan held out the bottle of bourbon. "Here, take it anyway."

CPSIA information can be obtained at www.ICGtesting.com
Printed in the USA
LVOW060833261112

308767LV00001B/24/P

9 781620 160039